Forbidden Lust in Paris

Age Gap Romance

Rachel K Stone

AS Holdings and Assets Publishing

GET YOUR FREE COPY of "FROM FRIENDS TO HIS."

Travel delays. A fake fiancé. And trying to muffle my screams of passion...while we share a hotel room...

A high school reunion couldn't have come at a worse time. Showing up flying solo was out of the question. So, I did the next best thing and asked my best friend to accompany me as my fake fiancé—bad idea.

Bryce Howard is that bad-boy billionaire, chiseled muscle type. We have been friends since college and he is always there for me in a pinch.

Travel delays have us stuck in a city with little hotel occupancy. We have to share a room and my mind is saying, cool it, he is your best friend. But the moisture building between my thighs wants so much more.

Get a free copy of the prequel, *From Friends to His*: https://hello.rachelkstone.com/welcome

bookbub.com/authors/rachel-k-stone

facebook.com/authorrachelkstone/

instagram.com/rachelkstoneauthor/

youtube.com/channel/UCbZdQqxw7X0FtMONG
Rmmlqg

Chapter 1

Giselle

"He was like a jackhammer. I felt like I was a piece of concrete he was trying to break through to get to the water main below," Maria groaned, waving her hands about for added effect.

Helena groaned loudly. "Right? He was the same way when he was with me. Wham! Bam! Bam! And not a 'thank you, ma'am' in sight!" she replied.

"How can a man who's so utterly perfect-looking be so bad in bed?" Maria asked.

"I don't know, but there's bound to be a string of disappointed women all over Paris," Helena said.

I stood there, looking from one of them to the other, not commenting. I tried desperately to keep myself from blushing as they discussed one of the local artists. They were right about his perfection, at least in looks. He was exactly the sort of man women fantasize about when they daydream of running away to Paris and falling in love with a French painter.

His name was André Boucher and he looked just as you would expect. He was slender and on the shorter side, but he wore an intensity that was hard to miss. His shoulder-length black locks and soulful deep brown eyes were mesmerizing. He seemed somehow fragile with his uncalloused hands and aristocratic features, but there was a sensuality to him that pulled you in, even me.

Of course, I wasn't so quick to jump into bed with him as my colleagues, but I could see why they had. I was also grateful I hadn't been seduced by his natural magnetism. From the sound of it, I'd have regretted the choice, likely more than they had. From the conversations I'd overheard between the two of them, this wasn't their first experience with less-than-thrilling sexual encounters.

André was a brilliant abstract painter. Though he wasn't quite famous, he was well-known, and his art was popular with the right people. You could see his work hanging on the walls of some very expensive mansions, not only in Paris, but around the world. It was only a matter of time before the most elite art collectors found him.

It would seem that his artistic talents didn't extend to his sexual prowess, however. It hadn't been that long since I'd heard Helena purring all over him while he was at the museum for a smaller showing of his work. She'd seemed quite smitten with him, but when he'd returned a week or so later, she'd avoided him like the plague. If she'd mentioned why, I'd not heard that particular conversation, but it all seemed to be coming out now.

"Then, when he was done, he bounded out of bed like his ass was on fire and washed his dick off in the bathroom sink," Maria continued. "I shit you not. The door was open, and he was in there with it just flopped over the edge, rinsing it off with soap and water. He dried it on the last clean face towel. I had to call the front desk to have more sent up after he was gone."

Helena let out a loud snort of laughter. "Oh, for fuck's sake. He did that to me, too! Like I was some sort of dirty whore and he had to get my corrosive juices off his cock before the rot set in! I wonder if he's like that with all the women or if it's just because we're filthy Americans?"

"I bet he does it to everyone. I don't know what he thought he needed to get off of there so quick. It's not like I had a chance to cum," Maria replied, rolling her eyes.

"Me either. I should have warned you. I didn't realize you were going to fuck him, or I'd have told you. Then again, I'm glad you did. Now I know it wasn't just me who had a dirty pussy."

"That's us, The Dirty Pussy Pack," Maria joked.

They both laughed as I stood awkwardly, pretending to look at some new pieces that had arrived. I had nothing to add to their conversation. I'd never slept with a French artist who was bad in bed. I'd never slept with anyone who was bad in bed. The truth was that I'd never slept with anyone at all, but I didn't want them to know that. It wasn't exactly that I was ashamed; I just knew they'd have a million questions I didn't want to answer.

I was both appalled and enthralled by most of their conversations. They were so sexually adventurous, nothing like me. I wasn't some prude who'd never heard anything sexual or risqué, but they really took the cake with some of their conversations. I was constantly shocked by the discussions they had with one another about their sex lives. They'd been bad in New York, where we all worked for the same museum, but they were off the chain now that they were in Paris with nothing to do but put in their work hours and get into trouble in their spare time.

As for me, I spent my time exploring Paris, enjoying the sights and the smells. The food was amazing. When I wasn't working in the museum, I made my way through the bustling streets, each building whispering tales of art and culture. I'd come to Paris for a once-in-a-lifetime opportunity. I'd been chosen as part of the team responsible for setting up a prestigious exhibition dedicated to the life and works of the illustrious painter, Rembrandt van Rijn.

My role as a museum curator had brought me here, and I couldn't have been more thrilled. The very thought of curating an exhibition that celebrated the genius of Rembrandt filled me with a sense of purpose and fulfillment. At 23, I was quite young for someone in my position, so I was determined to make the most of this extraordinary experience. I had a lot to prove and getting caught up in some sexual scandal wasn't on my to-do list.

Extricating myself from the debauchery of Marie and Helena, I headed out for the day. The air felt alive with the colors and smells of spring. Stumbling upon a charming café tucked away in the heart of the city, I decided to pause and savor the essence of Paris through a warm cup of espresso. The cozy atmosphere, complete with wrought-iron chairs and checkered tablecloths, oozed with old-world charm. The aroma of freshly baked croissants wafted through the air, mingling with the fragrant coffee.

I soon found myself eavesdropping on a nearby conversation between two French women that made the one between Helena and Marie look tame. Though my French was limited, I was learning quickly and thus able to pick up on quite a bit of what they were saying. It translated roughly into a discussion about one of them sleeping with her boss and the fallout of being discovered.

Apparently, they had been caught together by his maid and instead of ratting them out, she'd insisted on a raise. Then, several weeks later, she'd joined them in their little trysts. It was like something straight out of a porn movie before it unfolded into a drama that would make soap opera writers envious.

One woman told the other that her boss had eventually dumped and then fired her. She'd sought revenge by telling his wife about his affair and stealing his maid, not to clean her house but to keep her company. As it turned out, his wife didn't care. She was used to his philandering. She was only angry that he'd been careless with it.

"*Scélérat*!" the woman listening exclaimed.

She was right. He did sound quite like the scoundrel. I smiled, turning my head away so they didn't realize I'd been listening. I knew it was rude, but I suppose I had some sort of fascination for the sex lives of other women since I had no frame of reference myself. Even Helena and Marie, as much as they embarrassed me with their directness, were an endless source of fascination.

What must it feel like to be so sexually liberated? I wondered if I would ever know. Surely, I would. I mean, I wasn't inexperienced by choice. It was more fate, really. I'd never been in a serious relationship and didn't want to jump into bed with someone just to say that I had. While I admired the freedom other women felt sexually, I'd been raised in a fairly puritan household, and I guess some of it had stuck. I didn't think of myself as repressed or uptight, but I was picky—perhaps too much so.

With a chuckle, I returned to sipping my espresso and relishing the spirited exchange between the two women. So what if everyone in Paris was having sex but me. I suppose I should be grateful that at least I wasn't having bad sex or getting tangled up in carnal collisions. I firmly believe in always looking on the bright side of things. From my viewpoint, I might not have had any experience sexually, but at least I didn't have to deal with bad experiences.

As the two women behind me moved on to other topics of discussion, I finished my espresso and prepared to depart. They seemed to be in no hurry as they continued chatting happily away. I missed having someone I could chat with like that. My best friend from as far back as elementary school had moved to California last year after getting married and we'd mostly lost touch other than an email or text here or there.

The foul-mouthed Helena and Marie were the closest thing I had to friends now and though I adored both of them, we were worlds apart when it came to being like-minded. Perhaps when I get back to New York, I might put more of an effort into making new friends with common interests. For now, work was my priority. Besides, what would be the point in making a friend in Paris that I would soon lose touch with as well?

I often marveled at women who always seemed to be surrounded by friends, but those kinds of associations often seemed so shallow. I knew far too many women who went out to parties or bars with women they called friends only to cast them aside for the first man who showed them attention. Then, there were the petty women who were all too quick to undermine women they called friends.

Helena called those types of women "frenemies" because they acted like your friends but were very much an enemy who would stab you in the back. She had no use for such women. That was the one way that she and Marie differed. They both liked to go out and have fun, but Helena had a much smaller circle of trust than Marie. Of course, I suppose having a small circle was better than having no circle, like me.

Though she and Marie had invited me to go out with them while we were here, I'd so far declined. I just didn't think I could keep up with the wild lives the two of them seemed to lead and I didn't want things to become awkward with us being co-workers. I was just fine exploring Paris alone, though sometimes I wondered if I was missing out by not having someone to show me some of the local hangouts or activities I might be missing.

Little did I know that coming here would be the first step in a series of experiences that would challenge my notions of innocence and lead me down a path of discovery, both in the world of art and in matters of the heart. I was on the verge of opening up a whole new world that had so far escaped me.

Chapter 2

Giselle

The dawn of a new day in Paris brought a sense of excitement and apprehension. I awoke in my cozy Parisian hotel suite, the soft morning light filtering through sheer lace curtains and casting a gentle glow on the pastel-hued walls around me.

My mind buzzed with anticipation as I prepared for the day. I dressed in a tasteful yet chic ensemble, carefully chosen to convey professionalism and respect for the art world. Today, I would meet my international colleagues, each a luminary in their own right. We'd be surrounded by incredible art pieces that would soon grace the exhibition. I wanted to look the part that my museum expected me to play.

I couldn't help but wonder how I had become a part of this prestigious project. I was fairly new to the art world, having been with the museum for less than a year before lucking out on getting the position. My career as a museum curator had flourished, and now, I found myself in the heart of the art world, in the enchanting city of Paris. The scent of freshly brewed coffee filled the area around the small kitchenette in my suite as I poured myself a cup. I drank it with a quick breakfast of toasted croissant smeared with fresh butter before heading out.

As I made my way to the museum, the city's charm embraced me. The quaint cafes, boutiques, and centuries-old buildings never ceased to capture my imagination. The city's history seeped through the cobblestone streets, creating a surreal backdrop on my journey toward the museum. Paris was like a living canvas, a masterpiece in itself.

Arriving at work, I was greeted by an abundance of excitement. The space was a hive of activity as fellow curators, art experts, and technicians bustled about. I couldn't help but be overwhelmed by the art pieces being prepared for the exhibition. Paintings, sculptures, and artifacts from different corners of the world were carefully arranged, each carrying a piece of history and culture.

As I navigated through the museum's chambers, I encountered my international colleagues. Helena and Marie were there, as well. They were part of the team and key figures in making the event a reality. For all their naughty banter in private, they were both the epitome of sophistication and professionalism in this type of setting.

Helena's tall, slender form seemed right at home among the world's masterpieces. I marveled at her ability to seamlessly transition from discussing the most intimate encounters to handling priceless artworks. It wasn't unusual to watch her study a piece of work only to realize those around her were studying her instead.

Marie, on the other hand, brought an infectious energy to the surroundings. Her bubbly demeanor and blonde curls, perfectly coiffed, stood in stark contrast to the solemnity of the museum. It was as if she'd brought a piece of her vivacious world into the realm of art and history. They spotted me from a distance and waved enthusiastically.

"Bonjour, Giselle!" Helena's voice was melodious as she approached, embracing a bit of French dialog as her own. "I see you've made it in early, too. We were just discussing some of the pieces we'll be handling today."

Marie chimed in, her eyes twinkling with mischief, "Don't worry, darling. We won't be delving into any romantic escapades today, I promise." She gave me a playful wink.

I couldn't help but chuckle, feeling a sense of camaraderie that was unusual but invigorating. "I'm glad to hear that," I replied with a playful smile. "But I have a feeling today will be filled with discoveries beyond just art."

I wasn't wrong. The day unfolded with a whirlwind of activities. We inspected each piece of artwork, ensuring it was in perfect condition and meticulously documenting every detail for the record. These priceless pieces must be handled and protected with the utmost care. We were surrounded by security staff—sometimes private security hired by the owner for individual pieces on loan.

Our discussions were a blend of artistic appreciation and logistical planning. As we worked together, Helena and Marie's uninhibited approach to life became even more familiar. I found their spirited nature infectious. I marveled at how easily they transitioned from their public, respectable personas when surrounded by others to their carefree discussions meant for our ears only.

During these private moments, their conversations veered toward the risqué, leaving me to blush and, at times, roll my eyes. It was clear that their openness reflected their personal lives. While

I'd embraced the prospect of venturing beyond my comfort zone, I couldn't help but be amused and occasionally scandalized by their audacity.

"I have my eye on a tall hunk of manhood standing guard over that self-portrait we just inventoried," Marie said with a smile.

"You think you're going to tear him away from that $18 million painting to hook up in the coat room?" Helena laughed.

"Of course not. What sort of loser do you take me for? I'm a professional. I will wait until his shift ends and one of his counterparts takes over. Then, I plan to ply him with alcohol and tits until he submits to my will."

"Well, if anyone has the tits for that job, you do," Helena noted, mock bowing to Marie's chest. "Ass too, for that matter. I'd kill to have curves like that."

"You don't need curves like mine. You are a walking Statue of Venus. All you have to do is look at a man and he melts like butter," Marie replied.

Helena rolled her eyes and looked back toward the security guard in question. He stood across the room beside the painting he was assigned to protect. I looked too. He wasn't the most handsome guy you'd ever see, but he was tall and broad-shouldered. There was little doubt that beneath the suit he wore were abs of steel and muscles that rippled with every movement.

"Whatcha think?" Marie asked, noting my gaze. "He's doable, right?"

"Not really my type, but yeah, I can see how he might be interesting to someone else."

"What is your type?" Helena coaxed.

"I don't know. I'm not sure I have one, but I guess I'm more intellect over brawn."

"How do you know he's not an intellectual? He might be an art expert," Marie said, looking back up at him with a glimmer in her eye.

"He might be," I replied with a shrug. "I'm sure you'll let us know when you're done defiling him."

"Ooh, look who is getting into the girl talk now." She laughed. We both joined her, causing several heads to turn our way. We quickly resumed our somber faces and continued our work, but a small smile occasionally crept across our faces.

As Helena and Marie moved on to other things, my attention became more focused on the art being arranged in the gallery. It was a sight to behold so many priceless paintings all in one place. I had a hard time believing that someone found me fit to oversee such an undertaking, but here I was, and I had no intention of making a mess of things.

Plus, there was something that was just so breathtaking about it all. Throughout the day, I was drawn in by the allure of the art surrounding me. It was almost overwhelming to be among so many of his masterpieces. His paintings spoke to me, each brush stroke revealing a piece of the artist's soul. I was mesmerized by the way the art conveyed stories and emotions, transcending language and time.

Rembrandt was a notable storyteller. He captured the very essence of people on his canvas. His skill with light and shade created an uncompromising portrait of all he saw before him that was so real, so stark. He was, and sometimes still is, often criticized because he seemed to prefer the plain or the ugly over the beautiful.

Helena joined me again, her eyes fixed on the same painting. "Isn't it remarkable how a canvas can hold so much history and emotion?" She spoke with a reverence that contrasted with her earlier conversations.

I nodded in agreement. "It's as if Rembrandt's spirit lingers in every stroke, telling a story that defies time."

The conversation deepened as Helena and I shared our thoughts on art, history, and life. We discussed the challenges and rewards of curating such an exhibition and the weight of responsibility it carried. In that moment, the boundary between professionalism and personal connection blurred, and I found myself forming a stronger bond with her.

Marie joined us and I was equally enthralled with her knowledge of Rembrandt's work. Both women honestly did know what they were talking about when it came to art. I'd already known this about them, but it was even more apparent that they, like me, had studied for this exhibition so that they were well prepared for all aspects of their jobs here. It was impressive and gave me a whole new appreciation for both of them.

Once we finished, Helena invited me out to dinner, but I declined. It had been a long day and as much as I liked her, I really wanted to have a simple evening to myself and turn in early. Tomorrow would be another busy day for us all. Of course, Marie didn't seem too worried about getting a good night's rest. I saw her poised seductively against a pillar, talking to the security guard she was hellbent on bedding, and I smiled.

I left the museum that evening with a sense of contentment and wonder. The city had woven its magic, and I found myself once again immersed in the enchantment of Paris. I found a small patisserie I'd not yet frequented and stepped inside to enjoy a treat. I knew I would have to lay off eating so many sweets here, or I'd be forced to eat lettuce for a month once I got back to New

York, but I wasn't too worried about it. I was thin anyway and got plenty of exercise walking about the city.

Seating myself at a small table by the window, I watched people outside on the sidewalk as I nibbled at the plate of small French pastries I'd selected. I marveled as a woman came in with a perfectly groomed poodle on a leash and ordered at the counter. She sat the dog on the seat beside her as she sat down, occasionally giving it a nibble of her food.

I considered how novel it was to see a dog seated in a sweet shop looking at me with disinterest. It wasn't something you'd see in New York due to health codes. Of course, there was the rogue shop owner here and there who didn't mind, but overall, it was limited to service animals. This poodle seemed to just be a favored pet.

It truly was an amazing city, full of wonders to behold, glorious food to indulge in, and potential experiences to enjoy. I had to wonder how I would fit into a place like this on an extended basis. It was so far from my New York way of life in many ways beyond the mere distance between the two.

I contemplated the possibility of one day calling this city my home, of pursuing my passion in a place where art and history were woven into the very fabric of life. It was a thought that lingered, tucked away in the recesses of my heart, as my adventure in Paris continued to unfold.

Chapter 3

Giselle

The days flowed seamlessly in the enchanting city of Paris. As I became more deeply involved in curating the Rembrandt exhibition, my fascination with the art world and the allure of this exquisite city deepened. Paris was a treasure trove of culture and history, and every moment spent there felt like an exploration of the senses.

My connection with Helena and Marie continued to grow. Beyond our shared responsibilities, we formed a bond that transcended the boundaries of our professional lives. Despite the stark contrast between their audacious conversations and the world of art they expertly navigated, they remained integral to my Parisian experience despite being native New Yorkers like me.

One warm morning during a rare weekend off, I found myself strolling along the banks of the Seine, the river that wound its way through the heart of Paris. The sun painted the water with a golden hue, and the city's iconic landmarks—Notre Dame, the Eiffel Tower, and countless bridges—stood as witnesses to the history and culture that thrived along its shores.

My steps were unhurried, and the whisper of the river seemed to tell tales of love and art. I stopped to admire a street artist capturing the city's magic on his canvas, his brushstrokes breathing life into the scene. I couldn't help but smile, for I'd come to understand the beauty of art in a deeper, more personal way. It was as if being immersed in a world of genius had somehow rubbed off on me emotionally, if not creatively.

The truth was that for all my education and appreciation of the arts, I possessed little talent in that regard. I had a deep understanding of what it took to create a masterpiece but was incapable of doing so myself. My creative gene was more suited for home decor and small craft work, which paled in comparison to the work of the artists I constantly found all around me.

I was okay with that. I was fine with my place being to promote and highlight the works of the great artists of our time and beyond. They deserve to be remembered for their extraordinary contributions to the world. That was no more apparent than in the showcase I was putting together here in Paris. People would come from around the world to behold the paintings of Rembrandt in person.

Some of these paintings and etchings were on loan from private collectors who had never allowed the works to be publicly displayed, meaning that this exhibit might be the only chance many would ever have to see them. Much work had been done behind the scenes to facilitate the loans made to us. We had to ensure the complete security of all art in transit, on display, and during its return.

Some owners would only accept our terms if we allowed their privately hired security to remain with the paintings at all times. No expense had been spared to put this together, and it was coming together beautifully. The area set aside for the upcoming display was currently closed off while it was being put together and was heavily guarded with a mix of museum and private security.

Already, though, it was taking shape. Each time I stepped inside the gallery doors, I found myself in a breathtaking world of Rembrandt's creations. Each masterpiece, carefully arranged and illuminated, seemed to beckon me closer, as if it held a secret meant only for those who truly sought to understand. Rembrandt's works bore the weight of centuries, revealing the stories and emotions that transcended time itself.

In that hallowed space, I felt a connection with the artist beyond the bounds of history. I pondered his use of light and shadow, his ability to capture the very essence of his subjects. It was as though he had left a part of his soul on each canvas. His work was nothing short of pure genius, which I'd come to appreciate more and more during my work here.

I almost found it disappointing that we were nearing the end. In less than three weeks, we would open the gallery for a three-month exhibition. All these months of viewing would culminate in the first night's showcase and then my job here would be done. The wheels were in motion for other staff members to oversee the continued showing and return of all loaned paintings while I returned to New York to take care of some final details for an exhibition there.

Over the following weeks, I immersed myself in the art world. My days were a whirlwind of discussions, planning, and a newfound appreciation for the craft. Rembrandt's paintings seemed to come alive, and I reveled in the intricate details of his masterpieces. Like many people who would come to see his work, this might likely be the only time I'd ever see most of them firsthand.

As my days in France grew closer to an end, I found that I'd developed a love for more than just Rembrandt. I was in love with Paris itself. The city became my playground, my sanctuary of art and culture. I wandered through its cobblestone streets, discovering hidden gems and charming bistros. The city's cafes and parks became my solace, offering moments of respite from the intensity of my work.

Paris had cast a spell on me, and with every passing day, I found myself falling deeper under its enchantment. The thought of calling this city my home had slowly transformed from a mere aspiration into a heartfelt longing. How wonderful would it be to belong to this city? Its rich culture and vibrant nightlife had begun to feel like a part of who I felt I was becoming.

As I roamed the streets, I often found myself gazing at the grand architecture and ancient monuments, lost in the city's history. The Louvre, with its iconic glass pyramid, was a testament to the wealth of art and culture housed within its walls. The *Musée d'Orsay*, nestled in a former railway station, held a treasure trove of Impressionist masterpieces that left me awestruck. Paris was a city rich in culture and history.

But it wasn't just the art that captured my heart; it was the city's spirit. With their effortless style and passion for life, Parisians seemed to revel in simple pleasures—long lunches, strolls along the Seine, and evenings in quaint cafes. I yearned to be part of this vibrant tapestry, to live a life where art and culture thrived at every turn.

One evening, as I stood before a vibrant Van Gogh painting at the *Musée d'Orsay*, I felt a surge of inspiration. It wasn't just the art itself that moved me but the idea that art was a bridge connecting people across time and cultures. The emotion captured on the canvas resonated with something deep within, a universal language that transcended borders.

Returning to my hotel, I couldn't help but reflect on the life I envisioned for myself. Paris had ignited a passion for art and culture that had been dormant for too long. I wondered if this could be more than a temporary assignment, more than just a brief fling with the city. Could Paris be the place where I'd truly find my purpose?

The idea of living in Paris and being part of its artistic tapestry filled me with a sense of longing. But it was also a decision that could uproot my life and reshape my future in ways I hadn't anticipated.

As the days turned into weeks, I found myself standing at a crossroads of the path I'd always known and the one that beckoned with uncertainty lay before me. I'd grown to embrace the art world, Rembrandt, and Paris's intoxicating allure. The question that lingered was whether I was ready to take a leap of faith, to embrace a future that was both daunting and exhilarating.

It wasn't as if I had a reason not to stay. There was no one waiting for me in New York. My parents, who'd adopted me when they were already well into their fifties, were now living in Florida. Travel had become increasingly difficult for them now that they were in their seventies. So, visits were mostly limited to me flying down to see them. I could do that from Paris as well as I did from New York.

My small walk-up in New York was barely bigger than the hotel suite I was staying in, so the smaller apartments I saw for rent or sale in Paris were something I was used to already. There were so many reasons why I belonged here and not that many that prevented me from taking a leap of faith and just doing it.

For the first time in my life, I felt a sense of freedom, a newfound courage to explore my desires and embrace the unknown. The City of Lights had welcomed me with its artistic grace. I couldn't help but wonder if it was time to return that embrace, to make Paris not just a destination but a place I could truly call home.

I wasn't sure if I could ever honestly go through with it. It was one thing to become enamored with the city and consider it a potential new home, but another to take that leap and make the move. I loved the idea that I was the kind of woman who could just up and move to another country and find success of her own making, but was I truly able to pull it off? Did I have the courage to do so?

And that was how my infatuation with Paris came full circle. It was one thing to dream about uprooting your life, to make a new life in another country, but actually doing it involved so much more. There were the legalities to sort out. Plus, I only knew a few people that I'd met since working here during the last six months on this project. The language barrier was an issue, too. I needed to learn a lot more French than what I currently knew if I decided to relocate here.

The more I thought about it, the more I realized I wasn't being very practical. This was a lovely place, and I really enjoyed it, but I was letting my fantasies get the better of me. What woman didn't dream of moving away and starting over? Perhaps meeting a wonderful man who would sweep her off her feet and help her navigate her new city together? It was just silliness on my part.

My place was in New York. It was unlikely that I would land such a great job in my position at a Paris museum. I knew I could do the job I was hired for, but I also knew it was almost unheard of for someone my age to just walk into a position like mine with so little experience. I would definitely be starting on a lower rung if I tried to work in the same capacity in a city as renowned for its museums and galleries as Paris.

I regretted that my time here approached the end, but I also knew that I was deluding myself if I thought I could just waltz into a lovely life in Paris without taking more than a few steps back down the run on my career ladder. Right or wrong, my career was my main focus right now. Paris would always be here for me to visit when I wanted to enjoy the magic of the city again.

Chapter 4

Peter

The lecture hall hummed with the energy of a new semester. Students shuffled into their seats, exchanging greetings and sharing whispered excitement. As I stood at the front of the room, the morning light streaming through the windows bathed me in a warm glow.

"Bonjour, class," I greeted them, my enthusiasm apparent in my voice. "Today, we embark on a journey into the remarkable world of one of the greatest painters in history—Rembrandt van Rijn."

Eager faces looked up at me, notebooks ready and pens poised for notetaking. Of course, there were also a few who showed disinterest, as there always were when students were forced to take an art class when it wasn't their passion. Still, the overall number of students who seemed invested in the knowledge to come was always a gratifying sight. I knew the world of art had the power to inspire and transform lives.

We delved into the life and art of Rembrandt, discussing his use of light and shadow, the deep emotions reflected in his subjects, and the timeless quality of his work. The classroom was a hub of animated conversation, with questions and observations pouring in from all directions.

One student, a young woman with an infectious passion for art, asked, "Professor Dockery, what do you think it is about Rembrandt's art that makes it so enduring and universal?"

I smiled, appreciating her insightful question, though I suspected she'd borrowed the question from somewhere online to impress me. "Excellent point. Rembrandt's art goes beyond mere representation. It delves into the very soul of his subjects, capturing the time in which they lived and the culture they embraced. It portrays the human experience in a way that remains constant throughout the years following its creation."

Our discussion flowed like a river, with the students engaged in a deep exploration of art and the human spirit. Moments like these reminded me of the profound impact that art could have on the world and why I had chosen to teach the beauty and history of art rather than just create it.

I'd never expected to give up creating art at some point. Still, as my life became more about studying art and making lesson plans that would display how important it was to the youth of this generation, I'd let my creativity slip aside. At my home lay a dormant studio where I used to actively sculpt and probably would again, someday, if the urge ever returned.

After the class concluded, I made my way to a nearby café, a place that had become a sanctuary for reflection. With a cup of strong coffee in hand, I contemplated the upcoming Rembrandt exhibition I'd recently seen advertised. It was a limited exhibit of only three months. A special opening night was planned for a limited number of attendees. I'd managed to snag a dozen tickets for myself and some of my students as a freebie from the museum to the university. The anticipation had been building steadily.

As I sat in the café, my thoughts wandered back to my personal life. I was waiting for Sheila, a woman I had been seeing for the past few months. In the beginning, things had been amazing between us. We shared a passion for the arts and nature, leading to many exciting outings to galleries and beauty spots around Paris.

Sheila was beautiful and intelligent. I'd been enamored with her almost immediately, but familiarity had revealed a darker side to her. She was shallow and vain, her self-centered demands creating a roller coaster that dampened any feelings I might have eventually developed for her. It quickly became apparent that our only real connection was sex. She was wild in bed, and like many men, I let a lot of the drama slide because I enjoyed fucking her.

Still, there's only so much a man can take. I'd made up my mind to let her go. I'd selected this cafe to do so, thinking she'd be less likely to make an angry public spectacle of herself in the middle of it. That might spare me a lot of the venom I knew I'd receive in a private meeting. Some might paint me a coward for my choice, but I considered it an act of self-preservation for my mental health.

"Sheila," I said, standing as she approached the table and pulling her chair out for her to sit. I gave her a little kiss on the cheek, more a matter of polite greeting than affection.

"Peter. I'm surprised you'd want to have coffee after the way you acted last night."

I ruffled at this but said nothing. No sense starting a fight before I'd said what I came here to say. Last night had not been my fault. My crime had simply been to select a restaurant for dinner that she didn't like. She'd had a spat with the head chef there well before I knew her and felt he would take less than sanitary care with her food as a result.

I was livid. I'd attempted to make a reservation at the restaurant when we first started dating and learned that there was a long waiting list. Though my relationship with her was already on the skids, I decided to go once my reservation was available. There was no way I could have known about her previous experience since she'd never told me about it.

"I've been waiting nearly three months to get into this place, Sheila. I made the reservation when we first started dating, and today was the first opening they had to bring you here," I told her.

I looked around at the other people passing us by as we stood outside the establishment. She refused to even go in with me. My frustration had reached its overflow point, and it undoubtedly showed.

"And how was I supposed to know you'd choose to take me to the one place in Paris that I didn't want to dine? Honestly, you waited three months for a reservation. The last time I came, Don got us in with no reservation whatsoever."

"Well, *Don* was an international arms dealer, so I suppose he gets in wherever he wants at the drop of a hat. I, on the other hand, am a non-criminally aligned art professor without that sort of reach."

"He was not. Really, Peter, you have to get over this inferiority complex with my prior relationship."

"First of all, I do not have an inferiority complex about Don. You are the one who just tossed him into our conversation, and I replied accordingly. Secondly, he absolutely is a criminal. He has a record to prove it and you've told me as much yourself."

"I might have overstated his involvement," she said dismissively.

"Whatever, Sheila. At any rate, I've made our reservations for this restaurant. I've waited for months to try it. Instead, I'm standing outside arguing with you about your ex; that has nothing to do with this particular situation other than you once came here with him and fought with the chef. I imagine it is not the first or last the chef, or you will have, and he likely doesn't even remember it. Can we go in and just enjoy ourselves?"

"No. I'm not going in there. I told you why. You'll just have to respect that."

I took a deep breath and let it out slowly. If I loved this woman, I'd respect her choice, even if it felt like nonsense. However, I didn't love her, and I had really begun to dislike her, if I was honest about things. She might be a fireball in bed, but no pussy was worth putting up with the amount of shit she doled out on a daily basis.

"I do respect that," I told her, turning to hail a cab.

When the cab pulled up, I opened the door and helped her inside, leaning in to give the driver her address and some cash for the trip before closing the door. I could see the shocked look on her face through the window as the driver pulled away from the curb.

I was smiling as I went inside and enjoyed a fabulous meal. It was expensive, but I indulged in extra wine and a delectable dessert thanks to the money I saved on her meal. I knew I'd pay for this with a browbeating tomorrow. My phone was already lighting up with furious texts. I turned it off and finished my meal in peace.

I texted her after I returned home and asked her to meet me for coffee after my morning classes so we could discuss it. I had no idea what to say to her, but I knew I'd had enough.

As it turned out, she did the work for me. I could see how angry she was from the way she glowered at me across the table.

"I'm not the sort of woman you just stuff in a cab and send away so you can do what you want," she admonished me.

I was wrong about the public location keeping her under control. She was just as loud and overly dramatic as she wanted to be. The more people looked toward us, the more it encouraged her.

"Sheila, you were being unreasonable," I attempted to quietly interject.

"Unreasonable? Unreasonable!" she half shrieked, drawing the eyes of nearby tables. "If not wanting to eat at a place where the chef will likely spit in my food is unreasonable, then so be it."

I looked down at my now empty cup, wishing it was full again but of something stronger than coffee. I could really use a few shots of something at least 80 proof right now. When I looked back up, prepared to speak, she was way ahead of me.

"This just isn't working out. I should have known that a lowly art professor wouldn't understand how a woman like me needs to be cared for. We're finished, Peter. Don't call me. Don't text me. Don't even say my name out loud in the privacy of your home."

"If that is how you feel, Sheila," I replied, trying to hold back a smile of pure delight at her making this much easier than I'd thought.

"Don't be sad, Peter. We both know you wouldn't have been able to afford me in the long run anyway," she said, standing up and walking away in a huff.

Several other tables looked in my direction, some with sympathy and some with understanding. One elderly gentleman held up his cup of coffee and nodded in solidarity. I smiled broadly and stood up to leave, heading in a different direction from Sheila lest she decide I was stalking her for her next drama.

It was a relief to be done with her. I'd rather be a little lonely than deal with any more of her bullshit. Instead of dwelling on the bad experience, I refocused on thoughts of the future. I decided that my immediate plans would include attending the upcoming Rembrandt exhibition. It promised to be a night filled with art and intellectual conversations, surrounded by people who shared my enthusiasm for the timeless allure of paintings without the headache of having Sheila alongside me.

Returning to my apartment, I found myself surrounded by the sculptures and paintings that defined my space. Though none of them were overly expensive, they were tasteful and beautiful. Some of them were even my own creations. My home was a place of solace and inspiration, a haven where I could lose myself in the world of art and rediscover my true self. I realized that Sheila had cast a dark shadow on the peace I found here when she was present, another reason to be grateful for her absence.

Chapter 5

Peter

I'd invited my students to attend the upcoming Rembrandt display. Still, I was surprised when quite a few of them elected to attend. The tickets were quite pricey, so I felt it would be a shame not to have them go to use. Of course, if the students wouldn't go, I could always give them to other department or university staff members.

In the end, I was able to slate eight of the tickets for students and one for myself. I gave the remaining tickets to another professor for him, his wife, and her father to use. My lecture hall had transformed into a hub of discussions about it, with the students who would be going buzzing eagerly with anticipation. After my class ended, several approached me, their eyes gleaming enthusiastically.

"Professor Dockery, we're really looking forward to the Rembrandt exhibition. Do you think we'll have the chance to meet you there?" one of them asked.

I smiled, appreciating their eagerness. "Absolutely, I'll be available to all of you if you want to chat about anything. Feel free to approach me if you have any questions or want to discuss the artwork. It's going to be a truly enriching experience."

The students exchanged excited glances, and I couldn't help but be delighted by their passion for art. These moments reminded me why I loved teaching and sharing my knowledge with the younger generation.

After the class, I decided to take a break and grab a cappuccino at a nearby coffee bar. The aroma of freshly brewed coffee filled the air, and the warm, inviting atmosphere provided a welcome respite from the hustle and bustle of my classroom. This was the best part of my day. I loved it when the weather was nice, and I could venture out for this tiny bit of respite after classes. With the chaotic relationship that had clouded recent months behind me, I could once again enjoy these moments without poor company or phone interference.

I ordered a mocha caramel cappuccino and settled at a corner table, a book filled with notes in front of me. The event was rapidly approaching, and I wanted every detail to be perfect. As I sipped my drink and reviewed my notes, I contemplated my knowledge of Rembrandt. It was quite expansive, but given that some of my students would be attending, I wanted to brush up on it so I could answer their questions adequately.

The café's atmosphere, a harmonious blend of conversations and the occasional clinking of porcelain, provided a soothing backdrop for my review of the information. My thoughts wandered to the event itself. The exhibition was an opportunity to lose myself in the world of art, free from the complexities of personal relationships. I envisioned an evening filled with beauty, intellectual conversations, and connections with like-minded art enthusiasts.

I relished immersing myself in the art world, connecting with experts and fellow enthusiasts, exploring the intricacies of Rembrandt's works, and igniting my passion for art once more. It was a world where the boundaries of time and space blurred, a realm where the past became the present, and the genius of a painter touched the hearts of those who gazed upon his creations. Tomorrow night was the night, and I was more than ready.

After finishing my cappuccino, I returned to campus for my final class of the day and then made my way home. My apartment door was the gate that separated me from the hustle and bustle of the Paris streets, leaving me in my own little world. I appreciated the solitude. In fact, I probably appreciate it even more these days.

There would never be a part of me that didn't long for the type of deep, personal connection with a woman like my sister had found with her husband. Charlotte had met her husband in college and followed him back home to New York after their marriage the year following graduation. She and Steven had been happily married for more than two decades and had two teenage daughters together. I envied them that.

I'd love to find the sort of love they shared, but I knew I couldn't just command it to happen. I experienced no shortage of women willing to bed a lonely art professor, but I was a novelty item for most of them. They loved the eloquence of my words and intellect, but most didn't share my enthusiasm for it. It was easy for me to talk a woman into my arms, but not so easy to keep her there, and, for that matter, I'd met few I'd wanted to remain.

Perhaps I was just a romantic at heart. I wanted to lock eyes with someone across the room and be instantly drawn to them in a way that surpassed mere sexual interest. I wanted to love the same things, with just enough differences to make a life together exciting, but not so much that we were at odds. I definitely didn't want another Sheila in my life.

Even the thought of Sheila made me shudder. I moved away from any thoughts involving her. I refocused on the exhibition, picking out what I would wear and ensuring it was clean and pressed for the occasion. I couldn't very well arrive at such a momentous event looking shabby. With everything prepared for my classes tomorrow and what would follow that night, I went to bed, content that I was ready.

As I drifted to sleep that night, I imagined meeting a woman, someone unlike anyone I'd ever met. In my dream, we connected immediately, falling into an enthusiastic conversation about ourselves and our interests.

My anticipation was palpable when I stepped through the gallery doors the following night. The gallery had undergone a stunning transformation, with the works of Rembrandt meticulously arranged to showcase the essence of his genius. The soft lighting accentuated the details of each masterpiece, casting enchanting shadows that added depth to the experience.

As I stood by one of Rembrandt's iconic self-portraits, I marveled at how his eyes seemed to follow me, as if the artist himself were in the room. The atmosphere was electric, and the chatter of art enthusiasts filled the gallery.

I made my way through the exhibition, conversing with fellow art lovers, discussing the nuances of Rembrandt's technique, and reveling in the beauty surrounding us. It was a night when time ceased to exist, and the painter's genius took center stage. As expected, the students who'd come to the exhibit hovered about me like feeders, absorbing whatever additional knowledge I'd impart.

I couldn't help but feel a sense of fulfillment, sharing my passion with others and losing myself in the world of such a master. This night was a testament to the power of art. In this world, individuals came together to celebrate the timeless allure of paintings. I knew I'd continue to draw inspiration from the exhibition in the following days. I even hoped my passion for art would be reignited.

I spoke to my students enthusiastically, eager to dive deeper into the world of art and discuss, appreciate, and be inspired by the timeless beauty surrounding us. I was determined to make the most of this opportunity to connect with their young minds and kindle the flames of passion for art.

But as the night moved forward, they began to disperse, either finding their own way among the paintings or returning to wherever they dwelled when not beneath my wings. I enjoyed the paintings quietly, with no one to teach or impress. I was quickly lost in admiration for the techniques and histories of the paintings on show. Only when I tore myself away from the art did I find something else that caught my eye.

As I scanned the crowd gathered around me, my eyes fixed on a woman who seemed completely in her element among the art and the people. She was much younger than me. Though I was only forty-two, being surrounded by students most of the day made me keenly aware of my waning youth. I didn't feel like a middle-aged man—far from it, but I knew that students saw me that way. This woman wasn't a student of mine. She didn't seem to be a student of anyone's.

She wore a simple but elegant black dress that hugged her slender, curvy form. Her long legs led down to a pair of understated black pumps that only made them more alluring. Her thick auburn hair was pulled up in the back with a few loose tendrils framing a pale, slightly freckled face. Unlike many women her assumed age, she wore little makeup and didn't need it. She was a vision of perfection, a work of art in her own right among the masterpieces surrounding her.

I instinctively moved closer to her, gliding slowly among the paintings toward where she stood, speaking to a group gathered around her. She was definitely not a student. She was someone of significance, perhaps one of the owners of a Rembrandt being displayed or a staff member here at the museum. Maybe she was a tour guide explaining part of the exhibition to the visitors who seemed riveted to her as she spoke.

I could see her face better as I approached, which could sometimes be disappointing. That was certainly not the case with her. Her large green eyes were bright with intelligence. Now that I could hear her speaking, I was surprised to realize that she was American, speaking partly in English and sometimes in French, though the latter was minimal. I suspected she had practiced the few words she used well but wasn't fluent. What I did know was that she was a lovely creature.

I stood watching her, suddenly drawn more to her beauty than anything else displayed around the gallery. Her knowledge of Rembrandt rivaled my own and she spoke of his works with a certain eloquence as she moved from one masterpiece to the next. Whoever she was, she wasn't a typical tour guide. The small gathering of people around her seemed to be VIPs.

I carefully followed along from a slight distance so I didn't appear to be trying to infringe upon the group. However, I wanted to stay close enough to continue watching and hearing her as she spoke. I was absolutely enthralled by her beauty, grace, and knowledge. Though she was, no doubt, at least two decades my junior, I was captivated by her and couldn't make myself take my eyes off her.

Of course, I realized that I had to do just that. I couldn't just keep gawking at her like a love-struck stranger. The last thing I wanted to do was come across as some sort of pervert and be ejected from the museum by a watchful member of the security staff who didn't understand that I was harmless.

That was the last thing I wanted. How would that look to my students who might be floating around? Forcing myself to return my gaze elsewhere, I listened to her voice, only looking back when she stopped for a moment. She stood in front of the same self-portrait I had looked at earlier, waiting as her group studied it silently.

Then, something magical happened. She looked in my direction and we locked eyes. It was only for a moment, but it was enough to make my heart skip a beat. Had she felt it, too?

Chapter 6

Giselle

As the curator of the New York museum, I'd always been surrounded by art, but the Rembrandt exhibition was a different beast altogether. The anticipation was palpable as Paris braced itself for the grand event. Everything had to be perfect, and I couldn't afford any slip-ups.

My team and I worked tirelessly to ensure the gallery was immaculate, the lighting impeccable, and the security airtight. It was a lot to manage, but it was all worth it when I thought about the awe-inspiring artwork we'd amassed for display.

By the time the day of the grand opening arrived, I was a bundle of nerves and excitement. I selected an elegant, fitted, classic black cocktail dress for the occasion. My auburn hair was secured in a French knot, with small tendrils framing my face. I spent what felt like hours making sure everything about my appearance was perfect before I arrived at the gallery.

The Rembrandt exhibition was a prestigious event, and I was proud of the work my team and I had put into it. But the grand opening also meant I would be in the spotlight, mingling with art enthusiasts, critics, and potential donors. It was a chance for me to shine but also an evening filled with expectations.

The gallery was bathed in soft, warm light, and the crowd's chatter mingled with the faint strains of classical music, creating an elegant and enchanting ambiance. The anticipation in the air was almost tangible as guests sipped champagne and discussed the paintings surrounding them.

I moved through the crowd, offering welcoming smiles and polite conversation. The attendees were a mix of artists, collectors, and art connoisseurs, and their passion for Rembrandt's work was evident in their discussions. It was a night where art transcended time, where the past coexisted with the present.

Walking through the gallery, I couldn't help but steal glances at the masterpieces adorning the walls. Each painting seemed to tell a story, capturing the essence of humanity and inviting viewers to delve deeper into the emotions and intricacies of the subjects.

Then, while I was giving a mini tour to a group of guests deemed of utmost importance, I spotted a man watching me from just outside the group as I showed one of Rembrandt's self-portraits. Our eyes met momentarily, just long enough for a jolt of electricity to surge through my entire being. I quickly averted my gaze, returning to my group of VIPs.

When I finished with their privately guided tour, I moved about the gallery to mingle among the guests. I quietly walked through the crowd again and circled back, finding myself once more in front of Rembrandt's captivating self-portrait. It was then that my path crossed with the mystery man. As I stood before the painting, lost in its mesmerizing details, I became aware of a presence beside me. A slight electric current seemed to ripple through me.

I turned to find a distinguished-looking man standing there.
His dark hair was slightly graying at the temples. The salt in his
neatly trimmed beard beginning to overtake the pepper. His suit
was fitted to his tall, athletic frame. He was the man I'd seen across
the room earlier. I returned my gaze to the painting rather than
stare.

"Rembrandt's self-portraits are truly remarkable, aren't they?"
he said, his voice resonating with confidence and knowledge. I
noted that his accent didn't match most I'd encountered in Paris.
It was as if it had been somehow diluted, not quite American but
not quite French. Still, it had a lovely lilt to it. I found it somehow
soothing in a way I couldn't quite put my finger on.

I nodded, continuing to gaze at the painting as if I didn't feel
the need to study his handsome face instead. It took me a moment
to conjure up the words I needed to express any honest thoughts.
"Indeed, they offer a unique window into the artist's mind, a
glimpse of his introspection and self-exploration," I finally managed, hoping it didn't sound too contrived. I turned to look at
him finally.

He smiled, and it was a smile that held a depth of understanding. If I'd thought he was handsome before, I found that to be
even more true as his face lit up with the sincerity of his smile.
"You're clearly well-versed in art. I couldn't agree more," he said
as I glanced back at the painting again.

After a few seconds, I turned to look at him again. His dark
brown eyes held a twinkle of intrigue. His presence was magnetic.
He was likely twice my age, with an air of sophistication that was
hard to miss, but I was drawn to him in a way I couldn't explain.
It was as if this man had walked into my life out of nowhere and
I suddenly wanted to know every detail about him.

"I'm Peter Dockery, an art professor here in the city," he introduced himself.

"Giselle Martin, museum curator," I replied, offering my hand in greeting.

"You're the museum curator here?" he asked, seeming doubtful. "I'm surprised we've not met before now."

"Oh. No. I'm a museum curator out of New York. I'm only here for this particular exhibit. Well, I've been here for nearly six months now, but I've been working exclusively on this event. I'll be returning to the States as soon as tonight's opening is over."

"That's a shame," he replied, leaving the comment open-ended as to why. "At any rate, it's a pleasure to meet you."

He extended his hand in greeting, and I offered him mine in return. As our hands met, there was a spark, a connection that seemed to transcend the introductions. It was as if we both recognized in each other a shared passion that went beyond mere pleasantries and Rembrandt's embrace. There was something uniquely interesting about Professor Peter Dockery.

The conversation flowed effortlessly as we discussed art, history, and life. Peter's knowledge and passion for art were evident, and I found myself drawn to his intellect and the way he viewed the world through the lens of creativity. Unlike me, he'd spent a great deal of time sculpting.

"I'd love to see your work," I told him.

"Ah, you don't have to say that. I'm hardly on par with the kind of art you see on a daily basis."

"You might be. How could I possibly say for sure if I've never seen your work?"

"I suppose that is true. When do you leave Paris?"

"Ah, first thing in the morning. I have to get back to New York to tie up some loose ends for an opening there."

"That's a shame. I'd be happy to show you my art if you have the time. In fact, I'd love to show you around the city some more. Though I'd imagine you've seen a good bit of it already if you've been here for months."

"I have seen a lot of it, but there's nothing like seeing a place from the local point of view. I agree. It's a shame we didn't meet sooner."

"I guess I qualify as a local. I actually grew up in New York, too. My parents moved there when I was younger, and I only came back here when I went to college. My sister still lives there."

"Well, I might be too late to get a grand tour of Paris or see your work, but perhaps you'll visit New York to see your sister or parents again one day and we can have lunch or something," I suggested hopefully. I knew it was a long shot, but if fate had brought us together so unexpectedly tonight, surely there was a chance we could meet again.

"You never know. My parents have passed away, but I do visit my sister from time to time. Now I wish I had plans to see her sooner rather than later."

"Oh, I'm sorry about your parents."

"Thank you. It's been a while."

"Giselle?" came a voice from across the museum. I turned to see Marie motioning wildly for me to go where she stood.

"Will you excuse me for a bit? I'll be back soon," I told Peter, not wanting him to leave before I could return.

"Of course," he replied with a smile so captivating I found it hard to pull myself away.

After a brief confab with Marie about a problem with one of the painting displays and how to correct it, I returned to speak with Peter. We talked for what felt like hours, our words weaving a tapestry of shared interests and insights. The crowd around us seemed to fade into the background as we lost ourselves in the magic of the evening.

The evening was a whirlwind of art and conversation. As the hours passed, I couldn't help but be captivated by Peter's presence. He was a kindred spirit, and our connection deepened with each passing moment. Still, I felt the shadow of knowing that I'd be leaving before I'd really get a chance to spend any real time with him.

As the event continued, I again had to excuse myself to fulfill my role as the curator. It was a bittersweet moment as I left Peter, my newfound connection with him lingering heavily in the air around us. I had other guests to attend to, but a part of me longed to return to our conversation. He told me he would wait and maybe we could grab a coffee together when I was done. I was looking forward to that.

Unfortunately, I got tied up with some unexpected problems and lost track of the time as I worked with my staff to iron them out. The last thing I wanted was to leave behind a set of issues I'd have to try and deal with from afar. The longer it took, the more regret I felt at being stuck dealing with it. I wished I'd gotten some contact information from Peter in case he had to go while I was tied up.

I'd enjoyed our conversation immensely and wanted more time to explore the depths of our connection. The evening had been magical, but it was also a reminder of the fleeting nature of such encounters.

Once I could get away again, I made my way through the gallery, thanking the guests for their attendance and enjoying the conversations that followed. I looked for Peter but saw no sign of him. I felt miserable that he might have had to go, but that must be the case, as I didn't see him anywhere in the remaining crowd.

At the end of the evening, I stepped out of the gallery into the night air, pondering my last night in Paris. My thoughts lingered on the connection I'd shared with Peter. It was a spark that had ignited in the presence of timeless art, and I couldn't help but wonder if our paths would cross again, allowing us to explore the depths of our connection further. I'd always believed in serendipity despite never having experienced it for myself.

With the memory of our conversation etched in my mind, I began to return to my hotel, my heart filled with the magic of the night. The Rembrandt exhibition opened its doors to a world of art lovers. Within its embrace, I'd found a connection that held the promise of something truly extraordinary. Just as quickly, I had lost it. Such was the tragedy of life.

Chapter 7

Peter

I found myself disappointed that Giselle had been called away. I couldn't even remember the last time a conversation with a woman had captivated me so much. I was even more excited that she seemed equally taken with me. After she disappeared down a side hallway with one of her colleagues, I returned to study some of the paintings again. I even joined in with another small group being taken through the exhibit.

I'd just finished the walk-through and started looking for Giselle again when my phone rang. I tried to answer it but found that it was almost dead. I shrugged it off. I could call when I got back home. I looked around for Giselle again but couldn't find her.

After a while, I decided that maybe she'd gotten too busy to get back to me. I thought about leaving my number with another staff member but then decided it was pointless. The chances of us ever meeting again were slim with her living in New York and me living here. Though I did visit Charlotte there occasionally, it wasn't nearly enough for me to have any sort of relationship with someone.

I sighed, writing off my chance meeting with such a beautiful, intelligent woman as a cruel trick of fate. What was the point if we were so far apart? My phone rang again, only half a ring before stopping. I saw it was Charlotte, but I still couldn't connect due to my low battery. It wasn't like her to call me right back instead of just waiting for me to return her call later.

As much as I hated just leaving, I felt I needed to find out what was happening. I asked a nearby security guard to tell Giselle I'd had to leave, and he assured me he would do so. With that, I left the museum, leaving behind the most interesting woman I'd met in a while.

I returned home quickly and plugged my phone into the charger before going upstairs and changing out of the suit I'd worn to the museum. Coming back down the stairs, I picked it up and called Charlotte back with it still plugged in. There was no answer, so I left a message. Frustrated, I lay it down and went to the kitchen to grab a beer.

Sitting back on my sofa, I thought about Giselle and our conversation. I could only imagine what a woman like her would be like to touch. She seemed so soft and somehow innocent despite her intelligence. A few times during our conversation, she blushed a little when I was flirtatious or complimentary. It was really quite refreshing.

I closed my eyes and thought about her soft skin and long legs. I could feel myself getting hard just at the thought of her. I let myself imagine how we might fit together, how it might be to kiss her and run my fingers over her soft skin.

I imagined Giselle cooing softly beside me, stripped naked of the black dress that hugged her body so perfectly. In my mind, my fingers moved softly across her skin, connecting each and every one of her adorable freckles with an invisible line. I could almost hear the sound of her giggling at my touch, enjoying the pleasure I was giving her as she lay there and let me do as I pleased.

My little daydream unfolded slowly and sensually, with me taking my time exploring every inch of her pale skin. Soon, I'd moved on to kissing her, our mouths hot on one another as we lazily entwined them, drinking one another in and feeling our flesh pr essed together.

"I want you," she purred beneath me.

"I want you too," I replied, knowing that she might be the last woman I touched, the last woman I wanted to touch.

Our passion was ignited by lust but continued to be fueled by something deeper, something I'd felt since the instant I'd laid eyes on her. Giselle was a work of art in human form. She could have easily been designed by one of the masters that surrounded her in the museum. Her breasts were perfect, full but not too large. The swell of her hip was like a dangerous curve and her ass was a perfect a pple shape.

That didn't even begin to cover the delicate features of her face that made it beautiful or the non-physical aspect of her that appealed to me. Giselle was the total package. She was the kind of woman who inspired artists to create great works in hopes of capturing even an ounce of her perfection.

What must it feel like to make love to a piece of art? I wanted to know. I wanted to hold her in my arms and whisper to her softly while plunging into her depths. What would she feel like? I felt a little wrong for reducing such an incredible creature down to a sexual fantasy, but I couldn't help myself. I was mesmerized by her. I wanted her.

I allowed myself to imagine that we'd not lost one another at the museum, that I'd remained and she'd come home with me. We could have made love all night and parted ways tomorrow instead of sleeping alone. I reached down and began touching myself, stroking my cock through my pants as I imagined all the things I'd l ike to do with Giselle.

I could see her beneath me, her brow sweaty as we made love for hours in every way imaginable. I wanted to be on top of her, grinding slowly in and out of her perfect pink pussy. The ecstasy on her face while I plunged deep inside her until we both came like rockets bursting through the ozone into space.

Unzipping my pants, I freed my throbbing cock from its confines, continuing to stroke myself as I daydreamed about making love to the beautiful Giselle. What did she sound like during sex? Did she talk dirty? Did she beg? I'd love to hear her begging for my hard co ck.

"Please. Give me more, Peter. I want you so much. Fuck me," she would say.

It had been a while since I'd been this turned on by a woman. I wasn't exactly a womanizer, but I'd been with enough women to know the difference between just fucking for fucking's sake and really being excited by a woman. Giselle excited me. I wanted to make her scream my name, but I also wanted to feel her touch. That was what I wanted from Giselle more than anything. I wanted to f el.

I let myself remain lost in my fantasy, stroking my cock until I was on the verge of coming. I kept my focus on Giselle while slowly pumping my dick, wanting the pleasure to last for as long as possible. As my thoughts moved from the soft and gentle ideas of making love to Giselle to imagining myself fucking her hard and fast, listening to her beg for it, my strokes increased.

Soon, I could no longer hold back. I came so hard I couldn't stop it. I filled my fantasy Giselle with every sticky inch of cum I had to offer.

I let go of the little fantasy with a start, realizing I'd become completely lost in it. I reached for the box of tissues on a nearby table and cleaned myself up. Now that my flight of fancy had ended, I felt a little ashamed of myself for whacking off to such a lovely woman who'd done nothing to encourage such seedy behavior but be nice to me.

Tossing the dirty tissues into the nearby wastebasket, I wondered why I hadn't just hung around to see if I might have made this little dream of mine a reality. What was I afraid of? Did I fear that I'd get hung up on a woman who lived a world away and not be able to do anything about it or did I fear that sort of intimacy, in general.

It was true that my track record lately hadn't been stellar, but that shouldn't keep me from at least putting myself out there and seeing what happened, should it? People had long-distance relationships, even if they were a bit more casual than a truly committed partnership. I wondered if Giselle was the kind of woman who could handle something like that. The truth was, I didn't even know if I was the kind of man who could live with the woman I adored thousands of miles away across an ocean.

I was still contemplating all that when the phone jarred me from my thoughts. I glanced at it and saw it was Charlotte, so I picked it up. I could tell she was upset even before she began to speak, and when she did finally manage to do so, her words were garbled by the sounds of her sobbing. It took me the first minute or so of the conversation to get her calm enough to speak effectively.

"Okay, just slow down, Charlotte. Take a breath, honey."

Charlotte finally grew quiet on the other end. I could hear her trying to catch her breath. Finally, she began speaking again—this time quieter and calmer.

"There's been an accident. I tried to call you earlier."

"Yes. I was out and my phone was almost dead. What kind of accident?"

"Car. A car accident," she said, sounding like she might cry again.

"Are you okay? Are the girls okay?" I asked, feeling a bit of panic myself now.

"Yes. We're fine. I mean, we weren't in an accident. It was Steven."

"Oh. Okay. So, Steven had an accident alone."

"He was hit by a woman who ran a stop sign. It's not good. Oh, God. It's so horrible, Peter."

"Tell me. Is Steven okay?" I asked, my heart thudding against my chest.

Charlotte's husband, Steven, was a great guy. Some guys don't really approve of their sisters' husbands or get along with them, but that wasn't the case with us. In fact, Steven was like a brother to me. I cared as much for him as I did Charlotte and the girls.

"He's not good. He's unconscious and they are still running tests, but they know he has some broken bones. He has some head injuries, and they don't know..." She trailed off, her words replaced by crying.

"Where are the girls?" I asked.

"They're here right now. I didn't know what else to do. I brought them with me in case—" She stopped there, unable to finish the sentence. I understood what she meant.

"I see. What do you need me to do?"

"I don't know right now. I just needed to tell you what was happening. I'll know more when the doctors come back out to talk to us."

"Okay. I'll keep my phone close by. You call me the moment you know something or call me just because you need to. I'll be waiting to hear from you, so let me know something no matter what they tell you."

"I w-will. Peter, what if it goes bad? What if he doesn't make it?" she said, crying again.

"You can't think like that, Charlotte. Steven will be fine. Let's just wait and see what the doctors tell you before we get too twisted up, okay?"

"I'll try."

"Is there anyone with you there besides the girls?"

"No. Not right now. I called our neighbor, Tamara. She's going to come and get the girls in a little while and take them to her house for the night."

"That's good. So, just let me know as soon as you can."

"I will," she said solemnly.

"Okay. I love you."

"I love you too," she replied before ending the call.

Chapter 8

Giselle

I left the museum feeling pretty let down about having missed Peter. One of the guards told me that he'd left a message that he had to go, but he hadn't left any details beyond that, which I found surprising. Then again, what was the point? I was leaving in the morning, and I was hardly the type to meet him at his apartment for a last-minute roll in the hay.

Of course, Professor Peter Dockery had no way of knowing that, but perhaps he could sense it about me. It was late and all of the energy I'd felt during the exhibit had vanished. I took a cab back to my hotel and got undressed for bed, washing off my makeup and brushing my hair before climbing into the sheets.

Despite how tired I felt, I had trouble sleeping. My mind kept going back to Peter and wishing things could be different with us. I kept thinking about the attraction I'd felt for him. I'd not felt that for a man in my entire life. Sure, there had been men I'd been drawn to, but not like that. I'd connected with him on what felt like a purely instinctual level.

When I finally dozed off to sleep, I was surprised to find myself in the middle of a dream. It began with meeting Peter at the museum and went pretty much the same way things had in reality. The different part was what happened after the exhibition. In my dream, I'd met Peter outside, and we'd gone for a stroll, stopping at a bar for a few drinks and then returning to his place.

Then, things really heated up between us.

We were barely inside the front door when Peter pushed me against a nearby wall and kissed me feverishly. No one had ever kissed me like that, and I wanted it more than I'd ever imagined. His tongue tangled with mine, drinking me in, the remnants of alcohol providing fuel for our fire. My entire body felt heated by some invisible flame, pushing me toward a four-alarm fire that desperately needed to be quenched.

I let myself relax and enjoy the way he felt; his hard body pushed against me as we seemed to meld into one being. His hands roamed across my body, touching me in places I'd never been touched before, but I didn't stop him. I didn't want him to stop, but he did anyway.

"Is this okay? Are we okay?"

"Yes. Please," I managed, my words breathless with need and anticipation like I'd never felt before.

Peter hoisted me into his arms and carried me to his bedroom, putting me down beside his bed to slowly undress me. He unbuttoned the back of my dress, uncovering my body, exploring each inch with his lips and mouth as it became visible. I gasped as his mouth touched my warm skin, my hunger for him growing deeper as he continued.

As he slipped my dress down my shoulders, he planted small kisses across my back and shoulders. His hands ran softly down my arms, pushing the dress downward until it slipped past my hands and hips, falling in a pile to the floor.

"Beautiful," he muttered, continuing his sensual tour of my skin. Tiny goosebumps scattered across my breasts and arms; the tiny hairs rose to attention as he ran his hands down my frame.

I stood there, my breath shallow as he examined me, smiling with appreciation at my breasts and tiny waist. Finally, his mouth met mine again and his hands wrapped around my waist, drifting down to my backside to catch hold of my ass. He grasped my cheeks firmly in his hands and pulled me toward him, his erection pushing into me for a moment before he released me and reached upward to unhook my bra.

My breasts spilled forward, my nipples lightly brushing the hair on his chest. It was the most amazing feeling. Peter moved downward, his mouth wrapping around one nipple and then the other, sucking at them eagerly while pushing his hand down into my panties to slip his fingers along my wet folds.

I gasped loudly as he touched my most intimate parts, tensing momentarily and then relaxing into his movements. I opened my legs wider, giving him clearance to explore and he obliged. His fingers moved back and forth, teasing me before finally slipping inside. My nails dug into his back as he penetrated me with one finger and then another, moving them ever so gently in and out of m y pussy.

"That feels so amazing," I moaned against his ear, my hands now holding onto his shoulders to steady my weakened knees.

"It certainly does. Your pussy is so wet right now. I can't wait to taste you."

Peter pulled his fingers free of me, leaving me wanting more. It was only momentary, as he pushed me down across the bed and slipped my panties free, leaving me lying there in nothing but my heels. He left them on and centered himself in front of me, looking down at me as he once again began teasing me with his fingers.

I bucked forward against them, trying to get him deeper inside me, but he held back, making me wait. His thumb pressed against my clit, moving ever so slightly back and forth as he began to slip his fingers in and out of me, pushing my pussy walls apart as I cooed beneath him on the bed, my eyes closed as I enjoyed the way he was touching me. This was as close to heaven as I've ever been, and I wa nted to stay here forever.

"Carlton," he suddenly shouted. "Carlton!"

I looked up at him, confused. His face began to fade away right in front of me and then there was only darkness with a thin stream of light filtering in through a nearby window.

I awoke with a start, no doubt brought out of my sleep by people shouting at one another outside. I was surprised at how intense the dream had been. I hated that I'd woken up before I'd climaxed. It felt like I'd been cheated out of the best part. I lay lazily against the pillows and began touching myself. My dream might have ended too soon, but I could take care of that personally.

I closed my eyes and thought of Peter, imagining his hands stroking my clit and exploring my wet pink folds. There was nothing I wanted more than to enjoy his touch and know how he would feel inside me. How I could be so torn up after meeting a man only once was beyond me, but I wanted to experience every inch of him.

I took my time, touching myself just as he'd been touching me in the dream. I massaged my left breast with one hand while exploring myself with the other. I was just as wet as I had been in the dream, the fantasy bleeding over into my reality. If only Peter had been transported along with it, I thought as I continued to touch myself. I sank my fingers into my center, slowly moving them in and out just as he had.

I moaned into the loneliness of the room around me, desperate for release. I knew exactly how to touch myself. Though I was a virgin when it came to men, to having full-blown sex with one, I was very well initiated with my own body and how to get myself off. I'd heard Helena and Marie talk about how they'd rather have stayed home and pleasured themselves than have suffered sex with this one or that one. Still, I had a hard time imagining sex not being as mind-blowing as it was in my dreams.

Unlike them, I didn't own a vibrator or any other toys. It wasn't that I opposed them, but I couldn't imagine going into a shop somewhere and buying such things. I couldn't even see myself buying them online to be delivered in discreet little packages. I could only imagine visiting my parents in Florida and having one of them stumble across my browsing history while checking something online or on my phone during some emergency that required them to get into it.

I pushed the thoughts out of my head. They were ruining my focus on what was really important to me right now. I bit my lip and began massaging my pussy walls with my finger, crooking my index finger to hit the spot that always sent me over the edge. I cupped my breast, enjoying the weight of it in my hand as I milked my pussy walls for the desired effect.

My legs seized as my body prepared to give up the release I sought. I pulled my feet upward and dug my heels into the bed, bracing myself as I picked up the speed of my fingers slipping in and out of my center. My thumb pressed against my clit, rubbing it slightly as my entire body seemed to seize and then let go.

I twisted slightly in the bed with the force of my orgasm and then collapsed against the covers again. It had been satisfying, but unlike most of the times I got myself off, it felt like something was missing. I'd gotten so wound up in the dream, ready to be taken by Peter and feel the power of his body pumping into mine, that this all just seemed like a bit of a letdown.

I might be physically satiated, but I was far from emotionally content. In moments like this, I wondered why I was still waiting for someone like Peter to come along. It's like Helena and Marie always talked about—you could have great sex without an emotional connection. But even they would admit that sex with someone you loved and wanted was infinitely better.

I suppose that was just the way life was. You might find that, and you might not. Sex might just be sex, or it might be so much more than that. I didn't know if I would ever discover how truly magical it could be. The real question was whether I would finally settle for giving up my virginity to someone in some casual encounter, or would I find what I was really looking for?

My thoughts went back to Peter. The truth was that I hardly knew the man. I likely would never get a chance to find out if he was more than just some guy who talked a good game and caught my attention or if he had the potential to be so much more to me. Still, as I had met him, then surely there were more like him out there. Perhaps I'd been looking in the wrong places.

I was much younger than him, and I had always gravitated toward guys my age. They tended to be more into sex than substance, and without the latter, I'd never been interested in the former. I guessed that Peter had more experience and understood that having the connection made sex better than just getting laid by anyone out there.

Of course, he struck me as a man willing to go if I was, and that part of him was also interesting to me. I wanted both. I wanted the slow, smooth lovemaking that came with true passion, as well as the heated moments. I wanted it all.

I settled down into the covers again. At least, if I couldn't have the real thing, I could always dream about the French-American hottie I'd met tonight. There was nothing wrong with that. I drifted off into a deep sleep with a huge smile still on my face. Tomorrow I would leave Paris, but I could take my little "Giselle and the Professor" fantasy back home with me and enjoy it to my heart's content.

Chapter 9

Giselle

The sunshine on my face felt wonderful as I lay naked, wrapped up in the soft cotton sheets of my hotel bed. I smiled as I looked toward the Paris light, a sense of melancholy lurking just beneath my surface as I realized this was my last day in Paris. Today would be filled with the hustle and bustle of dealing with luggage and airports.

Though I was excited to return home after being gone for months, I'd miss my time here. I'd come to love Paris, but my work schedule dictated that I return to the art museum in New York. With the Rembrandt exhibit off to a great start, my part of the work here was done, and I was needed back at the museum.

I had to be back in New York first thing in the morning to oversee an event I'd been working on remotely, and now I must sew up the final details for it in person. With a sigh, I pushed the covers aside. I sat up in bed, for the first time realizing that the sun didn't usually hit so heavily through the window beside the bed first thing in the morning.

Picking up my phone by the bed, I gasped. After all the excitement last night and the sudden feeling of being tired that had taken hold once I returned to my room suite, I'd forgotten to set my alarm. Check-in for international flights would be closing in an hour and it would take at least half of that time to get to the airport. So much for arriving the recommended three hours before my flight. I reached for the hotel phone.

"I need to get a taxi to the airport," I told the desk clerk breathlessly.

"Absolutely, madam. What time?"

"As soon as one can get here. I'll be down in five minutes."

"I will find you one." She seemed to understand without me having to go into further explanation.

No doubt I wasn't the first person to call down for a taxi with that "I'm late for my flight" panic in their voice. I threw my hair up in a bun, tossed the few things I'd kept out for this morning into my open cabin luggage and closed it. Thankfully, I'd packed most of my stuff ahead of time. Giving the room a final once over, I darted out the door and hurried to the elevator with my three suitcases in tow.

"I've printed your final bill, charged your card, and hailed you a cab," the clerk said as I emerged from the elevator and juggled my bags.

"Thank you," I said, relieved to have even the least little bit shaved off the time it would take me to get to the airport.

My hopes were quickly dashed as we encountered heavy traffic and sat motionless, waiting for it to move again.

"How long are we going to be stuck in this mess?" I asked the driver.

He shrugged at me, speaking broken English with a heavy French accent. "If I knew that, I'd bet the races."

I sighed heavily and looked out the window at the unmoving cars. I was never going to make my flight, but what else could I do but try? I might get lucky, and it would be delayed too, or I would make it just under the wire. My heart thudded heavily with the anxiety I felt. What a disaster this was! All the hard work I'd done to ensure the Paris exhibition was off to a rocket start would be undone by missing the opening of the New York one.

Of course, most of the work on that exhibit had already been done by other staff members. I'd done most of my input remotely as needed. Now, I just had to finish up some final touches and clear up any remaining issues so we could open on schedule. If I missed my flight, that would put the success of that opening in jeopardy, and it would reflect poorly on me.

As if in response to my discomfort, the traffic began moving, and we were on our way again. I felt a tremendous sense of relief as the taxi resumed speed. I might make it, after all. Ordinarily, I wouldn't be too concerned. I'd just grab a room somewhere, spend one last night in Paris, and catch another flight. Unfortunately, I didn't have that luxury. I'd purposely scheduled my flight early in the morning so I could be back at the museum by early evening to check on final details for an event opening first thing the following morning.

It was going to be an absolute disaster if I missed my flight and couldn't get another. I bit my lip nervously as we proceeded along the Paris streets and breathed a sigh of relief as we pulled up to the curb. I glanced at my watch. It was going to be close, but I might just make it.

I retained hope until the very last moment when the woman at the counter shook her head from side to side and spoke the words I least wanted to hear.

"I'm sorry. Check-in for this flight is closed."

"Please, I have to be back in New York this evening," I told her.

"I'm sorry, but you're too late. You'll have to catch the next flight."

"When is that?"

"Two hours."

"Okay. I need to change my flight to that one."

"You'll have to go to the ticket counter for that," she told me dismissively.

I looked over at my pile of luggage and sighed. I'd have to haul it with me as I had nowhere to leave it where it would be safe. I turned and grabbed the handles, lugging them back to the ticketing area, and got in line. I made my way toward the counter with a sense of impending doom, losing all hope of things working out.

If the next flight was in two hours, then I was still cutting it close by getting my ticket now. That was assuming the flight wasn't full and there were tickets to be had. That only made me more nervous as I stood in line, waiting for my fate. There were quite a few people in front of me. I felt like screaming for them to hurry up as I waited impatiently for the next free ticketing associate.

Finally, it was my turn, and I wheeled my luggage up. "I need to change my ticket for the next flight to New York," I told the woman there.

She held out her hand and asked for my ticket. I handed it to her, and she looked at it before pulling up something on her computer terminal. After clicking through a few things, she shook her head solemnly. My heart dropped.

"There are no matching seats on that flight," she told me.

"Are there any seats on the flight?" I asked, the frustration in my voice no doubt apparent.

"There are still a couple seats left in business class. I can get you an upgrade for a change fee and the difference in pricing."

"And how much will that be?" I asked, daring to feel optimistic again.

"Twenty-one hundred euros."

I furrowed my brow, doing a little quick math in my head. "That's like $2200!" I groaned.

She said nothing but waited. When I didn't respond, she replied, "Yes. Would you like me to book the ticket?"

"I don't know. It's a lot of money. I'm not sure my employer will cover it."

"Perhaps you can call them and then come back. It may still be available if you don't take too long."

"May?" I replied.`

"Yes. I can't hold it for you while you consult with your boss," she said, sounding mostly disinterested in my dilemma.

I thought about this for a moment. I could call and check on reimbursement, but that might risk losing the ticket altogether. It would be far more hassle to miss final preparations for the event tomorrow than trying to talk my overlords into reimbursing me for the ticket. It was tricky, since I'd brought this on myself.

"Fine. I'll take the upgrade," I groaned.

She began clicking keys, finally asking for my passport and credit card to finish the transaction. Armed with an overly expensive plane ticket, I made my way through baggage check-in and security before taking a seat among the others waiting for my flight.

Even now, having a ticket in hand and waiting to board, I felt an overwhelming sense of anxiety. I would hit the ground running once I arrived in New York. I'd have to get my stuff home and get to the museum before it got too late. A night security staff member would let me in after hours, but only to a certain point.

It was one thing to stay past museum closing or return at a decent hour to take care of some business, but it became a whole new ball of wax to show up very late in the evening. That sort of behavior was suspect and would result in the director being called whether they let you in or not. That was the last thing I wanted.

I felt like I was on pins and needles and didn't think I'd feel any differently until I knew my timetable in New York. There could be delays in the flight that weren't yet posted or delays in the air. Either one could undermine my plans to get to the museum before it was too late, get my final review done, and get back home for a decent night's sleep before I had to be back in the morning.

As I sat in the airport waiting area, still pondering why I'd agree to such a tight schedule, I thought about my last night at the Paris museum. I really had done a fantastic job there and was proud of it. I wanted to be equally proud of the New York exhibit. In fact, I wanted it to be spectacular despite having handled it from afar with so many other things going on at an exhibition on another continent.

If I could pull both of these off with the appearance that I'd made it all so easy, then I'd be on the fast track for a higher position as soon as one was open. That was my ultimate goal. Though I enjoyed my job as a curator, there was so much more I could do as an assistant director or even as a director, eventually.

I'd started a few rungs up by nailing a curator position, but I didn't want to get stalled there.

What was the difference between starting in a low position, climbing up to curator, and starting as curator, then just being stuck there for as long as it would have taken you to get promoted? Either way, you weren't moving forward from the curator position. Of course, the higher positions were harder to come by. Our assistant director was a part of the family that owned the museum. The only reason he wasn't director was that the existing director had been there for years.

As things stood now, the assistant director had proved himself so incompetent that while he'd maintain his position, he'd never become director. So, it was just a matter of waiting for the director to step down before I could step into his shoes if I proved myself before that happened, which stood to be soon due to his advancing years.

I snapped out of my thoughts and looked around the waiting area. This place was packed. It was going to be a hell of a flight home.

Chapter 10

Giselle

My assessment of the flight wasn't at all wrong. Looking around, I was surprised I'd even gotten on the flight. The place was rammed with people waiting to board. I struck up a conversation with another American headed back to Virginia with a stopover in New York.

"Two months ago, I'd laughed at anyone who told me I'd be gallivanting across the globe at the drop of a hat, but here I am. In the past six weeks, I've visited Scotland, Ireland, England, Germany and France. I'm headed back home for a few months and then I'm off again! I'm going to the land down under!" she gushed.

"Wow. That's a lot of travel in only six weeks!"

"It is, but I've got nothing but time now," she said with a smile.

"Retired?" I asked, making an assumption based on her appearance. She was an older woman, maybe in her sixties. She wasn't quite old enough for retirement, but some folks called it a day early if they were fixed income-wise.

"Oh, no. I've never worked, at least not outside the home. My husband earned good money, but he was stingy. He never wanted to go anywhere, and he wanted me at home when he returned from work. We got married young and I spent the last fifty years tending to him, never to myself. He died a few months back."

"I'm sorry to hear that," I told her.

She smiled broadly again. "Don't be. He was a raging asshole. And all that money he hung on to with a tight fist? It's all mine now. Plus, the life insurance. I sold our house. It was a horrible big thing that took up all my time. I bought myself a little townhouse big enough just for me. I'm rolling in dough and I'm spending all but what I don't need to see me through to my end."

I wasn't sure what to say to this. I nodded, keeping a smile on my face but not convinced I should be smiling.

"Oh, honey. I'm sorry. You must think I'm awful. Maybe I am. It's just that I was married to that man while we were still in our teens. Folks did that a lot back in our day—you know, married while we were really still kids. Anyway, he was a mean son of a bitch. I'll spare you the sordid details, but I've earned every cent I got when that bastard died."

"Well, I'm glad you're enjoying it," I said, for lack of something better to say.

"Oh, I am," she told me with a chuckle. "I even got laid while I was in Paris."

I'm sure my face registered involuntary shock at this admission. She seriously had to be in her late sixties. Was everyone getting laid in Paris but me?

"I suppose that was too much information," she laughed, blushing a little as she spoke.

"It's okay. I've been in Paris for six months, and the women I work with tell tales that would probably shock a sex columnist."

"I just think it's great. Unless you count getting a little frisky with the minister's son when I was fourteen, I've never been intimate with anyone but my husband until three days ago. That's a long time to wait to have good sex. I envy you younger women who aren't afraid to sample the menu and don't get a reputation for it like we would have when I was your age."

"Oh, there's still plenty of that going around from certain people," I told her, thinking of all the slut shaming commentary I'd seen during my lifetime.

"I'm sure, but it's not nearly as bad. I see women on these social media sites talking about their sexual encounters openly. We'd have never been so bold. It's refreshing. I feel like I've just been handed a whole new, exciting life."

"I'm really happy for you. You seem to be enjoying it."

"I sure am. I'm even thinking about getting a tattoo. That's if I can find a place that's not too wrinkled to put one."

She laughed at this, so I joined her, not knowing what else to do. Our conversation was interrupted as they called for us to board, so we gathered our things and got in line. In the crowd, I got separated a bit from her, but I kept thinking about what she'd said. Here I was, waiting for the right man to come along, saving myself for someone special and now I wondered if it was worth all the importance I put on it.

Though it was horribly old-fashioned, I always fancied waiting until my wedding day to give myself to someone. How thrilling for your husband to be the first man you've ever shared such intimacy with, I thought. But how likely was it that you would be his first and how was it special for you if it wasn't special for him? Then again, what if he was bad in bed? What do you do if you're hopelessly in love with a man, marry him, and then spend your life having disappointing sex? That must be so depressing.

I thought about that all the way to my spot on the plane, finally taking a seat in the business class section. I was instantly spoiled. These seats were so much nicer than the economy seats I usually purchased. Even though I generally flew on the museum's dime when I traveled these days, their budget was very thick regarding procurements but very thin on travel, leaving me in the cheap seats on most trips.

Though Paris had been my first major project with the museum, I'd been on several trips stateside and into Canada. The flight to Paris had been cramped and long, with a ridiculously long layover during which I was stuck in the airport, biding my time with a book and headphones. This looked like it would be decidedly more comfortable, and it was a nonstop flight, so that would save me some time and frustration.

While I waited for the plane to finish loading, I pulled out the travel kit I'd brought to stow under my seat. I began putting on a little makeup, something I'd had no time to do after getting up at the last minute this morning. I was still shocked that I'd forgotten to set my alarm. Still, between the champagne at the gallery and the euphoria I felt after flirting with a handsome stranger, it had just slipped my mind.

I smiled as I thought about my dream about Professor Peter Dockery. I didn't have much time to consider it this morning once I realized I was late and became consumed with getting to the airport. Now that I was stuck on a plane for eight hours, I'd have plenty of time to think about it. I pondered it a bit as I began to apply my makeup.

I quickly dabbed on some BB cream, eyeliner, mascara, and some colored lip gloss. I never wore much makeup, so I had it down to a fine art. I pulled my hair into a messy knot and left a few tendrils down to frame my face. Satisfied that I looked presentable enough for travel purposes, I put my bag away and tucked my carry-on under my seat.

I settled in to look out the window, finally beginning to relax now that I was on the plane and headed in the right direction. I still wasn't happy with potentially losing the extra money it cost to get me in this window seat, but what was done was done. I'd be in New York in about eight hours and the time difference would work in my favor. I could grab the air train and subway home, but with my bags and already having lost time due to my delayed flight, I'd be better off grabbing an Uber instead.

I'd planned on having some time to rest and freshen up, but I'd have to settle for dropping off my bags, grabbing a latte, and heading into work. I was tired already just thinking about it.

"The show must go on," I muttered to myself as I watched airport staff moving about out on the tarmac below. They looked tiny even though the plane hadn't left the ground yet. I was always amazed by just how large airplanes were and that they even stayed in the air like they did. Of course, I wouldn't want to be on one that didn't stay in the air.

I glanced back inside the plane as people continued to get on the flight. Most of business class was already full, but there were still a few empty seats. So far, the one beside me was empty. If I was lucky, it was the remaining seat and I'd have this entire little area to myself. I took a moment to think about all the poor people further back on the plane in economy. With a full plane, they would be squished like sardines back there while I enjoyed extra legroom and a spare seat.

My newfound sense of entitlement amused me as I fished out my headphones and found music on my phone while waiting for boarding to finish. I went ahead and stuck it on airplane mode and started the playlist I'd saved. As the smooth voice of Norah Jones filled my head, I almost nodded off. At least that was one thing: I'd have plenty of room to spread out and catch a nap on the flight with the empty seat beside me.

Of course, I should have known I was wound up too tight for that to happen. Instead, my mind shifted into work mode as I pulled out the Filofax I kept in my bag. It was a running joke with my coworkers that I still relied on the vintage leather Filofax that had once belonged to my father. He'd gifted it to me when he retired. Like him, I preferred having physical notes that I could easily lay my hands on in addition to digital options.

I flipped through the notes of what I needed to accomplish tonight and put small dash marks beside them. The rest could be finished in the morning, and some would have to wait until then. It would be after business hours when I arrived at the museum, and I'd have to wait for some places to re-open in the morning before I could contact them for final checks.

It felt like there was still so much to do and no time left to get it done. The truth was that I really didn't know for sure. I might arrive to find that everything was in good order and I had relatively little to take care of. On the flip side, I might show up and realize the whole thing was a disaster that needed to be salvaged. My routine contact with staff led me to believe things were in good order, but I just couldn't be sure until I saw it myself.

I stopped to ponder whether the responsibility of becoming a director was truly what I wanted from the museum. If I had this many headaches as a curator, then a director must have massive migraines. Of course, I also knew he gave me a lot more responsibility than the average curator because he trusted me. Still, it was only a fraction of what he had to deal with on a day-to-day basis.

I closed the book again and lay it on my lap as I thought again about the woman I'd met from Virginia. I wondered if she was flying economy or first class. My bet was on the latter based on what I'd learned about her in a brief amount of time; for some reason, that made me smile. I closed my eyes for a moment and drifted away.

Chapter 11

Giselle

I awoke with a start, realizing that I had dozed off. I looked up to see people still dripping onto the plane. It felt like it was taking forever to get off the ground, but as I glanced at the time on my phone, I saw that it wasn't even time for takeoff, so I must have only fallen asleep for seconds.

A rather rotund woman clumsily tried to move her bags down the aisle and stopped to put them in the overhead bin. I watched her from afar, wondering how the size of that duffle even qualified as carry-on luggage.

My heart stopped in my chest.

Was I still asleep? Was I dreaming this?

Standing patiently behind the woman as she managed to settle in her seat stood the gorgeous professor I'd met last night at the gallery. He was coming toward me, a huge smile on his face. I tried not to gawk at him as he approached, but I didn't know where else to look, so I just kept my eyes on him and smiled through my confusion.

"Well, fancy meeting you here," he exclaimed as he punched a backpack into the overhead and sat down beside me.

I just stared at him in stunned silence as he continued to grin at me. Finally, I found my voice.

"Wh-what are you doing here?" I asked.

"Same as you. I'm flying to New York."

I contemplated this for a moment. How was he on the same flight—in the seat beside me? Was he stalking me? My mind ran through our conversation last night. I know I told him I was leaving this morning, but I hadn't told him what flight I was on. Should I be worried about this? I mean, he was insanely hot and very intelligent, but no one likes a creeper.

"How did you know what flight I was on?" I gasped, my mouth spewing out the thought in my head unexpectedly.

"Wait. What? No. I didn't," he said awkwardly. "I'm going to visit my sister."

"I thought you said you had classes today. When we talked last night, you said you'd have to go soon as you had to be in early to prepare for some kind of test." I tried not to sound as suspicious as I probably had a moment ago.

"Yeah. I had to put that in the hands of a proctor. My sister called me right before I left the museum last night. That's why I had to leave. My phone was almost dead and I wasn't getting a good signal in the museum. She kept calling and I didn't know if you were coming back, so I went home to put it on the charger and call her back. Anyway, to simplify, I have a family emergency. I had to catch the earliest flight I could get out. This was the last seat they had."

"Yes, I know. I missed my morning flight and had to upgrade."

"Ouch," he said knowingly. "So, you had to spend the big bucks for business class too."

"Yes. Ouch, indeed."

"Well, I guess we'll just have to look on the bright side. We're here now, and we have at least eight hours to continue our chat from last night."

"We certainly do," I said, forgetting all about the nap I should probably take instead.

One of the attendants briefly interrupted our conversation by making the usual pre-flight announcements. I used the time to try and gather my thoughts. I had the duration of the flight to put my foot in my mouth, and given my expertise at saying the wrong thing to men, there was a good chance I'd have it wedged there before the flight's end.

"Your family emergency—I hope it's not too serious," I said as the announcement ended.

"Yes and no. Charlotte—that's my sister—her husband was in an accident. He's going to be okay, but she'll need a bit of help with him and the kids for the next little while. Our parents are gone and there are only the two of us left. She has a ton of friends and neighbors, but not anyone dependable to stay with my nieces for an extended time."

"Oh, that's terrible. I hope the little ones aren't too upset about things."

"Little ones? Oh, you mean the nieces. They aren't little. Ellie is 13 and Anna is almost 15. They are at that age where they can mostly care for themselves but still need adult supervision."

"So, Uncle Peter to the rescue then," I said with a large smile.

"Yes, Uncle Peter is the most beloved uncle of all time."

"How many uncles do they have?"

"Just me," he said, chuckling.

"Aunts?"

"Not on our side of the family, but Steven—that's their father—he has two sisters. They're monsters."

"Oh, come on now. Monsters?"

"Yes, they have big sharp teeth and horns, and their eyes glow red in the dark."

"They're probably lovely women." I laughed.

"They're not. I promise you that they are exactly as I describe. They despise both me and Charlotte."

"I just don't see how anyone could despise you or your sister, if she's anything like you."

"Ah, flattery is always the way to my heart, but you'll just have to trust me when I say they dislike us immensely. Not to get too much into family drama, but they come from old money. Charlotte and I do not. We are beneath them."

"I understand. I run into the aristocratic sorts all the time in my line of work. It's always interesting to watch the people dynamics that come into play. Rich people. Poor people. Then some are rich and try to pretend they're starving artists and their counterparts."

"Those who are poor pretending to be rich," he finished.

"Precisely. They all have their own agendas for how they behave."

"And they're all predictable. I have the same thing in my classes. You wouldn't think it, but that sort of behavior seems to develop early on. I know their backgrounds from their student files, so they don't fool me, but they make a huge game of fooling one another."

"It must be so tiring trying to pretend you're something that you're not."

"It has to be. I had this one kid who actually traded places with another kid in my class. They were in their respective places academically—they didn't want to get tossed out of college, but one was the son of a wealthy diplomat and the other's father owned a barely profitable pub."

"I get why the struggling kid would want to step into the rich kid's shoes, but why the other one?"

"A woman. It's always about a woman, isn't it?"

"A woman?"

"Yes. The rich kid had his eye on this pretty little thing from Liverpool. Her father was a docker. He'd noted that she steered clear of the wealthier students, so he wanted her to feel he was someone she could identify with. He swapped everything with the other kid. A Porshe for a Fiat, a large apartment for a shared flat, even paid him enough to keep up appearances."

"And did it all work? Did he get the girl?"

"He did, but he couldn't keep her. No matter how hard he pretended, certain things about himself gave him away. By the end of the semester, they were seated as far across the room from one another as they could manage, and he'd moved back into his luxury apartment."

"That's crazy."

"It was. I had no idea about any of it until I heard the third guy in the mix laughing about it. It seemed that he walked away with enough cash to live a bit better while he was at college and ended up with the girl."

"I guess that's Karma for you," I said, laughing.

"I suppose it is. Anyway, enough about the pretenders of the world. Tell me some more about yourself. Who is Giselle Martin?"

Though it was a simple thing, I felt flattered that he remembered my last name without being reminded. Most men might retain your first name after meeting you once, but not necessarily your surname.

"I'm certainly not from old money. I'm not even from new money," I laughed.

"Still, you are quite young to be a museum curator. You can't be more than twenty-two."

"I'm twenty-three and will be twenty-four in a few months."

"Just starting out. I remember those days. I'm still coming to terms with turning forty a few years ago. It's like a slap in the face reminding you that youth is fading."

"Wow, I wouldn't have guessed that. You look much younger, maybe thirties at most."

"There's that flattery again," he said with a grin. "Thank you, but I am every day of forty-two. I have the mistakes to prove it."

"Divorced?"

"No. I have thankfully escaped the cliche of being a middle-aged divorcee with emotional baggage."

I wanted to ask if he had children, but I didn't want this to feel like an inquisition. He likely wouldn't have been able to drop what he was doing and help his sister in another country if he had kids of his own. Though, it was possible that they lived with their mother. Still, something told me that this man was an open book and would have mentioned them already.

Now, the captain came on the intercom, announcing takeoff as the plane began to rumble down the runway. I always hated this part of the flight. The takeoff and the landing were the worst. I didn't even mind a bit of turbulence in the air, but somewhere in the back of my head, I always felt a bit of foreboding about how rough it felt with the wheels on the ground.

"You can let go now," Peter said gently as the plane lifted into the air.

I was puzzled for a moment before realizing I had a death grip on the small folding armrest between us and, along with it, his hand that had been resting there. I let go and quickly moved my hand away, a deep red flush spreading up my cheeks.

"I am so sorry," I gasped.

He laughed. "Don't be. I'll hold your hand any day of the week. Maybe just not quite so hard next time. You're strong for such a little thing."

Now it was my turn to laugh, the awkwardness slipping away just as quickly as it had surfaced. "I'll keep that in mind."

"Can I buy you a drink?" he asked.

"I shouldn't. I have to hit the ground running when we land."

"Really? They won't even let you have the evening off?"

"Usually, they would, but we have a big event starting tomorrow, and I have to attend to some final details."

"Well, how about just one drink. We must toast having run into one another again and having all this time to talk on our travels."

"Fine. You've twisted my arm."

"That's my girl," he said.

There was something about the way he said it that made me a little giddy. For a fleeting moment, I thought of my dream about him last night and felt myself blushing. I quickly glanced out the window to regain my composure, commenting on a cloud formation like a dolt.

"I'm always amazed to see clouds below me instead of above me," I marveled, feeling the heat fade from my cheeks.

"Yes. They are a marvel. Quite a few things are lovely from above or below."

I noted the suggestive tone in his words but fought blushing again as I turned my attention to the flight attendant who had arrived at our seat. Peter ordered our wine before resuming our conversation. We continued to talk while the attendant fetched our drinks, and then we had another, but I declined the third, knowing I needed to keep at least some of my wits about me for the work I had to do later.

Then again, I might need my wits about me on this plane, given the turn our conversation was beginning to take.

Chapter 12

Giselle

As the plane made its way to New York, the conversation between Peter and me grew increasingly more personal.

"You've never had a serious boyfriend? Never?" Peter asked, seeming quite astounded by my revelation.

"No. Never," I admitted.

"How is that even possible? You're beautiful, you're talented, you're intelligent. I could go on, but I don't want to embarrass you," he said.

"Too late," I replied, feeling the heat spread up my cheeks again.

He chuckled and looked at me softly. "Seriously, though. You're a wonderful woman. Why would anyone not want to be in a relationship with you? What am I missing? Are you low-key crazy? A stalker? Am I already in jeopardy of being on one of those killed by true love crime shows?"

I laughed. "No, nothing like that. I'm not crazy."

"Spoken just like a crazy person," he teased.

I smiled at him. "Honestly, I don't think it's any one thing. It's a combination of things."

"Like what? Humor me. I'm fascinated," he said, his eyes keen with interest.

"Okay. Well, I'm driven. I spend a lot of my time at work. Before that, I spent a lot of my time studying. I was hyper-focused on graduating with honors. Once I accomplished that, I was even more focused on getting the job I wanted."

"And did you?" he asked.

"Did I what?" I said, my mind still contemplating the original question.

"Get the job you wanted."

"I did. I walked into the museum expecting rejection."

"Why rejection?"

"Because I'd already been rejected so many times. I must have applied to more than a dozen galleries and other museums before I landed at this one. I was always too young, too inexperienced ... too *something*."

"And what made this one different? What was it that got your foot in the door? The curation world is a tough industry to break into and even tougher to be successful in."

"Yes. Well, as it happened, they had fired their curator several days before and the assistant curator had stepped in. The former was really old. He'd been there for years and was set in his ways. He'd created a toxic work environment for staff and an inhospitable climate for acquisitions. The powers that be decided it was time to cut him loose."

"And the assistant curator?"

"Not much better from what I hear and from the brief time she spent there after I was hired. She had a good eye and some solid contacts but made promises she couldn't keep quite a bit."

"Promises?"

"Yes, she'd promise the higher-ups that she could get a certain exhibit or artifact on loan, but she'd never deliver. They'd waste their time looking into the value of bringing in the item, decide it was a good choice, and then she'd let them down."

"I see. So, did they fire her, too?"

"Not at first. I came in at just the right time. They wanted new blood and fresh ideas. They wanted someone who could take ancient artifacts and make them interesting to the younger generation."

"T-Rex meets Tech," he replied.

"Exactly. They brought me in as the new assistant curator, and she remained as curator. Less than a month later, she was gone, and I was in. I just showed up at the right time."

"I doubt it was that simple."

"I think it was," I replied, unclear what he meant by the comment.

"Perhaps you just haven't given yourself enough credit for being so amazing," he said with a soft smile.

He was at least partly right, of course. A part of me knew I wouldn't have been given the job if I weren't qualified and hadn't made a good impression. Though showing up when I did hadn't hurt my chances, I did possess the skills to be successful. I just didn't want to seem egotistical.

"I guess I'm just humbled by it all. I'm one of the youngest museum curators in the country. There are quite a few my age in galleries but not so many museums. So, I guess I feel like it's owed as much to chance as skill."

"Most things are. Just don't sell yourself short."

"I try not to."

Peter smiled and nodded. "So, let's get back to this lack of a serious relationship subject then. I get that you have been busy working on a career, and I know that your position at the museum must be time-consuming, but surely you've met interesting men in your line of work."

"Interesting? Yes. I'm not saying I've never had a date," I joked. "I'm just saying that nothing ever really worked out."

"Nothing?" he asked, a wry smile on his face.

I looked away, feeling suddenly bashful. My experience with men was limited and Peter was someone that I suspected had a very fulfilling romantic life. However, the fact that he'd never married said that perhaps he was a bit of a rogue. I reminded myself to be mindful of that fact.

"Nothing," I replied, looking down at my hands.

"Look at me," he said, a tone of commandment in his voice. I found myself doing as he said, meeting his soft gaze. His eyes were kind as he brought his face closer to mine, speaking quietly so as not to be overheard. "There is nothing wrong with that or you."

I smiled, feeling a little awkward at the conversation's turn. Still, a part of me was very interested in what he would have to say about my situation. What did a worldly man like Peter Dockery think about someone like me? Was it a turn-off to know I had no sexual experiences to speak of?

"I just feel like any man that I eventually do become intimate with will wonder why I haven't had sex with anyone in my life."

Peter laughed, already shaking his head back and forth. "Men don't care about that stuff, at least not normal men. I suppose you could come across certain kinds of men who would love the fact that their wife is a virgin on their wedding night, but most men live in reality. Not only do they understand that you're allowed to have just as lively a sex life as they've enjoyed—they appreciate that you are a sexual being."

"Then, on the flip side of that, I am not a sexual being and, therefore, not attractive to them?" I asked, feeling a bit offended by the notion.

"Not what I was saying at all," he replied with a disarming smile.

I waited for the rest of what he had to say, completely charmed by just the expression of understanding on his face. At that moment, I was quite certain that this man could end wars with his smile. Who could possibly be angry at one another with such a pleasant intervention?

"You don't have to be promiscuous to be a sexual being. You, for instance, exude sexuality," he continued.

"Me? I highly doubt that," I scoffed.

"No, you do. The way you dress, smile, rub a strand of your hair between two fingers when you're nervous..." he began to say.

I dropped my hand from my hair to my lap, causing him to chuckle. I hadn't even realized I was doing exactly what he said until he mentioned it.

He continued, "You have a way about you that says you're open to sex. Just because you haven't followed through doesn't mean you don't want to be bent over the nearest kitchen table and give in to wild abandon."

I blushed again. He was right, of course, but I wasn't used to a man being so direct. I wasn't sure how to act or what to say. My hand went back to my hair without even thinking about it. I noted his eyes as they dropped from mine to my fingers in my hair, a slightly bemused smile on his lips. I dropped my hand again, feeling subconscious.

"I j-just don't think about sex in such crass terms," I half stammered in an almost inaudible voice.

"You think what I said was crass?"

"A bit," I admitted.

"Tell me how it is you envision sex. You do think about it, don't you?"

"Of course I do. I'm not a prude," I replied, feeling a little defensive.

I had to remind myself that I wanted this conversation. I'd left myself open to it. Now that we were having it, though, I felt like I was way out of my depth and didn't know how to respond.

"So, tell me what you envision when you think about sex with someone."

"Really?"

"Yeah. Come on. We've got all the time in the world." He gestured to the plane around us.

"Okay. I just think of it in softer terms. I imagine being in love and making love in a bed, slowly and sensually—looking into one another's eyes and really feeling the connection between us."

"You're going to make a fine pastor's wife," he said, smiling broadly.

"Vanilla, huh?"

"Yes. Very."

"I suppose that comes from never having experienced it before. You know, I think that every woman thinks it will be magical her first time."

"And it rarely is," he added.

"So, I hear. I work with two fairly promiscuous women, and they're full of tales about great sex, bad sex, odd sex."

"It's just a part of the game, I suppose. If you're holding out for something meaningful for your first time, you may be disappointed. I suppose there's always a chance you'll meet Prince Charming and he'll sweep you off your feet. You'll both be completely in love and make love for hours under the stars atop his castle. There is always the possibility."

"Not very realistic though, huh?" I said, feeling a bit deflated but less defensive.

"No, not very. It's your life and how you choose to have sex or not to have sex is entirely your decision. There's absolutely no reason to let anyone talk you into something you aren't ready to do."

"Thank you. What about you, though?" I asked, eager to steer the conversation away from myself now.

"What about me what?" he asked.

"How old were you when you lost your virginity?"

"I don't know what you mean. I'm still a virgin," he deadpanned.

I laughed and raised an eyebrow in his direction to let him know I wasn't buying it for even a second.

"Okay. Well, I lost my virginity when I was twelve."

"Oh, my God! Twelve?" I gasped, not sure if I believed him.

"Technically, half when I was twelve and half when I was thirteen," he added.

"Huh?"

"My babysitter decided to give me a blow job the night before my birthday. My parents were away for the night, and she was staying with me and my sister. Charlotte had gone to sleep, but Fredericka, the babysitter, was still watching a movie with me."

"But you were a child."

"So was she really. Freddy, as we called her, was only fourteen. She'd been reading about oral sex and wanted to try it, so she decided it would make a nice birthday present for a boy about to hit puberty."

"Was it?"

"No. She was terrible at it." He laughed. "I mean, back then, I didn't realize it wasn't supposed to involve teeth and bruising...."

"Yikes!"

"Indeed. Anyway, after trying it for a bit, she didn't like it. I didn't like it either and we decided to move on to something else. She stripped off her clothes and let me explore a bit. That got me hard, something her oral skills had certainly failed to do, and she decided we should just go for it. I lasted all of about one minute, I think. The clock struck midnight just as I began to come, and she shoved me off of her so she didn't get pregnant."

"That's quite a story."

"It wasn't beautiful and magical," he laughed.

I couldn't wrap my head around losing his virginity so young. He was a child, but then again, so was his partner. We both laughed as the attendant began serving our meal, causing us to put our questionable conversational material temporarily on hold.

Chapter 13

Giselle

"So, I said to her, 'But you said you wanted whipped cream on it.'
"

Peter was on the tail end of regaling me with some of his sexual antics. I was quickly learning that he was no shrinking flower when it came to sex. From the time he'd first learned about sex, he'd been willing to explore it in all its forms. After his first experience with the babysitter, it had consisted mostly of masturbation and dirty magazines he'd snuck in and tucked beneath his mattress, but his college years had brought on a full-fledged sexual revolution for him.

"And you're okay with all these meaningless sexual encounters?" I asked him, fascinated.

"Meaningless? No, they've all meant something to me. I realize that in recounting them, they may seem like dalliances, and some of them were, if you want to get right down to it. But no, each has, in its own way, meant something to me."

"How so?" I asked.

"I find women beautiful. Each woman who has afforded me the opportunity to know her so intimately has possessed my heart and soul, even if it was for just a very short time. For instance, I met a woman in a bar in Spain. I didn't speak Spanish and she didn't speak French. Through a handful of broken English, we managed to chat a little, but we connected completely on a purely sexual level."

"Without having a real conversation? She must have been beautiful."

"Not especially. I mean, she was, but not in the way you're thinking. She wasn't a woman who made men turn their heads when she walked down the streets, but she exuded sexuality. It was the small things. She bit her lip provocatively when she looked at me. She leaned in a certain way. She touched my hand when she spoke."

"And, what happened?"

"We ended up fucking like rabbits in a dark corner of the alley behind the bar."

"What's memorable about that?"

"Well, here I am more than two decades later, remembering every moment of our time together. I have a connection to her that will always be with me. I can't remember her name, but I remember how she smelled and how it felt to be inside her. I remember everything about her."

"Except her name."

"Yes, except her name. I'm not sure I ever knew it. But it was never about the details. It was about the connection."

"I understand. You're saying that even a hookup can have meaning in the long run."

"Yes. For instance, if you and I were to get up from these seats and go into the plane's bathroom to have sex, you would never forget it."

"You're just that good at it," I teased, though I was wondering just how good it might be and finding myself interested in finding out.

"I am, but that's not the point," he laughed.

"What is the point?"

"We could have the worst sex ever in that tiny little plane bathroom and you would never forget me. Sixty years from now, I'd be the guy you joined the mile-high club with."

"That's a far cry from making love to my handsome prince on my wedding night," I laughed.

"It certainly is, but I bet it would be more memorable when you think back in the years to come," he said, winking.

"Once again, because you are so good at it," I replied playfully.

"I am quite good at it, as you say, but no. You'd remember it because your wedding night with Prince Not So Charming would turn into the same monotonous sex with the same man for decades until you could no longer remember the thrill of your first time. Hell, he might even be bad at sex, and you're stuck with that. Yikes!"

"Nothing wrong with monogamy."

"No, there isn't. But only having sex with one person in your life? Where's the joy in that? You can be as monogamous as you want once you've selected the man of your dreams, but what's wrong with having something to think about when it grows stale? Imagine that two thousandth time you've had sex with your prince being boosted by closing your eyes and remembering how you fucked a guy you met at a Rembrandt exposition in a British Airways toilet."

I blushed. "I think you discount love. I think that being in love with someone makes you want to enjoy sex with them every single time, whether it's the first or the two thousandth."

"Think is a good word to use. You might be right, but it's just what you think. You don't know how it will be. Why not have some experiences before you go down that one-lane road for the rest of your days?"

"It's a valid point."

Peter laughed. "You know I'm just talking, right? I would never be so presumptuous as to suggest you give up your virginity in any way other than how you decide."

"Oh, I understand that, but I think you've made some valid points. What if I end up with someone who isn't great at sex? I might not even know it!"

"That sounds more like an argument in your favor. It seems that if you're going to have bad sex, it is likely best to not know how much better it could be."

"Maybe, but I want to know. I didn't set out to hold onto my virginity until my wedding night, but I think that I've been so determined that it should be given to someone I loved that it's morphed into that. I actually love sex, at least with myself!"

"Now, there's a subject I'd love to hear more about," he teased.

I smiled at him, becoming increasingly comfortable and quite smitten with him, but it was more than that. I found myself wanting him. I wanted to know what he knew about sex. I wanted to know if he was as good at it as I imagined. Of course, it came back to the fact that I had no frame of reference, but I'd at least understand if I was enjoying myself. I felt emboldened somehow.

"Yeah? Well, here's something you'll love. I missed my plane this morning because I was so busy having naughty dreams about you that I forgot to set my alarm," I blurted, instantly feeling some mix of horror and liberation as the admission tumbled out of my mouth.

"Oh, yes. I do love this. Tell me more."

"No. I don't think I will," I replied, looking him squarely in the eye with a mischievous grin.

"Would you rather show me? I think the bathroom is available," he suggested.

I studied his face for a moment, my fingers rubbing the few strands of hair that had escaped the messy ball I'd put it in that morning. I thought about Helena and Marie. What would they do? That made me smile.

"See you there in one minute," I told him.

Peter smiled and unsnapped his seat belt. Without another word, he stood up and went to the bathroom door, slipping inside. My heart beat rapidly against my chest. Was I really going to do this? Could I really go through with losing my cherry to a man I hardly knew in an airplane bathroom?

Yes. Yes, I was. Before I could change my mind, I stood up from my seat and looked around to see if anyone was paying attention. They were all lost in books and movies; some were asleep. I made my way up the aisle and opened the bathroom door to find Peter standing to one side, a broad smile on his face. I flipped the lock and moved in front of him.

"Fancy seeing you in here," he quipped.

"Shut up and do me," I replied, shocked at myself but unwilling to back down.

The tiny bathroom on the plane didn't leave much room for maneuvering. Who knew how much time we had before someone decided they needed to use the facilities and began tapping on the door. I couldn't believe I was actually doing this, but I wanted it, and I wanted it with Peter.

Peter moved me around so I was positioned with my backside partly propped up on the small sink counter behind me. I let him strip off my panties, as I wasn't sure I could move enough to get down to them. I giggled as he plucked them off and handed them to me with a smile so we didn't lose them. I tucked them beneath the hand I used to prop myself up on the countertop for safekeeping.

Peter unzipped his pants and pulled them part of the way down. He was already hard, which I only knew because his erection was pressing against my leg. My line of sight was so limited, and we were so close that I couldn't actually see what I was getting into, but from the feel of it, I wouldn't be disappointed.

Pulling me forward just slightly, Peter kissed the tops of my breasts visible above my shirt. I'd casually undone a button as I headed for the bathroom, thinking I might entice him with some casual exposure. Of course, there'd been no real time for all that, but it had at least given him a bit of additional territory to examine. I grunted a little as Peter put his hands under my ass and moved me into position, then hesitated for a moment.

"Are we safe?" he asked.

"Yes," I replied breathlessly, grateful that I'd opted for the implant on the off chance that I might one day have sex.

It was all he needed to hear. He pushed forward, slowly entering me. There was a slight pinch and a tiny thread of pain, but it passed quickly. I had a moment of worry about whether there was blood, but then I forgot all about it as Peter began moving in and out of me, kissing me as we came together again and again.

It was all very awkward and yet so incredibly exciting. I loved how he felt inside of me and wondered why I hadn't done this sooner. Each thrust inside me felt amazing. I quickly became lost in him, everything around me fading into the distance as I enjoyed my time with a man most women could only dream of calling their first. Everything about it was perfectly imperfect. Outside the door, I heard someone shuffling about and got a little nervous.

"I think someone is coming, Peter," I whispered against his ear.

"Hopefully, it will be you," he joked.

I chuckled at his little joke as I pushed the thought of the outside world away again and became engrossed in the sensations going on with my body. I'd heard women talk about climaxing, and I knew the mechanisms, but it wasn't happening for me yet. Despite that, I was enjoying everything about this. Peter pulled me back into a kiss, his tongue tangling hungrily with mine as he pushed into me one last time. I gasped as he buried himself inside me to the hilt and flooded me with a warm stream of fluid.

I would have liked to have lingered there for a moment, but there was no time. The speakers outside the bathroom announced that we would soon land in New York. Peter and I hurried to get sorted out and return to our seats before the attendants began doing their pre-landing checks. Peter quickly had his clothes back on, kissing me softly before exiting the door to return to his seat.

I checked for bleeding and found there was a little, but nothing serious. I smoothed my clothes back down and looked in the small mirror, noting the mess he'd made of my hair. I looked around for the hair band I'd pulled it into and noted it had landed in the toilet. I left it there and just ran my fingers through my messy locks before stepping out of the bathroom, a huge smile of satisfaction on my face.

Though I hadn't cum, I'd enjoyed the sex immensely. I knew that my lack of orgasm was more about me than anything Peter had done or not done. *Maybe next time*, I thought as I slipped past him into my seat and fastened my seat belt.

Chapter 14

Giselle

"Any regrets?" Peter asked after a few moments of silence between us.

"Just one," I admitted.

"And that is?"

"I wish we had more time and space," I replied.

"Ah. Yes, that would have been nice," he replied.

"Yes. Still, it was amazing."

I wanted to suggest that we do it again in New York. I wanted him to come to my apartment and show me everything I'd been missing. I didn't want to be that woman who got a little taste of him and then expected more. I understood that he probably saw this as just another encounter he'd remember fondly in years to come.

I was still pondering how to approach that with him. Did it take away from our risqué bathroom boinking if I tried to make it into more? Perhaps this was all it was supposed to be, and I was being needy by wanting it to be more than I intended.

Fortunately, I wasn't the only one thinking about what should happen next.

"We could always do it again when we get to New York. I have to get to my sister's and help her with things, but I'm at the end of term. I'll be staying for a while, even once she's sorted out," he suggested, sounding more unsure of himself than what he'd presented so far.

"Only if you want. I don't want you to think you owe me anything because, well, you know."

"That's not it. I'd love to have more time and space too." His eyes met mine.

At that moment, I knew I wasn't the only one smitten. Perhaps we wouldn't be the love story of a lifetime, but there was definitely something there, and I wanted desperately to explore it.

"Then, we'll do that," I said, smiling broadly.

"Grand," he replied.

Our conversation resumed, but not about sex this time. Instead, Peter told me about his family a bit more. He'd been born in France but grew up in New York, which explained why his English was so perfect and his accent not as heavy as some of the others I'd encountered in Paris. His sister had remained when he returned to France to teach, as she'd met her husband and married by then.

We were still in animated conversation about our lives when the plane touched down. Any chance of further discussion was quickly lost in the hustle and bustle of retrieving our belongings and finding our way toward immigration control. We resumed our chat once we were in line. It was sweet how he stayed with me as long as he could before we had to part company.

In fact, his presence had kept me from obsessing about getting to work and sorting out whatever odds and ends I needed to take care of tonight. Though I hadn't pushed that entirely off my mind, I was now more interested in spending what little time was left with Peter. It was very uncharacteristic of me not to put work first, but then again, I'd never met anyone like him. I'd never found myself just so entirely enamored so quickly.

"Looks like we're going to have to go our separate ways now," Peter said, pointing toward where the line split off for U.S. and foreign passport holders.

"Seems so," I replied.

"I'll see you on the other side," he said jokingly. "Let me give you my phone number in case we miss each other. Just give me a call when you get settled. If I don't answer, I'm at the hospital. I'll call you back."

"That sounds good," I replied, pulling my phone from my pocket and unlocking it. I handed it to him and let him quickly enter his number just before the line split in separate directions. Peter returned my phone and kissed me lightly before moving in the other direction. Both lines began moving quickly, Peter growing farther and farther away from me. I watched, completely infatuated with him.

I wondered if this was the beginning of something and immediately chastised myself for it. No matter what Peter and I had discussed on the plane, I was still in that mindset where I would meet the love of my life and he would be the only one I knew intimately. I had to stop thinking that way.

Nothing was wrong with that, but he was right about one thing. Where was the sense of sexual adventure I should have? What had happened in my life that left me thinking that sex was so important? I'd heard the women at work talk about their experiences with more than a hint of jealousy on several occasions. There was no reason I couldn't have fun too—no strings attached.

I stood there, moving forward inch by inch as I considered that my liaison with Peter might mean nothing. We might meet again at the end of this line and make plans that ultimately fizzled. It could just be the excitement of meeting a stranger in Paris, rediscovering him on my flight, and throwing caution to the wind for once in my life.

I had to learn to let things just be what they were for a change. I'd lost my virginity and joined the mile-high club all at once. I didn't feel dirty or ashamed. I enjoyed every moment of it. If I never saw Peter again, he was right; he would become a cherished memory I would always carry with me.

Still, I wanted more. No matter how much I tried to convince myself otherwise, I still knew that I wanted that whole Prince Charming scenario, and right now, I wanted it with Peter. In my little fantasy world, we would meet again on the other side of this line and kiss goodbye once more before going off to tend to our separate issues.

Tomorrow, we'd meet back up and the magic would continue. We would begin to see one another all we could between my work schedule and his family's needs. By the end of the summer, we'd be in love. I'd follow him back to France and that whole Paris dream I'd tossed around might become a reality, after all.

"Excuse me, but the line is moving without us," an elderly woman said from behind, causing me to jump.

"Oh, my. I'm sorry. I was lost in my own little world," I told her as I hurried to fill the gap between me and the person in front. The woman moved along with me, looking at me thoughtfully.

"I can see that. He must be something special," she said knowingly.

I smiled, marveling at how much she could read from my expression. I glanced toward the foreign line to see where Peter was in it and couldn't find him. He wasn't in the line of people waiting and I didn't see him at any of the counters. Where had he gone? Had immigration pulled him to another room? I froze, thinking that he might be in some sort of bother. What if he got rejected and had to stay in France?

My imagination began to run wild. What if Peter wasn't what he seemed? I had no proof that he was an art professor. I didn't know for sure that he had a sister in New York. For all I knew, he was some sort of international criminal looking for riches.

But why would he have latched on to me? I wasn't wealthy. If he was some sort of love scammer, I had to say he was damned good at it, but he'd be sorely disappointed to see my bank account. I did okay for myself, but I was far from being someone he could bilk out of any significant amount of money.

I wondered if the number he'd given me was even real. The thought of it made me glance down at my phone. I realized I'd been so engrossed in watching him in line that I hadn't yet saved it. I unlocked the screen to see that it still showed the dial pad where he'd typed it in. I started calling it to see if it would ring but decided that would be weird of me.

Instead, I began typing in his name to save it to my contacts. I'd call him after I got through the line like a normal person instead of a crazy lady. That was precisely what I was being right now with my ridiculous thoughts about who he might really be just because I couldn't see him in line.

Of course, if such a thing were true, then he would undoubtedly be right about this being one of the most notable sexual experiences of my life. Obviously, no one forgets losing their virginity at my age but being able to say I lost it to some sort of international conman would put it on a whole new level. It might not be my proudest moment, but it would absolutely withstand the test of time in my memories.

I almost laughed out loud as I considered all of this and then discounted it all. There was no way Professor Peter Dockery was a fraud. I might not know him well, but I knew enough to know he was heartfelt and genuine. The way he looked at me had been enough to convince me, and the way he'd touched me made me feel as if we were meant to have the moments we shared.

Despite having been deflowered in a British Airways toilet, it had somehow felt perfect. It was romantic and sensual but also adventurous and carnal. We'd gone after one another like two exotic beasts in heat, kissing hungrily and getting right down to what we were there for. I closed my eyes and relived the moment he entered me, letting the slight twinge of pain I felt rocket through my center and then disappear, overcome by pure, unadulterated pleasure.

No wonder Helena and Marie enjoyed having sex so much. When you took out all the heavy meaning I'd been applying to it, there was just the act. It was like getting a massage or soaking in a hot bath. Your body just absorbed the joy and you felt amazing when it was over—wishing you could return and do it again.

I'd soon see if Peter was on the other side waiting for me. Though if he wasn't, it really didn't mean much. In fact, it might be better. My getting to the museum had already been delayed enough. I was going to need to get a move on once I got free of this line.

I shook off the thoughts and glanced down at my phone, his name poised on the screen. I had a work associate named Peter in London, so I began to add Dockery. It could be embarrassing to confuse the two.

"Best get your passport out, honey," the woman behind me said.

I looked up at her and then glanced toward the counters. She was right. We were almost there.

"Thank you," I told her again, pausing my phone entry to fish my passport out of my bag. In the process, I lost my grip on the phone, and it clattered to the floor. I frowned down at it as I pulled my passport free and then bent to pick it up. I was relieved to see that it wasn't cracked.

I looked up to see I'd reached the front of the line just as the woman called out, "Next." I approached the counter and presented my passport to be scanned. I was home.

Chapter 15

Peter

Making my way through the immigration line, I thought about Giselle. I watched her for as long as I could before finally losing sight of her. I also noticed her looking for me and felt a little warm, fuzzy feeling, knowing we were on the same wavelength.

I still felt slightly stunned by what happened between us on the plane. I had no intention of that taking place. It wasn't a case of being sorry that it did or feeling like I shouldn't have taken advantage. There was little doubt that she was firmly on board with the idea when I suggested it, despite it having been only in jest.

Despite our discussion about how sex was no big deal and how she was holding back for something that might not really be all that special once it arrived, I couldn't help but feel touched. While I might view sex as nothing sacred, she'd obviously seen it differently. For her to decide to take a chance and give me something she somehow cherished was a bit overwhelming when I thought about it.

I wanted her to never feel like it had been a mistake. Even if our time together wasn't something that ended in forever, I did want to see her again. I wanted to explore her every desire, but I also wanted more than that. There was something about her that I found mesmerizing. I felt a need to know everything about her. Though she had now broken past viewing virginity as something to cling to, there was still much for her to experience, and I wanted her to enjoy all the pleasures of the flesh with me.

So, maybe there was something to what she said about the power of knowing you were a woman's first lover. I wanted to teach her things and see what her heart would desire once she felt completely free to do whatever she wanted sexually. It wasn't as if she'd come across as repressed during our encounter. I could tell she was open and wanted me as much as I wanted her, but we could enjoy so much more together.

Once I finally reached the front of the line, I glanced up to see that she was still well behind me. The American line had been much longer than mine. I guess there weren't as many people visiting from France as people returning home to America from France. With summer just around the corner, I guess the tourists were wrapping up their travels to places like France and heading to the beaches around the world.

"Next," a voice called out from the far counter. I went down to her and presented my passport as she asked the usual questions. I was relieved when she waved me through. I always expected some sort of carnage when I traveled. It had never happened, but I wondered if a single soul traveled internationally without anxiety while passing through immigration.

Just as I cleared the counter, my phone buzzed. I smiled down at it, expecting it would be Giselle and I'd see her again once I reached the common area on the other side. It wasn't.

"Hey, Charlotte," I answered.

"I'm here. Where are you?"

"Just clearing immigration. I will be down in a few minutes."

"Okay. I'll meet you in the usual spot. I've got to get back to the girls. I left them at the hospital with their father."

"I'm on my way, sis."

We said a quick goodbye and I looked around for Giselle but didn't see her anywhere. I wanted to wait for her but couldn't with Charlotte already waiting on me and her situation. Instead, I headed toward the exit. I'd given Giselle my number so she'd call me if she wanted to see me again—which I hope she did.

She remained in my thoughts as I continued through the airport, looking for her everywhere I went. The flight had been crowded, so she might have passed me nearby and I wouldn't have known it with the throngs of people. Then again, the American line had been moving much slower than mine and she might still be lost in it.

I smiled at the memory, still fresh in my mind, of our encounter in the plane bathroom. I could still smell her scent on my skin, feel her hair brushing softly across my chest as our bodies rose and fell against one another. Her lovely curves were perfect. I could see that even in the dimly lit confined space where she'd given herself to me. Her skin was so soft, and I was completely taken with the tiny freckles that dotted her face and flowed down her arms and chest.

There had been great beauty in those moments we shared during our flight, inside the bathroom and out. What some might view as a tawdry hookup had been so much more than that. Giselle's beauty was rivaled only by her intelligence, and I was besotted by her. I had other things I had to deal with in New York, but I'd find time to see her as soon as possible for both of us. I closed my eyes for a moment and could see her as she turned her head to look up at me when I boarded the plane. It came to me in frames, as if each slight twist of her head was a still shot in my brain.

There was no doubt that I wanted to see more of Giselle. I'd likely be in New York all summer. My sister's house was immense. I pretty much had the entire third floor to myself when I visited, and I rarely took more than a change of clothes because I kept a closet full of things there. It kept me from having to pack a bunch of stuff and deal with baggage claim on my visit. I'd always thought it was a bit too much, but it had certainly come in handy for this trip's purposes.

I could easily fit Giselle into my life here. I was going to mostly be tied to whatever schedules the girls had. I'd get them off to school and activities while Charlotte was at the hospital or getting some rest. It seemed that Steven was going to be OK from what the doctors were telling her, but he'd have a long recovery even after he came home.

The way I saw it, I'd have no problem being there for Charlotte, which would have to be my first priority. I wouldn't dream of letting her down when she needed me. I'd still have plenty of time to see Giselle. I was looking forward to spending as much time with her as possible while in the city.

Of course, what did we have to look forward to past that? I was in Paris, and she was in New York. Extended long distance almost always spelled disaster for anything serious. Perhaps we were both better off in the long run if she never called. The thought of that made me feel a bit melancholy. The idea of being in the same city as her and not hearing from her wasn't something I even wanted to consider.

Why was I overthinking this anyway? I'd only just met the woman. What was the harm of having a little fling while I was in the city and calling it a day? Nothing, that was what. The problem was that something told me that Giselle wasn't the sort of woman you could just walk away from when your time together was done. I didn't mean she would be one of those women who gave you grief. I just knew her memory would haunt me like no other woman ever had.

"There you are!" Charlotte called to me as I approached, jarring me from my thoughts as I walked through the airport.

"Yes. Here I am. How's Steven?" I asked as she pulled me into a big hug.

"Cranky!" she announced. "He's in traction right now, but they say he'll be able to move about a bit more in a couple of weeks after they change his casts."

"Must have been a hell of an accident."

"Oh, Peter. You should see his car. The police showed me photos of the accident. You can hardly even make it out. It's completely mangled."

"Sounds like things could have been a lot worse."

"Yes. The man who hit him wasn't so fortunate. He caught the front of the SUV on the passenger's side but up toward the motor. No seatbelt. There was nothing they could do for him."

"How very sad," I told her as we approached the exit.

"I appreciate you coming on such short notice."

"Why wouldn't I? You're my favorite sister and brother-in-law."

She smiled at the all-too-familiar joke. I suppose everyone with only one sibling made similar remarks from time to time and thought it was funny.

"The girls can pretty much take care of themselves, but they have practices and events to attend, and I'll be going back and forth to the hospital until he's released."

"No need to explain. I understand why you called. Between the broken bones and the head injury, it's only natural that you want to be there as much as possible."

"They say the head trauma is just temporary swelling, no permanent damage that they can see. Thank goodness for that. I hated leaving the girls with him while I came here in case he has of the migraines it's caused, but their friend's mom is with them, so they aren't alone."

"I'm sure they're fine," I told her as we arrived at her car. "Let's go get them. We can grab a taxi back to your house so you can stay if you need to do that."

"That will work," she said, sounding as exhausted as she appeared, though I would never tell her she looked tired. I figured she must have been at the hospital all night and morning.

I looked around at the parking lot as we pulled away. I don't know where I thought I'd see Giselle out here, but I found myself looking anyway. I wanted to see her again. I wondered why she hadn't at least texted me her number but reminded myself that she'd talked about the busy evening ahead of her. I chastised myself for being so uncommonly needy.

She remained on my mind even as I climbed into Charlotte's car and headed toward the hospital. My sister chatted away, asking me about the flight and things back in Paris. I found myself unexpectedly telling her about Giselle, obviously leaving out the part about getting busy in the bathroom.

"Only you would pick up a woman on a transatlantic flight," she said, smiling a little.

"For the record, I didn't pick her up on the flight. I met her at the art museum last night and we just happened to be on the same flight today, seated beside one another."

"I'd be careful if I were you, little brother. That sounds suspiciously like either stalking or fate. You could land head over heels in love or six feet below ground with something like that, and I don't have time for any more carnage in my life," she joked.

"I can assure you that she is not a stalker. If anyone would be the stalker in this scenario, it would be me since I was the one who booked the last seat."

"Did you stalk her? Do I need to seek psychiatric assistance for you?" she said, teasing me.

"Not just yet. We'll see how it goes if she calls me."

Charlotte nodded and I found myself pondering the fact that I'd left everything under Giselle's control. She'd never told me which museum she worked at and if I went around trying to find her, then I would be the stalker, wouldn't I? Of course, if she called, the ball was in her court.

She would call. Wouldn't she?

Chapter 16

Giselle

"Damnit!" I said as I tucked my passport in my bag and finally looked back at my phone. The screen wasn't cracked, but it was cleared. Peter's number was gone, and I hadn't finished saving the entry. There was no way to get it back. I looked around frantically but saw no sign of him.

I was livid. How was I going to find him in New York? I knew where he worked in Paris. I could find him once he arrived back home, but how would I reach him while he was here? I wanted to look for him, but I had to retrieve my checked bags and take them home so I could get to the museum. The thought of work made me realize that maybe he would find me there. He knew where I worked.

I decided I'd have to leave it up to fate. I retrieved my things and called an Uber to take me home. I'd grab the subway from my apartment to work, but I didn't want to lug my bags onto the train and through the subway stations. I ordered a car from the app and headed to the pickup point where they would arrive.

As I sat there waiting, my mind went back to Peter. I wondered if he'd come to see me. There was still a chance that we were just a hookup and I'd never see him again. I found it hard to believe that. We seemed to have had such a solid connection. Was I imagining that?

My Uber arrived. I put my thoughts aside while the driver helped me with my bags. Climbing into the back seat, I settled against the cool leather, putting the airport and Peter in the rearview mirror. We headed to my apartment, sparking up some idle chatter as we made our way across Queens toward Manhattan.

It was already far past the time I'd expected to get home when I had left Paris. Was that only this morning? It seemed like so much had happened in only a day. I didn't bother to unpack anything other than just what I needed to get a quick shower and change for the museum. It would be closed, so I opted for jeans and a T-shirt rather than business attire. The night guards wouldn't care how I was dressed.

I started to dry my hair, but it took too long, so I left it damp and pulled it up in a clip before brushing on a light coat of mascara and lip gloss. Glancing in the mirror, I decided I was presentable enough and headed out the door toward the subway station a few blocks down. I could walk to the museum, but that would take longer, and I wanted to get in, get my work done, and get out.

The city felt alive all around me as I made my way further into Manhattan. A couple stood with their arms around one another, oblivious to everyone around them. I watched as they kissed and then chatted quietly, lost in their own little bubble. I'd never experienced that. I realized now that all of my relationships had been shallow and fleeting. I guess I'd already known it, but only now was the full realization hitting me.

I felt lonely in a way that I'd never experienced before. Is that what sex does to you? Does finding such an intense, instinctual connection to another person fill you with joy and then leave you deflated when it's over? That's how I felt. No wonder people were always searching for something that not everyone could find. I'd never been one to seek out a man to feel whole. I'd never felt alone doing my own thing. Now, I could see just how alone I truly was.

The subway arrived, staving off my thoughts for another moment. I boarded the train and found it packed. I stood, holding onto a nearby rail as it jostled back and forth along the tracks. I again considered how Peter had affected me and what it would mean for me. Would I always be looking for a connection like ours? Was there even another out there who could make me feel that way? Or was this just passing melancholy?

There was always the chance that I would run into him again, but New York was a big place and he said his sister lived somewhere in Brooklyn. I was tucked into the Sutton Place neighborhood outside the busier New York City streets. There wasn't a lot of hope for us to cross paths without planning to do so.

I was jolted from my thoughts as I realized we were almost at my stop. The last thing I needed was to miss it and suffer another delay. I moved toward the doors, pushing through the crowd and onto the platform. The museum was only a short walk away now. Usually, when I came to work, I felt energized and excited. I loved my job. Today, I felt weary to the bone. I was sure it was just as emotional as it was physical.

I moved to the museum's side entrance and rang the bell, waiting impatiently for one of the security staff to respond. It took only a few seconds for one of them to come on the speaker. I recognized the voice instantly.

"Name, rank, and serial number, please," Tucker's voice crackled across the speaker.

"You can see me on camera, Tucker. Let me in."

"No can do. You need the super-secret squirrel password," he responded.

"Let me in, or I'll have you transferred to basement duty," I teased.

I heard a click and a buzz as the door opened. Tucker stood smiling broadly at me on the other side as he waited for me to enter and closed the door behind me. We always played this little game of his when I arrived after hours and he was on duty. I knew he was checking the cameras surrounding me to make sure I was alone and didn't appear under any duress. The chatter was just his way of amusing both of us while he did so.

"The basement, huh? You wouldn't do that to me, would you? I'm just a little guy and a bit jumpy in the shadows."

By my estimate, Tucker was all of 6'5" and a sturdy 240 pounds. If there was anything in the basement to worry about, it was him. Still, like many of the other guards, they hated patrolling the basement. The artifacts down there for restoration were under lock and key at night, so they only had to check doors and hallways. Still, it seemed to give them all the creeps because the corridors were ill-lit and full of shadows from the display structures stored out in the open.

"I'll reconsider your assignment depending on whether you have any fresh coffee. I didn't have time to stop for some."

"Oh, you know the night shift always has coffee," he joked, motioning for me to follow him to the staff break room.

Two other guards sat there chatting when we came in and looked panicked when they saw me. They both started to push away from the table.

"Relax, guys. I'm not even here. I'm going to grab a quick coffee and go to my office."

"We're just on our break," one of them quickly offered.

"Then finish taking it as if I hadn't arrived," I told him.

I grabbed a cup, filled it with steaming black coffee from the nearly full pot, and took a sip. It was surprisingly good. I looked toward Tucker with a raised eyebrow, and he flashed me a sheepish grin.

"You know we can't stay up all night drinking that second-rate coffee the museum provides."

"Fair enough," I told him. "Thanks for the coffee, even if you did pilfer it from the VIP lounge."

"You're welcome," Tucker told me. "No basement, right?"

"Not today. See you guys when I'm ready to be sprung."

"See you then," Tucker said. The two other guards, Harry and Moses, said their farewells as I exited.

I went to my office and sat down with the paperwork left for my review. I was relieved to see that everything looked in reasonably good order. I made some notes about things I'd need to address first thing in the morning and then reviewed the pictures of the displays for the event. Because precious items were included, the exhibition area was locked off for the night, so I'd have to rely on these for my last-minute checks.

I breathed a sigh of relief as I finished, more than ready to be home in bed. I located Tucker to be let out and returned to my apartment, where I collapsed on the sofa for a few minutes, glancing at my phone. It was barely ten. It was hard to believe that I'd woken up in Paris this morning and was sitting on my sofa tonight.

It was even more unbelievable that I'd managed to have sex with a stranger on a plane, get my work done at the museum, and make it home at a reasonable hour. It would be a hell of a day tomorrow, so I'd need to get some rest.

Of course, I was still too wound up from my day for sleep just yet, so I decided to have some wine first. I retrieved a bottle from the small rack I kept in my kitchen, pulled a clean glass from the cabinet, and grabbed the wine opener before returning to the living room. On the way, I used the voice remote on my smartphone to beam my playlist to the smart speaker on a nearby shelf. The apartment filled with soft music as I sat down and opened the bottle.

I considered my unpacked luggage and decided it could wait another day. For now, I plan to just kick back, enjoy my Merlot, and do absolutely nothing.

Of course that nothing didn't exclude thinking about Peter. I found myself reliving our time on the plane together, going over our discussion that had led up to the encounter in the bathroom. Peter Dockery was unlike any man I'd ever met. There had been plenty of handsome, charming men, but I'd never felt the kind of connection with them that I'd found with him.

Even the night before the flight, at the museum. I'd been captivated from the moment I laid eyes on him, and his knowledge of art, especially about Rembrandt, had been quite impressive. I'd been reluctant to leave when I was called away and disappointed to find that he'd already gone when I returned. As shocked as I was initially to find him on the same flight to New York with me, I was thrilled to see him again.

Now, here we were in the same city, and I wasn't sure if I'd see him again. It wasn't that I didn't want to, but it seemed fate continued to step in at every turn. Fate had put him at the museum on my last night. Fate had put him on my flight. Now, fate had taken the chance I had of reuniting with him away. It was as if we were destined to meet but not spend significant time together.

The more I thought about it, the more I realized that perhaps our short time together was all we'd been meant to have. If that was the case, then who was I to try to fight back against the cosmos?

Chapter 17

Giselle

I desperately needed sleep, but it didn't seem inclined to grace me with its presence. Instead, I sat in my favorite chair by the window, sipping wine and listening to music. I tried my best not to think about things with Peter but failed miserably.

Instead, I switched on the television and flipped through the channels until I found a psychological thriller I'd meant to watch. I needed a diversion, but definitely not something full of romance or star-crossed lovers. Instead, I immersed myself in the drama of a woman who was housebound and being stalked by a stranger.

It was exactly what I needed to get out of my own head. Of course, I knew that staying up late watching the tube would haunt me come morning when I had to get up early and head to the museum. Still, it beat tossing and turning all night, especially if I thought about Peter during that time.

I soon realized I had no idea what was happening in the movie. My thoughts were like some big mash-up between Peter and the museum. I kept jumping from what I knew I would need to do come morning to flashbacks of moments spent with Peter.

Eventually, the drudgery of the museum won out and I focused on tomorrow, planning each step of my day so everything ran smoothly.

I considered that I'd already started putting Peter out of my head as I got back into my usual routine. I wondered if, wherever he was in Brooklyn, he'd already begun putting me in the rearview mirror, too. The more I thought about it, the more I realized that was what I should be doing. We'd hooked up on a plane, nothing more and nothing less. I wondered what Helena and Marie would have to say about it and pondered whether I would tell them.

A part of me wanted to share it because they were always sharing things about their sex life and I never had, but another part of me felt like it was personal. I wanted to keep it just for myself without anyone else knowing or commenting on it. I think the biggest thing is that I didn't want it to ever feel cheap and knew they would do that. My tryst with Peter would be placed on a shelf next to all the hookups they'd told me about over time and would be no more important than theirs. But, to me, it was important.

I moved away from thoughts about our bathroom antics and began wondering more about the man I'd found myself with. My mind conjured up what Peter's life must be like back in Paris. Based on our discussions on the plane, I imagined he was dedicated to teaching. He likely spent hours in the office creating lesson plans and grading papers.

I wondered if his teachings were purely academic or if he guided his students through creative efforts. I'd been in both kinds of classes. I knew there was a big difference between teaching art from the standpoint of learning creative techniques and teaching art appreciation. I assumed he taught the latter based on the things he'd said. In that case, I was probably right about my assumption that he spent a lot of time on lesson plans.

Peter was older than me and perhaps he didn't have to devote so much time to setting out how he would teach. Maybe he was knowledgeable enough to just stand before his class and share his knowledge with him. I could see that he was well-versed during the art discussions we'd had at the museum and on the plane to New York. That being the case, I imagined his work still required a great deal of test creation, grading, and plans on different ways to teach or make new discoveries about artists.

I wasn't sure why I was so curious about how or what Peter taught. I suppose I was just curious about anything involving him. So much of him was still a mystery to me. How would I ever find out all I wanted to know if I never saw him again? I still couldn't believe I lost his number, but I had to think he knew enough about me to find me again. Surely, he'd realize that something had gone wrong.

As the jet lag began to really set in, I realized just how tired I felt. I turned off the movie and lay my head on the sofa pillow, thinking I'd briefly rest my eyes. I wasn't sure when I drifted off to sleep, but I found myself in a dream once again. I was with Peter, but we weren't limited by the confines of an airplane bathroom this time.

Peter pulled me close, his face pressed against mine as we held one another closely. We danced slowly across the room, in no hurry to be anything more than what we were—two people attracted to one another who wanted to spend time getting to know all about one another's desires, up close and personal. Soft music played in the background and Peter hummed along to the tune, his vocals vibrating lightly against my skin.

It was just the kind of magical moment I'd imagined we could have together once we were back on the ground and had more than an eight-hour flight to get to know one another. As we danced across the room, he planted small kisses on my lips, moving quietly to my neck to linger for a bit before slipping down to feather more across my shoulder blades.

We stopped moving, our dance stalled in favor of enjoying one another's touch. I reached upward, running my fingers through his hair as his head bent to kiss the tops of my breasts. I could almost feel the sensation from our previous encounter. His hands unfastened the buttons on the back of my dress, slowly spreading it open to reveal more of my breasts until it fell loose to the floor around me.

I stepped out of it and moved closer to him as he unsnapped the front closure on my bra to fully expose my breasts and devour them with his mouth. His hands cupped each of them, pulling them toward his mouth and kissing his way around the soft globes until he reached my nipples. I gasped loudly as he nipped at them softly with his teeth, sucking one into his mouth and then moving on to the other. Back and forth, he took his time enjoying them.

I felt his erection pressing against me as I let him tour my bosom. Then, he moved down, pushing at my thong until I was exposed to him. He stepped back to admire my form as I stepped out of the thong and went to take off my shoes.

"No, leave those on. I love how you look wearing nothing but those," he said.

I did as he asked, letting him look as he began to slip off his own clothes, dropping piece by piece until he stood naked in front of me with a massive erection. He pulled me to him again, kissing me, lifting me upward as his cock pressed into my hip. I moaned into his mouth, aching for him, wanting him like I'd never wanted a man in my life.

Peter lifted me, carrying me to my bed and laying me across it. He pulled my legs apart, leaving me sprawled across the covers and spread open for him to admire. Taking one ankle in his hand, he began kissing his way down the inside of it, leaving ripples of goosebumps in his wake. I felt myself getting wetter, eager to have him inside me. My breath caught as he drew closer to my center.

"Oh, God," I moaned as his mouth closed over my clit, slowly licking it and teasing it with his tongue. I arched my hips, desperate for more, but he moved on, leaving me aching for relief as he slowly kissed his way down my remaining leg and then pulled me closer to the edge of the bed.

I watched him through a veil of passion as he moved his hands beneath me and pulled me upward so that my legs draped over his shoulders and my entrance was even with his throbbing cock. He balanced me with one hand and used the other to move his cock into place, teasing me with the tip as he rubbed it back and forth through my wet folds.

"Please, Peter. Please make love to me," I begged.

"Not yet. I love watching you while you're so heated up. The look of lust on your face is so beautiful."

I reached up and grasped my breasts, kneading them softly in my hands while he watched, still teasing me with his cock. Then, he slipped it ever so slightly inside me, sending me into another fit of pleasure-filled moans. He took his time, moving slowly further into me inch by inch and rolling his hips to seat his cock firmly inside while hitting all of my pleasure centers.

Then he pulled back. He moved his other hand back up to my ankles, holding each one of them in either hand now. He see-sawed back and forth, gazing from my face to where he impaled me with his cock. I writhed beneath him, desperate for him to make me come. I wanted to know what it felt like to have a man send you over that edge, spiraling out of control from the force of your own climax.

Our bodies swayed, pumping and grinding until neither of us could hold back any longer. I could feel the waves building inside me, growing more powerful as they stacked one on top of the other, growing like some sort of giant Tsunami wave ready to flood the beach of some quiet town.

"God, I'm so close," I squealed, feeling my body growing more and more tense. Then, there was no holding back. I unleashed the flood of my desire.

"So beautiful," Peter moaned, pumping into me hard and fast, demanding all he could get from me before he gave in to his own release and flooded me with spasms of orgasmic delight.

Afterward, he moved my legs down and lay on the bed beside me, pulling me closer to hold me tightly against him and kissing my neck softly. I was in heaven. I couldn't imagine ever being this satisfied by anyone or with anything ever again in my life. And even as sated as I felt, I still found that I would willingly begin all over when he was ready.

I lay in his arms, thinking about just how perfect this felt. How lucky was I that I'd found a man as incredible as Peter Dockery out of sheer luck?

But you lost him again, a voice rattled in the back of my brain. The idyllic room around me suddenly faded into a gray shell of nothingness. I stood in the middle of the floor alone.

"Peter? What's happening? Where are you?" I called out.

I awoke with a start, momentarily confused by my surroundings. Once I'd fully awakened and grasped my present state and my apartment, I felt disappointed that I was alone. With a sigh, I put away my wine glass and put a stopper in the bottle before heading to the bedroom to strip off my clothes and climb between the sheets.

Maybe if I went right back to sleep, the dream would return, but not that ending. The thought of the horrible way it had stopped made me shudder.

Chapter 18

Giselle

Nearly a week passed with no news from Peter. He was already beginning to feel like a distant memory, albeit a pleasant one. My days were full, though, and I hardly had time to agonize over losing his number and his likely assumption that I didn't want to see him again.

Or perhaps that was the other way around. I'd likely never be sure now. Our connection had felt real, but it may have only been fleeting—the heat of the moment. I'd come to accept it for what it was: a hookup in an airplane bathroom. I even shared it with Helena and Marie during a Skype chat as they packed to return from Paris. They'd be returning to oversee the return of artwork at the end of the exhibit there, but for now, they'd return here and let the museum staff in Paris handle the exhibit.

"Wait. You've been a virgin this whole time?" Helena said incredulously.

"Yes. I thought you knew that," I said.

"Girl, no. I had no idea. I just thought you weren't a whore like us," Helena said, causing both her and Marie to laugh.

I laughed with them and shook my head. "Honestly, I just thought I was saving myself for someone special. I wanted to wait until I was married to Mr. Right and all that. You must think I'm such a child."

"No, not at all," Marie said. "I think that we all think that for a while. We're taught that sex isn't something that you just jump into with whoever wants a turn. We're supposed to be good girls and not think about it or want it. Then you find some guy you think is 'the one' and give up your cherry. Next thing you know, you're on 'the one' number five, and all that seems so ridiculous."

"So, you're saying it's all downhill from here," I joked.

"No way. It's all a rollercoaster ride from here, baby," Helena chimed in. "You have nothing left to lose, so you can do whatever and whoever you want. Some will be so bad at it that you want to get up and leave in the middle of doing it, and some will be so good that you hope it never ends. You'll be in love. You'll be in lust. You might even go down a side loop of self-discovery and get into girls or whatever kinks suit you."

"And you might meet the man of your dreams and live happily ever after in a little house with a white picket fence. Of course, he'll love to go down on you anytime, and he'll have the best cock God ever made," Marie quipped.

"It could happen," Helena agreed, nodding and smiling. "Hey, we're just saying you can do whatever you want. All this old-fashioned saving yourself for marriage is hogwash. If you wanna go wild, do it. If you want to have sex with men you're in a relationship with, you can do that, too. No one should be telling you what's right for you."

"You two are like the big sisters I never had," I said, causing us all to chuckle.

"Hey, stick with us, kid. We'll get you in all sorts of trouble you won't want to tell Mom about," Helena said.

"Listen, I've got to go. The director is on the warpath again this morning, and I need to feed him some red meat or something."

"I suggest lacing it with rat poison," Marie groaned.

"Talk to you two when you get home," I told them, ending the video chat.

I stepped away from my desk and opened my office door. I'd closed it when they called, knowing the conversation would turn ribald whether I told them about Peter or not. As Helena put it, they were almost done "whoring" their way across Paris and ready to ride some Brooklyn boys. The pair of them were incorrigible and I loved them for that.

I headed down the hallway toward the director's office and knocked on the door frame. He looked up at me and motioned me in. I was keenly aware of how much he looked like a vulture with his sagging skin, pale blue eyes, and puffy red lips. He should have retired years ago, but he clung to his position like a barnacle on a ship.

"I was told you wanted to see me?" I said.

"Yeah. Let's talk about your expense report for Paris."

"Okay. Is there a problem?"

"Yeah. What's this up-charge on your flight? How do you go from a $860 round trip ticket to adding on another $2200 for the leg home?"

"Well, as I explained on my report, I missed my flight, and the only flight available that would get me back in time to oversee the opening here was two hours later and business class."

"You didn't think you should discuss this with me before paying such a huge fee?"

"Under normal circumstances I would, but I didn't have time. I was at the counter and ran the risk of not getting a flight until much later in the day if I didn't jump on what was available while I had a chance."

He grunted but didn't say anything, then he shook his head from side to side, "Why did you miss your flight?"

"My alarm didn't go off."

"That hardly seems like something that should cause the museum to incur another $2200."

"Listen, you insisted that I stay until the exhibit there opened, and you wanted me here to make sure the one opening was all in place. Anytime you put someone on such a tight schedule and they are trying to travel from one country to another, there's the potential for hiccups. My flight may have cost more than anticipated, but I'm quite sure that I was well enough under budget in other places to make up for it," I told him, feeling annoyed.

He seemed to contemplate this for a moment and then grimaced. "Okay. I'll approve this, but don't think it will be so easy if it happens again."

"Sure. Thanks. Are we done now?" I asked.

"We are," he replied.

I turned and walked out. I was all smiles as I exited his office. The truth was I'd been prepared to absorb the extra money myself, but Helena and Marie had convinced me to give it a shot. I was glad I did, and really, it shouldn't have even been a thing. I was damned good at my job and deserved a bit of slack.

The new event here in the city was coming along nicely. It had partly opened the morning after my return to New York with no major hiccups, which was a credit to the staff who had worked so hard to keep things moving in my absence. However, only a handful of people were currently allowed to view our curated collection. VIPS and top donors had been sent personal invitations to preview the work before the general public.

I was quite proud of what my team and I had accomplished. Though I'd been working on this opening during my time in Paris, my staff had been the ones who'd really brought the physical aspects of it home. Now, it was just a matter of ensuring the world knew about it and wanted to attend.

Tonight, I was working late. I'd spent a good part of my day making sure everything was perfect for a member of British royalty and his wife, along with their entourage. Normally, our well-versed tour guides show the work, even to VIPs. However, when dealing with royalty or heads of state, the museum wanted someone of higher standing to conduct the tours personally.

I'd been in the background when I started working for the museum, which was only about a year ago but now seemed much longer. Typically, museum curators worked more behind the scenes than I did, but my role here quickly escalated. The director was older and less hands-on than he'd previously been, often letting me speak in his stead or take on duties outside my purvey instead of those he felt were less successful in their roles.

While some might be less enthused about having to take on extra work, I embraced it. I wanted to learn and the more that was thrust at me, the more opportunities I had to do so. My job could sometimes be frustrating, making me wonder why I chose this career. Still, overall, I thrived in this environment. It suited my interests, my skills, and, sadly, my lack of a personal life.

"Thanks for the legal coffee," I heard a gruff voice say from my office door.

I looked up to see Tucker standing there with a big smile on his face.

"You're welcome. I can't have you guys getting in trouble for pilfering from the executive lounge. I'm not sure why someone was buying two grades of coffee anyway."

"Me either," he replied. "Anyway, just wanted you to know we appreciate it. I assumed you did it."

"You assumed correctly. Maybe you'll stop giving me grief every time I need in or out of this place at night."

"Doubtful. Where's the fun in that?" he said, chuckling as he disappeared down the hallway outside my door.

"Where, indeed," I said to myself, smiling as I finished working on new entries for our museum catalog.

I'd put the content creation for these aside while getting the upcoming event off the ground. We had several new acquisitions coming in for our general display and I needed to finish the research and information on them. It was something I always preferred to do after closing hours when there were fewer people present and, thus, fewer interruptions.

I was quickly lost in my work, all thoughts of anything but the art I needed to get cataloged escaping my grasp. When I looked up again, it was nearly eight. I'd done enough for one day and was ready to head home for the evening. I gathered my bag and locked my office before heading toward the security desk in search of Tucker or whoever was handling it.

"You know, all work and no play…" he began, stopping short and letting the rest fade into the wind.

"Yeah, I know, but I'm behind from being in Paris for so long," I told him.

"Of course. I haven't asked about your trip. How was it?"

"It was good, but it's always nice to get home again," I told him with a smile.

He examined my face and nodded. "Yes, it seems like it was really good. I hear your counterparts are flying home tomorrow."

"Counterparts?"

"Yes, Helena and Marie. I was told to expect them before opening tomorrow. They're apparently taking the overnight flight in."

"Right. I talked to them earlier while they were packing up for the trip home. Time does fly, doesn't it?"

"It certainly does. Before you know it, you'll be over the hill like me with a family and a mortgage to pay."

"Are you complaining?" I asked, wondering if I'd ever go down the path toward being a wife and mother. It seemed fulfilling in its own way, but so was my career, and I wasn't sure how good I'd be at balancing the two.

"Nah. Not a chance. You've met my wife. She takes good care of me. The kids are out of the house now and we're practically honeymooners again," he grinned.

I envied him at that moment. Tucker was a retired Marine. His wife, Maeve, was a former kindergarten teacher. They'd met and married while he was still in the service and survived years of deployments and moving to new stations. They lived a modest life outside the city in the suburbs.

"Give Maeve my best. I'll get out of your hair so you can start your nap," I teased.

"You know we never nap on duty, Giselle. We're always on watch."

"Of course," I told him, winking as he surveyed the cameras at the exit and then let me out. "Goodnight, Tucker."

"Night. I'll see you tomorrow evening."

"Probably," I said with a little laugh.

Chapter 19

Giselle

"Good morning, Sunshine!" Helena half-shrieked when she saw me coming down the hallway outside my office the following day.

"Well, good morning to you too. Where's your partner in crime?" I asked, genuinely happy to see her.

"Oh, she's around here somewhere. Barely back stateside and already got her eye on some man candy delivering a package. I think she's trying to see what other kind of package he has to offer."

"Of course she is." I laughed. "I missed you guys."

"We missed you too. There was no one to scandalize with our tawdry tales of carnal delight."

"I did miss those. Terribly enlightening," I teased.

"Don't you worry your pretty little head about it. We have more to share."

I smiled and she studied me a bit before finally pushing me for more information. "So, are you going to tell us more about this little airplane bang of yours?"

"Not yet. We'll wait for Marie. What are the two of you doing for lunch?"

"You're going to make us wait until lunch? When did you become such a masochist? Oh, my God. That's it, isn't it? You've become a dominatrix!"

Chuckling, I shook my head. "Not this week. Maybe next."

Marie appeared from a doorway behind us, all smiles. Her hunt for another package must have gone quite well. I waved toward her but made my excuses to Helena before she grew closer. I had work to return to and didn't want to get into a second inquisition from Marie.

"I'll see you two on the secret balcony at noon."

"We'll be there."

The secret balcony was what we called the little hideaway where we sometimes had lunch. Helena had discovered me eating there once and she and Marie had become my occasional partners in crime. The balcony was hidden behind an area where museum equipment and fixtures were stored for repair.

The area seemed chaotic, but our maintenance supervisor had once assured me that it was in an order that worked for him. It wasn't my problem how he chose to store things in limbo, so I'd taken his word for it. However, looking around during my early days of learning where everything was, I found the balcony behind a row of shelves.

"Is that balcony stable?" I asked.

"Yes."

"So, there is no reason for it to be closed off?"

"No. Not at all. It's kept locked so there isn't an open entry point into the museum."

"There are concerns of entry from the 4th floor?"

"Never underestimate the lengths thieves will go to is what security tells me."

"I suppose so. I suppose a bit of rappelling gear and a gutsy thief would see it as an opportunity."

Once I was more comfortable at the museum, I'd talked Tucker into giving me a key. I could enjoy a quiet lunch without being bothered by anyone, at least until Helena and Marie learned my secret. I later learned that Tucker had still done his due diligence by asking the director for permission to give me a key and added an extra security check specifically for this door in staff's closing rounds.

I smiled at the memory of my earlier times here at the museum. Though Tucker and I had vastly different roles here, we'd developed a great working relationship and even a bit of a casual friendship. He was in charge of the security staff and sometimes worked during the day but preferred the night shift.

I glanced at my watch and realized the morning was already flying by. I'd come in early to finish the cataloging I'd been working on last night. I sat at my desk and opened my computer to pick up where I left off, quickly becoming absorbed in the work. I was still hard at it over three hours later when Marie stopped by my door.

"So, I heard you have some juicy details to tell me and Helena at lunch."

"I'm not sure how juicy it is by your standards, and you already know about it anyway."

"Yeah, but we want to know every scandalous bit of it. I can't wait. I'm ducking out to grab some lunch for us. I'll be back to meet you at the usual spot by noon. You want me to get anything?"

"Thanks, but I brought my lunch today."

"How about a cookie? I'm going to that deli we like."

"Oh, you are a woman. Yes! One of the black and white cookies would be fantastic."

"Done. See you in a while."

I nodded and attempted to return to work but found I'd lost focus after the interruption. Instead, my mind turned to Peter and our tryst on the plane. I was amazed to find that even just thinking about it sent a little shiver of need through my core. I ached for more of him.

I closed my eyes and let my thoughts wander for a moment. I could almost feel his hands on my skin, his soft fingers caressing my breasts. His lips against mine. No one had ever touched me so intimately before. I'd never felt like I did in those moments with him. Even now, it seemed like I could still smell and taste him.

The thought left me feeling melancholy. I'd let Peter go. We shared a few moments in Paris and a memorable encounter somewhere over the Atlantic Ocean. It's like he said when he talked about the woman he'd met in a bar and had sex with; it might not mean forever. It was just the moments we had and then the memories of it for a lifetime. His effects on me would fade and I'd move on. He'd move on. For all I knew, he already had.

I felt a pang of jealousy as it occurred to me that he might have already hooked up with someone else, that our short time together had been more meaningless than I'd thought. I understood that it was my fault that I'd lost his number and couldn't call, but I felt like he'd have made some effort to find me.

Out of curiosity, I did something I'd never thought of before. I turned to my computer and googled my name and the word curator. There I was on the first page of results, including a picture of me. It was a link to the museum's staff page. So, Peter hadn't put in even minimal effort to locate me. That pretty much said it all, didn't it?

By the time Marie returned with food, I'd lost the urge to tell them more about my encounter with Peter. Reluctantly, I retrieved my sandwich and chips from the mini fridge in my office and headed up to the secret balcony to find they were already there waiting for me.

"I can't believe you didn't want one of these Cobb salads they make," Helena remarked as she took hers from Marie.

"Just not in the mood for one, I guess. I have a sandwich."

"And a cookie," Marie added, passing the large black and white I'd requested.

"Yes. Thank you," I told her. "I'll pay for it when I get back to my office."

"Don't sweat it. Just throw it in the food box."

"I will."

The "food box" was a wooden box I kept on a shelf in my office. Anytime one of us bought something relatively inexpensive for one of the others or just had some small change we wanted to dump, we tossed it in there. If you needed change for the drink or snack machines, you grabbed what you needed from there.

When the box began to get full, we'd cash it in at the bank for bigger bills and put it toward a nice lunch for all of us. We'd gone out for a nice meal before heading to France, so it was mostly empty except for a bit of change I'd tossed in there since my return.

"Enough about lunch money; tell us about what you've been up to while we were gone," Helena coaxed.

"I've just been working since I returned to New York," I said coyly.

Helen didn't miss my deliberate wording. "And what did you do before you left Paris?"

I smiled and replied, "Nothing at all."

They both scowled at me, and I laughed, feeling a little better than I had only minutes ago in my office. If I couldn't tell these two what happened, I couldn't tell anyone. I took a deep breath and held up my hands toward them in defeat.

"The only thing I did was join the mile-high club on the way home," I shrugged.

"Right, and we have yet to get any details beyond you hooked up in the bathroom on the flight. Tell us more."

"I met a guy at the Rembrandt opening and we chatted briefly. I got pulled away to deal with some VIPs and lost track of him. By the time the exhibit ended, he was gone. Then, he just happened to be in the seat next to me on my flight back to New York."

Helena shook her head. "You fucked a stalker."

"No. It was just a coincidence."

"Hell of a coincidence," Marie agreed. "Let me guess, he's been blowing up your phone since you landed."

"No," I said, my disappointment apparent in my tone. "He gave me his number, and I lost it. I was supposed to call him while he was here."

"Probably best," Helena told me. "The whole thing sounds a bit weird if you ask me."

I explained how things had unfolded so they understood why we ended up on the same plane and didn't think he was unhinged. I didn't know why I felt the need to explain everything to them, but I found that I didn't want them to think I hooked up with some loser.

I wanted both of them to know that he was wonderful and special, that I was lucky to have met them. I also wanted them to know I was livid and hadn't heard from him since. Mostly, I just wanted their input on what I should do. Should I use the fact that I'd lost his number as an excuse to contact him through the university somehow? Did that make the stalker if I did?

"I'm just disappointed that he didn't try to find me. I'm pretty easy to locate, given that he knows my name and that I work for a local museum."

"Wait, didn't you say he ended up in the last seat because he had a family emergency?" Marie asked.

"Yes. He didn't tell me what it was, but it had something to do with his sister."

"There you have it then. Whatever the emergency was, it probably kept him from looking for you. How long is he in town? He could still call you when things smooth out," she replied.

"Maybe," I said, taking a bite of my sandwich and considering this possibility. She might be right. I could just be making too much of him not having attempted to find me.

"Okay, so now that we got all that potential stalker business out of the way, let's get down to the important stuff. How was it? We need details," Helena told me.

I felt energized again now that I had reason to believe Peter hadn't just fucked me and walked away. I told them everything about my encounter with him. I knew I was gushing as I shared, but I couldn't help myself. I told them everything about how we talked to one another, and things got a bit suggestive.

I told them how I'd decided for once to just go with the flow and do what I wanted. So, when he suggested we hook up in the bathroom, I thought, why not? When would I ever have a chance like that again? Then there was the fact that I'd had to pony up $ 2,200 extra for the flight that I might not get back. I figured I might as well have something to show for my trouble. When I was done, they both just smiled knowingly.

Of course, I also left a few things out that they didn't need to know. I was okay with them knowing that I'd love to see him again, but I didn't want them to know how much I'd been obsessing over him. I told them what they needed to know about my time with Peter and my thoughts on being with him again, then left it at that.

"Congratulations. You've finally done something neither of us has done. I always wanted to join the mile-high club," Helena said.

"We could always hook up with each other on our next flight," Marie suggested.

"Does that count? If you do another girl? I thought you had to be fucked on the plane," Helena replied.

"I can pack my strap-on," Marie said.

We all laughed. It was good to have the two of them back and even better to have my own naughty story to tell this time. We finished our lunch while the two of them told me about their escapades, which made mine look paltry in comparison. If there was one thing you could count on from Helena and Marie, it was pure entertainment.

Chapter 20

Giselle

I always felt a sense of achievement on the first night of any large-scale event at the museum. So much work went into preparing for them. This one had been in the works for six months, much of that without me. The exhibition featured several Picasso paintings and sculptures on loan from various collections, some of which I'd arranged while in Paris.

I began my walk-through with the designer and coordinator, noting the greasy-looking fingerprints on the protective glass casing around the sculpture *Man with a Lamb*, which anchored one end of the display area's walkway.

"Where have those smudges come from?" I asked. The young display coordinator looked at it woefully. Nearby, a member of the maintenance staff quickly took ownership.

"I'm sorry. I had to replace one of the lights in the base. I think I touched it when I was putting the panel back in place," he groaned.

"Let's get that cleaned up before we open the doors," I said. The coordinator disappeared momentarily and returned with the cleaning staff, supervising as they polished the glass to perfection.

I checked the *Head of Fernande* sculpture to make sure the display glass there hadn't suffered any marks and found it pristine. We finished our review and prepared to open the museum and the exhibition. Unlike the one in Paris, I was not required to be such a public part of the event on most days. Now that it was underway, I could move on to the next project and ongoing museum work for a while.

Back in my office, I closed the door and sat down at my desk to work. Instead, I thought about Paris and the last large event I'd overseen. Things were very different here. There, we'd had a limited staff and had to wear hats that weren't usually a part of our positions. Here, there was plenty of staff to go around. I had to make an appearance later this afternoon at a special viewing, but mostly, others would take care of things.

It was a relief not to have to go out in the museum and schmooze with people for the duration of the event. I could get some other work done, change into the little black dress I'd brought for the event, and then I'd be done with any public engagements. Of course, I had to admit that it had its perks. If I hadn't been out on the floor, I would never have met Peter, and we'd not have shared such incredible moments.

I smiled as I thought of him. Our time together had been short but magical. What were the odds of meeting someone who made me feel so alive and free again? Leaning back in my chair, I let myself get lost in the memory for a moment and fantasize about what might have happened if we'd seen each other again here in New York.

I turned my chair, so it faced away from the door and closed my eyes, letting thoughts of him embrace me. Before I knew it, I was touching myself. I'd never done such a thing in my office before. The fact that my door was unlocked and anyone might walk in made it seem all the more risqué. I quickly moved from cupping my breasts, pinching my nipples through the soft material of my blouse, to slipping my hand into the band of my panties.

I stopped for a moment, not sure what I thought I was doing masturbating at work during the day, but I'd had a sexual adventure while crossing the Atlantic and been dealing with a lot of stress. I could use the stress relief. Before I knew it, I threw caution to the wind and slowly slipped my fingers into my pussy, moving them back at forth as I grew wetter.

I felt an odd mixture of inhibition and exhilaration mixed with the fear of getting caught as I grew bolder, finger fucking myself and stroking my clit, milking it until it was hard and fat, pulsing with need. I almost moaned aloud but caught myself, instead biting my lip as I continued to masturbate, my legs propped up on either side of my chair.

There was no masking what I was doing if anyone happened to come in, and right now, I couldn't really say that I minded. I suddenly felt bold and open to anything I wanted to do. What better place to release a little steam and shake off the tension of a day's work than right here in my office?

I cupped my right breast with my left hand, my nipple firmly pinched between my fingers as I rolled it back and forth, enjoying the hint of pain I felt. It only fueled the speed at which I stroked myself. I inserted two fingers deep inside and wiggled them, curving them ever so slightly to hit the spot I knew would send me over the edge.

It took me only a few minutes to get off; my legs seized and then shook violently with the force of my orgasm, sprinkling my desk chair with a spray from the forceful eruption that felt like it had come from my center mass. I collapsed into my chair, enjoying the relief I felt for a moment, knowing I couldn't remain like that too long.

The sound of the phone on my desk ringing jolted me forward. I awkwardly tried to pull my clothing back together and grab it, nearly sending the paperwork flying away in the process.

"Yes?" I said, my voice raspy.

"Is that your sexiest voice?" Marie replied.

"I, um," I stammered, trying to catch my breath and speak normally. "I'm sorry, I was just deep in work."

"Sounds more like someone was deep in you. You got a man in there?" Marie quipped.

"No. Don't be silly," I replied, feeling somehow seen and keenly aware of the shambles I'd made of my clothes.

"I don't know. It does sound like you've got your sexy voice on. Perhaps I should come and check on you."

"No!" I said a bit too loudly and she laughed, but dropped the subject.

"Listen, I just called to tell you that the celebrity tour has been moved forward. They're now going to be here at two."

"Two? I asked, glancing at the clock on my computer. "That's only an hour away."

"Yep. They said they have an early dinner to get to and want to do this beforehand."

I groaned. I was a wreck and now had to change for an afternoon viewing on short notice. "Okay. I'll be ready to meet them at the entrance."

"You should talk to them in your sultry voice. They'll love it," she teased.

"I don't have a sultry voice," I protested.

"Fuck yeah, you do." I could hear her chuckling as she hung up the phone. I smiled. Maybe I did have a sultry voice when I'd first answered.

At least now I didn't have to worry about fixing my clothes. I stood and walked to my door to flip the lock before stripping off my sensible gray skirt and bright pink top. I slipped into the black sheath dress I'd been wearing when I met Peter in Paris and topped it off with black and white heels.

I retrieved some wipes from my bathroom and cleaned off the seat at my desk, chuckling at what a mess I'd made and how much fun it had been to do it. I couldn't believe I had worked here this long and was only just now doing something so naughty. It made me wonder if Helena and Marie ever did anything like that. I suspected that they did, but I had no way of knowing for sure.

Using the desk mirror I kept in my drawer, I pulled out the makeup bag I'd brought to work for this purpose and began pinning up my hair. Once it was all in place, I returned to the tiny bathroom in one corner of my office, brushed my teeth and washed my face.

Sitting back at my desk, I applied some moisturizer and put on fresh makeup. Once I'd finished, I looked myself over and decided I was presentable enough for whoever I was escorting around the museum. I wondered if they'd be able to tell that I was fresh from getting myself off in my office. For a moment, I wondered if they'd be able to smell me. Horrified, I went back to my bathroom and freshened up a lot more than my face.

I had no idea who the celebrity was. The tour was booked by a publicist, and it could be anyone from some influencer I'd never heard of to a certain former NYU art student known as Lady Gaga. Of course, any celebrity usually comes with an entourage of family, friends, or associates. They'd all file out of some huge stretch SUV and pile into the museum or arrive in several unremarkable but expensive black sedans, sometimes flanked by security.

Tours like this, which took place during regular viewing hours, could sometimes get a bit hairy if there were any serious fans around, so extra security and whatever security the celebrity brought would be in place. My only job was to try not to make an ass of myself during it. I checked myself in the mirror again, smoothed down my clothes, and left my office to await their arrival.

Standing near the entrance where the guests were slated to arrive, I allowed myself to dabble in a bit of fantasy. Perhaps this handsome actor would be completely enamored of me and want to sweep me off my feet to join him at some upscale New York penthouse.

Of course, they were late, pulling up nearly fifteen minutes after they were supposed to arrive. I could have been doing something else while I waited—like giving myself another orgasm in my office, I thought. I chuckled at myself and walked out to greet the limo pulling up to the curb.

Chapter 21

Peter

"Hey, why don't we get out of the house for a bit today," Charlotte asked as we sat at the kitchen table eating sandwiches for lunch.

"Don't you have to be here with Steven?" I asked.

"Not for a while. His home health aide will be here all afternoon and the girls are in school. I have two tickets to a Picasso exhibit that the parents of one of my second language students gave me. Steven certainly can't go, and I know how much you love art."

"I don't know. I'd committed myself to staying here in my pajamas and maybe taking a nap until it was time to pick up your gremlins."

"Oh, come on. Don't be like that. I want to go, and I know you'll love it. Go get a shower and get dressed. I happen to know there are some decent suits in your closet in case of a funeral."

"I did not buy those suits in case of a funeral. In fact, I'm fairly certain you bought a couple of them and snuck them in the mix."

"Who knows. But you can never have enough suits. I happen to know you bought a black one on your second day here. Don't worry, I won't tell Steven," she said, winking at me.

"Well, in my defense, I didn't know how bad things were. I thought you might have just been downplaying how serious it was."

"Sure. Okay. At any rate, now that you don't have to save your new suit for a funeral, you can wear it to an art exhibition."

"But it's in the middle of the day."

"Are you a vampire? Have you been turned and just aren't telling me?"

"No," I laughed.

The truth was I'd been a bit down in the dumps lately. After I'd not heard anything from Giselle, I'd thought about trying to find her. There couldn't be that many museums in New York. It had been a serious consideration to just go to them all until I found her.

That was what I'd thought at first. Then I realized that I could probably find her online. Surely, she had some sort of social media or professional forum with some information I could use. I'd been so very close to opening my phone and doing a search, but I'd stopped.

I'd given Giselle my number at the airport. She'd never used it. Once we were separated at our passport checkpoints, it didn't seem like she had put much effort into finding me on the other side. At first, I'd just chalked it up to her being in the same kind of rush I was in. I had to get to Charlotte, and she had to get to the museum. Then, days had gone by with no word. Weeks later, I realized she simply didn't want to see me again.

I'd gone over and over it in my mind. Had I said something wrong? Was it something I'd done? The only conclusion I could reach is that I may have pushed her into doing something she wasn't ready for, despite her saying she was. I'd been foolish thinking someone who was still a virgin at twenty-three wouldn't have any regrets about giving it up to a stranger in an airplane toilet.

I hated that she might feel that way about it. For me, it had been truly special. I'd not only enjoyed the sex, but I'd also loved so much more about it than just the physical aspects. I felt connected to Giselle in a way I rarely felt with women. My disappointment at not hearing from her had really weighed on me and left me down in the dumps, though I wouldn't admit that to anyone but myself.

My sister knew, but that wasn't because I'd told her. It was because she knew me and understood when I felt a bit out of sorts over a woman. She'd tried to get me to talk about it a few times, and I'd blown it off. A part of me was ashamed that I'd let someone affect me so deeply when I'd only met them.

"So, what's the answer, sad sack? You coming with your sister to the exhibition?"

"Sure, why not," I said reluctantly.

"Good. Now, go get a shower, stinky. And while you're in there, trim your beard and brush your hair. You look homeless."

"Thanks. I just love how you always lift me up with your compliments," I said, my voice dripping with sarcasm.

"Anytime." She stood and left the table, presumably to shower and change for the exhibition.

Back in the guest room, I looked through my clothes, contemplating wearing something besides a suit. Who wore a suit to an afternoon art exhibition besides someone going there from work and already in a suit? Still, I knew my sister. She wanted me to dress up because she wanted to dress up.

I sighed heavily as I stripped down and went to get a shower. I thought about Giselle while I showered and discovered I had a huge erection. Definitely couldn't leave the room looking like that. I closed my eyes and thought about her as I stroked myself.

I could still see her standing there in the black dress. She stood out against the other women in the museum. Her auburn locks were pinned up carefully but softened by the loose strands around her perfect face. Unlike most women, she saw no need to apply heavy makeup to cover the freckles sprinkled across the bridge of her nose and dotting her cheeks.

She would have given off the image of someone much younger if not for the perfect curves that were evident even in her simple black dress. The light silhouetted her frame as she stood in front of one of the displays, giving clear definition to her rounded bottom and ample breasts.

That caught my attention at first, but then we spoke, and I realized there was so much more to her than just a lovely face and figure. Giselle Martin was intelligent, educated, and very well-informed when it came to one of my passions—the world of art. She knew more about Rembrandt than perhaps I did. It was all a huge turn-on, which was why I now stood in my shower with a raging boner.

I let the hot water spread over me as I leaned back against the wall and took matters into my own hands, slowly stroking my cock as I thought about how absolutely perfect she was. I think that, somewhere in the back of my mind, I'd thought there might be a chance we'd be on the same flight. I knew she'd been returning to New York that morning, just not what time.

However, I could never have imagined she'd be sitting right beside me, affording me another opportunity to learn more about her. And I certainly never considered that we would end up in the airplane bathroom throwing caution to the wind. The fact that she'd actually taken me up on my mostly kidding offer had astounded me, and I knew that perhaps I should have backed down. I knew she might have regrets about it.

Still, I couldn't resist having her. Even if it was for just that once in my life. I wanted to know how it felt to be inside of her. I wanted to hear her coo and moan as she gave me something precious that she'd been saving for just the right person. Whether that should have been me was debatable, but neither of us had turned back.

Those moments had been beautiful, despite the awkwardness of the confined space. The risk of being caught. The taboo nature of knowing we could get in serious trouble. And then there was just the beauty of touching such an incredible woman for the first time and knowing I was the only one she'd let get so close to her. My only real regrets about it were that we'd had so little time together and not been able to find more afterward.

Thoughts of her amazing body, the way she tasted, the way she whispered my name in my ear filled my head as I stroked my cock, quickly bringing myself to an orgasm. I milked every last drop and felt the emptiness of being alone settle back over me again.

Stepping out of the shower, I dried myself off and looked in the mirror. The face that looked back at me seemed old. My hair showed more streaks of gray at the temples and my beard was quickly becoming more salt than pepper. Fine lines were visible at the corner of my eyes and when I furrowed my brow.

"You're an old fuck, Dockery," I said out loud to the reflection in the mirror as I began trimming my mustache and beard.

I continued to contemplate the situation with Giselle. It occurred to me, too—that perhaps she'd realized how much older than her I was. Nearly two decades was a big age difference, but I didn't feel like a middle-aged man. I felt young at heart. It didn't change the way that she might see me, though.

I thought about my students. They treated me like I was their father or something. They weren't much younger than Giselle. The thought made me feel worse. I would never hook up with one of my students, but I'd been happy to do so with a woman barely older than the seniors in my class.

I pushed the thoughts aside and began getting dressed. I checked myself in the full-length mirror on one side of the room and nodded approvingly. I might be getting older, but I thought I still looked pretty good. I'd always been decent looking, and I kept myself in shape. There was nothing wrong with me.

My little pep talk made me feel a bit better. I shouldn't beat myself up. Giselle was just a woman I met and had sex with. She wasn't the first. She probably wouldn't be the last. In fact, I might even hook up with someone before I leave New York if I am lucky.

Somewhere in the back of my mind, I knew there was a chance that fate might take me back to Giselle again. The exhibition was at a museum. What were the odds that it was the one where she worked? As quickly as the thought entered my mind, I pushed it back down. It did no good to get my hopes up. The chances were likely slim, and even if they weren't, she'd already made it clear she didn't want to get in touch.

I sighed and headed back downstairs to wait for Charlotte. We still had a bit before we needed to leave, and she always took longer to get dressed. She appeared nearly thirty minutes later wearing a long navy skirt with a white blouse and a long silk scarf with blue and white polka dots.

"Well, don't you look eloquent," I said.

"Not bad for a middle-aged mother of teenagers, eh?" she said, striking a fashionable pose.

"Nope, not bad at all. You obviously come from a very good-looking family," I teased.

"Oh, you have no idea. You should have seen my parents. They were beautiful people. I do have a brother that, well, he might be adopted…"

"Hey now!" I said, smiling broadly.

I found myself feeling a little better already. Charlotte had been right. Getting out of the house might be exactly what I needed, after all. We made our way out to the car and drove toward the city, chatting happily as we traveled.

We parked in a garage not far from the museum and walked the last few blocks, climbing the steps and giving our tickets to the man stationed at the entrance to the exhibit. Charlotte linked her arm with mine as we sauntered in and began making our way through the collection.

Chapter 22

Peter

I felt a bit of tension in my shoulders as we walked through the exhibit. I enjoyed Picasso, and the works the museum had secured for the display were terrific. I hadn't seen most of them before and marveled at just how talented he was.

"Can you imagine being a stranger in a strange land with the police constantly watching you?" I asked Charlotte.

"No. It's just so fascinating that he could create such beauty amid incredible personal chaos," she replied.

"True. Are these the first Picassos you've seen?"

"Yes and no. It's the first time I've seen original pieces in an exhibition. I saw the cat he gave Ernest Hemingway once when Steven and I went on a tour of Hemingway's home in Key West."

"When did you go there? I don't remember you mentioning it."

"Oh, it was a while back, before we had the girls. We just decided to take a trip on a whim and did some sightseeing down there. I think it was about 2008 or so."

"Well, then, these are the first original Picassos you've seen."

"What? No. I would have sworn the guide told us that was a Picasso cat."

"I'm sure he did. I don't think they tell the whole story about that cat anymore, but the actual cat Hemingway was given was stolen in late 2000."

"Oh, no!"

"Yeah. If I recall, they don't know if it was during or after a tour, but the cat is missing. They replaced it with a replica."

"And the original cat was never found? Or did they just not want to put it back out after that? I mean, it was just sitting on a shelf for the taking."

"They did find it. Some guy tried to trade it for a boat or something that same year and they nabbed him. From what I heard, they recovered the cat, but it was badly damaged. I'm not sure where it is now."

"That's a shame."

"It is, but it was unclear whether Picasso created the cat anyway. Hemingway's wife found it in a box at some point after his death and said it was a gift from the artist, so everyone took her word for it. He and Picasso were friends in Paris, so it is possible."

"It certainly looks like a Picasso."

"That it does," I told her as we arrived in front of the sculpture known as *Head of a Fernande*.

Charlotte and I both stood there reading the description of the statue. I was familiar with the work. I'd seen it once years ago in Paris, but it still held just as much fascination for me. Charlotte seemed far less impressed by it.

"It's just so ... misshapen," she said.

"It's the shape he intended it to be," I replied.

"Sure, but didn't he create this in the image of his lover?"

"Yes. Her name was Fernande Olivier. She was quite the inspiration. He originally created this bust in 1909. He created 60 works that year with her as his muse."

"She must have been quite a woman, but you'd think he'd have made a bust of her a bit more flattering."

I chuckled, which seemed to only inspire her quiet tirade.

"Can you imagine? Some great artist tells you they've created a bust of you and then unveils this. Just look at it. One eyebrow sticks out, the other is carved in. There are all sorts of lumps and bulges, crazy angles."

"Would it be a Picasso if it looked like the Statue of Venus?"

"I suppose not, but I just can't imagine swooning if Steven were to call me over to an art studio and present me with this representation of me that looks like the Elephant Man."

I laughed, this time a bit too loudly. Only about a half dozen people were here, as they limited how many could come through at once. As much fun as Charlotte was having poking fun at this statue, I knew that she really had a great love for art and found it just as mesmerizing as I did. She just couldn't help but toss a bit of humor into the mix.

Charlotte's phone rang and she quickly grabbed it, looking around apologetically as the loud ringtone filled the gallery. She whispered quietly into the mouthpiece, her face falling as she spoke.

"Is she okay?" she asked, her voice elevated slightly. There were a series of acknowledgments as the person on the other end spoke and Charlotte's face turned into a scowl. She ended the call after less than a minute.

"I have to leave," she whispered.

"What? We only just got here," I said, feeling disappointed now that I was out and enjoying myself.

"I know. I'm sorry. One of the girls has a problem at school and I have to go take care of her."

"Problem? What kind of problem?"

"Just a problem. Listen, you stay here and enjoy the exhibit and the rest of the museum. I can come back and get you afterward."

"No. Wait. I'm worried. What kind of problem?"

"Good grief. A girl problem. Her first girl problem. Yeah get me?"

"Oh, yeah. Sorry."

"So, do you want to come with or stay?"

"I'll stay and let you get to her. I can find my own way home."

"Are you sure? I'm so sorry about this. I wanted us to have a good afternoon together."

"Don't worry about me. Go take care of the gremlin."

"Thanks. I'll see you back at the house. This family! They're going to be the death of me!"

I kissed her on the cheek, and she left the gallery, leaving me to ponder the works of Picasso alone. I drank them all in and then stepped out to venture around some of the other exhibits in the museum. Stopping to marvel at modern sculpture by a local artist, I found myself struck by the perfection with which it had been created.

It had been a long time since I'd sculpted. My desire to create seemed to have vanished over the years as I became more entrenched in teaching. Perhaps what I needed was a muse like Fernande. I wonder what my creation of a woman I loved would look like.

Once again, I pondered Giselle. I wouldn't say she was a woman I loved. I hardly knew her, really, but she was certainly a woman that I thought I could love. If we'd been given the time we deserved to truly get to know one another and weren't separated from one another on different continents. I could easily see us being together.

An image of her flashed through my mind. It wasn't the first time, but I kept returning to her sitting in her seat on the airplane. There were these individual moments that blended together to create one. She was looking ahead when I first saw her, then her head began to turn toward me until it finally rested on me with a smile of recognition. I could tell she was happy to see me, which had felt nothing short of amazing.

Letting the memory slip away, I continued to make my way around the museum, taking time to drink in all the beautiful creations displayed there. As I looped back toward the Picasso exhibit, I noted a woman who looked incredibly like Angelina Jolie exiting with a group of people. I chuckled to myself at thinking someone of such high stature would be just tooling about a daytime exhibit in a New York museum.

I turned to admire a gorgeous late nineteenth-century glass vase from the Tiffany Collection. It was meticulously crafted with all the expertise you'd expect from Louis Tiffany. I found myself wishing I could pick it up, feel the weight in my hands, and examine it closely. It was such an amazing piece of work. The part of me that had once fancied myself a creator wondered what it must have felt like in his hands when he was done. I was still studying it when I heard a familiar voice behind me.

"I hope you enjoyed the tour and thank you so much for coming today. I wish you had more time to enjoy more of the museum," she said.

I turned to see Giselle standing there. She had her back to me as she spoke to the group that had exited the Picasso exhibit, but there was no mistaking her perfect frame, her lovely auburn hair, and her voice. I debated whether I should make a hasty retreat before she saw me. I didn't want her to think I was stalking her across New York.

I froze in place, a part of me wanting to run and another part wanting to see what happened. I was no shrinking violet. I could handle rejection, but I couldn't handle being thought of as a stalker. If she'd wanted to see me, she would have called. She would have invited me here. I couldn't remember another point in my life where I felt so unsure of myself.

I was just about to make a dash into another part of the museum until I could sneak back out the front doors when she suddenly turned on her heel and began walking toward me. At first, it was as if she didn't recognize me. She seemed to be looking more past me than at me. Then she appeared to zero in. I realized I'd been standing in the shadows until she drew closer. She took only a few steps and then stopped dead in her tracks.

Here it was, then. Things were about to get grim for one or both of us. What a pitiful end to something that had once seemed so promising. I was sure she was going to want to get past what would be an awkward encounter as quickly as possible.

She wore a black dress like she'd had on when we first met in Paris, perhaps even the same one. I wasn't exactly a fashion expert. All I knew was it fit her lovely figure to absolute perfection. Dark tendrils of hair spilled over the clip in the back of her hair and a few framed her delightfully freckled face.

Yes, I could see how a woman could inspire a man to create breathlessly beautiful pieces of art that ended up in museums around the world. Looking at Giselle, I could see it quite clearly.

After the initial shock of seeing me seemed to pass, Giselle finally began moving toward me. The group behind her spilled out the front doors. I recognized the woman still beside her as one of the other women I'd seen at the museum in Paris. She remained beside Giselle as she approached. Instead of any anticipated coolness, I found myself looking at a beautiful smile spreading across her face.

"Marie, this is Professor Peter Dockery," Giselle told her before speaking to me directly.

"Oh, really?" Marie said, now breaking out in a smile of her own. "In that case, I have some urgent business matter to attend to. Pleasure to meet you, Professor Dockery.

"You too, Marie," I replied, not taking my eyes off Giselle as her associate disappeared down a side hallway.

I wasn't sure what she might have told Marie, but it was quite obvious that they'd discussed me in some capacity. That was the only explanation for her associate's quick extraction of herself from our presence. Now, I wished I'd been a fly on that wall. I'd love to know what she'd said and if it had been something that would delight me or something I'd wish I'd never heard.

I wasn't sure what I expected to happen if I did somehow find Giselle again, but I hadn't imagined it as the two of us just standing speechlessly staring at one another.

Chapter 23

Giselle

"I'm so glad you're here," I said, breaking my temporary paralysis and rushing forward to kiss Peter on the cheek. My heart was hammering so hard across my chest that I was sure he could feel it hitting his chest while I was near him.

"Really? I'm surprised," he replied.

"You mean because I didn't call," I said for the first time, realizing how that must have seemed to him. I'd been so busy judging him for not trying to find me that it never occurred to me that he might have thought I didn't want to be found.

"Well, yeah. I didn't expect you to call immediately, but I thought you would once you were settled in," he said.

His voice held no contempt or anger, just a sort of sadness. I knew how he felt. I'd been sad too, though I tried my best to just squash it down. It didn't seem real that he was here, even now. But he was here, and I wasn't going to let him slip through my fingers again so quickly.

"Peter, I lost your number. I was trying to save it and dropped my phone. When I picked it up, the screen cleared, and you were nowhere to be found on the other side of the immigration line. I didn't know how to find you. I'd hoped you'd try to find me instead."

"I thought about it, but I thought you had my number and were choosing not to call. I didn't want to be *that guy* that makes you change your number or quit work to escape."

"You could never be that to me. I just thought that when I didn't call you, you would realize something had gone wrong and look for me. I thought you were maybe glad I didn't call and had only given me your number because it was polite or something," I told him, my voice full of apology and regret.

We were both silent for another moment, just looking at one another. Then Peter moved toward me, pulling me into a deep kiss in the middle of the museum. It was completely unprofessional and I didn't care even one tiny bit.

"That felt good," he said, smiling down at me.

"It certainly did," I said, still lost in the way his lips felt on mine. I heard giggles from nearby and turned to see Helena and Marie making a hasty retreat up some nearby stairs. I laughed, as did Peter, who was looking in their direction too. "Are you here alone?" I asked.

"I am. My sister was with me, but she had to leave early."

"Well, I'm pretty much done here today. If you want to look around for a few more minutes, I can close up my office and we can go somewhere for dinner? That is, if you want."

"I'd love to have dinner with you."

"I'll be right back," I told him, already heading toward my office. I stopped only a few steps away and returned to kiss him again, this time lightly on the lips. His hand trailed down my bare arm as I pulled away from him. The hairs stood at attention and tingled in search of his touch as I walked away.

I quickly shut down my computer and shuffled everything into my bag. I thought about changing back into my work clothes but didn't want to take the time to redo my whole look again. I'd leave them in the office and take them home tomorrow.

I picked up my phone and called my boss. I was relieved when there was no answer. I left a message, hung up, and then called Marie. She answered with an over-the-top greeting that reflected her amusement at my PDA in the lobby.

"What's up, you sexy bitch?"

"I'm leaving for the day if anyone asks. I left a message for the director, but I don't even know if he's here."

"Good enough. Don't do anything I wouldn't do."

"That doesn't leave much, does it?" I shot back.

"No, not really. So, go wild," she said with a wicked little laugh.

"Thanks. I'll see you tomorrow."

"Oh, you bet you will, and I will want details. All of them."

I laughed and hung up the phone, grabbing my things and hurrying back out to the lobby. At first, I didn't see Peter, and my heart sank, but then he walked around a marble statue, and I felt a sense of relief rush through me.

"Ready to go?" he asked.

"I am." I took the hand he offered and walked out of the museum feeling like the world had finally been righted again.

We made our way to a little out of the way bistro near the museum and settled in for some wine and pasta, catching up on everything that had been going on since he arrived in New York.

"So, my family emergency was that my brother-in-law had a car accident and was laid up in the hospital. My sister needed help with my nieces, and I was the only one she trusted to stay with them."

"Is he okay now? Is he better?"

"He has some broken bones that will take time to heal, but he's back home. They have home health and physical therapy coming in regularly, so they can manage."

"Then I guess you'll be going back home soon," I said, already hating the idea of him leaving.

"Unfortunately. I'm leaving on Friday."

"Friday?" I repeated, frowning. We only have two days together. What cruel trick of fate was it that we were always given so little time?

"Yes. I could try to extend it a bit, but the fall semester is just around the corner. I have workshops I'm required to attend and planning I have to do."

"No. Of course. I understand. I just wish we had more time," I told him, pushing away the remainder of my pasta and finishing my wine.

"I guess we'll just have to make the most of what time we have then, huh?"

"I suppose we will." I motioned for the waiter to bring us the check.

"I've got that," Peter said when the server brought it over. He dropped some cash into the plastic tray and stood, holding out his hand for me to take.

"Your place or mine," I joked, feeling a lot more nervous than I thought I would about this now that the moment had arrived.

"Well, mine contains a temporary invalid, my sister, and two curious teenage girls who will ask you so many questions you'll wish you were dead," he joked.

"I don't have a death wish, so I guess we'll go to my place then," I told him, mentally cataloging what messes I'd left behind when I departed this morning.

"Wise choice." We exited the bistro and walked toward my place. We'd get there quicker on the subway, but it was a nice evening for a stroll and wasn't that far away. It would give me time to work up my courage to be a bit more adventurous.

As it turned out, I didn't need to worry about what my place looked like. I don't think Peter even noticed. He pulled me into a kiss the moment I closed the door and flipped the lock, dropping my bags in the living room on our way to the bedroom.

Bits of clothing were already being lost as we crossed the room and made our way toward my bed. By the time we arrived, Peter was down to his boxer briefs and I was in my bra and panties. Things suddenly fell into what felt like slow motion. The rush to get undressed was replaced with slow kisses and soft caresses.

Peter slowly slid the straps of my bra down my shoulders, freeing my breasts. We'd not even been able to do this much on the plane. We'd hardly undressed at all, and the most he'd seen of my body were glimpses of my exposed skin here and there as we went at one another like wild animals, urgent and instinctual. Now, we had time. We didn't have to rush anything.

Slipping my bra down, Peter reached around me, kissing me while unsnapping the back closures and letting it fall to the floor. His hands slipped into the band of my panties and began pushing them off until gravity took them to the floor. I kicked them away with my feet and reached for the tops of his boxer briefs, but he stopped me.

"Not yet," he breathed, picking me up and laying me across my bed.

Peter joined me on the bed, tangling his fingers in my hair as he hovered above me and kissed me. It was the kind of long, passionate kiss I'd always dreamed about. There was nothing about this that didn't feel like utter perfection. I quivered beneath him as he ran his hands along my sides, not in any hurry.

I wanted all of the passion. I wanted him to kiss me. I wanted him to touch me, but I also wanted desperately to feel him inside me. Our bodies moved together, mostly skin on skin, as we lay together on the bed and explored one another.

"You are the most beautiful woman I've ever seen," Peter breathed against my neck, planting small kisses that migrated slowly south toward my breasts. I gasped as the warmth of his lips slipped across my right breast and engulfed my nipple, softly sucking at it before moving to the left to do the same. I arched my back toward him, eager for more.

It was hard to believe this was finally happening. I'd thought I'd never see him again, and now, here he was, making me feel like an emotional wreck who might cry with joy at any given moment. I closed my eyes, enjoying the sensation of his lips and skin on mine.

I tensed for a moment as he moved down and he stopped, looking up at me wordlessly. I smiled down at him and nodded, unable to form any words. It had been only a momentary reaction to the unfamiliar touch of a man growing closer to my intimate areas. Though Peter and I had already had sex, it hadn't been like this. This was far more intimate, far more personal.

I shuddered as he reached my center, gently placing his hands on my legs and moving my thighs apart so I was exposed to him. He didn't move to touch my aching center just yet. Instead, he began placing soft kisses up and down my inner thighs. They were so light and velvety that they felt like a flower dragging across my skin.

I moaned quietly, loving every minute of it. Peter finally moved back upward, looking at me with a wanton smile. He kept his eyes on mine as he dragged his tongue slowly through my center, sending shards of electricity through my body and pangs of desire squarely to my very core. I grabbed the sheets, gripping them tightly as Peter took his time exploring me with his tongue.

My moans filled the room as he grew more and more aggressive in pleasuring me. I gasped loudly as he circled my clit with his mouth and sucked it, moving his mouth up and down it until it grew fat with longing. His fingers replaced his mouth, slowly pumping in and out of me as he continued to tease my clit.

I was close, so close. My body reacted to his manipulations, twisting in an effort to gain relief yet not wanting him to stop. He held me in place with one hand, lapping eagerly at my wetness as I finally exploded into a thousand pieces into his mouth, and he drank every drop of my pleasure.

Finally, I collapsed against the pillow. Peter moved up and kissed me, my juices still on his lips. He lay on the pillow beside me, touching me as I caught my breath.

"That was amazing," I half whispered.

"We've only just begun," he replied.

I smiled down at him and he pulled me closer into a kiss, the beginning of what I can only describe as a night filled with magic.

Chapter 24

Giselle

"Good morning," I said as Peter emerged from the shower the following morning.

"Indeed, it has been," he replied as he pulled me close to him, this damp chest hair dotting my t-shirt with water spots. I didn't care. I wouldn't have cared if I'd been in work clothes, but I'd called and asked to work from home for a few days due to an "unexpected guest" from out of town.

The museum had readily accepted my request. It was unusual for me to neglect work, but I'd get some things done here and there when Peter went to see his sister and check on things there. I wouldn't have to go in unless some sort of problem arose, and I knew that Marie and Helena would do their best to cover those without me since they knew all about my guest.

"What do you want to do today?" I asked Peter.

"You," he replied with a grin.

"I can get behind that." I leaned into him and kissed him softly.

He kissed me back. I felt like I was lifting off the floor, floating above it in some sort of blissful cloud. Peter pulled away and let go of me with a sigh.

"But it will have to wait for a bit. I have to go help Charlotte with a few things around the house. Then I can come back and help you with much more pleasant things."

"Okay. I'll see if I can get some work done while you're gone."

"Unless you want to come with me?"

"I don't want to be in the way, and you said the teens will be curious. I don't want them to think I'm some sort of tramp."

He laughed. "They won't be there, but they wouldn't think that if they were. My sister, on the other hand..."

I frowned and looked down at my feet. Peter put his hand beneath my chin and lifted it toward him. I looked at him, a somewhat wilted smile on my face.

"I'm only teasing you," he said. "My sister will adore you. Come with me."

"Are you sure?"

"Absolutely, but we'll take a cab. I don't want to waste time on the subway when we need to get there, finish my chores, and get back to one another."

"A cab it is," I told him, my smile broadening into something more genuine.

"You might want to change, though. The wet t-shirt might not send the right message."

"You should probably put on some clothes so you don't get arrested out on the sidewalk waiting for the cab," I retorted.

"Right. I have to do the walk of shame in a wrinkled suit. Where is it?"

"I think there's a trail between here and the front door."

"Guess I'll get dressed on my way out then," he quipped, dropping his towel to reveal his impressive nakedness and sauntering down the hall.

I laughed and went to my closet to grab another shirt, stripping off the damp one and replacing it with a pressed button-down that fell somewhere between casual and work quality. Despite the jokes, I really did want to make a good impression.

As it turned out, Charlotte and I hit it off right from the start. She was incredibly intelligent and quite knowledgeable about a great deal of art. She wasn't as well versed as Peter, but that was to be expected with his position as an art teacher. If I hadn't been so eager to return to my pace and have Peter all to myself, I could have easily seen hanging out with her the rest of the day.

I didn't have as much of a warm, fuzzy feeling for Steven, though it was through no fault of his own. He was still on pretty strong meds and not exactly up to chatting with visitors. I was relieved to hear that he would make a full recovery in time and offered my services to Charlotte if she needed anything once Peter was gone.

Back at my apartment, Peter and I were all over one another again from the moment we were behind closed doors. We only came up to order pizza, which I collected wearing a robe, and we ate curled against one another on the sofa. We did manage to watch a movie, or at least most of it, before Peter chased me back into the bedroom again.

"Sex pest!" I bleated before falling into a fit of giggles as he tackled me on the bed.

"You love every moment of it," he replied, flipping me over and grabbing my ankles to pull me back toward the edge of the bed.

I playfully tried to scurry away, but he held me fast, his hands fastened on either side of my waist. I faked a fight and then gave in, waiting to see what he had planned for me. I didn't have to wait long as his hands moved from my waist to slip beneath me on the bed, kneading my breasts with his hands and kissing my neck as I lay there waiting for him to do as he pleased with me.

I turned my head sideways and he kissed me on the cheek, dragging a finger down the side of my neck and pushing my robe away from my shoulder before finally pulling both sides down my arms and my body to leave me naked on the bed.

"What are you doing?" I asked, eager to find out what he had planned.

"Whatever I want," he announced with a little chuckle.

I laughed at this, too, as he ran his hands down my back and over my behind, continuing downward to slip between my legs and push them apart. I was already wet at just the thought of him inside of me again. We'd had sex several times throughout the night, and I was more than ready to do so again today.

"I love the curve of your breasts, the angle of your hips," he said as he trailed his fingers along one side of my body, letting the side of them glide softly along the trail he laid out on my body. "I love the freckles that crop up in the oddest places."

I smiled, my head still turned sideways against the covers, only half visible to him. What I loved was how he used the word "love" so fluidly. He wasn't telling me that he loved me; I knew that. But telling me he loved things about me was a close second in my book. Listening to him admire my body out loud made me feel sexy and wanted.

He began slowly kissing his way up my back, focusing on the center as he teased my heated skin with his mouth. As he neared my face, he bit softly into my shoulder, causing me to moan. It encouraged him and he began to nibble across my shoulder blade and onto the next. I wiggled beneath him, enjoying the sensation of having my flesh bitten, though it wasn't hard enough to really cause any real pain.

Peter slid his hands down the length of my back and onto my backside again, kneading my flesh there slightly as he pushed my thighs further apart with his knees. I could feel his erection as it brushed against my thigh. The hair on his legs tickled against my skin as he positioned himself to enter me. I let out a gasp of pure delight as he pushed inside me and began moving ever so slowly in and out.

I lay beneath him, enjoying our slow, lazy lovemaking as it built up to a crescendo. Peter was gentle, pumping in and out of me in long strokes until I was on the verge of exploding. I pushed back against his thrusts, meeting him each time until our bodies bounced back and forth in perfect rhythm.

The room filled with our grunts and groans as we picked up speed. I pushed myself upward, using my arms to help push back against him. I'd crossed the line from enjoying our docile little coupling to feeling like a wildling eager to be taken hard and fast.

"Harder," I begged, panting like an animal as Peter obliged, pumping into me hard and fast. I wanted to feel every inch of him driving deep inside of me, filling me with his manhood. It seemed so primal to be having sex with such wild abandon.

"I'm going to come," Peter groaned, still pumping into me with every inch of his sizable equipment.

I was on the verge too. I could already feel it welling up inside of me. I let out a loud groan as it rang through my center and shattered in forceful waves. Peter was quick to follow, releasing his own orgasm deep inside me. I relaxed, not quite collapsed on the bed as he remained inside me, coming down from the powerful climax.

Finally, he pulled free and rolled over to lay on the bed beside me. He reached over and played with a few strands of my hair. I could tell there was something he wanted to say, but I didn't ask what it was. There was a part of me that was terrified he'd talk about what would happen when he had to go, and I just wasn't ready to face up to that yet.

Some part of me felt like some miracle could keep us together. Perhaps he would change his mind about wanting to come to New York, and we'd only be apart temporarily. Maybe his sister would need him to stay longer, and he'd grow so enchanted with me that he couldn't bear being apart. I built up all sorts of fantasies in my head, but deep down, I knew they weren't realistic.

Peter and I were perfect together. Everything in my bones told me that. We had great conversations. We had similar interests that were different enough not to make them a boring topic of discussion. We were deeply attracted to one another, and the sex was off the charts fantastic. Still, the issue of our distance apart remained.

"I guess we should get some sleep," Peter finally said, shifting so that we could slip beneath the covers.

I loved that he didn't feel the need to jump up and wash our scents off like I'd heard Helena and Marie talk about. He was content to just curl up together, still smelling of sex and one another. We sank into the covers and Peter pulled me close, curling up against my back with his face in my hair. He pushed it aside and kissed me softly on the neck.

"You are an amazing woman, Gizelle," he said quietly.

"I have some pretty great inspiration by my side," I told him, feeling the pain of knowing that wouldn't last much longer.

"I'm glad I could bring such greatness out in you," he said, chuckling softly.

His breath against my skin was so comforting. I could see myself living a very long and happy life with Peter. Even well beyond when our bodies aged and changed—when we were old and no longer had the sexual urges that had painted our current days together—I could see us curled together like this.

Being in Peter's arms felt like a joy all by itself. I could be happy just lying like this with him, but as wonderful as it all was, I found myself lying awake until the wee hours of the morning filled with dread. The day ahead would be my last with Peter for who knew how long. How would we make this work when he was on a different continent, thousands of miles away?

I knew that I would ache for him, that my body would miss his, and the longing might be more than I could bear. How long would I want him? How long would I ache for him to hold me again? Would it ever pass?

Chapter 25

Peter

I woke up feeling like a heavy weight sat squarely on my chest. I watched Giselle as she slept, her auburn hair spilled across the pale blue pillowcase beneath her head. Today was our last day together. I would return to Paris, and she would stay here in New York. We'd both go back to our jobs, and time would erase the bliss we'd shared.

I desperately wanted to hang on to that and the memories would always be there, but I wanted more than that. I didn't want Giselle to be a memory. I wanted her to be my present. I dared to say she could easily be my forever. I found myself contemplating relocating to be closer to her.

Of course, that was all mad of me. We hardly knew one another. It was so hard to reconcile the way we fit so perfectly with how little time we'd spent together. I felt closer to her now than I'd felt with women I'd dated for months or even years. Though I'd never married, I wasn't opposed to the idea. I'd just never met a woman I wanted to marry—until now.

I shook off the thoughts. I had no business even thinking of this with any sense of permanence. It wasn't meant to be anything more than it was and I needed to remember that. Otherwise, I might do something stupid like give up my tenure to live with a woman I hardly knew.

I'd love to be someone who threw caution to the wind and took a chance like that, but experience has taught me not to rush into things, no matter how right they felt. It didn't make me happy, but I had to keep my wits about me. That was something very hard to do with a woman as intoxicating as Giselle.

There was a sense of foreboding in the air around us as we spent our last day together, trying to push away the impending gloom of our departure by getting lost in one another time and time again. As the hours passed, we neared the end of our time.

I pulled Giselle into my arms and kissed her, setting our passion alight as our tongues danced lazily with one another. Our kiss was filled with the longing of two people who knew this would be the last time for far too long.

It would be easy to dismiss my time with Giselle as some passing fancy, just a fling, but that would be inaccurate. It would be more apt to paint us as star-crossed lovers who desperately wanted to be together but couldn't find a way to make it work. If I could give myself to her and stay here forever, I would, but nothing was set in stone.

I was far more experienced than her when it came to love affairs and I knew no matter how wonderful things started, there was a lot of room for them to go wrong along the way. I had no doubts that Giselle was wonderful and beautiful, but love was fickle, and if that was where we were headed, it could end as easily as it had begun.

Perhaps a part of me wanted this to be a pleasant memory, to never experience the pain of losing her. Another part of me knew what it would mean for my career. I would have to start over. I'd lose my tenure and start at some minor university in New York, where I'd have to fight my way upward again. I was forty-two years old, and as much as I wanted to say I was willing to do that for Giselle, I knew I couldn't.

I felt selfish for it and wondered if I might even be wrong not to consider the possibilities. She was an amazing woman, but she was also only twenty-three years old. I was her first lover, and as much as she'd talked about saving herself for marriage and wanting to only be with one man for the rest of her life, that might change in time as she matured and began to wonder what she might have missed.

As much as it pained me not to be able to give us that chance, to not be willing to take that risk, I had to follow my instincts. I lost myself in her one more time, kissing her like she was the last woman on Earth. I could easily fall in love with Giselle. In fact, I was probably halfway there just from the limited amount of time we had together. It was all the more reason to put some distance between us and let things fall away with time.

"A penny for your thoughts," Giselle said softly beside me.

"I'm not sure they're worth that much," I told her, pulling her into another kiss.

I did my best to push away the pain of knowing our time had almost come to an end. Giselle nuzzled against me as I kissed her perfect, freckled skin, touring her body as if I was just discovering it for the first time before slipping my fingers between her legs. I propped up on one side, looking down at her as she lay sprawled across the bed, her legs open to me.

Her face was a vision of ecstasy as I explored her pretty pink pussy, slipping my fingers in and out of her as she arched her back, silently urging me to penetrate her deeper. I watched as she closed her eyes, lost in the sensations I created between her legs. I smiled down at her, enjoying how she cooed and moved beneath my hand.

Her eyes fluttered open for a moment, locking with mine, and I felt like I was being ripped into. How could I leave this woman behind without even trying? I pushed the thought from my mind, pulling my hand free of the slippery folds between her legs and leaning in to kiss her. I couldn't look into her eyes right now. I couldn't take it.

I pushed her onto her side away from me, spooning against her and kissing her neck. I moved my arm beneath her, wrapping it around her body to caress one breast while moving my other hand back between her legs to rub her clit. She stirred as I hit just the right spot, her tight behind rubbing against my rapidly growing cock.

I continued until she shuddered against me, lost in the throes of climax. I was so very hard, my cock pushing between her ass cheeks. I shifted down enough to enter her, taking her with one thrust. Our bodies rocked back and forth against one another as we fucked in slow motion. I was in no hurry to come. I wanted this to last. I wanted her to come again, to feel her spilling across my cock while I was inside her.

"Yes, that feels so amazing, Peter," she cooed, reaching back with one hand to touch the side of my face.

"I love your body. We fit together like perfect puzzle pieces," I moaned, slowing my pace once again as I felt my orgasm building.

Reaching across her body, I rubbed her clit again, sending her into a frenzy of gasps and moans.

"I'm going to come," she whined, encouraging me to push harder for her to do just that.

I quickened my pace inside her, thrusting deeply in and out of her center as she spilled her wetness across my cock, her body vibrating with the force of the release. I was ready to fill her with my own climax when she stopped me and pushed me back, climbing off of the bed and kneeling beside it.

"I want to taste you. I want it in my mouth," she said.

I was shocked at her boldness, but I suppose it was a part of learning about sex. She'd never tasted cum, and she wanted me to be the one to introduce her to it. I could understand that and was flattered by it. I offered her my cock and let her lick and suck however she saw fit. I was so close to coming it didn't take long for her to finish the job.

I sat on the edge of the bed, watching my cock as it exploded on her tongue. She had trouble taking it all, letting some of it drip down her chin and onto her breasts. It was a picture of perfection as far as I was concerned. She kept her eyes on me as she swallowed what she could and then wiped the rest from her lips and breasts, licking her fingers clean for my viewing pleasure.

"How was it?" I smiled down at her.

"Not too shabby," she grinned, climbing to her feet and taking my hand to pull me from the bed. She leaned against my chest as we stood in the middle of the floor, holding one another for a moment before we lay back down across the bed in each other's embrace for a while.

I dozed off for a bit with her in my arms; her hair spilled across my chest as she slept in my arms. I couldn't think of anywhere else I'd want to be and the longer I lay there with her, the more I wondered why I was leaving. We had so much more to share with one another and not just in the sexual arena. I wanted to take her to all the places I loved and show her why I loved them so much. I wanted to spend every spare moment of my day just being with her.

It was a wonderful dream, but that was all it was. A dream. I had to go and if I didn't do it soon, I might just stay here until I found myself wondering what I'd ever been thinking when I finally did.

"I have to go," I said softly as we lay against one another in her bed. A soft light seeped in through the window, casting a hazy glow over her face as she looked up at me with a certain sadness in her eyes.

"I know," she replied quietly. "You could stay the night. I could go with you to the airport in the morning and see you off."

"As much as I love that idea, we both know it's not for the best for either of us. Plus, I need to get my things from Charlotte's house and ensure she has everything she needs to get by without me before I leave."

She nodded, her head barely moving against the pillow. She took a ragged breath and I thought she might be crying, but she remained stoic. I was surprised when she addressed our situation first.

"I think it might be best for both of us if we didn't try to make this whole long-distance thing work."

"Are you sure?" I asked, not wanting to jump at her words but also not wanting to present any false hope.

"Yes. We're in two different countries and have careers we can't just walk away from. It's best to end things on a happy note and not suck the life out of how beautiful things have been between us during our brief time together."

"You're right. I know that and I know you know that. I just don't want you to think I didn't wish things were different."

"I don't think that. It's just how things are. It's been great while it lasted, and I'd like to remember it that way. I don't ever want there to be a day when we think of one another and have anything less than wonderful memories."

"That day will never come," I told her, pulling her close to me and just holding her for as long as I could.

Finally, I got dressed and left Giselle one final time, kissing her softly before walking out the door and forcing myself not to run back to her.

Chapter 26

Giselle

Three months after I watched Peter walk out my front door, I still thought about him often. I'd only heard from him once more after his departure. He'd sent me a text message once he was back in France.

Giselle, I have arrived safely in Paris. Thank you for our time together. I will never forget it. —Peter

I'm not sure what I had expected. Perhaps some long letter detailing his feelings for me, telling me how much he wished we could be together. I think a part of me wanted to hear that. Another part of me knew that it would only add more pain and he'd chosen the only words that could provide closure for both of us.

Perhaps it had been my feelings for him that led me to choose my next relationship. William Preston was handsome in the conventional sense. He was older, maybe in his early fifties. His chiseled chin was always clean-shaven. His mostly silver hair cropped closely in what Marie would call a "GQ" haircut, referencing the perfectly coiffed men who graced the cover of Gentleman's Quarterly.

When he looked at me, it was with the most piercing eyes I'd ever seen. They were almost clear, like glass, with what seemed like just a hint of blue that gave them an almost translucent quality. He towered over everyone around him. I guess he was likely six-four, maybe even pushing six-five. His broad shoulders were imposing, and his flat stomach led me to believe I'd find a six-pack of abs that would make a man half his age envious.

There was little doubt that he was likely the perfect man in the eyes of many women who beheld him. In addition to his good looks, he owned a successful business that he'd founded fresh out of college. It would be wrong to say he was self-made, however. William Preston came from what most would call old money.

The thing that put me off about him was that he seemed to know every bit of this. He was rich. He was powerful. He was handsome. Mostly, though, he was a smooth talker. He reminded me of an actor, always on cue, saying the right thing at the right time as if from a script only he could see.

William was an importer and liked handling certain aspects of his business personally. I met him while working on new procurements for the museum's permanent display. He'd taken an immediate interest in me, but I hadn't been so quick to reciprocate. I was still lost in the ghostly arms of my brief relationship with Peter.

"How about a platonic dinner for two?" he asked one day while meeting with me and my buyers.

One of them raised an eyebrow but pretended he hadn't heard the question, which had been posed while paperwork was being reviewed. I was caught off guard but had to admire his persistence. I found myself agreeing. I glanced sideways to see the buyer smiling slightly, but still feigning focus on the contract in front of him.

"Settled then," William said with a smile. "I'll call your office. I believe that's the way things are done these days."

"That will work," I told him, grateful when my buyer interjected to discuss the contract so we could move on to something else.

It wasn't that I didn't find William attractive. I did, but I just wasn't sure he was someone I could be myself with. Everything with Peter had seemed so natural. William and I came from two very different worlds. Sure, we had the work connection, but I feared that might be the only thing we shared.

When he called me three days later, I'd all but forgotten I'd agreed to go out with him. I debated whether his waiting several days to call was about a lack of genuine enthusiasm or he just hadn't wanted to seem too eager. Either way, it felt like a lukewarm move on his part.

Still, I'd already agreed, so I would give it a chance and see how it went. He was hosting a fundraiser and decided it would be the perfect opportunity for us to spend some time together. I was skeptical, as it was hardly a situation where we would be able to get to know one another. On the other hand, it prevented too much awkward one-on-one time.

On the night of the fundraiser, I was dressed to the nines. Rather than picking me up, William sent a car with his apologies, saying he was tied up with last-minute preparations. I arrived in the back of a limo and stepped out in front of what I could only describe as a mansion just outside the city.

The driver left me on the sidewalk outside the house without knowing where I was supposed to go. I thought William would at least make time to come out and greet me, but he was nowhere to be seen. After standing there awkwardly, pretending to be reading something on my phone so I didn't look as lost as I felt, I finally followed another arriving couple up to the large double doors leading into a grand ballroom built onto one side of the house.

"Invitation?" a man inside the door said to the couple and they handed him an ivory card with raised black letters.

I felt incredibly out of place already. Though I'd gone shopping for a suitable dress that had cost me a fortune, it still didn't seem as nice as those I saw on some of the guests already present in the ballroom. And now, I didn't have an invitation to show. Still, I approached the man as the couple moved away.

"Invitation?" he said again to me this time.

"I'm afraid I don't have one. I am a plus one, I suppose."

"A plus one for whom?" he asked, seeming disinterested.

"William Preston," I told him.

His eyebrows raised as he looked me up and down, making me feel somehow smaller. I raised my chin and met his gaze. He motioned toward a woman who stood nearby greeting guests and she came over.

"Maggie, do you have the overflow list?"

"Yes."

He nodded and turned back to me. "Name?"

"Giselle Martin," I said, every ounce of my willpower focused on staying here and not just turning to leave. I could get an Uber back to the city if I had to.

Maggie looked down at her list and flipped through the pages before shaking her head. "I'm sorry. You aren't on the list."

"You know what? That's fine. Thank you," I said, turning to exit the door.

I felt angry and annoyed. I'd spent a lot of money on a dress I didn't need, borrowed proper jewelry from a friend, and went to the salon to get my hair done. I wanted to make a good impression. It seems William hadn't cared enough to greet me nor make arrangements for someone else to do so in his absence.

I walked out the door and down the sidewalk, pulling my phone from the small clutch I'd bought to match my dress. I was in the process of calling an Uber to pick me up when someone came running toward me from the house and stopped short when he saw I was on my phone. I paused and looked at him.

"Giselle?" he asked.

"Yes," I replied dryly.

"I am so sorry. Maggie called to let me know they had refused a guest, so I came to find you."

"And you are?"

"I'm Arthur. I'm with Mr. Preston's security team."

"Well, Arthur. Thank you for coming out here, but I'm afraid I'm headed home."

"Headed home? The event hasn't even started yet."

"I won't be attending the event. I was ejected. Mr. Preston couldn't be bothered to pick me up personally, meet me at the car, or even make sure I was on the list to get inside. I think I'd like to just go back home and have a nice pizza and some wine."

"Please don't do that."

"Why? It's not your fault."

"It kind of is my fault. I was supposed to make sure you got here okay and get you inside safely. I got tied up with another problem and dropped the ball. He'll be livid if you go home because I messed up."

"That doesn't sound like my problem," I told him, still feeling annoyed.

"It isn't your problem. It's mine. Listen. I've only been here a few weeks. If you leave, I'm as good as fired, and I need this job. Do it for my toddler. I'm begging you."

"Emotional bribery?"

"Yes. That's exactly what this is. What's the worst that can happen now? You'll go in. Have some lovely food, free-flowing champagne, and be the belle of the ball on Mr. Preston's arm. That's got to be better than a ride back to the city, mediocre pizza and domestic wine."

I wasn't happy and tempting me with expensive food and wine didn't sway me, but his sob story did. I decided I could stand a night of indulgence despite my annoyance.

"Okay, Arthur. I'll do it for you, but only because your kid needs a roof over their head."

"Her head and thank you so much. I will repay you for this somehow."

"The only repayment I need is for you to walk me into that event and put me in the vicinity of William so I don't suffer further humiliation."

"Done. Shall we?" he said, motioning for me to walk with him.

"It really does look like a lovely party," I said as we strolled toward the house's front door, skipping the entrance line that had now gotten longer as people waited to be approved for entry.

"I'm sure it will be, and if you need anything at all during it, just find me. Any member of staff with a radio can call me for you."

"Good to know. Thank you."

"You're welcome and thank you too," he said as he opened the front doors and escorted me across freshly polished marble floors.

We headed toward the event, but this time through the door leading back into the house. As we stepped through the doors, I found William speaking with guests on the other side. Arthur quietly called out to him to get his attention, and he turned around, looking impossibly handsome in his tuxedo.

"Giselle!" he said happily, kissing me on the cheek. "I am so sorry I couldn't pick you up and bring you here personally. I trust that Arthur has taken good care of you?"

"The best," I said, feigning a smile.

"Excellent. Thank you, Arthur. You can go."

"Thank you," Arthur replied before disappearing back into the house.

"Come on. Let me introduce you to some people now that you're here," William said.

We spent the rest of the evening strolling from guest to guest. I hardly spoke as William preferred to do all the talking. I slowly realized that I might be more eye candy than companion, but I stuck with it because I'd promised Arthur I wouldn't bail.

And by the end of the night, I'd begun to feel that perhaps I had judged William too harshly. After he finished making the rounds necessary to secure donations, he began to focus more on me, apologizing if he'd perhaps chosen our first date poorly. Though things ended with just a kiss on the cheek, he drove me home himself and walked me to my door.

Chapter 27

Giselle

Despite the bumpy start, I found William to be more charming outside his business and philanthropy circles. Within weeks, we were spending much more time together. He could be distant sometimes and liked to be in control, usually dictating our plans rather than allowing me any input. I just chalked it up to being the nature of someone used to calling the shots in the business world.

He hadn't even pushed me for sex. I was grateful for that, as I wasn't sure I was ready to take that next step. A part of me still clung to the memories of Peter and how he felt inside me. I often imagined how it would be to feel his touch again, smell his skin as it pressed against mine.

It had only been after one night when William seemed particularly attentive that we'd finally ended up in bed together. He'd taken me on a trip to the country in upstate New York. It was the house he'd grown up in, though it made his current home look like a studio apartment in comparison.

With his father deceased and his mother in a very expensive care facility, he had the run of the house mostly to himself, unless you included the staff that maintained the place. Still, it was a beautiful home with elaborate carved banisters and marble pillars. Of course, my favorite part of the house were the expansive gardens that led to mysterious paths into the woods.

"I used to love to go down those paths and see what I could find in the woods. I think I spent more time out there than I did inside," he said, a far-off look in his eyes.

"I can't imagine my parents ever letting me roam through the woods as a kid."

"I imagine not, but you didn't grow up in the country, did you?"

"No. I'm afraid I was born and raised in the Big Apple. I'm a concrete jungle girl through and through."

"Life out here is very different. I never really took to city living. I love visiting the city and business has treated me well, but I've always preferred living just outside. If I didn't have to go in for meetings so regularly, I'd probably move back here."

"Sounds like you have good memories of this place," I replied.

"I have good memories of roaming through the woods. My parents, not so much."

"Oh. I'm sorry to hear that."

"It's just life. They were cold people. Probably the best thing my father ever did for me was drop dead."

I hadn't expected the bitterness and it caught me off guard. I couldn't imagine ever feeling that way about my parents. Even if I had issues with them, surely I wouldn't celebrate their death.

"I didn't mean to bring up something unpleasant," I said apologetically.

"No. Don't worry about it. I guess that sounded harsh. I suppose it was. Why don't we go inside? It's beginning to cool off down here and I don't want you to catch a chill. Dinner will be done soon."

We returned to the house to find it full of wonderful smells from the kitchen. Someone had already started a fire in the large den, and we sat on the sofa to warm ourselves from the cool fall weather outside. A woman brought us some brandy and we sat sipping it until we were called in for dinner, a lovely meal of roasted chicken, roasted vegetables, and fresh, homemade rolls.

Afterward, we returned to the den to sit by the fire. The staff departed for the night—all but the small security staff who had followed us up in a separate car. It seemed excessive to me that William surrounded himself with so much security, but he'd previously assured me it was with good reason.

"There are people in this world who would take me in a heartbeat, hoping to lay claim to money that doesn't belong to them. Money that they didn't earn," he had told me.

I listened, still feeling like he was exaggerating the danger to himself a bit. I didn't point out that he hadn't earned most of his money either. According to many, his business wasn't even as successful as I once believed. It wasn't failing, but it didn't net any significant wealth. So, the money and possessions he liked to flash around came from his inheritance rather than earnings.

I was keenly aware that I had a love-hate relationship with the man I was dating. There were moments when everything was fine. We were having fun and the things I didn't like about him seemed to fade into the woodwork. There was even a part of me that believed I judged him unfairly. I had no right to compare him to a man I'd only known briefly. There'd been no time for anything unflattering to come to light between us.

I did my best to give William a fair chance. As we sat by the fireplace, cuddled together, some of the issues I had with him melted away and there was just the comfort of having his arms around me. When he pulled me to him and kissed me, I welcomed it. I wanted him, or at least I wanted someone. I wanted to feel something.

That was the first time William and I had sex. I wouldn't call it lovemaking because there hadn't been any love involved. Like all things in William's life, he took charge and claimed what he thought was his with no thought as to how I might enjoy myself. He was rough and didn't spend a lot of time on foreplay.

Sex with him was perfunctory at best. He'd gone from kissing me, which had been the most pleasant part of the encounter, to fondling my breasts with all of the tenderness of tossing a football around the backyard. He preferred to have sex doggy style, so there was no face-to-face. I could have been anyone. He could have been at a glory hole, for that matter.

On our very first night, he stripped off my clothes. Looked me over as if he was grading an acquisition's worth and then pushed me forward over the side of the bed, spreading my legs and fingering me just enough to get a bit of moisture going. I soon learned he didn't like it if I got too wet. He said it dulled his sensation if I felt like a riverbed.

The truth was that William had a small penis. While I didn't have much experience with men, I knew he was woefully inadequate in that department. His penis was short and thin, negating pleasure from either length or girth. He also had no stamina.

By the time I felt we were really getting going, he was usually done—at least the first time.

If we went a second time, it would always take infinitely longer, and often, he couldn't manage another orgasm. He'd pump away at me and neither of us would come. Of course, this was my fault because he couldn't possibly be the problem. I kept thinking it would get better, but it never did, and I started to understand why women left men who were bad at sex.

Helena and Marie had talked about ill-endowed men but made up for it in other ways. Marie said she'd once been with a man who had a tiny penis, but she was not even phased by his like of a quality appendage.

"The man knew he was small, and he knew how to make up for it," she'd said whimsically.

"And how was that?" Helena asked.

I leaned in curiously, wanting to know what he did that made him so memorable for her despite his obvious shortcomings.

"The man had an amazing mouth. He could go down on you until your eyes rolled back in your head," she said, sighing.

"Still, that leaves out a lot of stuff you'd like to be doing, doesn't it?" I asked.

"Oh, honey. No. If a man accepts what he doesn't have, he's willing to fill in the gaps in other ways, literally," she told me.

"Like?" I pressed.

"Well, blow jobs on a tiny dick are a lot easier on the mouth, for one thing. You don't feel like you got reamed by a baseball bat after anal sex, either. As for plain ole filling up the pussy, there are toys for that—toys that don't go soft or come too soon. Toys that vibrate and toys that strap on and feel so real that you don't even know he's not fucking you with King Kong's dong."

"Wow. You have such a way with words," I said, feeling a bit scandalized by her graphic description.

"You did ask. You should know better by now," she said with an evil little laugh.

"Very true. I should."

In all honesty, it was good information to have if I ever ran into anyone like that who I wanted despite their inadequacies. Still, it did me no good with William. There's no way in hell he'd ever try any of that.

So, I did the next best thing. As someone once supposedly suggested, I closed my eyes and thought of England. Except in my case, I thought of Paris. I thought of Peter and how he'd felt. It was hard to focus on that, with William's rough handling ruining the fantasy, but it got me through things, and I could slip out of bed once he went to sleep and continue my little daydream in the bathroom while I satisfied my own needs without William's assistance.

Things never got better with William, though, and there was only so far dreams of Peter could take me. Yet, I stuck with William, lying to myself that it might get better soon. I always knew that wasn't true, but I guess I just didn't want to be alone again.

I think it was because I dwelled on things with Peter that I missed some pretty obvious signs that William and I weren't right for one another. I let it go when he made plans for us without consulting me. I mistook his expectation that I would go along with him as just him getting more comfortable with me and wanting me to be there. He manipulated me in ways I didn't even notice.

I quickly learned that the people in his sphere were equally as conniving when they needed to be. More importantly, I found that I was more hurt by their betrayals than his. It was one thing for a wealthy man to feel he could do as he pleased and lie as he saw fit, but it was another for someone you considered an equal to do it. I'd seen it play out while we were still at his childhood home.

We walked back toward the house, passing Arthur along the way. He and a few of his fellow security staff were the only members of staff we'd brought with us. The rest were already here as caretakers. A cook had come in for meals, but she lived in the area and was only called in when William visited.

"Arthur, can you secure the grounds for the evening?" William told him as we approached.

"Yes, sir," Arthur replied, already moving away to tend to his duties.

"He seems like a very good addition to your staff," I said. "I hope he works out well for you."

"Huh?" William said, seeming confused.

"Arthur. He's new, isn't he?"

"New? No. He's been with me for almost ten years."

I was sure my mouth fell open in disbelief. Arthur had lied to me. On that very first day, when I would have walked away from William and never looked back, Arthur had stopped me with a lie. Of course, could I really blame him? It seemed everyone around William lied out of self-preservation, including me. The only difference was they were lying to others. I lied to myself.

Chapter 28

Giselle

"Why are you still with that man?" Helena asked as I ate lunch with her and Marie on our secret balcony.

"Because he's gorgeous and filthy rich!" Marie interjected.

"I don't care about his money or his looks. I don't know why I'm still with him. I think I've just gotten used to him," I said.

"That's the problem," Helena groaned. "You've gotten used to how he acts."

"He's busy. I don't think he means to be so cold."

"Please. You're a plaything for him. He picks you up when he's bored and puts you back in the toy chest when he isn't in the mood to play. If the truth was told, you're probably not even his only toy," she half hissed.

"I don't think that's true, but he does seem to prefer money over anything else. He gets so involved in business dealings sometimes that he forgets we have plans."

"Does he call and cancel them in time for you to do something else?" Marie asked.

"Not always," I admitted.

The truth was that he'd often tell me he was running late and ask me to wait for him, so I would wait. After a while, it would become clear that it was too late for us to go and do what we'd originally intended. I'd eventually get a call or message telling me he'd gotten completely caught up in something and wouldn't make it. There would be apologies and promises to make it up to me.

Then there was the sex. It was bad. I knew that. I began to realize the full weight of what Peter and I had once discussed about women who ended up in a relationship where the sex was horrible and, because they had no experience, never realized how great it was meant to be. They might spend years being unsatisfied sexually and not even know it until their partner was gone and they finally learned the truth.

The problem was that I already knew the truth. Sex with Peter had been wonderful. I often thought about him after a horrible night with William. For that matter, sometimes I thought about him during sex with William. It helped me get through what I had now come to view as an ordeal to be tolerated rather than anything pleasant I wanted to remember.

"Why are you still with this clown?" Marie asked.

"I'm not sure. Some things between us are good. I've met a lot of people that I like and if I get rid of him, they'll go too."

"Ah, yes. The division of friends. I never understood why folks still can't socialize with both halves and feel they must choose one or the other," Helena said.

"Because it leads to awkward social situations where both sides turn up and they're forced to make sure they're dividing their time equally," I replied.

"I think it is far simpler. They choose whoever they find more beneficial to them. If their interests are financial, they will go with whoever is more powerful or has more money. If they're looking for emotional support, they will choose the person who gives them that," Marie offered between bites of her sandwich.

"So, you're saying I am of lesser value to most of the people I've met through William?" I asked, frowning.

"Sorry, but yeah. He has all the money and all the power. Anyone who stands to gain from being his friend or is in danger of losing money by dumping him will abandon you. You'll likely end up with a handful of their wives, girlfriends, or boyfriends who will sneak around and have lunch with you because they like you but won't want to be seen with you in too public a place."

"Like a mistress," I laughed.

"Without even a reach around," Marie said.

"Crass," I replied.

"You're welcome."

"I just can't believe people are so cold," I admitted.

"Believe it. Look in the mirror. If you're staying with William because you don't want to risk losing friends that might be able to further you somehow, you're just like them," Helena offered.

"Of course, I'm not. I've just met some people I genuinely like," I said, appalled that she might think of me that way.

"And if they feel the same, they'll still be your friends. Do you really need them if they bail just because you split with William?" she asked.

"I suppose not."

"Listen, here's the bottom line. I know you don't have much experience with relationships, so I'll share what I've learned with you. I once stayed with a man for two years because I loved his mother. I grew up in a house with no mother and three brothers. His mother embraced me and made me feel like I was special. I stayed with him so I didn't lose another mother," she said.

"But you weren't happy?"

"I thought I was. Every time he invited me over to her house for dinner, it was magical. We were like one big happy family. Then we would leave, and he'd be the same dull man he always was. Even the sex was mediocre, but we had a life together. I'd moved in with him and given up my party ways for a safe little house in the suburbs. I thought it was what I was supposed to do."

"Why did you finally leave?"

"I didn't. He left me."

"What?" Helena and I both gasped, almost in unison.

"Yep. He met some little girl on a business trip to the West Coast and dumped me like yesterday's lunch. Can you believe that?"

"You must have been devastated, though. Like you said, you had a life together," I observed.

"I was, for a bit, but that's the point of the whole story. I didn't lose anything, really. I was in a bad relationship that I tried to pretend was good just because a small portion of it suited me. When he was gone, I realized I didn't miss him. I missed his mother. I missed our house. I even missed trips to the seaside. What I didn't miss was him," Marie told me.

"I think I see where you're going with this delightful little tale," I said with a smile.

"Of course you do. It's up to you whether you stay, but if William doesn't make you happy, you'll miss the life you felt you had with him, but you won't miss him. All you need is to find what *does* make you happy, and you'll not think twice about him again," she said.

"You're probably right. I just hate to have to deal with it. I don't think he's the sort to be dumped and take it lightly."

"You could always just make yourself unappealing, so he dumps you," Helena joked.

We all chuckled, but I had to admit that I considered it. If he dumped me, he wouldn't feel so defensive about it. I'd learned enough about him and his previous relationships that he didn't like to be rejected and set out to make those who did leave him miserable at any opportunity. I'd be the bad guy and he'd make sure everyone knew it, even if his version was incomplete or skewed.

After lunch with the girls, I gave some serious thought to our conversation. I knew Marie was right in saying I would miss some aspects of our relationship but not him. In all honestly, I'd begun to prefer it when he was busy and couldn't see me. While his canceling plans at the last minute used to annoy me, I now find it to be a relief.

The last time he canceled, I ordered a pizza and opened a bottle of wine. I found that I was much more content here alone. Sitting on the sofa enjoying my meal, I realized it had been months since I'd done this. The last time I ordered a pizza was when Peter was here. The thought of that made me smile, remembering our last weekend together.

The memory of sitting around in my robe with Peter, having a casual dinner between romps in the sheets, was always comforting. Underneath that feeling of happiness, though, the sadness of losing him always lurked. I wondered if there would ever be a time that I thought of him and didn't feel that twinge of pain or if it had become a part of our story that would always remain.

It wasn't that I didn't enjoy my memories of him. They were special to me, and I never wanted to forget any of them, but they left behind a certain melancholy that I couldn't quite bear. It always took me to a darker place where I felt alone and wished I could somehow change how things had turned out.

I found myself wondering where he was now and what he was doing. Was he happy? Was he with someone else, someone who didn't come with the pitfalls we would have faced just trying to make things work? It was a strange sensation. I wanted to think Peter was happy, but I didn't really want to believe it was with someone else. I couldn't bear the thought of him belonging to another and I knew that was selfish.

In my mind, I still imagined him reappearing one day, coming back to my apartment and telling me he'd made a mistake. I longed to hear him tell me he was coming back to New York to live, that he'd taken a job here and wanted to spend the rest of his days with me.

I wondered if everyone had a happy ending story that they told themselves about the one they lost. I remember Peter teasing me about my fantasies of a Prince Charming and making love on top of his magical castles, but he hadn't really been wrong about that. I'd wanted exactly that, and I still wanted it, only in my current version of that tale he was my handsome prince, and I didn't care if the castle was my tiny apartment.

I closed my eyes and imagined Peter touching me, kissing me, making love to me. I missed him. Perhaps I would always miss him. Here I was with a man who most women would kill to be with and all I could think about was a man I couldn't have. Of course, the women who wanted William Preston didn't know what they were getting into. The shiny exterior he presented was dull and rusty on the inside.

William Preston possessed a sort of human rot that had permeated his soul. His years of having everything handed to him on a silver platter gave him the impression that everyone was inferior. He had no time to acknowledge or examine his own faults and, therefore, no time to address them. Instead, he spent his time projecting his issues onto other people, and they let him do it.

Even me. I allowed him to blame me for anything he saw as unfit in our relationship. If we were late, it was because I took too long to get ready, not because he'd arrived late to pick me up. If the food was bad, I shouldn't have suggested the meal. The petty reasons for his disdain for everyone around him were endless, and the longer we were together, the more of a scapegoat I became.

Was this really how I wanted to live my life? Did I really want to spend it with a man who saw no fault in himself and believed everyone around him was incompetent and inferior? I was pretty sure that it wasn't. I knew I had to excise myself from William Preston very soon. I contemplated it further while eating my pizza and drinking my wine, eventually shuffling off to bed. I began to appreciate that I was the only one in my bed, considering the alternative.

Chapter 29

Giselle

"I thought we'd stay in tonight," William said as he picked me up the following weekend.

"Oh? I thought we were meeting friends for dinner?" I asked, not relishing spending hours couped up alone with him.

"We were, but I have a really early day tomorrow, so I canceled."

I couldn't help but wonder if they'd gotten any more notice than I was getting. Not only was William inconsiderate of my time, but he was the same to his friends and work associates. Only those he deemed important to him were spared his disregard, which said a lot about how he viewed me.

We rode the rest of the way back to his place, mostly in silence. I knew how the evening would go already. He'd have his chef make us a meal that suited his preferences, which meant the food would be healthy and mostly tasteless. William didn't like a lot of sauces or spices on his food, so it tended to be bland. That was fine when we went out and I could order my food separately, but

I was mostly relegated to using salt to give it a hint of flavor during meals at his house.

After dinner, he would want to sip some brown liquor in the den. He'd want to go to bed early since he had already cited an early work day tomorrow. He'd paw at me long enough to deem what he was doing adequate foreplay and then we'd have sex that was perfunctory, at best. He'd cum. I wouldn't. He'd roll over and go to sleep while I stared at the ceiling for hours until I dozed off too.

I used to slip out of bed after he was asleep and go back downstairs to watch something on TV or scroll through the news and social media on my phone. The last time I'd done that, he'd woken up and come down to complain about my absence. It had resulted in my going back to bed and being subjected to another round of lousy sex that ended without an orgasm for either of us. It was just him trying to get off and failing before giving up and climbing off me to go to sleep.

I really didn't want that. So, instead, I just lay there in the darkness and thought about Peter. The memory of sex with him somehow made this seem more tolerable. It was as if the good memories helped me get through the current bad situation. I began to realize, though, that my memory of our time together was starting to fade. The detail was becoming fuzzier despite my feelings for him remaining intact.

What was I still doing here? Why was I lying next to a man who didn't make me happy in any way? It was that thought that got me up and moving. I picked up my phone from the bedside table and glanced at it—nine o'clock.

I got out of bed but did not slip downstairs to entertain myself. Instead, I got dressed and put my phone in my bag. William didn't stir as I left the room and went downstairs to order an Uber. I waited quietly for the message that it would be there soon and then slipped out the front door. Arthur appeared out of nowhere, causing me to jump.

"You scared me," I told him flatly.

"I'm sorry about that. What are you doing out here?"

"I'm leaving."

"I thought you were in for the night. Mr. Preston said no one would be leaving before morning."

"Mr. Preston was wrong."

"Does he know you're leaving?"

"Does it matter?" I asked as my phone dinged to let me know the Uber had arrived.

"No. I don't suppose it doesn't."

"Then goodbye, Arthur. I would say that I hope your little girl is doing well, but it seems she doesn't exist," I told him, my parting shot.

He seemed a bit surprised but accepted the comment for what it was, an acknowledgment that I knew he lied to me. He had to also know that in doing so, he let his boss off the hook for bad behavior that would only continue. If he'd been with William for over ten years, he obviously knew how his relationships went.

Of course, it wasn't Arthur's fault that William was an arrogant asshole. Still, he certainly wiped his backside enough to be complicit in the game. I walked past him and climbed into my Uber, leaving him to stand outside the house and debate whether to wake William and tell him now or let him sleep and find out on his own tomorrow. The answer came the following day when William called me at the museum.

"Hey, I'm sorry I missed you this morning. Arthur said you had to get an early start and had taken an Uber out. You should have told me last night. I could have had someone drive you."

I thought about how to best handle this. Despite my disdain for Arthur, I honestly didn't want him to lose his job. William was the sort who would fire him over even a slight as small as not telling him I'd left last night. Of course, I found it fascinating that he didn't even realize I was no longer in his bed before waking up this morning.

"I didn't need you to have me driven in. I can handle my own transportation."

"Um, okay. You seem a bit on edge. Is everything okay?"

"Yes. I'm just busy. You called me while I'm at work."

"I always call you at work," he replied, his voice conveying that he didn't see any problem with that.

"Yes, you do," I said flatly. "What do you need?"

He seemed oblivious to my tone as he responded with a light-hearted invitation to meet him for lunch. However, he wasn't as blind to the tone of my reply.

"No. I have other plans today."

"Other plans? Like what? Eating a sandwich with those two trollops you work with?"

I wasn't sure what I found more offensive, his disregard for my making plans of my own instead of dropping them for him or the demeaning way he referred to Marie and Helena. It wasn't the first time and it seemed to only apply if he felt they were somehow taking attention away from him. For such a rich and powerful man, he was incredibly petty and thin-skinned. I made a hasty decision. As much as I wanted to have a conversation with William, work was not the place to do it.

"I will call you tonight when I'm off work. I have to go right now."

I hung up the phone without waiting for an answer. No one dismissed William so abruptly. There was little doubt that he was stewing over it. My phone rang immediately. I glanced at it and saw his number, so I let it go to voicemail. A moment later, it chimed with several text messages, but I ignored them too. Instead, I stood up and walked out to check on our progress in setting up a gallery for an upcoming exhibition.

When I returned to my office more than an hour later, I picked up my phone to see a litany of messages from William. I deleted the voicemails he left without reading or listening to them. I considered what I might have left at his place that I'd need to retrieve and decided there was nothing I couldn't easily replace. I'd prefer never to step foot in his house again.

After work, I went home and mentally prepared myself for the conversation I needed to have with William. There was so much I could and wanted to say, but the more I considered it, the more I realized it didn't matter. It wouldn't make any difference and William wouldn't care. There was no point wasting my breath on him anymore.

I took a deep breath and dialed his number. There was no answer. Typical of him to try and put the ball back in his court. Rather than leaving a message, I simply hung up and decided to call again later. Instead, the phone rang as I was about to lay it down on the table nearby. It was him.

"I missed your call. Did you call to apologize for being so short with me today and not returning my calls?"

"I am calling you back now, and no, I didn't do so to apologize," I responded.

"I swear, Giselle. What is up with you lately? You've seemed a million miles away and now you've become borderline rude to me."

"I don't want to see you anymore, William," I stated flatly.

"What?"

"You heard me perfectly fine." My heart hammered in my chest.

Though I knew William and I were over, and I had no feelings for him, I still felt the stress of the situation. I'd never had to dump anyone before. Here I was on the verge of turning twenty-four and just now having my first official breakup. I felt like a frightened teenager about it. The worst was that I knew William wouldn't make it easy for me by just going away.

"You can't leave me, Giselle," he said quietly.

For a moment, I thought he might actually have some feelings for me, even if he wasn't demonstrating them properly and took my presence for granted, but then he continued.

"Do you know who I am? Do you know how many women would kill to be with me?"

"I know exactly who you are and don't care who else wants to be with you. It's not my problem anymore."

"I should have known better than to date beneath my standing. How could I have even thought that some low-class museum curator could ever fit into my world?"

Some would have taken this as a personal insult, but I'd grown used to William's behavior since we'd started dating. If you rejected him, you must be at fault for it and had to be put in your place. Whether he believed what he was saying was irrelevant. He was only saying it because he thought it would be hurtful to me.

"I don't know, William. All I know is that this is over. Don't call me anymore."

I ended the call and put my phone on silent before turning it to face downward on the table. He would call back. He would text. There was no doubt of that, and none of it would be because he cared or didn't want this to end. I was just another pretty thing on his arm, and he'd have me replaced by morning just to prove he could do better. That was how his mind worked.

And all the while he was off showing his associates his new arm candy, he would still be calling me to chastise me for giving up someone as amazing as him. He wouldn't try to get me to come back because he couldn't have me saying he stooped to begging. And, of course, he didn't want me back. He wanted me to say I'd made a mistake and ask him to forgive me and take me back so he could be the one to reject me.

I didn't answer my phone for the rest of the night. I left it on silent mode and had a relaxing evening in by kicking back in a long hot bubble bath and sipping wine. Afterward, I curled up in bed with a book I'd been meaning to start reading and got pulled into the pages until I could no longer hold my eyes open and fell asleep.

Chapter 30

Giselle

My phone was full of hateful messages from William the following morning. I read a few of them and then deleted the rest without bothering to open them. I confirmed what I suspected. With William now receding in my rearview mirror, I got ready for work and headed to the subway, feeling truly at peace for the first time in a while.

It would take nearly two months, though, to put the William disaster behind me. He spent the first week or so sending me hateful texts and voicemails. I finally just blocked his number to put a stop to it. That resulted in him calling me on the office phone a couple of times and me hanging up the moment I heard his voice.

Only when he showed up at my apartment did I begin to wonder if he might be more unhinged than I expected. I turned to the only person I knew who could help me and owed me the favor of doing so.

"Arthur? It's Giselle," I said when he answered the phone.

"This is unexpected," he replied.

"You gave me your number a while back when William and I were together. I'm sorry to use it now, but I need your input on something."

"Is he still harassing you?" he said immediately.

"Yes. How did you know?"

"He always does it. I'll talk to him."

"And you think he will listen to you?"

"He'll pretend what I say doesn't matter, but he's smart enough to know when I'm right. I'll handle it, and I'm sorry."

"Thank you."

"You're welcome. Take care, Giselle."

With that, we ended the call. I didn't know what Arthur said to William or how well it was received, but there were no more attempts to contact me or give me any grief. As predicted, most of our mutual acquaintances kept a distance. Though they weren't rude, they were merely cordial if we crossed paths and made a hasty retreat.

Nearly two years later, my director told me he was sending me back to France. It wouldn't be an extended stay like last time, but I'd be there for a couple of days to meet with a collector and view a piece of art he might be loaning the museum. Though I tried not to think about Peter, I wondered if I should try to see him while I was there or if that was just drudging up things for both of us.

This time, my flight was nearly twelve hours due to a layover in London. It was frustrating to be stuck there long enough for it to be a delay but not long enough to do anything more than grab a bite to eat and maybe a glass of wine. Plus, it was an overnight flight, so there wouldn't be much to do anyway.

Of course, due to the shortness of the trip, I didn't have any pull in advocating for a more expensive direct flight. I'd used up all my brownie points when I'd gotten the museum to foot the bill for my business class upgrade back home last time. I knew I was pushing the envelope here, but the museum could better afford a $2200 upgrade than I could, and if I hadn't had to be back so quickly, I could have waited for a later flight.

As I had told him, it wasn't my fault I'd been put in such a position. Still, I knew how closely he watched the museum's bottom line and he wouldn't be so accommodating if there were a next time. While he might be a bit lazy when it came to the day-to-day operations and content to let me take on extra duties he chose to avoid, he was very much on top of the budget.

By the time my flight landed in Paris, I was exhausted. I decided to get to my hotel and just go to bed. I didn't bother to set my alarm since my meeting wasn't until later the following evening. When I woke up, I was confused. My surroundings made no sense at first, but as the sleep faded from my eyes, I remembered where I was. I looked at my phone and saw it was barely nine in the morning.

I thought about sleeping in a little longer but was wide awake. Slipping out from between the covers, I showered and put on a pair of soft jeans and a nice sweater before venturing onto the Paris streets. It would be nice to visit some of the lovely patisseries and shops I'd come to love during my time here.

It would be even nicer to share a meal with Peter at one of the lovely cafes, but I wasn't sure if I wanted to open that door again. I'd love to see him. Of course, I would, but I didn't want to open an old wound for either of us. Instead, I went to a little vintage boutique and browsed through a rack of silk scarves. I'd developed a particular fondness for them during my previous stay. It was hard to believe that it had been four years since I'd first visited Paris.

"Those are lovely. Yes?" a very eloquent woman said as she approached me.

"They're divine," I told her.

"This one would look lovely with your complexion." She pulled one I hadn't noticed from the display. It was eggshell blue with a small beige floral print. Though it was hard to know without seeing them up against one another, it looked as if it would match perfectly with a skirt and jacket I'd bought in this same shop on my last trip.

"It's perfect. Thank you for pointing it out."

"Shall I take it to the counter while you continue to browse?"

"Yes, please."

I left the shop about twenty minutes later with the scarf and a lovely blouse that matched the floral print. It would at least match the blouse if it didn't match my suit.

I sat at a nearby cafe looking out the window as I enjoyed a freshly baked croissant with loads of butter and a hot cup of coffee. My mind drifted back to the night I'd met Peter and how disappointed I'd felt to find him gone after the exhibition. It had seemed like a missed opportunity and seeing him on the plane had felt like destiny.

Now, here I was in Paris again. How could I not try to see him? Even if he said no to me, would I regret not having tried? I'd deleted his phone number to avoid the temptation of calling him on lonely nights. So, I'd have to call the university to reach him. If I was going to do it, I needed to do it before he left for the day.

My hands shook as I pulled up the university's webpage and located the staff directory. I sat looking at Peter's photo for a moment before switching to the keypad on my phone and dialing the number and his extension. I hadn't realized I was holding my breath until I heard him answer on the other end. I exhaled slowly.

"Professor Dockery," he said.

"Hello, Peter. It's Giselle." There was silence. I waited for him to speak again for what seemed like an excruciatingly long time. "Giselle Martin," I added.

"Giselle," he repeated. "This is unexpected."

I couldn't quite make out anything from his tone. My heart raced and I wished I hadn't called. This felt so awkward compared to how natural things were between us before.

"I'm just in Paris for a couple of days and thought I'd see if you wanted to grab a bite of lunch with me tomorrow," I said.

The words rolled off of my tongue as if they had a mind of their own. It was like they'd become self-aware and believed they would never be uttered if they didn't get out and get out fast. I paused and waited again, holding my breath as I awaited his response.

"I'd love to have lunch with you," he said at last. "I have classes until noon and then a staff meeting at one. Could it be a late lunch? Like around two?"

"Two would be perfect. We could also get together tonight for drinks if you like. I have to meet with some people at six, but I should be done in about an hour or so."

"That sounds nice too, but I'm afraid I can't make it for drinks. Lunch will definitely work for me, though," he replied.

His voice was pleasant enough. Past what I suspected was some initial shock at hearing from me after so long, he sounded genuinely happy to talk to me. I certainly was excited to be talking to him again. Of course, I felt a little let down that he didn't want to go for drinks tonight because it told me there was likely someone else.

Having lunch with a former lover at a public cafe in broad daylight was quite different from having drinks together after hours. Things could go very differently than a hug and polite goodbye when neither of you had anywhere to be and might end up alone together, exploring familiar territory. Part of me hoped for just that, so his sticking to lunch would probably be best for all concerned.

"Very well. Lunch it is. Do you know *Au Vuex Paris d'Arcole?*" I asked, wanting to go someplace I wouldn't get lost trying to find.

"I know it well. I'll meet you there at two."

"Great. See you then."

"Giselle?" he said, sending a little chill through me as he said my name.

"Yes?"

"I'm glad you rang. I'll see you tomorrow."

"Bye, Peter," I replied, ending the call before I said something dumb.

I felt torn the rest of the day. It would be so lovely to see Peter tomorrow, but I was almost certain he had someone in his life now. I couldn't be sure. Perhaps he wanted to make sure things remained platonic because he didn't want to start up something we'd have to leave unfinished once again. Maybe I would find out when I saw him.

I spent the rest of the day trying not to think about him. We were old friends getting together for a bite to eat. Nothing more to it than that and I'd be doing us both a favor to remember it. With that in mind, I went about rekindling my love of the city, walking around for quite a bit longer before returning to my hotel to get ready for my meeting.

I changed into my dress clothes and pulled my hair up into a tight knot at the base of my neck, leaving only a few tendrils to fall around my face. I wanted to look professional but not strict. I took one final look in the mirror. Then, I made my way down to the lobby, stepping back onto the Paris streets to make my way toward a small gallery where I was supposed to meet with the broker who'd set up the meeting.

An hour later, we were finished, and I'd succeeded, securing the loan of a rare piece of art that had never been lent to an American venue. I was quite pleased with myself as it had been a difficult procurement, and I had pulled it off. The director would be happy with that.

I started back to my room but then changed my mind. Just because Peter couldn't join me for drinks didn't mean I couldn't have them. I ducked into a little bar near the hotel. I sat in a small cubbyhole at the back and sipped a few martinis while listening to the music before finally returning to my room.

Chapter 31

Giselle

Perhaps it was the martinis or the thought of seeing Peter tomorrow that made me feel so melancholy, but I couldn't shake the feeling of gloom that hung over me. I lay across my bed, thinking about what I would say to him. It wasn't something I had to do before. Our conversation was always natural and flowed easily. After the stilted chat on the phone earlier, I wasn't sure that would be the case tomorrow.

Perhaps I'd been wrong to call him after all this time. What was I hoping would happen? I smiled to myself at the thought. I knew exactly what I would have liked, but that didn't seem likely now. I closed my eyes and thought about Peter smiling down at me as he pushed strands of hair away from my face. The memory of his kisses raining down across my face and the feel of his hands roaming across my skin washed over me.

I sighed and stood back up, opening my laptop and returning to Peter's photo on his university faculty page. I pulled my sketch pad from my bag. It pretty much lived there these days. I rarely unpacked it between trips as I hardly drew anymore. But tonight,

I felt inspired. I fished around until I found the charcoal pencils in a side pouch, sat down at the table, selected some quiet music from my playlist, and began sketching.

There'd been a time when I would have been an artist. I was constantly sketching something, but once I'd finished college and begun working within the art world, I never seemed to have the same enthusiasm for it that I once possessed. I think a part of me felt some sort of imposter syndrome. How could I call myself an artist when surrounded by so many masters?

I couldn't remember the last time I'd picked up these pencils, much less a brush. I'd never been one to sculpt, but I'd previously fancied myself a decent painter. Now, my life's work has become to highlight the work of others. Was I selling myself short by embracing the work of others instead of pursuing my own? Perhaps, but I couldn't deny that I loved my job. I got to see priceless art up close and personal, without the protective barriers around it that kept the public at a distance.

But it wasn't just the work of famous artists that lured me in. I also loved the work of more contemporary artists who remained undiscovered. It was a dream of mine to help bring them into the spotlight. I'd wanted to someday own my own gallery where I could present their sweat and tears to the public and provide them with the accolades they deserved for their hard work and inspiration.

I'd lived in New York all my life and seen many great artists selling incredible works for spare change on sidewalks across the city. Our society doesn't value art like people used to in the days of the greats. Ask most Americans my age to name a contemporary artist, and the only name they'll be able to come up with is

Banksy. You'll find few who know who Penny Hardy is despite the incredible sculptures she creates.

Then there are the people who fancy themselves artists but aren't using any traditional form of media. They're creating digital art in software built for that purpose. They have talent and may earn a great living creating graphics for several businesses, but it's not collectible. The NFT market took a stab at that but quickly fizzled out. The game seemed to take a piece of substandard art and flog it to as many social media personalities as you could find. It was as if you "say" it's art; people accept it as art, even while looking at it and feeling no emotion whatsoever.

Others aren't even putting in that much effort. They merely type words into a generator that creates an image for them. Granted, it takes a bit of practice and skill to create something that doesn't have extra digits or distorted features, but it isn't going to sell for millions at auction. Those lucky enough might make a few bucks by selling it on a merchant site plastered on cups or t-shirts. Still, no true art curator would ever take their efforts seriously.

I began humming along with the song playing while I continued sketching. I might never be able to sell any works I created for any amount either, but I was content with that. I knew that my work was merely average compared to most. I just hoped I could do something for someone who was more serious about their efforts and wanted to use their talents to make a living. I'd not be able to accomplish that as a museum curator, but my credentials there would help me eventually open my own studio. That was my dream.

I looked down at the sketch of Peter. It wasn't bad at all. It didn't reflect much of the man in the photo I'd used as a guide, but more of how I saw him in my mind. His picture in the staff directory was serious, unsmiling. My sketch was how I remembered him in my mind, looking at me with a wide grin, almost mischievous. His eyes twinkled when he was like that as if a spark had been set off in them.

I liked to think I caused that spark in him, that I was the one who gave him such joy. That might have been true once upon a time, but it wasn't the case anymore. Now, someone else lit that fire in him and I'd missed my chance. After my previous stay here, I'd considered making Paris my home. Why didn't I just do it? Why didn't I take a chance to come here and see what happened?

I'd felt like doing so somehow made us indebted to one another when the truth was that I could have come here on my own and given us a shot. It had simply been a matter of timing. I wasn't ready to make the leap and give up my career to move across the ocean. I couldn't convince myself that I should do it just because there was the possibility that a man might want a relationship with me if I did.

I pondered what might have happened if I had. I certainly would have missed the unfortunate experience with William Preston. I could be here and happy with a man that I found incredible in every way. Instead, I was just meeting him for lunch as friends, where I would likely hear him tell me that we could never be more because he'd moved on.

I lay the sketch pad aside and went to the bathroom to wash my face and undress for bed. Lying beneath the covers, I began to touch myself, but I just wasn't feeling it. I removed my hand and lay it flat on the sheets beside me. I barely had time to consider why I'd lost interest in pleasuring myself before I'd fallen fast asleep.

When I awoke the following morning, I felt like I was on pins and needles. I was looking forward to seeing Peter, but I still sensed that there had been reluctance in his tone when we spoke. I'd called him, anticipating we might have a bite to eat and enjoy a nice chat about how we were and what we were doing. I suppose that was still possible, but in my mind, the day wouldn't stop there.

I envisioned lunch turning into an afternoon stroll that would turn into dinner and drinks. We'd end up back at his place or at my hotel, and just how much we'd enjoyed being with one another would all come back to us. We'd make love for hours and fall asleep in one another's arms. The following morning, I'd awaken, and we'd have one last send-off in the shower before he had to go to work and I had to catch a plane back to New York.

My thoughts had trouble making it very far past that point. I didn't want to consider the reality of the situation. The part where we only had one day together and then returned to our worlds wasn't a part of my little fantasy. Instead, I considered that this time might be different. We'd realize how well we fit together and not want to be apart.

I wanted to start my own gallery. Couldn't I do that as well in Paris as in New York? Was I ready to give up my cushy job at the museum to strike out on my own? I'd been saving up and had some backing, but their potential interest was formed around me putting down further roots in New York. They knew I was a part of the art world there. I knew people and people knew me. My reputation as an art expert was what they were investing in, and I might not be able to drum up that kind of support in Paris.

I had trouble reconciling the part of me that desperately want-ed a real shot with Peter and the part that knew it wasn't meant to be. Our fate was to meet, enjoy a short time together, and then go our separate ways. In my heart, I knew that.

I think it was so hard to find someone who felt so perfect and I think he might be as good as it ever got. After knowing Peter, William had only been a bigger disaster than he would have been anyway. The string of casual relationships and lovers I'd had since then had never compared to how Peter made me feel. Was it just because he was my first lover? I had others since him that were great in bed. I'd met men who were fantastic to be around. In some cases, I'd encountered men who were both.

Still, my heart continued to cling to Peter. I compared everyone to him, and no one measured up. Marie and Helena assured me that when someone came along that I felt truly drawn to, I'd finally let him go and move on, in the truest sense of the word. I hoped they were right because even though I had stopped longing for him, I still felt he was the one who'd gotten away.

I showered and dressed, taking my time to make sure everything about me was perfect. I wore my hair down, something I rarely did anymore. In fact, I'd been thinking lately that I might cut the long Auburn mass of hair I'd had since I was a girl. I was a woman now and a professional woman at that. Perhaps it was time to change my style to match my ambitions.

I finished my makeup and looked in the mirror, pulling my hair into different mock styles I might consider. None of them felt right. Anyway, that was a decision for a different day. I used the hot brush to tame my wild locks, making them wavy and smooth. I gave myself one last look in the mirror before making my way out the door.

It was still early, but I wanted to stop somewhere for a glass of wine or perhaps two. I had a feeling I would need to calm my nerves a bit before I sat across the table from the man that filled my dreams and fantasies on far too many nights for me to count. Though I wasn't in the habit of drinking in the middle of the day, today seemed like the perfect day for it as far as I was concerned.

Chapter 32

Giselle

My first impression wasn't what I'd expected. I guess I still had the vision of Peter in my head exactly as he'd been the last time I'd seen him. Now, I couldn't help but note how tired Peter looked. He was still quite handsome, but the darkness beneath his eyes and the thin lines across his forehead revealed that all was not well with him. His suit seemed a bit less perfectly fitted than usual, as if he'd lost some weight.

"Giselle, it's such a pleasure to see you. You look as stunning as always," he said as he approached me.

"It's good to see you too, Peter."

He pulled me toward him and kissed me on either cheek. Nothing overly personal, but a typical Parisian greeting you might receive from any acquaintance. The immensity of the moment flooded over me. I wanted to run away. All I could think about was what a horrible mistake this had been. Why had I tried to stir something up that was long dead?

"Shall we get a seat and order some food? I don't know about you, but I'm starving," he said. I couldn't help but notice that his voice sounded a little nervous. Was I imagining that?

"We can't have you starve to death. Sure, let's get seated." I tried to smile despite the sickness I felt in my stomach.

I mentally chastised myself, asking what had I expected. I'd lived this moment so many times and it was always so thrilling for us both. We were always so elated to see one another again. The conversation was lively and the sexual tension between us was palpable. In my imagination, not a day had passed since we were so enthralled with one another.

This moment had none of those qualities. It was lukewarm and awkward. I took a deep breath and slowly exhaled as a young hostess showed us to a table. I needed to get a grip. We hadn't seen each other in several years. Things were bound to be a little stiff at first. Once we got seated and began talking, we'd find a more comfortable vibe.

I ordered another glass of wine and Peter ordered a beer. It made me feel better that he'd not opted for coffee or tea, like perhaps he needed something to calm his nerves too. After ordering two portions of the daily special, simply roast beef, sautéed vegetables, and roasted potatoes, we chatted a bit. The knots in my stomach finally began to subside.

"So, tell me what you've been up to," he said, leaning slightly forward and studying my face a bit closer. My heart fluttered.

"Not that much. I'm still at the museum."

"As a curator?" he asked.

"Yes and no. I'm still a curator, but the director has been grooming me to take his place when he retires next year."

"Is that what you want?"

"Yes. No. I don't know. It's okay for now, but I have other things I want to do."

"Like?"

"Like open my own gallery. I'd be able to show what I want when I want."

"But can't you do that as a director?"

I couldn't quite pick up what he might be thinking. He seemed to be just going through the motions, asking questions and acknowledging answers as if on autopilot. I got the impression that he was having some difficulties knowing what to say. At least we still had that in common.

"I can, to an extent. There's a board that resides over the museum. Even though I can suggest certain exhibits, it's up to them to approve them or not. I want to feature local artists a lot more than they allow. The museum mostly caters to the masters and their collectors."

"You want to bring tomorrow's masters into the light," he observed, knowingly nodding.

"Yes."

"That's refreshing. I spend so much time talking to my students about how the great artists paved the way for future creators, but no one wants to support them when they get out there on their own. Of course, many students in my classes have no intention of being an artist. Some are there just to collect the humanities credit they need for their degree. Others lack the drive or the talent."

"But there are some artists," I added.

"Absolutely. Every once in a while I run across a student who could find great success with their work if given the opportunity.

It's not enough these days to be gifted. You have to find a way to get your work out there and show it to the right people."

"Yes. That's what I want to do. Anyone can curate the Picassos and Rembrandts of the world. I want to find new talent and put them on the map."

"But why?"

"What do you mean 'why'?"

"Why is that so important to you? Are you in it for the money, glory, or personal satisfaction?"

"I'd say the latter. I want to be a part of the journey. Of course, the money is always nice too, if I can make ends meet. I'd prefer not to go broke trying to start a business of my own."

"Of course. It defeats the purpose of starting a failing business," he said, flashing a sincere smile.

The server brought our food, and I pondered what to say next. I hadn't missed that Peter kept the conversation focused on my work life, not my personal life. So, it seemed that I should follow suit. I ordered another glass of wine and somehow wasn't surprised when Peter asked for another pint of beer.

"And how's your work going?" I asked, keeping things safe.

"It's good. Not much has changed there. I've cut back on the number of classes I teach to have more time for some personal things that have arisen."

And there it was. There was the opportunity to move the conversation away from polite acquaintance chat to something more intimate. I hesitated though, unsure that I really wanted to go down this path. Then again, I knew I needed to know, so I took a sip of my wine and prepared myself for the answer.

"So, tell me. What personal things have you too busy to teach?"

Peter hesitated for a moment, taking a bite of his food and looking at his plate as if to buy himself a moment before answering. Finally, he swallowed and said the last thing I wanted to hear from him.

"I got married."

Now it was my turn to take a bite and postpone any commentary. I wasn't even sure what I wanted to say. There was only the obvious, expected reply, so I went with that.

"Congratulations. I didn't know that," I told him.

"Thank you. We've been married for a couple of years now. Her name is Jillian."

"I'm sure she's a wonderful woman. Do you have a photo?" I asked.

"I do, as a matter of fact," he said, pulling his phone from his pocket and scrolling for a moment before holding it out to me.

I took it and examined the photo of what appeared to be them on some tropical beach. They were both smiling at the camera, the sun shining on their faces as they stood there leaning into one another. Her long dark hair spilled over her bare shoulders and onto the strapless bikini, partially covered with a sarong.

"You look incredibly happy," I told him, returning the phone.

I did my best not to convey what I felt inside. My heart was broken. While I'd dabbled with men I viewed as inferior to him, he had moved on to find a woman he loved enough to marry. I was too late. All my daydreams about refueling our fire and somehow finding a way to live happily ever after were officially dead.

"We were," he said, looking quietly at the phone for a moment, then putting it away.

"I'm happy for you. You deserve every happiness," I said, trying desperately to sound like I meant it.

In truth, I did mean it. I did want him to be happy. I'd just hoped he would find a way to be happy with me one day. Now, I knew that wasn't going to happen.

We made small talk for a bit, finishing our food and our wine. I was tempted to order another glass but knew it would put me in danger of becoming a babbling brook of emotion. I needed to keep my personal feelings to myself very much today. I stuffed them down and focused on getting through the rest of the meal.

If anyone had told me I would feel relieved when a lunch with Peter was over, I'd have called them crazy. Yet, here I was, thankful that this was nearing an end. He insisted on paying the bill and then we headed back out of the cafe together.

On the sidewalk outside, Peter once again kissed me on the cheek. This time, however, he gave me a lingering look that made me wonder what was going through his mind. I'd like to think he had some regrets too, but I knew it didn't matter if he did.

I would definitely need more wine, but I had no business being out and about in a bar in my current vulnerable state. Instead, I bought a bottle on my way back to the hotel. There were no wine glasses, so I drank it from a coffee cup as I sat and looked out the window at the city beyond.

Now, the picture of Peter that had always been stuck in my mind had been replaced. Instead of seeing him looking at me affectionately like he had the last time we were together, I could only see the photo of him and his wife, smiling happily on a beach somewhere. As I considered this, an echo of his words seemed to sail across my brain.

When I'd handed Peter back his phone, commenting on how happy they looked, he hadn't said, "We are." Instead, he'd said, "We were." Though I'd been too devastated for his words to really sink in at the time, now I realized what he had said, and I had to wonder what it meant. Was it possible that Peter was in an unhappy marriage? There had been no indication that they had separated or divorced.

So, why the past tense response? I considered this a bit longer and finally decided it didn't matter. Whether Peter Dockery was happily or unhappily married did not change the fact that he was currently married to another woman. Even if she didn't currently make him happy, she had at some point. He'd been happy enough with her to marry her in the first place.

I'd always heard that couples go through rough patches and green fields. It could be as simple as them currently being in a rough patch, which was the source of the comment. The truth was I could spend all kinds of time obsessing over the meaning of his comment, just as I'd spent years clinging to the memory of a man who had moved on within a year or so of our parting and found someone he loved enough to marry.

The fact that Peter had been my first lover, the first man I'd felt a connection to, it was well past time for me to accept that it was yesterday. I had to stop comparing people to him, and I had to stop daydreaming about what might happen if we ever met again.

Today, we *had* met again. He was married. That daydream was dead and there was no resurrecting it unless you believed in miracles—I didn't.

Chapter 33

Giselle

I didn't know how long I sat looking out my window, but the sky had already grown dark above the emerging city lights below. I felt unusually tired. The mid-day wine and delayed effects of jet lag were beginning to catch up with me. I was grateful I didn't have to return to the museum for a few days when I arrived home. With the time change and the layover again in London, it would be Friday evening when I arrived. I'd need the weekend to recover from the whirlwind trip.

My flight was another early one and I was keen not to make the same mistake I'd made before of missing it. I set my alarm and plugged my phone into the charger before stripping off my clothes, climbing into bed, and opening my phone to scroll through social media and the news. I needed a diversion, and this was the most I felt like doing right now.

Still, it wasn't enough to keep my thoughts from returning to Peter. It was amazing how I'd gone from being so pumped up about meeting Peter when I thought of doing so to how deflated

I felt now. It was as if someone had zapped every bit of strength from me and left me a hollow shell.

As I once again thought about our lunch together, I realized how unhappy Peter had seemed. I understood that he was married and probably a bit reserved because of that, but he'd seemed unnaturally so. Was he so afraid to be himself around me because I might make more of it than it meant? That didn't seem like him at all. Perhaps he didn't trust himself with me and held back.

I considered the latter for a moment. I once again considered whether Peter was unhappy in his marriage. Was there a chance they were on the skids, and it might end? It would explain why he'd been willing to meet with me for lunch. Perhaps he wanted to keep the door open for us but not quite step through it. There had been a lingering look when we said goodbye and that would all make sense.

"Oh, stop it," I said out loud to the empty room around me, frustrated that I had to once again remind myself to stop agonizing over Peter.

There was no reason for me to go down that road. I'd held on to some little shred of hope that Peter and I would get reacquainted since the day we parted in New York. I had to stop and just accept that he was gone. If someday—no. There would not be a someday. Peter was over. We'd enjoyed one another briefly, and that was all it was meant to be.

I made a decision. I would indulge in my memories of Peter tonight while I was here in Paris, but in the morning, I'd let him go forever. It wasn't if I was obsessed with him, but he crossed my mind far too often for a man I couldn't have. I'd pushed that down into the dark recesses of my mind while I was dating

William, but as our relationship soured, Peter's memory resurfaced. That is all any of this was, a memory of something better.

I glanced at the time. It was still early afternoon in New York. I called Helena's extension at the museum. No answer. I hung up without leaving a message and called Marie instead. She answered on the second ring with her cheery, "Hello, Marie Vaughn speaking."

"Hey, Marie. It's Giselle."

"Oh, our fair lady of gay Paris," she quipped. "How's it going over there?"

"Well, I got the art but not the guy," I told her.

"No. What happened?"

I'd texted Marie while waiting for Peter to tell her I was meeting him. She'd been as excited about it as I was.

"He's married," I said flatly.

"Married! That was fast!"

"No, not really. He didn't tell me how they met and married, and I didn't ask. I don't think I could stomach it. He did show me a picture though. She's beautiful. It's been enough time since he was in New York, though. He's had more than enough time to date and be married."

"For some people. It depends on who you ask," she countered.

"I suppose," I said glumly.

"Oh, I'm sorry, honey. I know that isn't what you wanted."

"It's okay. It's closure, isn't it? I can stop daydreaming about Peter and get on with my life."

"I thought you'd been getting on with your life anyway?"

"I don't know. I thought I was getting on with things, but a part of me was holding back. Peter was always in the back of my mind. I compare everyone to him, and they don't measure up."

"I get that, but I think you and William were doomed without Peter."

"Yeah, of course. I'm not talking about him. There were others that I just completely blew off that might have been better, though. You know?"

"I do know. So, at least now you can let go of the Peter fantasy and find a new one. Hey, if you wanna get laid, I know a painter in Paris that you can call."

"Very funny. I think no sex is better than bad sex."

She laughed. "When will you be back in New York?"

"My flight lands at three tomorrow afternoon."

"Coming into the museum?"

"No. I'm off until Monday. I've emailed the details on the acquisition already."

"You should come out with Helena and me this weekend then."

"That sounds entertaining, but I'm already exhausted. I think I'll be half dead by the time I get home and just go to bed."

"Good idea, but we aren't going out until Saturday. You should be all resurrected by then."

"Thanks. I just might."

"All right. I'll give you a call Saturday afternoon with details. We don't go out until late, so you'll have plenty of time to decide and get ready if you want to go. Are you okay right now, though?" she asked, her voice full of concern.

"I am. Just need some rest."

"Okay. I have to run, but call me back if you need to. You've got my cell number."

"I will. Thanks, Marie."

"Bye for now."

I said bye and ended the call before returning to my scrolling. I soon realized I wasn't really absorbing anything I was seeing. Instead, my mind had gone back to Peter. I could still smell his aftershave on my skin from where he'd kissed me on the cheek. What if he really wasn't happy and we came back together, after all? I allowed myself to drift into fantasy one last time.

I wondered what my wedding with Peter might have been like. Would we have had a simple wedding in New York? An elaborate one in Paris? Perhaps a destination wedding at some exotic location in the South Pacific.

I decided that my marriage to Peter would have been a fairytale come true, and thus, it deserved a fairytale wedding. I saw myself in a lace mermaid-style dress with a long train flowing out behind me as I walked down an aisle littered with rose petals toward my husband-to-be.

Of course, Peter would look nothing short of dashing in a tuxedo with a cummerbund that matched the color of the ribbons running through my bouquet. The mischievous twinkle in his eyes would be noticeable as I approached him, waiting to declare my undying love for him.

I couldn't quite imagine the ceremony, the part where we pledged our love and said our "I dos" to one another. My mind wouldn't let me put myself in that much pain and pulled me back, only allowing my fantasy to go so far, but it didn't stop me from traveling backward in time, imagining making love to Peter in my bed.

I could still see him standing in front of me in his robe, smiling broadly as he watched me drop mine to the floor, inviting him to take advantage of me. When I closed my eyes and really thought about it, I could almost feel his lips on my skin and his hands roaming freely across my body.

I longed to feel him inside me again, making love to me so slowly and tenderly that I wanted to cry tears of joy. It had all felt like such perfection to me, and I longed to find that again. If not with Peter, then with someone else I could care about as much as I had him. I think that was the hardest part of all this. It was the lack of sex. I could find good sex if I was willing to look for it, but that connection that we had.

There was something else about Peter that I'd never felt with another man. I'd found him to be beautiful in a way I didn't ascribe to others. It isn't uncommon to see a man and think he's attractive, but with Peter, I often found myself looking at him and thinking he was beautiful. I was mesmerized by the twinkle in his eyes and how his lips curled into a half smile when amused.

For all of my denials, I'd been in love with Peter. I've always been one of those people who balks at those who say they fell in love at first sight with someone. I don't think I ever really considered that I'd done exactly that with Peter, but hindsight told me it was very much true. That very first day at the museum, when I spotted him across the room, I'd fallen for him.

I hadn't looked at him and thought he was attractive or interesting. I hadn't wondered what he was doing looking at me and smiling. I knew. I knew all of it. From the moment I laid eyes on him, I realized he was beautiful in a way I'd never seen a man before. I knew I wanted him and not just in the carnal sense.

I'd been Cinderella at the ball, and he'd been the handsome prince dancing with me until the clock struck twelve and we had to part. Only my story didn't get a happy ending. Instead of a glass slipper, I got a kick in the gut with a pointed-toe boot. The dream was over and there was no longer a chance that it might recur.

Peter Dockery was married to a beautiful woman and they looked very happy together. Perhaps they were, perhaps they weren't. It was hard to say from merely seeing a photo, but whatever the situation, they were married. He'd chosen someone easier to be with and I'd been forgotten. I'd spent too much time dreaming of Peter while he'd been relegating me to a memory bank filled with experiences like having sex with a hot woman at a bar in Spain.

Was I no more than that to him now? Had I ever been more to him than that? Our relationship had lasted mere days—and I was still obsessing over it because it had been my first real taste of what it felt like to be in love and enjoy every intimacy with a person.

I lay back against the pillows and closed my eyes, letting my thoughts of Peter slip away. I knew there would never be a time when I didn't remember him fondly. I just couldn't let those thoughts overwhelm me or interfere with my moving on.

"Goodbye, Peter," I whispered out loud. "I'm letting you go. Just as you've already done with me."

Chapter 34

Peter

"Did you have a good day?"

"It was fairly uneventful. Just classes and lunch with an old friend," I replied.

"Anyone I know?"

"A curator from a museum in New York that's here on business for a couple of days."

"Oh, so you'll be able to see them again," Jillian replied.

"No. Today was the last day they're here," I told her.

I wasn't sure why I was keeping the conversation so gender-neutral. Jillian wouldn't have minded if I'd told her I was meeting a woman for lunch. She'd never been the jealous type. She wouldn't even have cared if I told her the woman was an old lover. In reality, it was a fling, but it was a very meaningful one for me.

The truth was that after I'd returned from New York, I'd been devastated to be leaving Giselle behind. Even though I knew it was way too soon to ask her to come with me or for me, I'd been tempted. I hadn't wanted to spend a single moment without her.

I'd even returned to New York a few times since then to visit Charlotte and her family. Every single trip, I'd thought about calling Giselle. Initially, I'd even looked into transferring to a university near the city to be with her. I'd talked myself out of it, unwilling to start over for the chance at a romance that might not even work out. I often found myself wondering if I'd made a mistake.

Then, I'd met Jillian, and everything had changed. She'd blown me away from the very beginning. I'd traveled to the south of Spain during a long weekend with the intention of just winding down on the beach in La Barrosa. It was there that I spotted her walking along the beach in the early morning hours.

She wore a conservative black bikini with a flowing sheer white dress pulled over it. Her dark hair spilled over her shoulders in long, silky layers. Her dark eyes caught the sunlight as it rose in the sky. She was nothing short of beauty coming to life, and I knew I had to meet this Spanish beauty.

As we approached one another, walking along the water's edge from opposite directions, I smiled and greeted her in Spanish. She returned the greeting in French. I was surprised that she somehow realized that I was French and stopped to ask her how she knew. Much to my surprise, she began grinning broadly.

"Because you speak Spanish with a French accent," she told me in broken French.

"Really? No one has ever told me that," I replied, my Spanish a bit faltering.

"English?" she asked.

"Yes."

We laughed over the fact that we had to switch to a third language to better communicate as I turned to walk the other way down the beach with her as if I'd been headed that way all along. As it turned out, she was Spanish but had moved to Senlis last year to help care for her elderly father, who passed away a few months ago.

"I am so sorry for your loss," I said.

"Thank you," she replied.

"I take it you've moved back here after his death?"

"No. I'm just here for a few days to finish moving my things from a friend's house. My father left me the house in Senlis, so I'll be returning there at the start of the week."

"I live less than an hour away from there," I said, feeling a little giddy as I stopped to face her.

"Do you?" she said, pausing beside me.

"Yes. I teach art in Paris. I've visited the museums and beauty spots in Senlis many times."

"You should visit them with me when you get back," she suggested, her eyes on mine as she spoke.

"You're right. I should. How about dinner tonight so we can talk about it?" I offered.

"That would be lovely. I might even put on some clothes for it," she replied seductively.

"Don't feel you need to do that on my account."

She laughed and we began moving down the beach again toward my hotel. I thought about being bold enough to invite her to my room for a drink, but I didn't want to come off as some sort of cad. Instead, I merely kept walking with her past it until she stopped again.

"This is me," she told me, stopping at a small villa not far from where I was staying.

"Very well," I replied. "Shall I meet you back here at six? We can walk together to dinner."

"Make it six thirty and you have a date," she replied.

"Perfect. I'll see you then."

She kissed me on the cheek, and it seemed to flow through my entire being like the tingle of an electrical current. I felt euphoric as I returned to my hotel. It was as if there was an instant connection that I hadn't experienced since I'd met Giselle.

From the moment we met, Jillian and I were inseparable. She was younger than me, but only by seven years. I proposed within six months of meeting her, and we married less than three months later. All of that had fallen apart in the span of one day when Jillian had come to me and told me she was leaving me. We'd been married less than two months at the time.

"What? Why?" I'd asked, bewildered and heartbroken.

"I've been to the doctor and the news is not good. I can't put you through such a tragedy."

"Tragedy? Doctor? What are you talking about?" I'd asked, my heart already sinking deep into my belly.

And then she'd said the most hateful words a man can ever hear from a wife he loves with his entire being.

"I have ovarian cancer. I didn't want to tell you until I knew for sure, and I don't want you to suffer this misery with me."

At first, I was too stunned—no, too devastated, to speak. When I finally found my voice, I could hear how shaky it was as I spoke.

"No. You are not going to do this, Jillian. You will not leave me to suffer alone like some sort of unwanted dog. I love you. You and I will get through this together."

"I don't want to cause you that pain," she said, holding in her own tears.

"And you think that me sitting somewhere alone, wondering how you are doing will take that pain away? You're my wife, Jillian. Thick or thin. Remember? We will get through this together. Sit down and tell me everything. Let's see what we can do about this."

Jillian sat down at the table and gave me all the details. We planned our fight despite our lack of any real weapons against this monster she carried inside her. It had a name—epithelial carcinoma.

We cried together after they took away any chance that we might have children. We shared hope during her chemotherapy. I cried alone in my office after learning that we were losing the battle and she refused to continue treatment, but I respected her choice to do so. And we got through all those things together, no matter how hard it was for either of us.

"Mr. Dockery, I'm getting ready to leave now," the home health aide told me as she stepped into the room, shaking me free of my thoughts.

It was code for me to follow her so that she could update me on how Jillian had done that day. We never discussed Jillian's health in front of her anymore as she was well aware that she had little time. Jillian neither wanted to hear how much worse she was getting nor to suffer the indignities of me listening to the details of her intakes and outputs, among other things.

The aide walked me through Jillian's day. It was no different than the past three, which in our world was good. No significant change meant that she was hanging in there. I felt selfish for wanting to hold on to her for as long as I could, knowing she might be in considerably more pain than she'd tell me about. I said goodbye to the aide and walked her to the door before returning to Jillian's room.

"So, what's the good news? Can I go salsa dancing later?" Jillian asked, attempting to sound chipper despite her current condition.

"I think you might need to wait until the weekend," I replied, sitting by her bed and taking her hand.

"Okay. That will give me time to have my favorite dress cleaned."

"The red one?" I asked.

"Yes. The one you love."

"I'd love a burlap bag if you were wearing it."

"That's sweet. Perhaps I'll find one and test that theory." She sounded incredibly tired.

"How are you feeling?"

"Over-medicated," she replied. "I can hardly keep my eyes open."

"Don't fight sleep because of me. If you're tired, sleep. I'll be here when you wake up."

She smiled and nodded slightly. I knew she was just as aware as I was that she might not wake up. She'd reached the point where it was a real possibility that something might fail, and she wouldn't come back to me. I tried hard not to think about that, but the knowledge was there whether I wanted to acknowledge it or not.

"I love you, Jillian," I said.

"Love you too," she replied, already drifting away.

I sat with her for a few more moments, watching her sleep. Then, I slipped quietly out of the room and went to my office down the hall. Sitting at my desk, I opened my notebook to make notes for tomorrow's class but instead found myself lost in a flood of tears.

I was filled with anger, hurt, and fear at the thought of losing Jillian. We'd barely had time to get to know one another before we had so much to deal with. I looked down at the blank page in front of me, now tear stained. I ripped it out of the notebook and waded it up, tossing it in the trash can beside me.

My poor Jillian, I thought. I considered what sort of asshole was out having lunch with an old flame while his wife lay dying in a bed at home. Why had I even gone? I wasn't sure. All I knew was that when Giselle had called me, I'd seen a chance to have lunch with someone and feel something akin to normalcy for a little while. Instead, I'd found myself drawn to her again. She was just as beautiful as the last time I'd seen her.

Even worse, I'd desired her, and I was ashamed of that. I'd not acted on it, but I'd wanted to, which was unacceptable. Jillian would be so hurt knowing that I'd even thought of such a thing. I'd spent the entire lunch fighting my urges and trying to be better than the carnal creature that lurked inside.

I might have succeeded at not breaking my marriage vows, but I certainly hadn't excelled at it. Then, there was Giselle. I'm sure she'd expected more from me. If she'd not been looking for a rekindling of our previous flame, she'd at least expected more friendly banter that I couldn't conjure. She'd tried to hide how uncomfortable she felt, especially after I told her about my marriage, but I'd seen the hurt behind her eyes.

Good job, Peter. Hurting two women at the same time. Aren't you a peach?

I closed the notebook and went back to check on Jillian. She was sleeping, but her expression was pained. It grew more so every single day and with her increasing pain grew my despair. I turned off the light beside her bed and went to the living room for a drink.

Chapter 35

Giselle

"I think he's gay," Helena said between bites of her salad.

"You say that about everyone who doesn't want to fuck on the first date," Marie chided.

"He's not gay. He's just old-fashioned. He doesn't want to hop in the sack with every woman he dates," I said in defense of my latest love interest.

"What sort of person is still holding out after two months?" Helena asked.

"He's not holding out. We've only been out four times; two were lunches at the hospital cafeteria between his shifts," I said.

"And the other two?" she asked.

"One was a work event here. You know that because you met him. I believe you're the one who asked if he wanted to see your vagina."

Marie chuckled and Helena grinned. "I did do that, didn't I? He *is* a gynecologist. I thought he could check me while he was here and save me a trip," she laughed.

"Right. I think it was more a case of you'd had too much of the wine being passed around," I told her.

"She had, but it does bring up a point. Maybe he doesn't want to have sex because he spends all day looking at hoo-hoos and they've lost their appeal for him," Marie said.

"The two of you are scandalous. Stop talking about my sex life," I told them.

"You mean your lack of a sex life," Marie noted.

"Very funny," I said. "So, what's going on with the two of you then?"

"Oh, Marie has gotten herself all loved up with a graffiti artist," Helena said.

"He is not a graffiti artist. He paints murals!" Marie bleated.

"Did he or did he not get arrested for graffiti at one point?" Helena said.

"He was a kid and some dude paid him to paint that wall. He had no idea it didn't belong to the man!"

"Why would someone pay him to paint a wall they didn't own?" I asked.

"Because the wall belonged to the man his wife had an affair with, and he wanted to make a point. He just lacked the talent to do so," Marie said.

"I'm probably going to regret asking this, but what exactly did he have him paint on it?" I asked.

"It was abstract in nature. It wasn't so much about the art as it was the writing in the center. It was in Latin and Sean was only seventeen. He had no idea what it meant until the man filed a complaint, calling it graffiti and insisting it was threatening. Sean said he can't remember the exact words. The man gave him a piece of paper with them written down. According to the police report it translated to "I will kill you slowly."

"Oh my God! Did he go to juvey for it?" I asked, trying not to laugh.

"No. When the guy found out who was really behind it, he dropped the charges against Sean. He said it wasn't right to hold a kid responsible when he didn't know he was being used to commit a crime."

"What a story, though," I said, finally laughing now that I knew he'd not been charged or locked up for it.

"Right? He said that it taught him not to do murals in foreign languages without knowing what they meant and to always confirm that he was dealing with the owner or someone with permission to have work done."

"So, how serious are things with this Sean guy?" I asked, wondering why I'd never heard about him when Helena obviously had.

"I don't know. We'll see," she said.

"We'll see, my ass," Helena scoffed. "They've been hot and heavy for months now. I only found out because I caught them all cuddled up at the same restaurant I was in with my sister. I had to practically waterboard her to get anything out of her," Helena said.

"Fine. It's serious. I really like him, and I don't want to jinx it," Marie replied.

"And what about you, Helena? Who are you seeing or doing or whatever," I asked.

"No one at the moment. I'm celibate," Helena said, sounding earnest.

"My ass," Marie scoffed.

"It's true. I've decided that I let too much of my romantic life be dictated by my nether regions. I want to sit back and focus on myself for a bit," Helena said, sounding slightly defensive.

"Fair enough," I told her. "But why are you giving me grief about someone not jumping into bed with me right away if you're doing the same thing."

"Because I can," she said, chuckling.

I threw a grape from the small bowl I'd packed with my lunch at her. It bounced off her arm and then sailed over the railing. She glanced at it and then back at me, still smiling. "Madam, you are a murderer. You have killed that innocent grape!" she joked.

"It had it coming," I retorted with a shrug.

We finished our lunch and headed back to work. I couldn't help but think how far my friendship with these two had come. They used to completely embarrass me with all their talk about sex and men, but now I was right in there with them, telling them all about my own experiences, good and bad.

Of course, I didn't always tell them everything. If I'd told them I was thinking of breaking it off with the gynecologist, a man named Carter Gray, there would have been a lot more discussion of things I just didn't want to discuss. Sometimes, I valued their input and other times I made up my mind and didn't need the back and forth over what I considered a done deal.

Since I'd been dating Carter, I'd felt next to nothing for him. He was decent looking and kind, but that was about all I could say for him. He wasn't overly affectionate, and I found that off-putting. I'd previously told the girls about the lack of sex thing. I continued to defend his not wanting to jump into the sack too quickly, but I hadn't told them it extended well beyond the bedroom.

Carter had never kissed me on the lips. Every date had resulted in a polite hug or kiss on the cheek. When I tried to push the issue by kissing him, he pulled away and made an excuse about garlic for lunch. Another time, I'd tried to cuddle with him while watching a movie on my sofa and he'd hastily gotten up to go to the bathroom. When he returned, he'd claimed he was on call, which he hadn't previously mentioned. He got a text to come to the hospital for some emergency.

Though he was a nice guy and I enjoyed going out with him, he just seemed like someone who was more friend material than anything. In fact, he might very well be gay, and if he was trying to hide it from the public by dating women, I wasn't going to be the one to out him. He'd find his way. Of course, there could be a million reasons why he acted as he did. The thing about it was that I wasn't invested enough in having a relationship to even spend much time wondering why.

The more I thought about it, the more I realized dating him was a waste of time for both of us. I thought about what Helena said about focusing on herself and decided that might also be a good idea for me. Since my return from Paris and learning that Peter was married, I'd thrown myself into a string of short relationships in hopes that someone could ignite the same spark in me that he once had. It hadn't happened and maybe I was trying too hard to make it happen.

A week later, I broke things off with Carter as politely as I could. In all honesty, he seemed relieved. I couldn't blame him. I felt relieved too. I had a new event in the works at the museum and wouldn't have much time for him in the coming weeks anyway, so it was good timing. I could spend time getting some serious work done and doing some self-contemplation.

I quickly became absorbed in updating the museum's catalog with new acquisitions and preparing for the new exhibit. We planned on putting it in a wing that hadn't previously been used. It had been in disrepair and closed off for years until the director decided to finally sink some money into restoring it for public use. The finished product was stellar for displaying the new modern art exhibition we were planning.

For now, though, it was empty. I walked through the space to get a feel for it. In my mind, I positioned some of the various paintings I had in mind on the walls. It would ultimately be up to the designer to lay out the space based on the curations, but I had a lot of input since her ideas were centered around my acquisitions. I smiled as I looked up at the walls. They were like a blank canvas on which I could create my own masterpiece.

"This is a lovely space, isn't it?" a male voice asked from behind me.

"Yes," I replied, turning to see who had ventured in.

I didn't recognize the attractive stranger standing there. He was what Marie would call "messy," with tousled brown hair and sleepy eyes that revealed just a hint of green between the slits. He wore old jeans with paint splotches and a t-shirt that said "Sixties Original, Unrestored" which, if true, put him in his fifties or maybe even early sixties.

"Are you Giselle Martin?" he asked.

"I am," I replied curiously.

"I'm Graham. I was told to check with you and make sure the space was to your liking."

"Oh. Yes, it's perfect. You are with the construction crew?"

"Something like that. Just let me know if you need anything further and I'll make it a priority." He offered me a business card.

"Absolutely. I will. Thank you so much," I said.

He said his goodbyes and walked away. I found myself watching him go. He had the swagger of a man who wouldn't kiss me just on the cheek after a date, and after my last relationship, I could appreciate that. I glanced down at the card.

Graham Tollenger, Chief Architect
Tollenger Architecture LLC

I smiled and tucked the card inside the notebook in my hand, reminding myself that I was not pursuing men at the moment. For all I knew, Graham Tollenger was married or just not interested in general. I didn't plan to find out. If I called him, it would be because I'd discussed any issues with the space he'd renovated for us with the director and been asked to do so.

As I returned to my office, I passed Graham in the hallway again. He stopped to look at a pillar that was splitting down one side and had been for some time. When he saw me, he motioned toward it.

"How long has this been splitting? Do you know?"

"Not exactly, but it's been growing more obvious over the past year or so."

He nodded his head, his brow furrowed. "I'll talk to the director about securing it. Can't have this building falling down on such precious contents." His eyes riveted on me for a second before looking away. He gently patted the pillar and then walked toward the director's office with a broad smile.

Despite myself, my heart did a little flip-flop in my chest. I stood there watching him swagger off again for far too long before pulling myself away and returning to my office for more catalog work. I had no time for Graham Tollenger. I didn't.

Well, maybe I did.

Chapter 36

Peter

I watched as Jillian lay sleeping. We no longer shared a bed and hadn't for some time. As her disease progressed, I'd had to bring in a hospital bed to better care for her. Though she was easy enough for me to lift, given the horrible amount of weight she had lost in the past six months, I was afraid that her frail state would result in injuries. The bed allowed me to tend to her needs without as much movement.

A nurse came every day now and checked her vitals. Jillian had been unconscious for the past week and wasn't expected to make it much longer. I tried to tell myself that I was ready for the end, that I was ready for this to be over for her. The truth was that I wasn't. What romance and intimacy Jillian and I had once shared had been over for quite some time. Cancer had robbed us both of that, but I loved her and didn't want her to go.

I'd called her sister, Ariana, to come. She'd arrived yesterday to spend what time she could with Jillian. It wasn't her first visit, and I was thankful for that. Jillian had enjoyed seeing her when she was still alert and able to talk with her. They'd had many private conversations that I'd not asked about, letting it remain between the two of them. If it concerned me, I was sure I'd be told by one of them.

I was on a sabbatical from teaching, determined to spend every moment I could with my wife. I'd only left her side briefly when Ariana was with her or the nurse was tending to her each day. Often, my short escape from the sense of impending doom I felt was just stepping outside to get some fresh air for a few minutes.

Watching Jillian lie there, the life slowly draining from her, was devastating. It took a mental and physical toll that I hadn't expected. After her diagnosis, I'd hoped for a mistake. I just knew that we would go back to her oncologist one day and they would explain that they had made a mistake; it was a shadow on the scan or some anomaly that was easily corrected with meds or even minor surgery.

Then, there had been the hysterectomy. Jillian had been more devastated at the loss of her ability to have children than she was at the broader issue of possibly dying from cancer. The worst part was that the surgery had been unsuccessful. The cancer had already spread too far. She'd ignored the symptoms for too long while taking care of her father.

By the time she met me, she had gotten used to the discomfort until it got far worse. At that point, we were married, and she'd developed other symptoms. That's when she finally went to the doctor and found out the cause of her distress. A biopsy confirmed the diagnosis and they suggested the surgery that they knew would likely only buy her time. Still, we were hopeful they might find things weren't as bad as they thought. Instead, they found they were far worse.

So, we started chemotherapy. There was never any hope that it would magically shrink her cancer to the point that we could hope for remission. It was only an effort to buy Jillian more time to put her affairs in order and spend the time she had left doing what she wanted. Most of them still went undone. She was always sick, weak, and exhausted. All of her dreams faded away and she faded away with them. Today, we were at the end. The nurse had come to check her vitals and this time she stayed with us for a while longer than usual.

Just after lunch, Charlotte arrived from New York. She'd come to see Jillian for one last time too, but she was also there to support me. She knew I would fall apart when the end came. I'd held myself together for too long. I'd remained as stoic as I could for Jillian. I didn't know what I would do when she was no longer there, needing me to be strong.

I remember her words to me before she got so sick. She'd told me to go on with my life, to find someone who would make me happy. I'd told her I didn't want to talk or even think about that, but she'd made me promise. I'd told her I would. It might be the only lie I ever told Jillian. I could never see myself moving past her.

"I will be just fine. Don't you ever worry about me," I'd told her.

"I do worry about you. I'm so sorry that I can't stay with you forever. I wanted to grow old together."

"Jillian, we will grow old together whether you are in this world or the next. You will always be with me; that is all we need to say about this."

I knew she wanted to talk about it more, but I was selfish. I wouldn't let her. I couldn't let her tell me about what she wanted me to do when she died. I didn't want to think about that, and I still don't, but time grew closer, and I'd be forced to live in that fresh hell without my precious Jillian.

"Mr. Dockery?" a voice said from behind me. I jumped. I hadn't heard anyone come outside.

I turned to see the nurse standing outside the front door, waiting for me to respond. I was frozen. I knew why she'd come out. I didn't want to go in there. I couldn't make myself speak or move.

"Mr. Dockery," she repeated. "I need you to come inside now."

"Is she—" I managed to choke out. I couldn't finish the sentence.

"No. Not yet, but it's only a matter of time. I think you'll want to be there," she said quietly.

I nodded, holding back tears. The moment had arrived, and I was no more prepared for it than I had been the day she'd told me she was sick. I felt my body move toward the front door, past the nurse, and into the house. Then, I stood in the bedroom with no memory of walking through the house to get there.

Ariana sat on one side of the bed, holding Jillian's hand. Charlotte sat on the other. She stood and helped guide me onto the chair she vacated, then moved behind me and put her hand softly on my shoulder. I took Jillian's hand. It was frail and limp. She remained unconscious, heavily dosed on morphine to keep her as comfortable as possible.

Her chest rattled up and down, filling the room with her jagged breaths. It had been like this for the last few hours. I knew the sound. I'd heard it before when my grandfather had passed. They called it a death rattle. It came at the end when it became harder to breathe, but it had slowed in just the short time since I'd stepped outside, coming in shorter, hitched gasps.

Then, it finally just stopped. I held my own breath, waiting for her to breathe with me, but it never came. I let out my breath, tears rolling down my face as I sat there quietly, not knowing what would happen now. The nurse took over, stepping to the side of the bed and checking Jillian's vitals one last time.

"She's gone," she said. "I'll give you all a moment."

The nurse disappeared out the doorway and left us alone with Jillian—Jillian's body, my mind corrected. My wife was dead. I was a widower. The enormity of the loss was already settling around me like a wet blanket. Charlotte moved in front of me and pulled me toward her into a hug. Ariana lay her head over on the bed, sobbing into the blankets. I felt like I should go to her, but I couldn't move.

"Help Ariana," I managed to say to Charlotte. "Help her."

Charlotte understood, moving toward Ariana and pulling her upward into her arms. Ariana turned and wept onto her shoulder. I found enough strength to stand on wobbly legs and make my way out of the room. The nurse was finishing up a phone call in the front room. She turned toward me when I entered.

"Mr. Dockery, I am so sorry for your loss. I've made arrangements for your wife. The coroner's people will be here shortly. You can give them any final instructions you haven't already provided."

"Thank you," I told her.

Jillian had already taken care of everything. She'd insisted that I not be bothered with funeral decisions and wondering if I was doing what she wanted after she was gone. I'd gone with her to the funeral home, and we'd made the arrangements together. I'd been opposed at the time, not wanting to deal with such macabre things. Now, I was grateful for her foresight. I couldn't imagine having to go through that so soon after losing her.

The nurse returned to the bedroom to make her final preparations for the men who would take Jillian away, and I poured myself a drink. A few minutes later, Charlotte came in, leading a still weeping Ariana toward a chair. I poured them both a drink and another for myself. We all sat down and sipped our drinks, waiting silently for what would come next.

I felt completely empty, gutted that my beautiful Jillian was gone. I'd be lying, though, if I didn't admit I also felt relief. A part of me was glad it was over, for her and for me. It had been so hard for her. There had been so much suffering. It was horrible of me to feel grateful for the end, but I had to believe that most people in my shoes felt the same when they lost someone who had suffered a long-term illness.

I was glad she was no longer suffering. I was glad I no longer had to watch her endure the undignified manner in which cancer takes a person or feel the discomfort that I could never begin to imagine.

The three of us remained in the front room as the nurse took the coroner and his men to the bedroom to retrieve Jillian. They emerged only minutes later with her on their gurney. She was covered by a white sheet as they wheeled her toward the long black hearse that would transport her to the funeral home. Then, they were gone, disappearing in the distance with my most precious cargo on board. The nurse said her goodbyes, taking the remaining equipment loaned to us by Home Health with her and leaving us in the empty shell of a home.

The dam finally broke, and I collapsed into a nearby chair, weeping like a baby. Charlotte tried to comfort me, but there was none to be had. Ariana did the same, despite feeling what I could only imagine was an equal grief to mine. I pulled them both toward me into a hug. Time seemed to fade and distort around me. I wasn't sure how long we remained that way.

Finally, I regained control and went to wash my face. I would need to make some very difficult calls now. Jillian had left me a list. Charlotte offered to do it for me, but I felt it was something I should do personally. The simple truth was that I needed something to do, even if it was having difficult conversations with other people who also loved Jillian.

I retrieved my cell phone and the list tucked into an envelope on a kitchen shelf. There were other envelopes to be opened. Some addressed to me, and some addressed to others. Some were instructions for taking care of things that would need to be addressed after her death; some were notes to various people she wanted given to them at her funeral.

I unfolded the list and looked down at the carefully written names and phone numbers, some for people I knew and others I didn't. I steeled myself and dialed the first number on the list.

Chapter 37

Giselle

The new exhibit was coming together nicely. I spent the better part of the last month putting everything in place and was quite proud of how it turned out. The new space was a marvelous canvas for the artwork being displayed. Graham Tollenger and his crew had done a great job of it.

He'd done an even better job of charming me. We'd been seeing one another since shortly after I'd met him. He'd returned a few days after our initial introduction to assess the crack in the pillar he'd been looking at and to get his crew started. The director insisted they do it at night while the museum was closed, and I'd been working when they came in.

I'd asked if he'd like coffee once he'd started with the work. We'd sat in the administrative break room, sipping our cups and chatting. Soon, the conversation turned personal. I'd learned that Graham Tollenger was fifty-seven and a father to three boys, all grown and on active military duty. Their mother lived in Australia. Graham said she moved there to get as far away from him as possible.

"Why is that?" I'd asked. "Are you a bad man?"

"No. I'm just a man who likes money. I'm married to my job. I worked long hours to pay for nice things that I thought we both wanted. It turns out she wanted a husband more than dresses and jewelry. You sometimes learn these things the hard way."

"So, now you're alone."

"I'm never alone," he said bluntly.

I smiled at him, not sure how I was supposed to respond to that. He laughed, causing me to raise a questioning eyebrow in his direction.

"I'm not saying a womanizer. I'm saying that I'm always working, so my crew is around."

"I see. So, you're still a workaholic who likes nice things," I observed.

"Yeah. Pretty much. Why not? My wife is gone, and my boys are off living their own lives. I have a very nice houseboat and spend my money however I see fit. Sometimes, I spend it on pretty women who enjoy good company without getting too attached. You know anyone like that?"

"Yes. I think they're called sex workers," I told him, a wry smile on my face.

He laughed again and shook his head. "You're funny. How about I just stop beating around the bush and ask you out?"

"How about you do that?"

"Giselle, would you like to go to dinner with me this Saturday?"

"I'd love to," I told him, surprised at how easy and simple things seemed with him.

And just like that, we'd begun dating, but it was never serious. Both of us were focused on our work. In fact, I think it was part of our draw to one another. We saw each other here and there for a casual dinner or drinks. Sometimes we went to a club or out dancing. Mostly, we just had a lot of sex. It wasn't uncommon for us to meet up for lunch and a quickie before returning to our jobs.

It wasn't true romance, but it worked. Helena and Marie thought it was marvelous. Marie had become completely devoted to Sean, and Helena was seeing an old friend she'd been in love with since they were in first grade. It was as if I'd switched places with them. They were the ones who were looking for real love and I was the wild one, just doing whatever felt good.

Today, I was fresh off a tryst with Graham at the renovation of a high-rise he was working on. I'd dropped by to see the progress at his invitation and found the crew gone for the day. Graham and I had taken advantage of the view from the mirrored windows in the unfinished penthouse. Then I returned to work on the new exhibition.

"Giselle, can you help me downstairs. I need your expertise," one of the other curators said as I finished some work at my desk.

"Sure. I'll be right down. Which exhibit?"

"The Abstract Romantics," she told me.

"Okay. I'll be there in about five minutes."

"Great. Thanks." She walked back out the door and disappeared down the hallway.

I finished the listings I'd been working on and went downstairs to help her with whatever she needed. I was just finishing up and about to return to my office when a woman stepped away from one of the Ming vase displays and approached me.

"Giselle?" she said.

"Yes?" I replied, looking in her direction. She looked familiar, but I couldn't quite place her at first.

"Charlotte. I'm Peter Dockery's sister."

Hearing Peter's name was like a punch in the gut. I'd finally put him behind me and now here was a reminder of him in the living, breathing flesh. I suppose I should be surprised that we hadn't run into one another before now. Charlotte enjoyed the museums.

"Yes, Charlotte. Of course. How are you?"

"I'm okay. How are you? It's been a long time, but I recognized you instantly. You're just as beautiful as ever."

"Oh, thank you," I replied, a flush spreading up my cheeks.

"Have you spoken to Peter?"

"No, not in a while. I was in Paris a few months ago and we met for a quick lunch. He told me he had gotten married. He seemed very happy."

Her face dropped at the mention of Peter's marriage. She shook her head sadly from side to side.

"He didn't tell you," she said finally.

"Tell me what?"

"His wife, Jillian. She had ovarian cancer. She died last month."

"Oh, God. I'm so sorry. Please give Peter my condolences."

"I will. He'll be glad to hear from someone he cared for so deeply."

I looked at her, puzzled. Sure, Peter and I were good together, but our time was too short for it to have meant much to him. It meant much more to me because he had opened up a whole new world. He'd allowed me to live a much freer, richer life. I had to honestly say that I was no more than a fling for him. Perhaps Charlotte was just trying to make me feel better.

"He meant a lot to me too. I hope he's coping with things well."

"Peter will be fine. He's a tough cookie, my brother."

"Yes. He is," I replied.

In truth, I couldn't bear the thought of Peter being in so much pain. He must be devastated. A part of me wanted to catch the next flight to Paris to comfort him. That was hardly appropriate, though, was it? He likely didn't want me there anyway. I knew Peter well enough that he wouldn't want me to see him in such an emotional state. That was why he couldn't tell me about her, and it explained why he'd said we "were" happy.

"I'm sorry. You're at work. I'll get out of your way. I was just stopping by to see what was new while I was in the area and then I saw you."

"I'm glad you said hello, and please do give Peter my best thoughts."

"I will do that."

I watched as she walked toward the exit. All I could think about was Peter and how he must be feeling right now. I ached to know he was hurting so badly. I knew how it felt to lose someone you cared about. I'd lost him, after all. That was no comparison to how it must feel to be in love, get married, and then watch your spouse die from such a horrible disease.

I wondered if I should do more. Should I call him? Should I send a card? I didn't want my only acknowledgment of his loss to be dependent on his sister remembering to tell him that I'd sent my condolences. I returned to my office and looked up his email, thinking I might send him a note, but I didn't have his home email address. I'd have to send it to him at work. It was the same with a phone call; I'd never asked for his number again when we met for lunch and would have to call him at work.

In the end, I decided to do what ordinary people did in this situation. On my way home that evening, I stopped at a card shop and spent nearly an hour picking out a card that didn't seem too personal or too impersonal. I took it home and practiced what I wanted to say on a separate piece of paper, finally deciding to keep it simple.

It took several attempts ranging from an entire paragraph to only a few words, but I finally landed on what I felt was appropriate to the situation. I reread it, crossing out "your wife" and putting "Jillian" instead. I didn't want it to come across as too impersonal, but I also didn't want it to look like I was already trying to move in on him.

In fact, the last thing that crossed my mind was that I might have another chance with Peter. Not only had that ship already sailed, but it was crass to even think of such a thing given the current circumstances. My only thoughts were platonic for a friend who was broken-hearted and in pain.

I rewrote the words from my pad of paper onto the card.

Dear Peter,

I am so sorry to hear about Jillian. All my thoughts are with you, always.

Giselle Martin

Satisfied, I sealed the envelope and laid it on the table, realizing I didn't have his home address either. I'd have to send it to the university, after all. I frowned over this, but it was the best I could do. I looked up the address for the university and finished addressing the envelope so I could take it by the post office tomorrow and get it on its way.

I felt like I should do more, but I also knew I shouldn't. It wasn't my place to repair what was broken with Peter. The truth was, it never had been. He'd never been mine at all. I'd come to realize that, once I was able to let go of my naive fantasies about him.

My focus now was work. My goals didn't revolve around a relationship with Peter or anyone else. Graham was fun, but that is all he was. I enjoyed our time together. I liked the simplicity of seeing one another when we felt like it, and no one was upset if the other one had other plans or was busy with work.

There was no jealousy on either side of our relationship. In some ways, it was healthier than any committed relationship I'd attempted, including my brief fling with Peter. I'd spent so much time pining for something that wasn't meant to last that I'd missed out on just enjoying myself.

It's not that I didn't still care about Peter. Obviously, I did, and it hurt to know he was suffering through such an emotional storm. I was very well aware now that my romantic feelings for him had disappeared after all this time. It was bound to happen someday and had come much later than it should have.

I lay the envelope on my bag and got ready for bed. Tomorrow, I would mail it and life would go on for both of us in our different worlds with an ocean between us—just as it had since we last held one another and parted ways.

Chapter 38

Giselle

Graham and I lay cuddled in bed early one Sunday morning after an evening together. It was a rare event for us. We didn't usually spend the night with one another, preferring to just part ways after our trysts so we could wake up in our own beds the next morning.

"No walks of shame on my watch!" he teased.

"Especially on the boat. It would be my luck that I'd stumble into the harbor and drown."

"Oh, please don't do that."

"Why? Would you miss me?"

"Because I'd be the last person who saw you and end up trying to beat murder charges," he said with a chuckle.

"I see how you are now," I told him, pretending to pout.

He smiled and pulled me closer, nuzzling his face into my neck and planting small kisses there. We lay there for a moment longer and I glanced at the clock. It was almost time for the sun to come up.

"It's almost dawn. I have to get going."

"Are you a vampire? Got to get home before the sun comes up, do you?"

"Yes, that is exactly it." I pulled away and sat on the edge of the bed. "Seriously though, I need to get home and change for a meeting."

"On a Sunday?"

"Yes. I'm looking at a little place down by the docks in Hell's Kitchen."

"Little place for what? To live? Are you trying to move closer to me?" he asked, seeming to like the idea if his smile was any indication.

"No. I'm working on getting funding together to open my own gallery. It's early stages, but I'm looking into what kind of spaces I can afford in different areas of the city."

"You should have asked me. I can help you with that."

"Thanks, but I'm fine. I'm really just window shopping right now."

"Okay, but you'll tell me when you're more serious. I know where you can find all sorts of buildings that might suit you and probably get you a good deal on one."

"I'll take it under advisement and as far as moving closer to you, I don't live that far away as it is."

He shrugged and sat up, leaning on one elbow and smiling at me. "It's damned hot to find a woman who's as absorbed by work as I am, you know."

"Weirdo," I said, pulling on my clothes and looking down at him with a bemused look.

"Yep. All right. I've got some shit going on the next few days. I'll call you about Thursday or so. Cool?"

"Cool." I leaned across the bed to kiss him softly before climbing up to the top deck and putting on the shoes I'd left there the night before. The sun was up now, reducing my risk of falling into the Hudson River. I stepped off the boat and made my way out of the marina toward the subway.

I was already excited to look at the place I'd lined up for today. I'd been creating a business plan to present to potential banks and investors. I'd been saving up for my own gallery for some time. I'd thought I would be promoted to director at the museum by now and make more money to put toward my dreams, but there didn't seem to be any retirement in sight for the current holder of that position.

I could stay and wait for it to come to me someday, or I could move ahead with my own plans. I'd decided that I couldn't wait for someone to dictate my career to me. Even if I wasn't yet in a position to open one today or tomorrow, I could at least spend some time doing the groundwork.

Of course, today wasn't the day I'd find my dream location. I arrived to find the place far too derelict for recovery. It was cheap enough to secure for the gallery, but the work needed to be done on it would eat up the money I saved. I was running into a lot of that with the places I'd viewed, which meant I would have to increase my budget for that part of my venture.

I returned home and made some notes. I was still a bit geared up to take some actual first steps toward starting my gallery and doing more research online. Though I still had a way to go, I felt optimistic about succeeding. It just meant I wasn't quite there yet and would need to keep working at the museum for a bit longer.

That wasn't necessarily a bad thing. Each day I spent there gave me additional experience and exposed me to people within the art community. I was well respected; many of them sought my opinion on potential artwork for their homes or offices, even outside exhibitions. Then, there were the artists I ran across. We were often approached by up-and-coming artists looking for a showing.

Unfortunately, our museum didn't really show work of complete unknowns. To make a space for them, they had to at least be well enough known that they'd been shown in local galleries and had a fan base. Even then, their exposure was limited. They might be displayed in one of the smaller galleries as part of a collection of artists with a common theme.

At home, I had a list of artists and contact details. I visited outside art shows and sought out what I liked to call feral artists showing their work out on the streets. Some of them were quite good and I hoped to bring them into the public eye more in the future.

Of course, there was currently a rise of individuals who called themselves artists, but they created images using artificial intelligence. While it did take some skill to create a quality image that lacked unintentional distortions, some had taken to creating the images, printing them, and then painting over them to give them the effect of original artwork. It was a slippery slope. To the naked eye, you might see paint on canvas and be completely unaware that the art had been created using someone else's original work.

Then again, you also ran that risk with original paintings. It wasn't uncommon in the art world for someone with talent but little imagination to rip off the work of a lesser artist and sell it as their own. It was easily done by purchasing the original painting for pennies and then simply recreating it with another signature.

Many in the industry were appalled by the use of AI to create art, but it wasn't all bad news. Some efforts had seen lost art recreated from x-rays that showed the original faded or damaged art or art that had been painted over. Several projects have developed a method of taking this kind of data and then using a mix of AI generation and 3D printing to recreate masterpieces down to individual brush strokes. It wasn't yet perfected, but it was quite promising in the case of art that would otherwise be lost.

It was still quite costly to create, so you wouldn't likely find a copy of *Two Wrestlers* by Van Gogh hanging in someone's one-bedroom flat. It was pretty realistic, though. To the naked, untrained eye, it might even look like it had actually been painted by hand. I'd seen only one of these paintings firsthand; the detail and strokes were nearly identical to the original piece of art. However, there was little chance of it being confused with the original—at least for now.

My phone chimed, pulling me away from my research. I glanced down and saw that it was from Graham.

—How'd it go?—

I typed a response. *—No go. Back to the drawing board.—*

—Maybe next time—

—I have plenty of time— I replied before putting my phone aside and closing my laptop.

I'd been so absorbed in researching that I hadn't realized how late it was getting. The sun had already begun to set over the city. I poured myself a glass of wine and took the bottle with me to sit in my favorite chair near the window that overlooked the city. It reminded me of Paris, looking out the window at the city lights below.

Thoughts of my time in Paris brought Peter back to the front of my mind. I wondered how he was doing. Was he alone or with family...either his or Jillian's. He must be in so much pain right now. I teared up just thinking of him that way and wiped the back of my hand across my eyes to clear them.

My thoughts shifted back to me. I wondered if I would ever find that kind of love. If I did, I hope I never had to experience the grief of losing it. Of course, I suppose we all did eventually unless we were the ones who went first. I wasn't sure what was worse, losing someone you loved, knowing you were going to die and leave them behind, or never experiencing the joy and pain of loving someone so much.

"Poor Peter," I said into the empty room around me. "Poor Jillian."

I sat drinking my wine and just looking out at the lights outside. My phone dinged again. I was sure it was Graham, but I didn't pick it up. I liked Graham. He and I were very much alike. What we weren't was in love, and as much as I enjoyed his company, I knew that our time would likely come to an end soon. Nothing had happened to sour me on our relationship. It had simply run its course.

I finished the wine and went to wash up before slipping naked into bed. I had a busy day at work tomorrow and needed to get some sleep. I hadn't gotten much last night on Graham's boat. I wasn't complaining, but I needed to get in some tonight if I didn't want to be a zombie tomorrow. I didn't worry about that for very long. My lack of sleep and wine combined worked their magic and I was fast asleep almost as soon as my head hit the pillow.

Chapter 39

Peter

The days following Jillian's funeral were the hardest of my life. I would venture to say that the funeral itself had been less difficult than the hours of emptiness that followed. At least during the service, I was surrounded by people who loved Jillian. Knowing that so many cared about her gave me a sense of solace.

Charlotte stayed for nearly a week afterward, cooking and cleaning for me and Ariana, who had also remained. She wouldn't be leaving anytime soon. Jillian and I had agreed that her younger sister would take the house and I would move back into the city when the time came for such a change. I had only relocated here after our marriage because it was Jillian's childhood home. It was also Ariana's, and it was only fitting that it remain with her instead of me.

It might be the one thing I was looking forward to in all the grim days that lay before me. I'd never quite taken to the solitude of our home in the French countryside. The city suited me better and I was eager to get back to some small flat amid the rows of other small flats where I could walk to the bakery on my way to work and wouldn't need a car. I was leaving that with Ariana, as well. It had been Jillian's more than mine anyway.

Charlotte helped me pack for my move before leaving. There wasn't much. I took only what I'd brought when I moved here and the things Jillian had given me, along with a few mementos of her. Ariana would take care of the rest. What she didn't want to keep, she would give to charity or relatives. We agreed that if this was too much for her, living in the house where both her father and sister had died, she should sell it and not feel guilty about it. It was hers to do with as she pleased.

I suspected that she would keep it, though. Like Jillian, Ariana was strong and wouldn't dwell on what had happened here. She was much younger than Jillian, the product of a second marriage ending in an amicable divorce and a half-sister with a different mother. That had never made a difference between the two girls. They loved their father and one another equally as they had their mothers.

She and I spoke briefly on my last day at the house. I packed my things into a small moving van to return to the city where I'd bought a small flat. It was a bit rough, in need of many repairs, but I'd been able to buy it without additional financing, and renovating it would keep me occupied during the hours that invited too much loneliness.

"I hope you will find happiness here," I told her.

"I will. I can remember being here when I was young. Mom and Dad didn't divorce until I was nearly eighteen. It seems like yesterday that Jillian was reading me bedtime stories. She always seemed like more of an aunt than a sister when we were young because she was so much older. She was almost eight when I was born. Always so beautiful..." she said, her voice trailing off.

"She was. Yes. I'm going to miss her."

"I know you will. You do. Are you sure you want to give up this house?" she asked one last time.

"Yes. There's nothing for me here without her. We had so little time to really enjoy our lives together. We were barely married and moved into this place when our lives were filled with doctors, tests, treatments. I have more bad memories here than good, I'm afraid."

"I can understand that, but you're always welcome to visit. Maybe once the wounds heal a bit, you can find some happier memories of this place to cling to."

"Thank you, Ariana. I will come back, if only to see you."

"I'd like that. Very much."

We hugged each other tightly for a moment. Then, I got in the van and drove away, glancing only briefly in my rearview mirror at the house and life I was leaving behind. It was more appropriate to say it left me behind as I had no choice in the matter. Tears streamed down my face as I drove. I brushed them away with the back of my hand and kept facing forward. That was all that was left for me to do now.

My thoughts were full of Jillian as I drove. I tried to focus on the better memories I had of her. I could still see the lovely woman who had captivated me that first day on the beach. I could picture her laughing as she sprayed me with a hose while working in the garden after we moved to her father's house. I could hear her words as she read to me from a favorite book as we lay in bed.

I was mesmerized by Jillian's beauty from the start, but she was so much more than that. She'd been smart and funny. I found her always ready with words of wisdom or advice when I needed it. I couldn't have designed a woman more perfect for me. If I had any regrets about my life with Jillian, they were only that we were robbed of what our marriage could have been.

Reflecting back on our dating life and the days before her diagnosis, I could see that the signs of trouble were already there. Jillian had felt ill more often than usual. She'd chalked it up to some sort of gastric distress that she couldn't quite shake. At first, she'd believed it might just be from months of the stress from dealing with her father's demise. When it had persisted, she'd thought it might be an ulcer or some new allergy she'd developed.

I hadn't realized how much distress she'd been in before being diagnosed that she'd simply hidden from me because she didn't want to come across as a hypochondriac. She'd even considered that it might be psychosomatic. She'd gone from burying her father to planning a wedding within a year and considered that it was just all in her head, a result of having too much on her plate too soon.

I'd offered to slow things down, put the wedding off, or simply elope and be done with planning altogether, but she wouldn't hear of it. She wanted her big day, even if it was just a simple wedding at a small wedding gazebo with a few dozen friends and family in attendance. I told her we would do what she wanted, and she'd powered through with the wedding.

The memory of our ceremony made me smile. She'd been a beautiful bride. She'd worn her hair pinned up in loose curls. Several tendrils fell down in perfect spirals that framed her beautiful face. The dress she'd selected was stunning. It was fitted to her every curve and trailed behind her in a short lace train. The pearls pinned into her curls were dotted with tiny glass beads that caught the light around us.

We'd spent our honeymoon in Crete, strolling along the beaches as we had when we'd met in Spain. We'd made love night and day, enjoying one another as only newlyweds can. It was blissful and remained so for a while—not long enough.

I stopped myself short of going down the road where we'd gotten the bad news about her cancer. I couldn't relive those horrible moments just yet. I wanted to remain in this little bubble where I remembered how we were and fantasized about how we might have been instead of what had unfolded.

The past two years of watching her fight to stay alive against all odds had been dehumanizing for both of us. There is a special kind of hell to be found in knowing you don't control your destiny or that of someone you love so much. You feel helpless, powerless, and dehumanized. So, I tried to focus on what came before that.

Arriving at my new flat, I unloaded the small moving van and carried everything inside. There wasn't much, but that was okay. I needed to do some additional work before I could properly furnish the place anyway. I put everything in one corner of the dining room for now and went to return the van to the friend I had borrowed it from. I'd told him I would be back by six and he was there waiting.

"Thanks so much for this," I told him as I parked it in the lot and handed him the keys.

"No problem, Peter. If you need anything else, just let me know. I would have been happy enough to come with you and help you move your things."

"I know. It was just something I needed to do alone, I guess."

"I understand. Do you need a ride back to your place?"

"No. It's not far from here. I'll walk. I could use the fresh air."

"Are you sure?"

"I am. Thanks again."

"Anytime. Call me soon. Okay?"

I nodded and made a hasty retreat to the sidewalk. People meant well, saying everything they could to support you without acknowledging what was wrong in your world. I was just in a place where I needed to be alone. I stopped by a bar on the way home and had a few beers. They were welcome after the tough day I'd had, both from physically moving things and the emotional toll it had taken.

"Hi. Mind if I join you?" a woman said.

"Go ahead," I told her, motioning to the stool beside me.

"My name is Therese. I'm here on vacation."

"Peter. Somewhat native," I replied.

"Somewhat?" she said with a fetching smile.

I smiled back, contemplating whether I could really just sit here and flirt with some woman so soon after losing Jillian. There was a part of me that craved intimacy. I wanted someone to touch me and make me feel good without any of the emotional stuff that came with it. Who better than a tourist? She was attractive enough and coming on strong enough for me to believe she was willing.

Jillian and I hadn't been sexual for a very long time. Shortly before her diagnosis, her pain had increased to the point where she didn't want sex. Then, the physical and mental toll of her condition had combined to bar anything more than cuddling together. The better part of the last two years had been sexless, and I didn't blame Jillian for that. I could never blame her for something so unexpected and devastating, but it sealed our relationship's fate. We'd lived a platonic existence where there was immense love, but we could never be lovers again.

"I'm sorry. I have to go," I blurted, standing up and dropping cash on the bar for my drinks and a few rounds for her. "Have a few drinks on me."

"Did I say something wr—" she began to say, but I was already at the door, making my way back to the sidewalk that would take me to the safety of my new home.

Once inside, I leaned against the cool surface of the front door and took a deep breath, exhaling slowly. I'd never felt so alone in my life, and I knew it would be a long time before I would ever truly consider doing something about it. Instead, I went upstairs and began painting the bedroom. I'd sleep downstairs on the sofa that had come with the place tonight while it dried. I had a week to get this place in some semblance of order before I returned to work. I was looking forward to being too busy to think.

Chapter 40

Giselle

"I'm going to need you to go to Egypt for six months," the director said.

I blinked at him, trying to process what he'd just said. A month ago, the idea of going to Egypt for half a year would have been a dream, but now I had things on my plate that made it a nightmare.

"I can't," I told him.

"Giselle, I need you on this."

"For what project?"

"We're doing an Egyptian sculpture exhibit there and I need someone to curate it.

"I'm not an Egyptian expert. Surely one of the other curators is more qualified."

"I considered Sandra. She certainly has more extensive knowledge of Egyptian art, but she's not as capable as you are when it comes to the overall process."

"You mean you can't use her to fill the boots of several different positions to save a dollar," I replied in a sour tone.

"What's up with you? Lately, you seem to balk at doing the slightest thing you deem beyond your responsibilities."

"And the issue with that is what? I was hired to do a job and I do it. In fact, I do it well. I shouldn't have to fill in the gaps you've left in your employment roster to boost your budget numbers to the board."

"I don't appreciate the insubordination," he growled.

"And I don't appreciate being used however you deem fit. I've been on several foreign trips to help further the presence of this museum, and I've never minded, but the extra effort has not been reflected in my salary, bonuses, or in the form of advancement."

"I shouldn't have to reward you just for doing your job!" he said indignantly.

"Yes, you should. That's what employment is all about! I do my job well, and I demonstrate my ability to excel. In return for that, I should be rewarded for my efforts."

"Well, be that as it may, we are on a tight budget. I can't afford to raise your profile or salary now."

"You've not raised anyone's salary or profile in five years. People are about to start walking, and you'll be left tending foreign exhibitions by yourself soon."

"Is that a threat?"

"No. It's a promise and I'm not going to Egypt. You can ask Sandra or go yourself, but I won't be available. Are we done here then?"

"For now, but this isn't our last conversation. I think you and I need to have a much longer discussion about your future here, Giselle."

"Ain't that the truth," I hissed, standing up and walking out.

I walked down the hall away from his office with my head high. Beneath my crisply pressed blouse, I was sweating, and my heart thudded loudly. I was the proverbial duck, calmly unruffled on the surface but paddling like mad beneath the waves. I'd never spoken to my boss in such a manner, but I'd had enough, and I was on my way out the door anyway. I just wasn't quite ready to tender my resignation. Another meeting like that and I might find it filled out on my behalf for me to sign.

I'd barely gotten settled back into my work when the phone rang. It was Helena. The gossip mill was already in full swing, and she'd heard about my little temper tantrum, for lack of a better word. I felt completely justified in what I said, mind you, but I probably could have delivered my message with a bit more composure.

"I heard that you yelled at the director," she said.

"I didn't yell at him. I just told him how I felt."

"What did he say?"

Helena didn't have to ask what I had said. She had a good idea already. I'd talked with her and Marie over lunch enough to know we all had the same thoughts. I also knew we weren't alone. Everything I said had been completely true. I'd only left out names. It wasn't my place to speak for other people.

"Not much. You know him. He muttered about a lack of money in the budget and got all red in the face at being spoken to in such a way. Same old bullshit as usual."

"He'll be raging all week now."

"Yeah. Sorry about that."

"Don't be. Someone needed to tell him what a huge pile of cow dung we think he is," she said with a low laugh. "Shit. I hear him coming down the hall. Gotta go."

She hung up without another word and I smiled knowingly. She was right about the raging. He'd be barking at everyone in an effort to reassert his dominance over us. I'd be the last on the list, though. He'd need to lick his wounds and feel like he was back on top before he came back around to me again. I felt some satisfaction in that.

I should have moved up to director long before now or at least to the assistant director position, which had been left vacant almost since I'd started work here—especially since he wouldn't let the director position go. He was doing a terrible job of it. That hadn't always been the case. Once upon a time, he was very much on top of things and well respected. Only after he'd gotten a late life divorce did he seem to change, taking his personal frustrations out on the staff and paying less attention to our needs.

He'd also begun to date a string of wretched women who demanded more of his time than he had to give, leaving his work to suffer. It put more responsibilities on his underlings, and we weren't receiving any acknowledgment through promotions or raises. To make matters worse, each time someone who wasn't absolutely essential left, he shifted their duties to existing employees. People, including me, were sick of having bits of former job positions farmed out to us as if they didn't take up additional time.

The fact was that minding the budget was the only part of his job he still did. He'd always been a stickler for watching the bottom line and continued that even as he ignored everything else. There was only so long you could chip away at one portion of the overall budget to feed the lacking parts before it all imploded. He crept closer to that every day.

Perhaps I shouldn't have barked at him like that, but I was tired, and it seemed like there was no respite lately. Graham and I had decided to stop seeing one another. He wanted more and I didn't. I was focused on opening my own gallery and didn't have time for a serious relationship. I missed having someone I could call when I felt lonely, but I wasn't in love with him, and honestly, I didn't see that ever changing.

Of course, I often second guessed myself. Perhaps just enjoying him being around was as good as it would ever get. Not everyone gets that fairytale romance they seek, and I might very well be one of those people. At one time, I would have said that Helena and Marie would be party girls forever, but they'd settled into relationships where they were happy and fulfilled. Was I still being too picky about what I thought a relationship would be?

Whether I was destined for true romance or not, I did know that now was not the time to pursue it. I was very close to getting the gallery I wanted. I'd put a bid on a building that was in a great location and required very little work other than cosmetics. With a bit of paint and new flooring, it could be up and running quickly. As soon as I had the go-ahead that it was mine, I'd be buried in getting it ready and lining up the artists I wanted for my opening.

Overall, I felt pretty good about how things were going. The job I'd been lucky to get and had once loved here at the museum was beginning to wear on me, but I expected to be out of it by the time things went well and truly south. I'd not intended to have today's little outburst, but the thought of putting my plans on hold for six months while I toiled away in Egypt for no personal gain had made me a bit unhinged.

I worked until about six and then left for the day, passing Tucker as he came in for the evening. He smiled at me and gave me a wink.

"Feeling feisty today, were you?" he asked.

"I swear, there's not one single little thing that remains untold in this museum, is there?"

"I'm sure there is, but it's rare. Is it true you took a swing at him?"

"Come on," I said, laughing.

"Now you know it's not as exciting if you just got into a bit of a pissing match. There has to be blows exchanged."

"Are they really saying that?" I asked incredulously.

"Not yet," he said, grinning.

"Well, if you're going to start a rumor, tell them that I kicked him right in the ass with my high heels. I want them to have a good image to go with their tale," I teased.

"Consider it done," he laughed. "I'll see you in the morning. I have a staff meeting after the night shift."

"That's a very long night."

"Yep. It's six to six, and then there's a seven o'clock roundup. I'm off tomorrow, though."

"Big plans?"

"Only if you consider sleeping all day a big plan."

"I don't know if it's a big plan, but it sure sounds good. Give my love to Maeve and the kids."

"I will," he said, walking down the hall as I headed for the exit. I heard him still chuckling to himself as he turned the corner.

On the way home for Chinese takeout, I stopped and grabbed wine from a nearby bodega. After today's nonsense, I could use a chill night to just regroup. I took it home and sat at my small kitchen table for two. I rarely saw a guest these days, and I opened my food to take a few bites before uncorking the wine.

I'd barely settled into my meal when my phone buzzed. I glanced over at it lying beside me on the table and saw that it was an unknown number. Curious, I answered.

"Miss Martin?" a woman said from the other end.

"Yes?" I replied.

"This is Terri Hanover with Vine and Brown. I'm sorry to call so late, but I thought you'd want to know immediately. My client has decided to accept your offer on their property."

I didn't respond right away. I had expected them to take bids through the rest of the week and not to have news until after that.

"Miss Martin?" she prompted.

I suddenly realized I was smiling into the void rather than responding. "Oh. Yes. This is great news."

"I thought you'd be pleased. Can you come by the office tomorrow so we can firm up the sale and get the paperwork moving?"

"Yes, absolutely. What's a good time?"

"I'll be in from eight until noon and then again after three until about six."

"I'll be there at eight!" I told her.

"Fantastic. I'll have a bagel, coffee, and some papers waiting for you."

"That sounds perfect. Thank you so much for everything! Goodbye!"

I hung up the phone and just sat there for a moment, smiling happily. It was finally happening! Was I ready? Yes. I was ready. Of course, I was ready. Wasn't I?

The truth was that I was ready, but I was also scared to death. I knew that sooner or later I would nail down the property I needed for the gallery, but I hadn't expected it to be so soon. Now, I had no choice but to get the ball rolling.

Chapter 41

Peter

It had taken weeks to get the flat finished. Every room seemed to have issues I'd not expected and had to be repaired before I could make other renovations. It slowed the overall process, but I couldn't deny that I was okay with it keeping me busier than expected. Though, I was proud of all I'd accomplished when I was done.

The outside would need a bit more work, but someone with a higher skill level than me would need to be employed, and I wasn't in a huge hurry to tackle it. I only had a weekend left to finish unpacking and get my things together for the first day of classes.

Somehow, I knew this would be the hardest part of my move. Though I'd left most of Jillian's things with Ariana to handle as she saw fit, I'd still managed to keep more than I realized. I found several boxes that contained things that reminded me of her.

I'd made the mistake of not marking all the boxes and mixing the contents, so I constantly ran across Jillian things as I tried to sort and separate everything to go into different rooms. I laughed. This is why she'd helped me pack my old place. She'd caught me tossing things in different boxes without rhyme or reason. When she was done, every box was organized and marked for which room it needed to go to for unpacking.

Of course, I'd done the packing, but it had been under her careful direction. It made getting things out of the boxes and into place so much quicker. Left to my own devices, I'd spend twice as long unpacking half as much. It would be comical if I weren't so frustrated with myself for not having learned the lessons she taught me.

I lifted a silk scarf to my nose and sniffed it. I could still smell her scent on it, but it was already fading. Each time I found one of her things, I put it in a nearby box that I'd begun to fill with her stuff. When I was done, I discovered I had nearly five mid-size boxes of her things. I put them in the small cubbyhole beneath the stairs and pushed them toward the back until I could bear to look at them again.

I hung my clothes in the wardrobe in my bedroom and placed a single photo on my dresser. It was the photo of her and I on the beach. She had her head back laughing and I was smiling broadly. It was the only way I wanted to remember her now.

Looking around the flat, I decided it was in pretty decent order. I'd need to get some more things for the kitchen and some additional decor. I'd probably replace the shabby furniture that had come with the place at some point, but for now, I was content with having a couple of throws tossed over it to dress it up a bit. It wasn't as if I intended to have much, if any, company.

Satisfied that the place was livable, I left to retrieve some food for the fridge. It felt so strange being out in the grocery store alone. While Jillian was sick, I had groceries delivered and only ducked out for the odd thing I'd forgotten to order or hadn't been sent for lack of stock. Before that, we'd always gone together, and she'd picked out most of the food with occasional input from me on preferences or cravings.

Without Jillian's special dietary needs to consider, I didn't feel like particularly healthy eating right now. I'd get back to eating healthier foods, but today, my shopping consisted of microwavable meals, pizza, coffee, and beer. I had wine at the flat I'd brought from the house. Ariana didn't drink, so I saw no need to leave it for her.

Back at home, I put the pizza in the oven and the beer in the fridge. I set a timer on my phone so I didn't forget my food and grabbed a bottle of Merlot before realizing I hadn't packed a corkscrew despite having had several at the house. I grumbled and fished out a cheap sangria with a mushroom-topped cork. I could wiggle it out without a corkscrew. I knew there were other ways to get a corkscrew out, but I couldn't be bothered to look them up.

Fortunately, I remembered to pack wine glasses. There'd been a box of them that had never been opened. They were a gift from Charlotte to use on special occasions. I guess being widowed and moving back into a cheap apartment alone was close enough. I filled one with some of the sangria and checked on my pizza. It was almost done, and I noted that I didn't have a pizza cutter or oven mitt either.

"Really?" I said out loud. "You are the worst packer ever."

I grabbed one of the tea towels I'd unpacked to use as a potholder and used a butcher knife to cut the pizza into quarters. I put two on my plate and took it to the living room to eat in front of the small television I remembered to bring. I'd purposely left some of the things for Ariana, but there was a lot I'd simply forgotten in my despair.

There were some things that I realized either Ariana or Charlotte had packed for me, knowing that I'd need them because I knew I didn't bring them. I was grateful to them for caring for me as much as possible. They'd packed the tea towels, plates, and most of the kitchen stuff I hadn't even considered. I folded one of the large slices of pizza in half and took a bite before sitting it back down and wiping my fingers on the paper towel I'd remembered to buy at the store.

I turned on the television and found a movie to stream while I relaxed for a bit. It was an older crime caper that I'd not seen before. It sounded like exactly what I needed. Something that was mostly action and didn't get too blogged down in the plot. Reaching for my briefcase nearby, I pulled out a pad of paper and a pen to start a list of things I'd need to get for the flat, adding to it here and there as I thought of things while eating my dinner and sipping the far too sweet sangria.

With most of what I could do around the flat completed for now, I finished my meal and the movie, then moved on to my lesson plans for school. I was grateful to start with a fresh semester instead of trying to take over my classes after someone else had already been teaching them for months in my absence.

I worked into the late hours until I was too tired to hold my eyes open and then I went to bed, hopeful that I could sleep. I was grateful when I dropped off right away, but it didn't last. I awoke at around three a.m., a scream caught in my throat from some horrible nightmare I was already beginning to erase from my mind.

I thought about getting up but decided that I would only regret the lack of sleep tomorrow. Instead, I lay back down and tried again. I tossed and turned for what felt like hours, but eventually dozed back off. This time, my sleep was uneventful. I awoke several times but was able to get back to sleep without too much delay.

Still, when I woke up the following morning, I felt exhausted. I suppose that would be a constant state for me for a while yet. I'd done a lot of work in the past week getting this place together and my emotional state was incredibly tiring in an unexpected physical sense. But all I could do was put one foot in front of the other and keep moving forward.

As the weeks ahead progressed, it seemed like things would never get any better. I thought of Jillian all the time and I missed her terribly. I dreamed about her and often thought I heard her voice in crowds. I always looked for her in those moments, even though I knew she wasn't, couldn't, be there.

Gradually, I began to find my feet again. I wasn't over Jillian. I doubt I ever really would be. I put our photo away. I couldn't bear looking at her face every morning when I woke up and every night before I went to bed. She was gone, and I had to stop dwelling on my life with her. That life was over, and I'd have to start a new one.

I eventually did the unthinkable. I met a woman, Katie, a member of the administrative staff at the university. She was kind and attractive. Nothing about her reminded me of Jillian. Katie was petite and curvy with shoulder length, shaggy blonde hair, and big green eyes. She seemed like a woman who didn't spend much time worrying about where a relationship was headed and instead seemed content to just go out and have some fun.

So, I asked her out. I thought it was just what I needed. Perhaps I would even take her home with me at the end of the night if it seemed she was willing. I made reservations at a little sushi bar I loved without asking and found it a mistake.

She didn't live far from me, so I walked to get her, and then we strolled to the restaurant. The chat was light and enjoyable. She'd worn a fitted dress that accented her curves and revealed a great deal of what I can only describe as fantastic cleavage. Everything seemed off to a good start until we arrived at our destination.

"Sushi?" she said, frowning at the sign out front.

"Yes. You don't like it?"

"No."

"That's okay. They have other food. You don't have to have the sushi."

"No. I can't go in there," she bleated.

"Why?" I asked, confused.

"I'm allergic to shellfish. I'll swell up and stop breathing just being around it."

"Oh, God. I'm so sorry. I didn't know. No problem. We'll find someplace else to eat."

"Yes. Please," she said, seeming to calm down.

Every place we went was rammed. We ended up eating at a little bistro that only had sandwiches and crisps. They didn't even serve alcohol. Some women would have found the little mishap funny or charming, but Katie didn't seem to be one of them. She picked at her food and barely made conversation.

"I'm so sorry about the restaurant. I should have asked you first. It's been a while since I've dated."

"Yes. I heard that your wife died," she said bluntly. "Cancer, I heard. How awful."

"It was, but let's not talk about that," I said, trying my best to salvage this date.

"Why? Did you not love her?"

"What? Of course, I did. Why would you ask that?"

"I don't know. I heard that you weren't married that long before she got sick. I'd think something like that would kill the romance right off the bat." She shrugged dismissively.

I was shocked by how glib she was being about something that had hurt me so deeply. How had I missed that she was an insensitive person? Her behavior took me right back to another woman who'd caused a stink over a restaurant. I just couldn't do this again. Without thinking, I stood up from the table and tossed some money down onto it.

"Your house isn't far from here. I'll let you get yourself back there."

"Are you fucking kidding me?"

"No. I have to go," I said, turning and leaving the restaurant.

I was fuming all the way home. Thankfully, she worked in a building I didn't frequent very often, so I wouldn't have to see much of her in the future. So much for attempting to get back out there. Instead, I went home, sat down with a beer and cried.

Chapter 42

Giselle

I was surprised by how fast things began to move once I took possession of the building for my art gallery. Despite breaking things off with Graham, he'd been very helpful in handling a few unanticipated problems at the gallery. I'd insisted on paying him, but he'd refused to charge me more than a nominal amount for materials.

Within the span of two months, I'd closed on the property, completed the required repairs and anticipated improvements, and began setting up display areas. The gallery signage arrived this week and will be installed tomorrow.

On the backend, I'd been working on lining up artists and creating a marketing campaign and grand opening to guarantee a full house. Though the gallery was much smaller than what I was used to in the museum, it had enough space to house three separate areas. One would be view-only artwork on loan from local collectors. Another would showcase an individual or small group of similar artwork intended for purchase.

The third would be strictly a sales floor where local artists would sell their work on consignment. Work would be rotated as items sold or reached their agreed-upon pull date. Though I'd personally review work that I thought fit for the market, there were bound to be some works that didn't hit right and had to be returned without sale.

In addition to these areas, there would be a limited amount of art purchased by the gallery for resale. This would include original paintings, sculptures, and high-end prints. I wanted the art in my gallery to be of great quality but affordable to everyone interested. So many of the galleries in the city were set up to cater only to the rich. I also wanted to provide art that the average person could afford.

This all played into my desire to promote local artists, who were often very talented but sold their paintings for far less due to lacking an outlet willing to give them a chance. The gallery was designed to bring in people of many tastes and means. I only hoped I could succeed at it. Especially since I'd already resigned from my position at the museum, this would now be my only means of income.

I hadn't planned on giving up my position just yet. I intended to take a vacation to oversee the gallery's opening and then give it a chance to get on its feet and begin producing income before I left my job. Instead, I'd been called to the director's office shortly after our little spat.

"I've thought a lot about what you said about your position here, and while I understand your concerns, I cannot currently do anything to address them to your satisfaction. What I need from you is a bit of flexibility in your position until I can. I am sending you to Egypt."

I started to object, but he raised his hand to stop me.

"I don't want to hear about why you can't go or how it isn't your place. I've already heard your complaints. Now, I need you to do as you are asked—no, do as you are told and make arrangements to take care of the Egyptian exhibit for this museum."

I bit my lip, trying to choose my words carefully. In the end, I was just done with this whole argument. "I can't go to Egypt because I'm turning in my notice. I won't be available. You'll have my signed resignation on your desk within the hour."

I stood to walk out, and he stopped me, his brow creased with anxiety. "You can't resign so suddenly. I'll need time to replace you."

"I'm only required to give you two weeks and you have other curators. We both know that you will probably see this as yet another opportunity to cut costs by making them do extra work instead of replacing me. So, I guess you better decide how you want to dole out the work or do it yourself. I'll finish what I can on current projects and leave you a file with details on anything left pending with my departure."

This time, I did walk out the door. My heart hammered loudly, but I felt good about it. Was I scared? Of course. But I was also thrilled that I would be out of the rotten climate of this museum soon and could focus on making my gallery a success. If careful, I still had money saved in the bank and could float my bills for up to a year. I had time to accomplish my goals.

Soon, more of the staff were leaving the museum. Helena resigned from her position to pursue a second degree. Marie was still shacked up with her graffiti artist, who was becoming quite well-known in the city. Marie had resigned from the museum and now functioned as his manager, sorting out all the details of his upcoming work and making sure he didn't get into any bother with unsolicited or inappropriate work.

In fact, I'd commissioned work from him for my art gallery. I was on the end of a row of buildings, and he'd created a large collage of popular local artists mixed in with their more famous counterparts. It turned out quite well and was eye-catching to traffic passing by. I'd already had a few patrons who mentioned that it had drawn them in, so it was money well spent.

Initially, I didn't have the money to hire employees, but as my collection grew, I required security. I turned to Tucker for a recommendation as I knew he was familiar with many of the other security guards at area galleries and museums.

"I'm hurt that you'd ask me to refer someone," he said over the phone.

"I don't understand. Why?" I replied, confused.

"You don't seem to have even considered me in your search for a quality security guard."

"Oh!" I replied, comprehending what he was getting at. "You were my first thought, but we both know I can't afford you."

"Try me. What are you offering?"

I told him what I could afford to pay, and he laughed. I smiled at my phone. I knew that would be his reaction.

"You're right. You can't afford me, but I'll tell you what. I'm getting too old for this big old museum and dealing with this bunch of wild animals I have to keep up with over here. If you throw in an extra week's vacation and the occasional free lunch, I think we can come to terms."

"Tucker, I appreciate your willingness to come with me, but I don't want to sell you short. I can't afford to pay for health insurance or any real benefits like you're used to."

"I don't need insurance. Maeve still works, too, and I'm covered under her policy. She's tired of me being gone all hours of the night. You hire me for the day shift, and I'll find you a couple solid youngsters to trade out the night shift and weekends for basic security wages. I make a little less money but get a lot more loving at home."

I laughed at this but knew I couldn't do better than having Tucker watching my gallery for me. I took the deal.

"Welcome aboard, Tucker. When can you start?"

"You know the drill. I gotta give these ass hats my two weeks' notice before I go, and then I'm all yours. I can send some guys your way to fill any gaps you have in the meantime and keep my eye on them from afar if you add that good coffee to my benefits."

"You drive a hell of a deal, Tucker," I said. "I'll take it."

"Fantastic. I'm off tomorrow. I'll come by and we can sort out the details."

"I'll be here and thank you so much, Tucker. Knowing this place will be in such great hands is a relief."

"You know it," he replied, ending the call.

I lay my phone on the counter and smiled. I liked that he was joining me, not only because I knew I could trust him but also because I knew the director would be furious when he learned I'd stolen him.

All in all, the gallery was doing well. It was doing far better than I'd expected. I wasn't making any real money, but I was earning enough to pay the bills without digging too deeply into my savings. I felt good about that, especially since most businesses spent years in the red before turning a profit. I wasn't in the black yet, but I was right there on the edge of it and inching closer by the day.

I hadn't been certain when I'd decided to do this if I could be successful at it, especially in a city like New York where there were so many galleries. My advantage was that I sold more for less. While many of the galleries here relied on selling high-dollar items that might take months waiting for a buyer, I sold things almost daily. I had a steady stream of ordinary people looking for one-of-a-kind artwork that didn't break the bank and I was delivering it to them.

They didn't care if the lovely abstract they thought would be perfect for their living room was painted by Picasso or Paul Lasso. They loved that it suited their space, was original art, and was affordable. And the people who came into their homes and saw it wanted one too, which only increased Paul Lasso's profile and padded his wallet.

I knew many gallery owners would thumb their noses at someone who catered to clientèle and artists like the ones I sought, but that was the beauty of it. No one in the area around me was doing what I was. They were selling cheap prints, or they were selling priceless art. I was selling art to folks on a budget.

I quickly moved several artists up in the world by putting their art on living room walls and boutique easels for people to see and enjoy instead of languishing at art shows attended by snobs who couldn't be seen buying art by some nobody. But something unexpected had also happened that even I hadn't considered.

As the art in my gallery became more popular, some of the wealthier art collectors in town began to take notice. Those who didn't feel they needed to check some box with a collectible name were coming in and buying pieces they couldn't get anywhere else. They were commissioning some of the artists I promoted directly.

I was proud of all I was accomplishing. I'd worked hard for this. Soon, I'd have to expand my reach and pull in more artists from further away to maintain the diversity I liked to be present in my gallery. There was always more to do and more to share with the world as far as I was concerned.

If I had any complaints about my life, it was that I was incredibly lonely. I'd been tempted to give Graham another shot at things, but nothing had changed about my feelings for him. I didn't want to give him any false hope. I'd love to have someone in my life who really sparked my enthusiasm, but it seemed like it just might not happen for me. The last time it had was still Peter, and I'd had to let that go.

Feeling a bit down in the dumps despite the excitement of everything going on around me, I decided to call it a night and head to bed. Perhaps a good night's sleep would help me feel more energized for the coming weeks. I'd be busy and wouldn't have time to consider being lonely soon.

Chapter 43

Peter

It had taken me nearly a year after Jillian's death to decide to feel like a halfway normal person again. I'd not been on a date since the disaster with my colleague. I'd rather be alone than suffer the awkwardness I'd experienced with her. Though I knew that had been more about her crassness than anything I'd done, I could have handled it better. I was just in no place to do anything but react. I didn't want to find myself in that place again.

However, the loneliness remained. I'd just learned to live with it. I considered the two of us to be old acquaintances now. I thought nothing of eating dinner alone, watching movies alone, or even attending events without a plus one. People made exceptions for you when you were a widower. They didn't ask why you hadn't brought anyone or try to fix you up at every opportunity.

But now, I'd had time to adjust, and those who cared about me were beginning to encourage me to find someone again. I continued to push back. "It's too soon" was my go-to, but I knew they were probably right. Even Jillian had told me she didn't want me to be lonely. It seemed easy in practice but much harder to do when faced with asking someone out, showing up, and managing not to cry during dinner because the waiter suggested a dessert that used to be your wife's favorite.

Then I met Barbara. She was a tall, slender redhead with a wicked smile and an art collection that made me drool. I attended a garden party at her home to celebrate her birthday. Though I didn't attend alone, I didn't have a date. Instead, I'd gone with a friend from work whose husband was deployed. She rightly assumed that I wouldn't hit on her and needed to get out of the house and out of my head.

Barbara's date had cancelled on her at the last minute, citing a problem at home he had to deal with. A follow-up phone call from his wife, who had hit redial, led Barbara to cancel their relationship, as she had no idea he was married. Despite her troubles, she was a perfect host, with no indication she was dismayed about the situation. I only learned about it when she'd discovered me eating cake in a quiet corner away from the crowd.

"Not enjoying my party?" she'd asked, approaching me with a glass of wine in one hand and the half-empty bottle in the other.

"I am. I have cake," I said, instantly realizing how stupid that sounded.

"I can see that, but why are you eating it in a corner by yourself."

"I just needed a moment," I replied. "It's a lovely party, though."

She smiled and sat down beside me, taking a slow sip of her wine. I started to ask her why she was hiding in a corner of her garden, but she decided to tell me before I could.

"I guess I did too. I thought no one would be back here," she admitted.

"I'm sorry. I can leave and let you be alone with your wine if you'd like," I said, grinning.

She raised an eyebrow in my direction, likely assessing whether I was taking a dig at her drinking or trying to be funny. She grinned too.

"No date?" she asked.

"Yes and no. I came with a married colleague, but she got lost in the crowd somewhere."

"Ugh. Never date married people!" she exclaimed, frowning.

"It's not really a date. She just didn't want to come alone. Her husband is deployed."

"So, she conned you into being her escort for my party and then abandoned you here. Do you even know anyone?"

"I do now," I told her, flashing her my most winning smile.

"Well, I suppose if we're going to hide here on this bench together, we should introduce ourselves. I'm Barbara Holden. Today is my 40th birthday and my date stood me up to stay home with his wife."

"Ah, thus the advice not to date married people. Okay. My name is Peter Dockery. It is well beyond my 40th birthday and my date has dumped me to chat with friends. I think she's hoping I'll meet a nice girl while I'm here."

"Single then?" she said, noticing me more now.

"Yes."

"No wife at all? Not separated. Not at home with the kids? Not plotting revenge after a bitter divorce?"

"No wife. No kids. No plotting. I was married, but now I'm widowed."

She frowned at this. "I'm sorry. Look at me putting my whole foot in my mouth."

"It's okay. You didn't know."

She was quiet for a moment, sipping her drink while she considered this. She noted my empty sparkling cider cup sitting nearby.

"Non-drinker?" she asked, nodding toward it.

"Not at all. They handed me that and cake, so I took it."

"Shall I replenish it with something with more potent grapes?"

"Yes, please," I told her, holding my cup up toward her. She filled it with white wine and topped up her own glass before sitting the empty bottle by the bench.

"Cheers," she said, holding her glass up for a toast. I mock-clinked my small plastic cup to hers and took a sip of my wine. It was quite nice.

"Aren't we a pair then. You're widowed and I am an idiot."

"I doubt that," I replied, not really knowing what else to say. Her judgment might be questionable if she was dating a married man, but it hardly made her an idiot.

"No. I am. I saw the signs and ignored them. He owns an international hotel chain, so when he wasn't available for days on end, it was plausible that he was away on business somewhere. He didn't answer calls at night but said it was because he liked being free of work calls. And we never, ever, went to his house."

"Okay. Maybe you are an idiot," I teased.

She looked at me with a scowl and then started laughing. I joined her, and we dropped the subject altogether. Instead, we talked about what we each did. She owned several clothing boutiques and a beauty salon, which explained her impeccable appearance.

"How about we get some more wine?" she offered after an extended chat.

"Sure. I'm sure there are folks here wondering where the hostess is by now anyway."

"True. I'll make a sweep through and then we can hide from them some more," she said cheerfully.

"Fine by me. I never was one for large crowds."

It was a great start to a promising relationship, but within weeks, it had quickly soured. Though Barbara was everything a man could ask for in a woman, she had one fatal flaw—at least where I was concerned. We'd only been dating a few weeks when she was ready to go all in. She was talking about our futures together, perhaps living together or getting married.

"Barbara, I'm just not ready for any of that," I told her.

"Why? Aren't you happy with me?" she asked, confused by my reluctance.

"That's not the case at all. I love being with you, but I'm just not ready to get married again."

"We don't have to marry. We could live together," she said hopefully.

"I'm just not ready for that either."

"Do you think you'll ever be ready?" she asked, the testy edge to her voice very noticeable.

"I don't know. Maybe. Maybe not. I'd just like to take our time and see where things take us."

"I see," she'd said, ending the conversation.

It was the first of several similar exchanges. One of which included her basically shaming me for putting her off when she wanted kids.

"I'm not getting younger and if we want to have children, we'll find ourselves out of time in a few years. Do you really want to be raising children in your sixties?"

"Children? Are you serious right now? Don't you think it is way too early to talk about kids?" I gasped.

"Are you not listening to me. I just turned forty. I don't know how much longer I have before I lose that possibility and your sperm count is going to start dropping like a stone if it hasn't already."

"Dear God, Barbara. I don't even want to be having this conversation. If you fear losing a chance to have kids, freeze some eggs, but don't rush me into fatherhood."

"I don't want to freeze eggs and risk having to have a surrogate, potentially even a different father, if you can't fertilize them," she half shrieked at me.

It was then that I saw it—a certain madness in her eyes. Barbara wasn't a bad person, but she was desperate. She'd never been married, which should have been a warning to me. She'd talked to me about her previous relationships; they'd been failure after failure, some her fault and some not. Whatever the reason she'd remained unmarried, it was clear that crossing that line into her forties had really shaken her.

"Listen, Barbara. I understand where you're coming from. I do. But I'm not ready to get married again and I don't even know if I want kids. If I change my mind and decide I'm willing to raise them when I'm still in my sixties, then I'll do that. If I have to adopt them or raise stepchildren because I married someone who already has children, then I'll do that."

"Well, that just doesn't work for me," she said, sullen.

"I'm sorry, Barbara. Truly, I am. Let's take some time apart to sort out our heads and what we truly want."

"I don't need time apart. I know what I want! You're the one who's unwilling to compromise."

"You aren't asking me to compromise, Barbara. You're asking me to commit to getting married and having children when I'm not sure if I want to do either. We've barely had time to get to know one another as well as we should before getting married."

"You said you proposed to your former wife only three months after meeting her!" she growled.

"I did. I loved her and I wanted to marry her."

"And you don't love me?" she said.

"I've never said I did," I said, feeling horrible about being so cold to her.

She began crying and I wanted to hold her, tell her I was sorry. I knew it was a mistake to do so, no matter how bad this felt. Instead, I turned and walked away.

I returned home in a state of complete frustration. I hadn't wanted things to go that way, but she was being unreasonable, and we'd been headed toward a breakup for some time. Up until today, I thought it was me, that I was the problem. I felt like I was holding back and not letting myself get too close to Barbara because I feared falling in love and losing her as I had Jillian.

Now, I knew the truth was I'd picked up on how rushed things felt. I hoped Barbara would find what she was looking for, but I couldn't give her what she wanted. I might not be able to give it to anyone, but I certainly couldn't so soon into the relationship.

Back at home, I did something I hadn't done in a very long time. I opened the box that held my sculpting tools and went out to fetch some new clay. I hadn't created anything since before Jillian and I met. Perhaps it was time to spend some time alone with my craft.

Chapter 44

Giselle

I stepped off the plane in Paris, ready to tackle the world. I'd been open for nearly five years and was doing a nice business for myself and several local artists. I was so proud to say that I'd been able to give some of them the boost they needed to be seen and appreciated. Now, it was time to expand my horizons beyond the local talent.

While working for the museum in Paris, I came across several talented artists whose work I was interested in buying for resale. I'd contacted a gallery owner I'd met previously and asked her if she could set up a showing with some of them. She suggested that she might include some artists she felt worthy of viewing, and I accepted her offer.

"Giselle! It is so lovely to see you again!" she said as she swept in from the back of her gallery.

"It's nice to see you too, Mia. It's been far too long."

"It certainly has. When did you get in?"

"Yesterday morning."

"Oh, good. I'm glad you've had time to sleep off a bit of the jet lag."

"I did. It's such a long flight," I admitted.

"Yes, but why are you here so early? The showing isn't until six."

"I know. I just wanted to stop in while I was nearby and see if things were coming along okay."

"Splendidly. We're working on getting it all properly displayed in the private showing room and the artists will be here for you to meet."

"Perfect. I won't hold you up then. I'll see you at six."

"Yes. Wonderful." She escorted me back out the door.

I knew I'd caught her off guard. No one wanted a potential buyer turning up before the art to be presented was displayed perfectly to their satisfaction. I hadn't really been thinking when I'd decided to step inside to say hello before the showing. I headed back toward my hotel, intending to nap before the event. Though I'd slept off some jet lag last night, I'd been up early today and still felt slightly tired. I wanted to be fresh for the viewing.

Back at the hotel, I stripped down and climbed beneath the sheets after setting an alarm so I didn't oversleep. A smile crossed my face as I thought about the last time I'd overslept in Paris and what it had led to. There was Peter again, creeping back into my thoughts. Then again, how could I be in Paris and not think of him? I wondered if I should attempt to contact him again but decided against it.

Instead, I rolled over and settled down into the covers. I hadn't realized how tired I was until my head hit the pillow. I was out cold until my alarm went off nearly two hours later. I climbed out of bed feeling ready to tackle the world.

I'd already laid out my outfit for the evening, forgoing a skirt or dress in favor of what I liked to think of as a power suit. It was a pair of tailored black pants with wide legs and a matching pea coat style jacket. I paired it with a bold red shirt and black and red wide-heeled shoes. I completed my ensemble with my hair pinned in a classic bun at the nape of my neck and simple makeup.

I took a look in the mirror one last time. This was it. It was important to me that I looked like a successful gallery owner who could give the artists I chose what they deserved in terms of exposure and profit. I wanted to project an image that said I was professional, trustworthy, and capable of delivering on my promises. I had developed a keen eye for art, and I needed the artists I chose to promote to believe in me just as much as I believed in them.

Stepping into the crisp Paris evening, I grabbed a cab back to the gallery. I'd walked it earlier but didn't want to arrive looking rumpled. It was in one of those places that wasn't too far away but was just far enough to be a bit of a hike. I watched the lights flash by as we drove through Paris. Even after all this time, I loved this city. Long ago, I decided it wasn't the place for me to live, but I always enjoyed coming back here again.

"Here we go," the cab driver said as he pulled up to the front of the gallery.

I paid him and stepped out, all smiles as I looked over the gallery in front of me. It was lit up on the outside and people were milling about, sipping glasses of champagne and looking over art displayed on the other side of the large plate glass windows. I stood straight and went inside, looking for the gallery owner. She spotted me first.

"Ah, Giselle! There you are. You look positively radiant. Are you ready to meet some artists and spend some money?"

"I certainly am, Mia. Show me what you've got," I replied.

"Okay, we'll start with the paintings and then we'll move to the sculptures. I'll spare you the awkwardness of meeting any artists that don't suit your fancy and just introduce you to the ones you want to meet with."

"That sounds great. Let's go.

Mia and I walked through the empty display room to review the work she had to present. Some of it seemed uninspired despite the skilled techniques employed by the artist. However, there were several pieces of work I found genuinely captivating.

"Can I see more from these three artists? Are these their only pieces?" I asked.

"Oh, no. They have more," she said, motioning toward two employees nearby.

She spoke to them, and they immediately went to work. One began moving rejected work off easels, and the other disappeared into an adjacent room. He returned in a moment carrying two more paintings, set them up on one set of easels, and then left again, followed by the other employee. While Mia and I began looking at the first artist's additional work, they set up the pieces they brought back on the other easels.

"Yes, these three are great. I want to talk with them and discuss prices on their work."

"Perfect," she said, motioning again toward one of the employees. He disappeared and returned with three artists, two men, and an impossibly tiny woman.

After introductions, I spoke privately with Mia and each artist to propose purchase terms for the paintings I selected. I would commission more if they sold well, but I'd start with just these. With my selections here secured, we moved on to the sculptures.

"I'm truly impressed by some of these," I said as I looked through the sculptures she'd arranged in a separate viewing area. However, I didn't find anything that jumped out at me. They were good, but I didn't see what I was looking for. Then, I spotted a series of sculptures that grabbed my attention.

"These are fantastic," I said, looking over the three clay busts in a semi-circle. They seemed to capture a woman as she turned her head to one side and upwards. I wondered what she was looking at. Was she looking up to the sky? The expression on her face told me it was more than that.

"Yes. They're by a new artist. I saw them at a smaller display and encouraged him to let me present them tonight. Aren't they divine?"

"They are and they seem so familiar."

"Do they? I've not seen any like them," she said, puzzling at them. "Do you think he's copied someone?"

I could tell she was upset that she might have suggested an artist who had merely stolen someone else's idea and she had missed it. As gallery owners, it was our job to thoroughly research any art we selected for presentation or purchase so we didn't find ourselves in a sticky situation.

"Oh no, not at all. It's not that the art itself looks familiar. It's more like the woman he used as his model is someone I know or have seen. I would like to know who he used as his muse for this piece.

"We'll bring him in and ask him about that. Are there any others you'd like to discuss?"

"No. I'm just not feeling it with any of the others. They are well done and the marble one is very well crafted, but they just don't feel like anything special to me. I'm sorry."

"That's fine. You win some and you lose some, right?"

"True," I acknowledged, still mesmerized by the sculptures that had caught my eye.

I continued looking over them as Mia went to speak to one of the employees. He disappeared and she returned with two glasses of champagne, handing me one before taking a sip from the other.

"I have some other pieces I didn't select if you'd like to review them. Everyone has different tastes, and you may see something more there. I have the alternates displayed throughout the gallery for a secondary showing once we've concluded our business, but I'll gladly give you first pick.

"That would be lovely. You never know," I told her. "Do you have any more pieces by this artist?

"No. From what I understand, he isn't a full-time artist. These were only shown before because a friend convinced him to put them out at an acquaintance's art show to fill in a hole left by a fickle artist."

"That's a shame. These are so lovely. If all of his work is like this, I'd likely buy it too."

"I'm surprised. I wasn't sure if I should place these as he's not really looking for representation, but he did express an interest in having them seen. Honestly, I'm not even sure he will go through with the sale. They seemed rather personal to him."

"So, you don't think he'll want to give them up?" I asked, curious as to why she would show pieces that weren't procurable.

"Perhaps I shouldn't have, but I was doing a favor for a friend who really felt that if he got a boost in his work if he saw that someone like yourself found it appealing, it might encourage him to do more. It would seem that he's had it tough for the last few years and has become a bit of a loner. I agreed. They are quite good, and I figured it couldn't hurt for you to see them and maybe talk to him."

"Then you think he might be interested in selling them after all?"

"You can ask. Here he comes now," she said, "Giselle Martin, this is—" she began to say, but I finished her sentence for her.

"Professor Peter Dockery"

I stood with a look of shock on my face, rivaled only by the one displayed by Peter.

"You know each other?" she asked.

"You could say that," Peter said, a broad smile replacing the momentary surprise of being face-to-face with me.

"I'm sorry. I feel like I've missed something here," Mia said, looking confused.

"Peter and I have met before. Would you mind if we had a moment to speak privately?"

"Oh, of course. But I'm supposed to be present during negotiations for art through the gallery," she half stammered.

"Not a problem. The negotiations can wait a moment," I told her. "I'll find you when we're ready.

She nodded silently and disappeared, waving for her two employees to follow. For the first time in years, I found myself standing face to face with Peter again; for the first time ever, I wasn't sure how I felt about that.

Chapter 45

Peter

"Giselle, what are you doing here?" I asked immediately.

"I'm buying art for my gallery," she told me. "What are you doing here?"

"I have no idea. My friend told me I should show this art at an earlier art show and then he convinced me to let Mia show it to some gallery owner coming in from New York, but they never gave me a name. I had no idea it was you. When did you open a gallery?" I said, genuinely happy to see her.

About five years ago now, I guess. Peter, these pieces are beautiful. I love how they seem to move as you walk past them, as if she's looking up at something."

"That's exactly what she is doing. She's looking up at me," I replied softly.

"Jillian?" she asked.

I was surprised she could still remember my wife's name after all this time. Even more impressive that she couldn't recognize herself in another form. I smiled and reached for her, half expecting her to flinch, but she didn't. I cupped her chin lightly with my fingers, moving her head slowly sideways and upwards to match the statue's pose.

"She's you," I said softly.

"No way. No, she isn't," she said, pulling away and turning to look again at the series of busts I'd made.

"She is. I created her from my memories of you. Not a perfect likeness, but I like to think it's close," I told her, looking toward the busts now that I had the live model in front of me. "It's from the day I got on the plane and saw you sitting there. You turned to look up at me. This is that moment."

I watched as she poured over them again, slowly taking in the details. "Do you mind if I touch them?"

"Of course not," I replied, noting that there was a bit more of a cordial nature to her voice now. If I had never fully realized that I had hurt Giselle, I was certainly realizing it now. She studied the likeness of herself with the cool gaze of an art professional, much as Mia had looked at them when I brought them in for her scrutiny.

When she was done, she turned back to me and nodded her approval, though she said nothing about the fact that they were based on her. It was as if she didn't want to really acknowledge the work's origin, and how could I blame her? "They are incredible. I'd like to buy them. Are there more?"

"More? Yes, a few. Not of you, though."

Once again, she made no comment about any of my work being about her or not about her. She could have been commenting on statues of anyone, even someone who didn't exist. She was all business as she spoke.

"I'd like to see all of your work. Could we perhaps do that tonight? I'm leaving tomorrow."

"Of course," I said, keeping my tone professional to match hers.

"Are you available after the showing?"

"I am," I said. Something told me that the way I felt right now was how Giselle must have felt that day at lunch when I was so cold to her. I also knew she wasn't doing it to get even with me. She was practicing self-preservation, and I didn't blame her one bit.

"Perfect. Then, if you can bear with me, I will tie up the rest of my business here and we can see what else you might have that I want to procure for the gallery."

"Absolutely," I replied.

"It's good to see you, Peter," she said quietly. "You look well."

"Thank you. It's nice to see you looking so well, too," I replied, feeling more than a little dejected.

I watched as Giselle left the room and motioned for Mia to join her. The two women spoke for a few minutes and then continued away from me to walk through the gallery. My heart sank to my feet. I'd not expected to see Giselle here, and then when I did, she overwhelmed me. She was just as stunning as the last time I'd laid eyes on her.

The memory of our last lunch took me to a darker place. I'd been in such a state of turmoil that day and seeing her had torn me in two in various ways that I'd refused to acknowledge. I knew that I'd been cool to her just as she was being to me right now. Perhaps it was now she who was the married one. I hadn't asked and it had been a while. It was insane to think she'd remained single all this time.

I pondered this for a while. She wasn't wearing a ring, but that might be because she was traveling or looking at art for purchase.

Some rings could be substantial and a tiny bit of carelessness when getting too close to art could cause damage. It was obvious that Giselle liked to get close to the art to really look at it, so it would make sense for her not to have on some huge rock or matching band.

I looked back toward the statues. It had never been my intention to sell them. They were the very thing that brought me out of my pain. I'd started with the intention of sculpting Jillian. I had so many pictures of her to work from, but each time I began to create her, I ended up in tears. I could never see her face without remembering those final days when her beauty had been ravaged by pain and illness. It was too much to take.

So, I'd gone back to memories that didn't end in tragedy, at least not one with the finality of death. I remember Giselle and how she looked up at me as I arrived next to her on the flight to New York. She'd been a picture of perfection as her head had slowly moved from looking ahead to looking upward at me with a smile of recognition. I'd seen her before she'd seen me. I watched her while the woman in front of me put away her bags.

Those are the moments I had captured in these statues. I'd created the first one and decided it wasn't exactly how I remembered her, so I moved on to the second one. It was nearly six months later before I created the third and final piece. When I was done, I realized that they formed a sort of flow from how I first saw her when she didn't know I was there to her wonderful smile when she finally spotted me.

A while later, she and Mia returned, and we discussed the terms of sale for the three sculptures. I was shocked to learn what they felt they were worth, but I wasn't selling them for the money. In my mind, I was now selling them to the woman they belonged to. If she chose to sell them to someone else, that was her call. With contracts signed and our business out of the way, Giselle suggested we look at the remainder of my work before it got too late.

We grabbed a taxi back to my place, not really talking much on the way. I felt grateful that it wasn't very far if things were this awkward between us. We were nearly there when she finally asked me a simple question.

"Would you have sold them if it hadn't turned out to me that was looking to buy?" she asked.

"I don't know," I told her and that was as honest as I could be about it.

The sculptures had been sitting in the small shed I'd repurposed as a studio when a colleague had come over to borrow some tools. As we'd walked out my back door and into the attached shed, he'd noted them and insisted that I show them.

"These are incredible, Peter," he'd said.

"You think so? I don't know. I just feel like they aren't quite what I was looking for."

"What were you looking for?"

"I guess I was looking for the real deal," I'd remarked.

He nodded in acknowledgment and studied the busts again. "Who is she?"

"Just someone I knew a lifetime ago."

"Ah, an old flame."

"Something like that," I admitted.

"What are you going to do with them?"

"I don't know. I haven't thought much about that."

"You should show them. I bet these would sell in a heartbeat."

"Eh, I hadn't even thought about selling them."

"They are too big for this little hobbit house of yours."

"Hey, now. I love my little flat. Don't be knocking it. I could always put one in a corner of each room."

"No, you couldn't. Breaking them up destroys the flow of the piece."

I shrugged, and we both stood there studying the sculptures. They were large but not overly so. Still, to display them together, you would need a decent space to do so. They were only busts, so they'll need to go on pillars or a table, at the very least.

"I have a friend who's sponsoring an art show. You should put them in her exhibition in a couple of weeks."

"Art show? Exhibition?" I laughed. "They're hardly worthy of all that scrutiny."

"Don't sell yourself short, Peter. You've always done that. You started teaching art because you studied the greats and felt like you didn't measure up. When was the last time you even attempted to create something of your own before these?"

I grimaced. He was right about at least part of what he was saying. I liked to believe I was talented, but when I looked at the great artists that I gave lectures on, I saw none of their incredible talent in myself. Perhaps an exhibition might give me some perspective on how others viewed my work.

As it turned out, they did create quite a bit of interest. Several people were interested in them but rejected them for precisely the same reasons I couldn't display them in my home. If someone of means had seen them, perhaps they'd have sold, but people who lived in smaller accommodations weren't interested in dedicating such a large portion of a room to an art installation.

I was surprised when Mia contacted me based on the earlier exhibition and asked if I'd be interested in showing them to a potential buyer from New York. She explained that they had a prestigious gallery owner looking for unique pieces to sell. I hadn't asked the buyer's name, but my friend had encouraged me to agree to show them and come in for the exhibition so the buyer could meet me if interested in the work.

As a teacher of the arts, I found it quite interesting to be on the side of art where your work was being considered and accepted or rejected. I wondered how many people had rejected artists that we considered masters in their early days of work. I don't think I would ever consider myself worthy of standing beside such greats, but I'd like to think I was no hack, either.

Finding myself face to face with Giselle again had been much more than I'd bargained for. It was like fate had decided to take over and bring her back to me again. Of course, I'd never considered starting things with her again. There'd been so much water under the bridge since we'd last met. It wasn't that I didn't think of her from time to time, but nothing had changed for us.

I was still tied to France, and, as far as I knew, she was still tied to New York. Even if I'd ever hoped to rekindle anything with it, I knew it would only end the same way it had the first time.

Chapter 46

Giselle

"Ready to go?" Peter asked as I reappeared from finishing up my dealings with Mia.

"I am," he replied, seeming a little on edge. I suppose that was expected, as I felt a little nervous, too.

Outside the front doors, I stopped and waited for Peter to take the lead. Instead, he stopped too, looking softly down at me. "What is it?"

"I don't know which way to go."

"Oh! Of course. I'm sorry. It's a bit of a haul. We'll get a car."

We made small talk while he hailed a cab. I was grateful that it came quickly. It was amazing how you could be so at ease with someone and then see them again, only to not know what to say or how to respond. It didn't take long to get to his place, so I wondered if he was just trying to spare my outfit or save us from a more awkward time together as the car pulled up in front of it.

"How long have you lived here?" I asked, realizing I could be arriving at the house he'd shared with his late wife.

"Not long. I bought it and refurbished it shortly after Jillian..." he said, letting his words trail off.

I felt a sense of relief, though I wasn't entirely sure why. Something just seemed wrong about stepping into the space he used to occupy with his deceased wife. I waited as he unlocked the door and showed me inside. It wasn't exactly a pad you would find on the cover of Homes and Gardens. Still, it was tastefully decorated and immaculately clean. I realized it was the first time I'd ever been in any of Peter's personal space.

"Are you sure you live here?"

"Yes, of course," he said, looking momentarily confused.

"It just doesn't seem like a bachelor pad," I said, a smile forming.

Peter paused as we stood in the still open doorway and looked around before finally nodding in agreement. "I guess I can see that. I watched a lot of home decor videos for ideas. I didn't want it to look like a man lived here alone like some sort of old hermit."

"*Do* you live here alone like some sort of hermit?"

"Pretty much, but I didn't want it to look that way." He laughed.

"Fair enough. Well, let's get to your work so I can let you get back to that," I said, eager to see what else he'd done and just as much wanting to distance myself from the attraction I still felt to him. I was purposely not trying to be overly friendly, so I didn't give him the wrong idea.

"Sure. Some of it is scattered about the house. I'd have put it all in one place had I known I'd be having an at-home showing today."

"It's not a problem. I wasn't aware that you even sculpted."

"I didn't for a long time. I just got an urge to pick it back up one day and begin creating smaller pieces," he said as we walked into his living room. He flipped the lights on for me to see better and directed my attention to a set of shelves on the far wall, which displayed several smaller pieces for me to review.

"These are magnificent," I said, looking them over.

"You don't have to be kind just because it's me."

"I'm not. These are truly incredible. The detailing is wonderful, and the overall creation is masterful. Are you interested in selling them?"

"Which ones?"

"All of them."

"Perhaps. Would you like to see the rest?"

"I would."

He led me toward the back door and out to the makeshift studio, where he had started working on something not yet taking form. I glanced at it and followed him toward a nearby table with several finished pieces. Unlike the busts he had created of me and the romantic pieces of couples downstairs, these were darker works. A raven was overlooking what appeared to be a man fallen in the snow. A vulture stared blankly ahead with a twisted human corpse in his claws. Finally, there was a man and woman, but unlike the romantic pieces downstairs, they were turned away from one another.

I leaned down, getting a better look at their faces and then looked back up at Peter with a raised eyebrow. "Are they—" I began to say.

"Yes. They are me. Those three were my first sculptures after everything fell apart. They are a bit too grim to put in the house."

"They aren't as detailed as the ones in the living room."

"No. I was struggling for a while, Giselle. I couldn't focus on Jillian's face, so things came out a bit. I have some early work, but it's in my office at the university."

"These are different, but they would appeal to a certain demographic. You'd like to sell them?" I asked, having difficulty not pulling him into a hug and not letting go.

"Yes. If I don't, I'll likely destroy them at some point."

"I understand. Should we go back inside?"

"Yes. Listen. I'd like to sit and just chat for a while if that's okay. Would you like a glass of wine?"

I considered this, decided it was a bad idea, and then found myself saying "yes" anyway. Peter led me back to the living room and motioned for me to sit while he disappeared to retrieve the wine. I sat nervously on the sofa for a moment and then got up, returning to the sculptures on the shelves. They were incredibly detailed, and though we hadn't discussed their origins before, I realized something when I examined them this time.

"These are—" I began to say, but Peter finished for me.

"Us," he replied, handing me my glass of wine.

"But why? We haven't seen one another for years, and every time we parted badly. Once, I lost your number. Once we agreed not to see one another due to distance, and the last time, well, you know."

"I do know and I'm sorry for any pain that may have caused you. The truth is that I never forgot about you. I tried to push you from my mind, but you were always there, and after Jillian died, I couldn't bear to remember her face. I'd try to remember the woman I'd first met. Instead, I could only conjure up the emaciated, unwell vision of her that I never wanted to think about."

"I'm sorry. I know the entire experience must have been horrible for both of you. I can't even fathom what it was like or how it would have affected you."

"I hope it's something you never have to understand," he said, drinking his wine.

I sipped mine, too, and moved back over to the sofa. He followed. Things finally seemed to thaw between us as we began discussing everything that had happened in our lives to bring us back to this point. Before I knew it, the hour had gotten late, and I needed to return to my hotel.

"Why don't you stay?"

"Stay?" I asked, my heart suddenly racing.

"Yes. Stay here, with me."

I thought about this for a second. Rather than waiting for an answer, Peter moved closer and pulled me into a soft kiss. I didn't resist. In fact, I melted into him, kissing him back with just as much passion as I'd felt for him all those years ago.

Everything happened quickly after that. There was no thinking about whether we should or shouldn't. I'd wanted him for so long that I wasn't about to pass up the chance to be with him again, regardless of the outcome. We practically ripped one another's clothes in our eagerness to get to one another and satisfy our needs.

Peter took me right there on his sofa, pulling me down on his lap to impale me on his throbbing, hard cock. It felt amazing sitting on top of him, taking control as I rode him slowly up and down, enjoying every hard inch of him inside me. His hands cupped my breasts softly, holding them and gently flicking my nipples as they bounced up and down with my movements.

I could feel him pulsating inside me and began to slow down, wanting this to last. I wanted to cum like only he could make me. I rode him in long, slow strokes, grinding my pussy down so his cock was buried deep inside me.

"You're still so beautiful," he told me, pulling me downward into another deep kiss. We stayed that way for a moment, kissing deeply as I barely moved on top of him. Finally, I pulled away and we resumed our rhythm, making love at a slow, easy pace until our need grew too much to hold back.

Peter grabbed my waist and began guiding me down on his cock, no longer content to let me lead. He pumped into me hard and fast, using his grip on me to meet each thrust so our bodies bounced up and down with wild abandon. I could feel the pressure of an orgasm building inside of me as he fucked me like a man who hadn't enjoyed sex for a while, and I wondered if that might be true but pushed it out of my thoughts.

"God, I'm coming," I moaned, closing my eyes and just letting myself feel him moving inside me. His cock pushed at my pussy walls, spreading them apart and letting them relax again before hitting all the right spots again. I dug my nails into his legs as my body quaked with the power of my climax.

"That's it. That's my girl," he told me, still pumping in and out of me passionately, milking me for all I had to give. As my orgasm began to subside, he let loose with his own, filling me with his own powerful stream of ecstasy.

We continued to move slowly up and down for a moment, milking one another for all we had to give, and then we were still. I leaned forward against him and held him to me, finding it hard to believe I was really here with him and that we'd really just had sex on his sofa like two horny teenagers.

I smiled at that thought as I laid my head on his shoulder, clinging to him while I could. I didn't want this to end, but I knew it would. It always ended the same way, with Peter and I on opposite sides of an ocean that left us stranded without one another. My smile faded.

But then something happened, something unexpected. Peter pulled away and I did the same. We sat there looking at one another, me still poised on top of him. He smiled at me and pushed some of my hair away from my face.

"I can't tell you how happy I was to see you tonight, and I was terribly afraid for a little while that I'd lost you forever. I could feel how distant you were at the gallery, and it hurt. I realized it must have been how you felt when you met me that day for lunch. I knew you'd come here with some hope, and I dashed it as if it were nothing. I didn't even explain my situation to you. I treated you like a stranger."

"I was a stranger. I'm still a stranger now, really," I said quietly.

"You are not a stranger. We've not spent much time together, but it's as if I've known you all my life. I fell in love with you the moment I laid eyes on your freckled face in that museum where we met. And I was a fool to think anything in my life was more important than moving heaven and Earth to be with you."

"It's okay, Peter. I understand. Life just isn't always fair."

"True, but I've changed. You have no idea. I love you, Giselle."

I stared at him for a moment, tears falling down my cheeks, and though I knew that perhaps I shouldn't, I replied.

"I love you too, Peter."

Chapter 47

Giselle

"I don't want to part ways again," Peter said as he leaned on one elbow, running his fingers idly across my collarbone as he spoke.

We'd managed to move from the sofa to his bed, cuddling together and talking as we contemplated what this might mean for both of us.

"I don't know how we can avoid it. You can't leave your tenured position, and I can't walk away from my gallery when it's just becoming successful," I said, knowing it was best just to put things on the table.

"If I've learned one thing in the years since we met, it's that there are some things that matter and some that don't. I don't care about my tenure anymore. I'll find what I need at a university in New York. If I lose a bit of financial security in the process, that's okay. I'll just get me one of those sugar mamas I always hear about in the States."

"Aren't you getting a bit too old to be someone's boy toy?" I teased.

"I don't know. You tell me. I hear there's an up-and-coming gallery owner in New York who might just keep me in the style I'm not accustomed to," he shot back, leaning in to kiss me.

"You keep that up and she just might buy you some new clay to work with."

"I do love fresh clay," he purred, kissing across my chest.

I moved toward him, and he pulled me into a kiss. It was long and passionate, our tongues flicking back and forth against one another as he held me tightly against him. My breasts pressed firmly against his chest and his erection grew larger, pulsing against my belly as if it had a life all its own. We were hungry for one another, eager to devour one another again.

Our kisses grew more passionate, heating us both to our core. Peter kissed my neck, nibbling at my ear lobes and then stopping to lean in and kiss my breasts. He pulled a nipple into his mouth, teasing it gently with his tongue. I moaned loudly, encouraging him to move on to the other.

Peter continued to kiss my breasts before finally moving down to push my thighs apart with his hands. I was soaking wet as he began to explore me with his fingers, all the while continuing to enjoy sucking at my breasts.

"Skip the foreplay. I need you inside me," I panted, pushing him to fuck me again. I suddenly wanted him in the worst way, and I wanted him now.

I opened my legs to him, and he didn't hesitate, climbing on top of me and entering me with one swift stroke. His hard cock slipped in and out of my slick warm pussy, causing me to groan loudly. He moved slowly at first but quickly picked up speed at my urging. I pleaded for it, wanted it. He was finally mine and I wanted him to take me like I belonged to only him.

"Yes. Harder. Yes," I begged.

Peter happily gave me exactly what I was asking for. His bed creaked loudly as he pounded into me while I pleaded for more. My body bucked wildly beneath his, my legs weak and trembling. I felt like an animal in heat that needed to be satisfied. Peter was all for it, giving me inch after rock-hard inch until we both exploded. I came so hard I thought I might pass out.

We both fell apart on separate sides of the bed, each trying to catch our breath. I felt embarrassed at having been so out of control and slowly turned to look at Peter. He was leaning on his side, looking at me with a wicked smile.

"I guess I got a little crazy, huh?" I said bashfully. "It's just been so long, and I wanted you so much."

"Oh no. You can get out of hand with me anytime you want, but remember, I'm getting to be an old man. You might give me a heart attack."

"Very funny. You aren't that old," I laughed.

"I will be. I'll be old and wrinkled, and I won't be able to get it up anymore," he teased. "What will you do then?"

"Well, Helena and Marie assure me I can buy toys if needed."

"Oh? I would ask how this conversation came about, but I don't think I really want to know."

"You are correct. You'd never want to know about my conversations with those two."

"A bit harsh on me, were they?"

"Oh, no. You misunderstand me. They are just foul. You'll never meet two fouler women in your whole life than those two," I said with a little laugh.

Peter smiled at me and reached out to stroke my cheek thoughtfully. "I can't wait to meet your foul friends, and what about your parents?"

"Ah, the parents. Yes. They are going to despise you."

"What? Already?"

"Yes. Absolutely. Why wouldn't they? You're so hideous and uneducated."

"I am those things," he said, laughing, and I joined him.

"My parents will love you because I love you. Of course, I don't know when you'll be able to meet them. They're very busy for two geriatrics. I hardly ever get a chance to talk to them. Instead, I get emails from all around the world. They've retired to Florida for some time, and now they've decided to travel the world and see everything they haven't had a chance to see before they shuffle off their mortal coils."

"They sound like my kind of people. Perhaps we will surprise them by turning up on their next vacation to the last place they expected to see us one day."

"That would be great. They'd get a real kick out of it."

"It's after eleven. Does this mean you're staying?"

I glanced at the clock and back at him. "That depends. I'm starving. Those hors d'oeuvres at the gallery were deeply unsatisfying. What do you have to eat around here?"

"Oh, madam! You are in luck! I have leftover quiche and wine that I was too nervous to eat earlier."

"Nervous? What could you possibly have to be nervous about?"

"I was meeting some high-powered gallery owner about selling my work."

"Yeah? How'd that go?"

"Woman obviously doesn't know what she's doing. She bought everything in my collection and asked if there was more."

I smiled at him. "You must have given her something she liked."

He smiled too. "I promised her some quiche."

"No wonder she couldn't resist your work," I teased.

Peter kissed me on the nose and climbed out of bed, slipping on a t-shirt and pajama pants, laying near the bed before rummaging in a nearby drawer. He produced another t-shirt and similar pants with a drawstring waist for me and disappeared out the door. I heard him padding downstairs and rummaging in what sounded like the kitchen.

Climbing out of bed, I slipped into the baggy pants and t-shirt. I felt a little ridiculous in them but loved that he'd given me his clothes to wear instead of my having to put back on my over-pressed outfit, which I realized now must be horribly wrinkled. If I stayed the night, I'd have to wear it back to the hotel in broad daylight tomorrow morning—my first true walk of shame.

I went downstairs and looked for my purse, collecting my other clothes along the way and spreading them out the best I could. Inside, I found my phone and set my morning alarm so I didn't forget. Of course, I was now in a much better position to upgrade or change my flight, but I had things to tend to in the city and would prefer not to miss it.

"I have an iron for that if you need it," Peter said as he entered the living room and spotted my suit.

"It'll be fine. I'm sure I'm not the first woman the hotel has seen arrive looking disheveled and wrinkled after a night out with some French rogue."

"I'm a French rogue now?"

"You prefer naughty professor?"

"That would make you the slutty student and that just feels terribly wrong considering that I *am* a professor, and my students are getting to be a third of my age."

"I'll cross that fantasy night off the list," I told him.

He laughed and then seemed to focus on the phone in my hand. "Calling an Uber after a bad one-night stand?"

"Not a chance. I was setting my alarm. The last time I missed a flight, it cost me a fortune and I ended up hooking up in the bathroom with a stranger."

"That's a horrible position to be in!" he joked.

"Tell me about it. Those bathrooms are tiny. I think I still have a cramp all these years later."

Peter smiled, his eyes glazing over with the look people get when remembering a favorite tale. He reached out toward me. "Give me your phone."

I looked at him with a puzzled expression but handed it to him. He began typing something into it and then handed it back to me. "It's for you."

I lifted the phone to my ear, and it began ringing someone else's line just as his phone went off on a nearby table. He picked it up and said, "Hello, Giselle."

I heard him across the room and in my speaker. "Hello, Peter."

We both laughed and hung up, but I was still a little confused as to why he'd called himself from my phone until I glanced back down at the face of mine. He hadn't only called himself but also entered his name as a contact on my phone.

"Now, you have my phone number. I have yours. We both know where the other lives and works. There is no reason in the world for us not to be able to find our way back to one another again. You can call me all you want, even to talk about absolutely nothing."

"That sounds like a plan," I said.

"Good. Our quiche should be warm now. Let's eat a bite and talk about how we will make this long-distance romance work while I make plans to never be apart from you again."

And that's exactly what we did. Peter and I sat at his kitchen table and discussed his relocation plans and how long that might take. We might spend some time flying back and forth while he found suitable employment and got moved over, but we would split that. He'd come over as he could and I would come back in search of more artwork by Paris artists, which I'd already planned to do anyway.

The prospect of a long-distance relationship could be daunting, but now I knew that Peter and I truly did belong together, and we would work it out one way or another. We finished our makeshift meal, had some wine, and went back to bed, making love again so softly and slowly that I couldn't imagine ever being touched by anyone but him, ever again. Afterward, I fell asleep with my head resting in the crook of his arm, feeling exactly like the princess who finally got her happy ending with Prince Charming.

The next morning, Peter and I parted ways again, but I was content believing it would be the last time. He would apply for jobs in New York, and I would continue with the gallery while I waited for him to join me. Who knew what would happen between us while we waited or once he managed to get moved over? But we were both willing to take a chance and give things a real shot.

As my plane departed France this time, I knew that spending the night with Peter had been the right decision. I hoped I would never have to be apart from him again.

Chapter 48

Peter

I stood fidgeting nervously as I waited for Giselle to appear. Everything about my life was different now. I was living in New York, teaching at an upscale art school rather than a mainstream university, and I loved it. More importantly, I loved the woman about to join me in this park.

We'd been planning this day for months and though it wasn't my first wedding, I felt vastly different than I had when I'd married Jillian. As much as I didn't want to think of the pain that had come with my marriage to her today of all days, it was a part of me and always would be. She and I had at least partly mistaken love for lust, and I knew that now. We'd been so enthralled with one another that we hadn't waited for the passion to dwindle so we could see another side of one another, the non-sexual people that we were.

So, when the sex had ended so abruptly with her illness, we'd really not had that much in common. Of course, I had no regrets about marrying Jillian. I did love her in my own way, and she loved me too. Despite the pain that came with our marriage, I am glad it happened. I couldn't imagine her having to go through her illness alone. Things might have ended differently if we hadn't married when we did. I wouldn't have left her, but she might have left me. I had resisted as a husband, but she might have been more insistent if we hadn't been betrothed.

Now, here I was on the other side of my life with her. I was finally doing as she had asked. I'd found happiness again with someone else, but not just anyone else. I'd returned to the woman before her, who I'd never quite been able to get off my mind, no matter how hard I tried to push her away.

I knew now just how much Giselle had always meant to me. I'd clung to her memory in the hardest times of my life, even when I felt guilty for doing so. It was Giselle who brought me little shards of joy during my loneliness and set me on fire when we were together. I was happy to finally play the role of the prince in her happily-ever-after fairytale. I had no reservations in believing we would be exactly that—happy forever.

Now, here we were, finally getting married. We would begin our real journey on this day. For better, for worse. For richer, for poorer. In sickness and in health. It was a lot to accept that you would endure with another person, but if you couldn't make those promises to someone, how empty of a life must you live? I was firmly on board with my commitment to Giselle.

In addition to becoming her husband, I had previously joined the ranks of artists she promoted. My work was prominently displayed in her gallery and at home. In the gallery were the dark pieces, too dark for purchase but very much a topic of discussion among patrons.

The original pieces that had drawn her attention were displayed in our foyer, greeting visitors to our home and showing them the way inside with a forward glance toward the inner portion of the house. At least, that's how we now saw the three busts of Giselle, though both of us knew their true meaning. I'd been surprised to find she'd decided not to sell them. Nor had she sold the other work she'd insisted on buying from me. Only the work I created after we were together again had been sold, and I was elated to say that it sold quite well.

There wasn't a lot of pomp and circumstance at our wedding. Still, it was well attended by various New York friends and family we had made in the two years it had taken us to make it to the altar. When we discussed venues, the common suggestion was The Boathouse in Central Park. We both loved going for walks there and found the venue charming.

As the music began, I looked up, squaring my shoulders. A smile crept across my face as her bridesmaids marched down the aisle, including my sister Charlotte and my two nieces, who had only fallen more in love with Giselle in their adult years. My groomsmen consisted of my brother-in-law, Steven, and a couple of work colleagues with whom I'd become close. Helena and Marie were there too, looking somewhat hungover from the drunken party they'd given Giselle the night before.

As Giselle finally appeared at the back of the walkway toward me, I caught my breath. She was stunning. Her hair hung in long curls across her shoulders, the copper color in stark contrast to the white lace against which they lay. As the wedding march began, she moved toward me; I felt nothing short of ecstasy.

Everything that morning seemed to move in slow motion until now. Then, it was as if someone pushed fast forward. The wedding and the reception were incredible, but they seemed to go so fast when compared to how long it seemed to take to get to this point. The whirlwind ended with us emerging from the boathouse, showered by bird seeds and cheered on by our guests as we stepped into the waiting carriage outside.

It felt magical as we rolled through the park, taking in the smiling faces of those who watched us head toward a future that I could only believe would be worth the wait we'd had to get there. When we arrived at the park's edge, we shifted into a limo already loaded with our things. We made our way to the airport for a honeymoon in Cancun.

Sitting in first class on the plane, we clinked our glasses of champagne. The lovely dress Giselle had changed into for the reception flowed softly about her long legs as we waited to take off for our destination. We'd been flying for a bit when I turned to her to ask a question.

"I wonder how many people have joined the mile-high club more than once?"

"Well, many people have private planes, so probably more than you think," she quipped.

"Yeah, but how many have gotten a second chance on a commercial flight and taken it?"

"I couldn't say."

"How about we make it at least one couple that has done it."

"Peter! We're too old to be getting dirty in an airplane bathroom," she admonished playfully.

"Old is a state of mind and you aren't anywhere close to old anyway."

She chuckled for a moment and glanced around. Most people were either engrossed in the little movie screens in front of them or asleep. She turned back to me and nodded. "See you in a couple of minutes."

With that, I pulled myself to my feet and casually went to the bathroom. A moment or so later, Giselle had done the same. The first-class bathrooms on the plane were much bigger than the one where we'd originally gotten frisky on a flight to America. Instead of the cramped little space with just a toilet and a hand-washing basin, these were divided into two sections. One had a toilet and the other had a washing up and changing area.

A few moments later, Giselle opened the door, quickly stepping inside and locking it behind her. I pulled her close, putting my lips on hers and pulling her into a deep kiss. My tongue parted hers to engage her in an erotic dance that quickly had us both heated up. We might have more space here, but we didn't have more time.

I moved away to quickly unbutton the top of Giselle's dress, exposing the perfect moon of her cleavage. I decided not to stop there and unbuttoned it further until I could reach the full measure of her beautiful breasts. I bent slightly to pull one of her nipples into my mouth, sucking at it until it turned into a tight pink rosebud perfect for flicking with my tongue. She let out a familiar light groan of pure delight.

Eager to please her, I dropped to my knees on the bathroom floor, pushed her dress up, and slipped her panties down her legs to drop to the floor. She stepped out of them and spread her legs open to me. I kissed her thighs, licking and nibbling my way toward her sweet, wet pussy.

I didn't waste any of our precious time, getting right to business, lapping hungrily at her hot pink folds, making long strokes through them as I eased deeper toward her center. Her hands tangled in my hair, guiding me to where she wanted me as much as I'd allow her. I looked up at her, our eyes locked lustfully together as I lapped up her juices and began teasing her clit with my tongue.

She bit her lip, trying hard to stay quiet so we wouldn't be heard in the cabin on the other side of the flimsy door. I knew we were short of time, but I wanted to make her come. I'd failed the first time, but I knew exactly how and where to touch her now, and I made quick work of it, sucking at her clit and moving my fingers in to hit her sweet spot until she was exploding in my mouth.

Her breasts rose and fell as she panted heavily after her climax. I moved up and kissed my way across her breasts again, kissing her again with the taste of her cum still on my lips. I entered her with one fluid move, causing her to grunt much louder than expected and then bite her lip again to stifle her noises.

She leaned back against the wall as I continued to kiss and fuck her, enjoying the way her tight pussy hugged my cock, milking my own climax with the powerful muscles she possessed. Our quiet moans filled the small space as we joined the mile-high club again, this time as man and wife. I groaned loudly as I came inside her and began to slow my strokes until we stopped.

We remained locked together, kissing and looking at one another, until a knock at the door made us both jump and then laugh. Giselle called out to the unexpected visitor in her smoothest voice.

"I'm sorry. I'll just be a few more minutes."

There was no response, just the sound of them moving away. We both chuckled and began getting ourselves together before slipping out of the bathroom and quickly returning to our seats. I moved a blanket over the two of us as we leaned against each other, still coming down from our little bathroom adventure. No one seemed to have noticed we were even missing for a bit, except for one.

As Giselle and I rejoined the passengers in first class, an attendant gave me a knowing smile. I smiled back before we took our seats. I had no regrets and appreciated that the staff on the plane had no intention of causing any stir over our antics as long as we weren't creating a problem for them.

I marveled at how much things had changed in my life. The first time I'd joined this club with Giselle had been great, but this time had been spectacular. We both knew each other's bodies so much better now. And while I'd not made her come the first time, she'd exploded like a volcano this time. It was beautiful.

I glanced over at my lovely new bride, satisfied and content, as she leaned against the seat beside me and closed her eyes. I couldn't imagine my life without her anymore.

Epilogue

Brandt

"The gallery looks lovely," the woman said as she stepped inside and looked around.

"Thank you. I've made a few changes," I replied, noting how her high ponytail swished across her bare back as she walked around.

"These are interesting. What do you know about them?" she asked.

"They are by an artist named Peter Dockery. They represent the deep pain and sorrow he felt at the loss of his wife."

"They're beautiful. I love darker works. Are they for sale?"

"I'm afraid not. They have been maintained by the family as part of the gallery."

"I didn't realize it was a family-owned establishment."

"Yes," I told her.

She nodded in acknowledgment and continued to look around. There was something about her that I found interesting. She was pretty in a way that most girls my age weren't, possessing some confidence that made her carry herself a certain way. I wondered if she was really so self-assured as she appeared.

"Can I help you look for anything? Is there something in particular you have in mind?"

"Perhaps. As I said, I prefer darker work. Do you have anything else like the Dockery work on display?"

"Not from him, but there is another artist that is quite similar I can show you. Follow me."

I motioned for one of the other members of our staff to take over the till and stepped out onto the floor. The girl followed me up the stairs to an addition made to the shop last year to house additional art that didn't quite fit in with the general vibe of the gallery areas below.

Before I could even point her to any particular piece of work, she gravitated toward the small sculpture of a woman that sat atop a center shelf at the back of our displays. I smiled as she stood before it, marveling over the structure of the wrought iron piece carefully crafted from reclaimed metals.

"This is amazing. Who's it by?"

"No one you've heard of. It was created by an artist named Remi."

"Remi. That's such an interesting name," she said as she examined the statue. "Can I touch it?"

"Of course," I replied, watching as she ran her hands carefully over the sculpture, caressing its rough edges and smoother surfaces.

"I think I'd like this one," she said finally, not bothering to look at anything else.

"No problem. I'll get it packed up and brought down for you. It won't take long if you want to look around more.

"I will do that, though I don't think I'll find anything more spectacular than that," she said, seeming to really look at me and take me in for the first time.

I think it was what I'd found so unusual about her. I was barely eighteen, but girls always flocked to me without knowing me. My mother said it was because I was such a beautiful child. I scoffed at that notion, but I knew she meant it. She often referred to my father as a beautiful man and I looked very much like him with my dark hair and even features. It was funny how you thought of people in terms of symmetry when immersed in the art world your whole life.

This girl, though, had walked in and not batted an eyelash at me. She was here for the art, and I was only an afterthought. Perhaps she, too, appreciated symmetry. Now that she'd found what she was seeking, she seemed to notice me more as I removed the statue and placed it in a box surrounded by soft straw to protect its more delicate components. She made no move to return to the lower gallery, instead watching me as I packed away her soon-to-be purchase.

"My name is Melody, by the way," she told me with a large smile.

"Brandt," I replied, glancing up at her as I finished closing the box and turned back to face her.

"This is my first piece of art. I mean, I have some stuff that my parents bought me, but this is the first piece I've ever bought for myself. I really love it."

"I'm glad you do. Let's go down and ring it up for you," I told her, beginning to feel awkwardly a certain way that I should not be feeling alone, upstairs, with a customer.

We made our way downstairs and I rang up the purchase, placing it in a large bag for her. It wasn't very heavy, but our policy was to always offer assistance with art transport.

"Do you need some help getting it home? I can arrange delivery if you like."

"No. That won't be necessary, but thank you, Brandt. I really appreciate you showing me this. You should put more like it down here in the shop."

"I will let the owners know you suggested it," I told her with a broad smile.

"I'll come back again. Are you here often?"

"More than I care to be. I'm starting college this fall, so I'll be working here all summer until then."

"Wow. Me too! Where are you going?"

"NYU. I've been accepted into the school of arts."

"Ah, that makes sense. I guess working in an art store gives you a feel for it all, huh?"

"Very much so."

"I'll be at NYU too, but I'll be over in the engineering department. I think that's why I like this piece so much. It combines art with industrial metals," she joked.

"That it does. Maybe we'll run into one another on campus then," I said hopefully.

"Oh, you can bet we will. Here, let me write down my number. And don't wait until fall to call me. We can hang out over the summer and maybe check out the campus together."

"I'd like that," I told her. "I'll talk to you soon, Melody."

"I hope so," she said, turning to leave just as my father came in.

"Remi, where did you put the rest of the Carthridge prints?" he asked.

I saw Melody, still within earshot, as she stopped in her tracks and turned back around, returning to the counter. "Remi?" she said curiously. "I thought you said your name was Brandt?"

"It's both. I have bizarre, artsy-fartsy parents who named me Rembrandt. Most people call me Brandt, but they like to call me Remi like I'm still a two-year-old," I groaned.

"Hey, I am not an artsy-fartsy parent," my father protested, but Melody seemed not to even notice him.

"Then you created this statue," she said, holding up her bag.

"Guilty," I admitted.

"Why didn't you say so?"

"I don't know. I was just enjoying how much you liked it without knowing you were talking to the person who made it, I guess."

She smiled knowingly, nodded, satisfied with my answers, and finally looked at my father. "I guess you being an artsy-fartsy parent paid off, huh?"

He laughed. "I suppose it did. His mother will be thrilled with his assessment of us when I tell her. I'm Peter Dockery, by the way."

Her eyes grew wider as she glanced sideways at the dark piece on display she'd first noticed. She turned back to me again with a confused look. It took me a moment to realize what the question she thought too personal to mention might be. "His first wife."

"Ah." She glanced back at my father sympathetically.

"Well, I think I've learned enough about the Dockery family gallery today. I'll see you again the next time I visit. Maybe I'll even get to meet the artsy-fartsy mom unit next time," she quipped as she turned around and walked across the gallery and out the front door.

"She certainly seems like a bit of a spitfire," my dad teased, tussling my hair like he had done all my life.

"Stop that!" I said, laughing as I tried to smooth my hair back down.

I watched Melody disappear down the sidewalk, a massive smile on my face. "She was something else, huh, Dad?" I said.

"Seemed to be," he said idly, looking beneath the sales counter for something.

"I'm glad you liked her. I think I'm going to marry her one day," I told him.

My father stopped and stood back up, glancing toward the windows, though Melody was already well out of sight. He sighed and shook his head, smiling from ear to ear. "Well, when you know, you know, son. I'll let your mother know to start planning the wedding now. She might be done by the time the two of you future lovebirds graduate college, and you actually propose."

"What if I can't wait that long?" I asked.

"Oh, you'll wait. If she's the right woman, you'll wait until you find a way. Trust me. I waited on your mother for years."

"Waited on his mother to what?" Giselle said as she emerged from a nearby entryway.

"Nothing, my love. Peter and I were just discussing his future wedding plans."

"Wedding plans? He can't get married. He's barely out of diapers!" she exclaimed.

"Mom, please. Don't ever say that in front of people," I groaned.

My parents laughed as only the two of them seemed to do. I'd never met another set of parents who seemed to just enjoy one another's company the way the two of them did. I hoped that when I did eventually get married, I would be as happy as they always seemed. I'd never known them to argue or even seem angry with one another over more than a play fight over who forgot to buy milk or some other nonsense.

As they disappeared upstairs to look for the missing prints my father had been seeking, I could hear them giggling like two teenagers in love, making me smile. Someday, I knew my parents would be gone, and I would be running this gallery alone. But I knew it would always echo with the laughter and playful banter they filled it with during the nearly twenty-five years they'd been married, with plenty of years left to add more.

If you loved "Forbidden Lust in Paris," then you will love "**Unbroken Seal.**"

Release: Availalble Feburary, 2024

A retired Navy SEAL.
A caretaker half my age.
Delicate hands caring for me in all the right places.

I spent most of my life at sea, witnessing war on almost every continent. Some places were so remote, they aren't even on a map. Throughout all that time, I never sustained a major injury. That was, until the North Korean incident, which nearly ended my life and left me with limited mobility, a bad demeanor, and the need for round-the-clock caretakers.

My most recent caretaker is Selena Torrence, a twenty-three-year-old with long golden wavy hair, hazel eyes, and a five-foot-six tight, full build that would turn any man's head. Luck has brought her to me.

She torments me because I can't have what I desire. I am broken and not the man I used to be. I need to let go of my fantasies and realize once and for all that she is only here as my helping hand and nothing more. But when the lights go out, how can one focus on being an employer when your assistant is so skilled at tucking a battle-hardened Seal into bed?

SNEAK PEAK CHAPTER ONE

"You should have been with me last night. I had some hot rugby player balls deep in me for most of the night," Jane said with a huge smile.

The waiter who had just arrived cleared his throat. It was hard to say who was more red-face, him or me. He hurriedly took our order and made a hasty retreat. I looked back at Selena with my lips pursed.

"I swear, Jane. You are so foul. And why would I have wanted to be there for your sexcapades?"

"Not for that, but for before. He was visiting over from the UK with some of his teammates. You could have lost your virginity with a hot British stud with an ass so tight you could—"

Her words were cut off as the waiter reappeared with our drinks and quickly disappeared again, obviously wanting to steer clear of overhearing any more of the conversation. She started to finish but I held up a finger to shush her.

"Just stop. You spend more time worrying about my virginity than I do," I chastised.

"Well, someone has to worry about it. You're 23 fucking years old and still haven't gotten laid! You must be the oldest virgin in Florida. Everyone else got their cherry popped by some college dude on spring break. Shit. I can't even remember the guy's name that did me on the beach."

"I do. It was Torrence Parker. He was a freshman at UNT."

"How the fuck do you know all that?"

"Because I was there before you ran off from the party with him. You told me all his details in case he was really a serial killer and drowned you in the ocean after you did the deed. Plus, he was extremely proud of his UNT cup because it had a green handle and looked like it said 'cunt' from a certain angle. Real winner, that guy," I replied, taking a drink of my sparkling water.

"Right," she said, laughing at the memory. "Seriously though. You need to let loose and get some."

"I'll have sex when it feels proper and with the right person. Besides, I have other things on my mind. I start a new assignment tomorrow with Warrior Care. I'll be helping a wounded veteran around his house while he recovers."

"Honestly, Selena, why won't you just go and get a real job?" Jane said between sips of the wine she had ordered.

"I enjoy what I do. Getting paid isn't everything," I replied.

"Getting paid is everything if it helps you move out of your grandparent's basement," Jane groaned.

"They don't have a basement," I snapped.

"You know what I mean," she replied.

I did know what she meant, and it wasn't an uncommon discussion between us. I still lived with the grandparents who raised me. They lived on the lower level where it was easier for them to get around and I had most of the second floor to myself. There were a couple of rooms that were used for storage, along with the attic, but I had a large bedroom and bathroom to myself. The bedroom beside me had been converted to a workshop and office area which I used to run a small online crafting business that provided enough income for my day to day needs but not much more.

"You spend all your time in your room or your shop like a sulking teenager," Jane pointed out.

"I like my room. There's nothing wrong with wanting to spend time alone and when I'm in my shop working. So, actually I do have a "real" job," I told her defensively.

"You spent too much time alone and you spend more of it in your room than you do working or playing," Jane replied.

"I don't. I'm out with you right now, aren't I?"

"Yes. Do your grandparents know? I bet they wouldn't approve," she said with a smirk.

"Of course, they know. What's not to approve of. You're my oldest friend," I said.

"That's exactly the problem. They think I'm a trouble maker and a bad influence," she told me.

I watched as she stabbed a plum tomato with her fork rather fervently and then bit it to it with particular vengeance. Jane was no fan of my grandparents, and she was completely correct in what she was saying, still I protested her claims.

"It's not as bad as all that."

"If you say so," she replied, moving lettuce around on her plate as she spoke.

"My grandparents need me there, Jane. They aren't as young as they used to be, and they could fall or have some sort of episode. What if something happened to one of them and I wasn't there to help?" I said, taking a bite of my own salad.

"That could happen right now while you are having lunch with me, Selena. It could happen while you're asleep. One of them could stroke out while you were standing there talking to them," she pointed out.

"What an awful thought!" I gasped.

"It is, but I'm just saying that you can't keep things from happening to them. If they are going to have a problem, they will have one. Nothing you or anyone else can do to stop it."

"That's true, but I can be there to make sure they get whatever help they need right away."

"Look, I understand that, but you can't babysit them all the time, Selena. You need to have a life of your own too and if they weren't so afraid you might get one and not come back, they'd encourage you to do so too. Just because they are a couple of bible beaters, doesn't mean you have to be one."

"They aren't that bad," I scoffed.

"They are that bad. You've never even had a boyfriend because you are terrified that they will be disappointed in you for sinning. I'm not even talking about sleeping around. I'm talking about just dating, for fuck's sake. I still remember them almost coming unglued when you suggested you might go to the school dance with Timothy Sanders. My God! Like anyone would be worried about you doing the nasty with the likes of him," she ranted.

"I thought he was sweet," I said, a fond smile on my face.

"He was sweet. He was also six foot six in eighth grade and had red hair and freckles. Oh, and buck teeth!"

"Don't be so shallow. He was really nice, and I liked him. He liked me too."

"My point is not that he was unattractive. My point is who would possibly look at him and think they couldn't trust him with their granddaughter at a chaperoned dance. He was awkward and scared of his own shadow."

"You know, Timothy Sanders is a doctor now. He got braces in college and keeps his red hair carefully cropped instead of in those wild curls he used to have. I wouldn't exactly describe him as a stud, but he's not so bad anymore. He kind of has a Conan O'Brien sort of thing going on."

"Is he still single?" she asked, sounding hopeful for me.

"No. He's married and has six kids."

"Six fucking kids! Damn. He made up for all those years he couldn't get laid. That's too much child bearing for my taste though. It sounds like you dodged a bullet."

"Maybe my grandparents knew what they were doing, after all," I suggested with a grin.

"I wouldn't go that far. I'm sure they would love to be swimming in great grandchildren, but they'd have to let you loose to do that."

"You act like they are holding me captive."

"Aren't they? Emotionally, at least?" she said, looking me directly in the eye.

"You just don't understand. I don't expect you to, but I don't want to discuss it any further. Let's change the subject."

"You want to hear more about me sexing up hot British men then?"

"No. I think we can be done with that conversation too," I groaned.

I knew that Jane would never see my point of view on this. She and I had grown up in exactly the same kind of household. We were raised by families who attended our Southern Baptist churches every Wednesday evening and twice on Sundays. I had towed the line, only rarely ever dipping my toes in potentially dangerous waters. Jane had rebelled. She snuck out at night to meet boys or lied about where she was to go to parties.

As we'd grown older, my grandparents had grown wary of me spending time with her. By the time we were juniors in high school, I was forbidden to see her outside of school. The handful of times I had gotten in hot water with my grandparents were when I had disobeyed them to spend time with her. It had been my belief that I wouldn't be caught, but we always seemed to run into someone from our church who would then mention seeing us and I'd end up grounded.

Unlike Selena, who didn't seem to care if her parents were angry with her or what punishments they doled out, I cared how my grandparents felt. Perhaps it was because they were all I had and my fear of becoming my mother. She had disobeyed them, and she ended up pregnant, giving birth to a child she didn't want and then running away completely, leaving me in the care of her parents. With no idea who had fathered me or if my mother would return, they had simply raised me. They might have been strict, but they were just trying to protect me from repeating the mistakes my mother had made.

"Look, I don't mean to bust your chops. I just worry that you aren't doing what makes you happy. Your whole life has revolved around you tiptoeing around your grandparents. At some point, you have to stop being that scared little girl they created and become a woman in your own right. You want to be a virgin forever? So be it. You can become a nun if that suits you. I just want you to get out of that house and live whatever life is suited to you—not just the one your grandparents expect from you."

"I appreciate that, Jane. I know you love me and are just trying to watch out for me, but I am happy. I don't expect you to understand. You are more daring. I admire that you just grab life by the horns. We just don't think about things the same way."

"Okay. Fair enough. I'll lay off about it," she said.

"Thank you," I told her, relieved to have the discussion over and done with.

"Did I tell you that I'm moving?"

"Moving? To where?" I asked, feeling alarmed that she might not be around soon.

"Not far. I've had my eye on that old Victorian over on Sands Hill Lane and they accepted my offer."

"Wow. That's huge!" I gasped, feeling a mixture of relief and just a bit of envy.

"It's going to be a lot of work. It's really run down. When the Mancombs died, it just sat derelict for years. I know a guy who owns a contracting business, and he looked through it with me. He says it doesn't have any serious defaults other than the plumbing and electric will need to be upgraded."

"That still sounds like a lot of work and money," I observed.

"It is, but I got it for a really low ball offer and I'm going to move in as soon as the electric and plumbing are done. My rental agreement ends next month, so I'm not going to renew it. I can live in my rough looking new house and work on it during my spare time."

"You sound really excited about it though," I told her.

"I am. You're welcome to come over and help," she laughed.

"You know I will," I replied.

"Perhaps you can even stay over sometimes and have a breather from the old folks home," she teased.

I smiled at her and raised my bottle of sparkling water to toast her wine glass. "Here's to us, besties till the end."

"Always," she said, tapping her glass against my bottle.

bookbub.com/authors/rachel-k-stone

facebook.com/authorrachelkstone/

instagram.com/rachelkstoneauthor/

youtube.com/@asholdingsandassets